By the same author:

Cover design: *Raymond McCullough*
Cover painting: *Ken Riddles*, Bangor, N. Ireland

Not the End

of the

World

Gerry McCullough

Published by

Precious Oil
PUBLICATIONS
www.preciousoil.com/publications

ISBN 13: 978-099929432 7 1

ISBN 10: 099929432 7 2

First published **2016**

**10a Listooder Road, Crossgar,
Downpatrick, Northern Ireland BT30 9JE**

Not the End of the World

A bit of Orientation

Sometime in the future, who knows how far away, all the things which people have been dreading and issuing warnings about for years are beginning to happen.

The planet earth has finally become one political unit. Its capital city is now called Nexus Luxuria. Luxury, after all, is clearly the thing most people have been aiming for all their lives.

Life has developed in an almost exactly similar fashion to the threatened forecasts. The world has at last achieved all those marvellous things we've at present only started to acquire for ourselves – global warming; over-use and exhaustion of fossil fuels; a third world with slave labour factories; globalization of commerce until just seven multi-national companies are running the entire planet (under a titular World President with seven Vice Presidents – a Government with no real power, but considerable wealth and status); and a population kept happy by recreational drugs, which are no longer frowned on but instead encouraged. In fact, an other-earthly paradise – not!

Oh, and at a guess the future time when all this is happening is about a hundred years ahead of ours.

Or is it only fifty?

Thanks to my husband, Raymond, for cover design, editing, proof-reading and general encouragement.

Chapter One

It was the end of the world.

Great monstrous lumps of falling universe crashed through the air. Faint shrieks signalled disasters far enough away to be ignored. Chunks of exploding heads in many bright colours – the scarlet of blood, pink, brown or black of flesh, red, blonde or black of hair – were all around.

Merc Swingly, pushing his untidy brown hair back out of his eyes, jumped to one side to avoid a passing dishwasher, and seized his wife Seraphina by the arm. He screwed up his face in horror, momentarily altering the youthful innocence of his normal expression to a less boyish mixture of apprehension and angst.

'Run!' he yelled in his wife's ear. 'Run!'

Seraphina's dark wavy hair floated wildly in the fierce wind, as her long tanned legs covered the ground at tremendous speed. Her slim athletic body in its highly trained state, was nevertheless finding it hard to keep up while carrying their daughter Lucy. Seizing the baby from her arms, Merc bolted in no particular direction, glancing back anxiously every few seconds to make sure Seraphina was still there. Lucy wriggled in his tight grasp and pulled happily at the hank of hair which was falling down over Merc's forehead.

Merc would have felt marginally happier about the situation if it had not been someone else's hair.

This was not amusing. It was fine to say, 'Run!' The question remained, 'Where to?'

The crashing noises on all sides intensified.

The dangerously huge and heavy lumps of concrete which had previously been the foundations and buildings of the vast city of Nexus Luxuria continued to miss Merc and his family by inches. Ahead of him he could dimly see what might be a cave, or might not so long ago have been a cellar.

'In here!' he shouted, and ducked his way inside.

It was pitch dark.

Beside him, he identified the funny little catch in her breathing which meant that Seraphina had been running too hard and had probably just missed the bus.

'What on earth are you doing, Merc?' came the familiar voice. 'How could you have let this happen?'

Yep! It was her.

Merc didn't attempt to answer.

'Let's go further in,' he suggested. 'It might be safer.'

'Waah!' said Lucy.

From the back of the cave, or cellar, a weird, delicate light shone out of nowhere.

Merc jumped several feet.

'Merc.'

A strange voice.

Human? Please!

But to Merc it sounded more amphibian. If he had much real idea of what an amphibian voice would sound like.

Had he imagined it?

No! There it was again.

'Merc!'

Hitching Lucy up more securely on his hip, and taking Seraphina's arm, he moved forward a few paces, straining to see something – anything – in the dim light at the back of the cave.

For some reason, the light, like some slightly out of date wall paint, had a hint of green.

'Yes?' said Merc. His voice, he noticed with annoyance, was quivering slightly.

Pulling himself together, he asked again, making his voice firm and confident, like someone at a job interview, 'Yes? Is someone there?'

A figure moved towards him.

In the darkness of the cave, Merc could just about see the creature, in the green light which apparently emanated from itself.

He was looking at a cross between a large crocodile and a medium sized dragon, with touches of gorilla and human. The human bits, Merc decided, were definitely the most terrifying. There were scales, large flappy wings, strong, muscular arms, some reddish hair round the head, and a face like Nosher Boggs, the ex-boxer who ran Nexus Luxuria's most successful bookies.

Lucy, recognising something which resembled the illustrations in her favourite dinosaur book, gurgled happily and stretched out her arms to grab at this enormous new toy.

Seraphina, most uncharacteristically, said nothing.

'Merc Swingly, we have a job for you.'

'I have a job already, thank you,' Merc heard himself replying politely.

'It appears that the world has come to an end too soon,' the creature went on, ignoring him. 'At least another decade of the present state of affairs was scheduled. There are people dying now out there who have never been given a proper choice. My instructions are that this should not have happened.'

He coughed, and added hurriedly, 'Oh. Sorry. I have failed to introduce myself. I am Gryphon Longfellow, Third Degree Representative.'

'Representative of what?' Merc wanted to say.

But didn't.

He wasn't altogether sure that he wanted to know.

'I might comment,' continued the Third Degree Representative, clearing his throat impressively, and thus making the bumps on the top of his head swell to an angry red in a rather alarming manner, 'that some of us fail to see the need for any further delay. In our view, the sooner the whole sorry mess comes to an end the better. Some of the human activity we are forced to observe here in this world is unacceptable to the last degree, as you must be aware. However, the decision does not rest with me, I am glad to say. A further chance, and the right to make choices. That's the requirement from up top.'

He paused.

Merc said, 'And what do you intend to do about it, Mr. Third Degree Representative? I should have thought all this was a bit past fixing.'

He gestured vaguely backwards to the flying blocks and collapsing mountains outside the cave, and the faintly screaming voices.

'Can you, for instance,' said Merc, 'put his head back on Silo Clotson? I saw it disintegrate with my own eyes.'

His tone of voice displayed, against his will, the pent up anger which was trying to spill out of him.

'Merc! Not in front of the baby!' Seraphina said sharply.

'She saw it too,' Merc said briefly.

'Oh, I can't do anything!' said Gryphon Longfellow reasonably. 'I'm only the errand boy. That's the job we have for you. He wants you to do it. To put the world back together again.'

The green light screamed in Merc's eyes.

Lucy began to howl in his ear.

Suddenly, taking advantage, with a well developed skill, of Merc's preoccupation, she wriggled down from her father's arms with a bump, and staggered across the floor, holding out her hands towards Gryphon with a beaming smile.

Seraphina screamed and rushed forward, managing to obstruct Merc's similar urgent leap in his daughter's direction.

Lucy reached up to grab what she was convinced was a fluffy life size toy dinosaur.

Seraphina, sobbing gustily, managed to reach her baby, and snatched her franticly to safety.

To her surprise, this was quite easily done. The Third Degree Representative, stepping back in some alarm, showed no inclination whatsoever to hold on to the child.

'Leave her alone!' panted Seraphina. 'I won't let you hurt her!'

'My dear Madam,' said Gryphon Longfellow with an air of exasperated patience, 'I haven't the slightest desire to hurt her.'

He saw the amazement on the faces of both parents. 'Oh, I assure you!' he said. 'Strictly forbidden, you know. All sorts of dire punishments attached. Millstones come into it, I believe, whatever millstones are. No need to worry!

'This is getting rather difficult,' he muttered to himself. 'Perhaps we should leave it for now. Just remember what I said, will you? Second chance. A choice for the people who haven't had one.'

At that moment Lucy reached over, and, gurgling happily, stuck her finger into Merc's eye, and cooed triumphantly into his ear.

'F***!' Merc said.

Seraphina, who had apparently reverted to normal, said, 'Merc!' sharply, in his other ear.

And then Merc woke up.

Chapter Two

Instead of the voices of his family, he could hear the alarm going off loudly beside him. Seraphina was already up. She had been dealing, he supposed, with Lucy, whose interior alarm clock seemed, for some unfathomable reason, to be set two hours earlier than Merc's.

He could hear a clatter of dishes downstairs in the kitchen. There was a smell of coffee.

Merc blinked his eyes, rolled over and stretched out one hand to switch off the alarm, and decided not to have another doze.

What a horrible dream!

Sinking back into it was definitely not an option.

He forced his eyes open, swung his feet out of bed, stood up, yawned, and stretched.

Half an hour later, Merc was feeding Lucy from a jar of baby food with one hand, while mopping up the remains of his egg yolk with a toast soldier grasped in the other.

In the intervals of scooping up spoonfuls of goo, to push into the baby's mouth, he waved a fluffy cat in her direction.

'Pussy!' he said. 'Pussy cat!'

'Uck!' said Lucy.

Merc listened carefully. His eyes glazed.

'Pussy cat?' he eventually mumbled.

'Uck!' said Lucy again.

Merc gulped, and felt a great joy flooding through him.

Lucy, under his patient tutelage, at still only 14 months old, had just attempted to say, 'Duck,' he was pretty sure.

Well, it was 'Duck,' or something very like that.

Not 'Cat,' certainly.

So.

'Seraphina! Sweetie! Come and hear!' he yelled.

Seraphina, her hair falling over her face, emerged in a cloud of steam from the utility room, where she was extracting clean clothes, mostly for Merc and Lucy, from the drier.

'If you don't get a move on, you'll be late again,' she observed.

However, the news of Lucy's amazingly intelligent achievement distracted her from any further comment on Merc's punctuality record.

Both parents hung dotingly round Lucy for the next five minutes, trying (in vain) for a repeat performance.

Then Merc, with a horrified glance at his watch, sprang to his feet, grabbed his briefcase, and with a quick kiss for both his wife and his daughter, rushed out of the door.

A moment later he rushed back for his car keys, and Seraphina took the opportunity to wipe the splash of orange coloured baby food from his cheek.

Then he was finally gone.

Driving through the heat and fury of the crowded rush hour traffic in his electric automobile, Merc rehearsed explanations and apologies for his inevitable lateness.

The truth was that, since the human race had finally run out of oil some time ago, the mortgage had definitely been called in (after years of blood curdling threats to take the matter of all these overdue repayments to court within seven days of the date of this letter); and the planet seemed to be due for re-possession any day now. Traffic, now all the cars were powered by electricity, had become so bad, not only multiplied by thousands but also draggingly slow, that the only way to arrive on time for work would be to leave in the early hours of the morning, before anyone else was up. Like Buzzo Lurker, the creep.

Or walk to work, like Sebwall Norton, the super creep.

Merc had not yet reached the stage of crawling to management to that extent.

If only old Cawny Screed was still in charge. Screed would have understood. Screed had been late as often as not himself. He understood about the current traffic problems.

Chapter 2

Screed was a relic of the old days, before the last take-over, when the bottom line, if important, wasn't quite so terrifying in its consequences. He was a fat, pleasantly red faced man with a mop of snow white hair who knew that life occasionally contained other imperatives than work, and was prepared to allow his employees at least some small amount of time to enjoy the valuable experience of life which took place outside the office.

Cawny, forced into early retirement, had been followed by Buster Panter.

Merc wasn't quite sure what had happened to Panter.

The turnover rate for Chief Executives in the Company was more than that of a princess trying to sleep in a bed full of peas. Or even fleas.

Buster Panter had been bad enough.

Merc had been happy to hear that he was gone.

But the new boss, arriving at head office after the recent take-over, was different again.

And how!

Merc suspected that this new boss, Flacker Winterbotham, stayed in the building all night in some little private hideaway he had set up, counting paper clips. Certainly, he was inevitably last to leave at night and first there in the morning.

One of Winterbotham's first actions on his appointment, after sacking fifty per cent of the workforce, mostly the older ones, had been to introduce longer working hours, starting an hour earlier and finishing an hour later.

Merc, who had little enough time to spend with Lucy in the evening as it was, had been pretty gutted about this. So had most of the rest of the staff.

But it had been made abundantly clear that choice did not enter into the matter. So the mainly gutless staff had said nothing.

Anyone who was unhappy about the new hours, had said Winterbotham – smiling in his own individual way, which reminded Merc of crocodiles seen on television nature programmes – was perfectly free to leave whenever they liked.

There were many eager young people out there, had said Winterbotham, who would be only too delighted to step into the jobs left vacant.

No-one on the staff was keen to lose their job. There weren't any going outside the seven Companies, since that last take-over.

The new hours were established.

So much for the unions. Which had been pretty obsolete for some time now anyway, come to think of it.

And now the Company – Company One, Worldwide Productions – produced everything that had to be produced, and was the most important of the seven great multi-nationals; the others being Planetary Banking and Insurance; Planetary Building and Construction; Worldwide Weapons (mainly operating in the third world countries); World Health and Chemicals; World News and Recreation; and Cultural Education and Indoctrination. Between them they controlled and/or produced just about everything on the planet.

Including hair styles, skirt lengths, insurance, politics, football matches and Happy Honey pills, electric cars, and weapons of Mass Destruction.

Oh, and soup.

Well, food, really.

But it often seemed to boil down to soup.

Made from soya products.

Merc looked round and grunted in annoyance as one of the slow moving electric bus-trains snaked its lethargic way past him.

Normally, nothing moved more slowly than a bus-train, except perhaps yeast. Today, Merc seemed to be the exception that proved the rule.

The heat was growing more intense as the traffic built up. All this climate change and global warming, Merc thought vaguely. Nice in some ways, though not in traffic. But how far could it go?

He parked in the employees only car park, noticing that he'd managed to get just about the last space. The huge building which was the company headquarters leered over him. It had once been a bank, at least a century ago, and it looked appropriately and criminally threatening. The lofty walls, topped by a frieze carved with famous figures of bankers from the past, one of the ugliest pieces of artwork, in Merc's opinion, which had ever graced Nexus Luxuria, blocked out much of the sky.

The thick oak doors embossed with strong iron bands sat open. In another ten minutes they would swing shut, and would remain like that for the rest of the working day. Access would only be by means of the personal card issued to all employees, which when entered in the appropriate slot opened the doors, and also recorded the time and the name of the card holder, so that money could be docked as necessary from the end of month salary. Merc, who couldn't afford to lose any of his not enormous income, was relieved, though surprised, to see the doors still open.

He was even more amazed and delighted to reach his desk that morning before running into Flacker Winterbotham or one of Winterbotham's many sycophants.

'Hi, Hyacinth,' he said, as he hurried into his office, carefully avoiding, as usual, any danger of saying, 'Hiya, Hya.' He smiled at his assistant administrator as he slid into his chair and switched on his computer screen. 'How's it going?'

'Great, MS,' responded the junior analyst enthusiastically.

Hyacinth was slim, young and blonde, a popular combination.

Merc reflected, not for the first time, that if he was that way inclined, he could probably have a red hot affair with her.

And then Seraphina would find out about it, and she would either walk out or throw him out, in either case keeping Lucy.

Was it worth it?

No way!

His good friend Ben Gunther had been through all that. Ben's red hot affair, Merc remembered, had left him covered in third degree burns. It made Merc even more reluctant to take the risk. In any case, he still loved Seraphina – didn't he?

Sometimes, when Lucy was definitely settled to sleep, and Seraphina, warm and inviting, rolled over towards him in bed, he had no doubt whatsoever about it.

At other times, when they had one of their frequent arguments about nothing, he wasn't quite so sure.

But whatever the case, he knew one thing for certain. He didn't want to lose Lucy.

Or Seraphina either, he was pretty definite.

What woman would be any better as a lover?

Not Hyacinth Duckworthy, for sure.

'FW wants to see you, MS,' his assistant now said, smiling be-witchingly. It wasn't the moment for a bewitching smile to work. Merc, collapsing backwards into his unfortunately rather uncomfortable ergonomically designed computer chair, had frozen with horror.

'FW?' he croaked. 'Oh. Sure.'

Hyacinth smiled sexily. In vain.

'He rang through twice. An hour ago, and then half an hour later. I said,' she added demurely, shaking back her thatch of long fair hair sexily, 'that you were in the loo. And then that you were in the middle of a really crucial phone call with Brace Heatherspud from Planetary Banking and Insurance, which might go on for some time.'

'Um… thanks, Hya,' Merc mumbled. 'Thanks. I owe you one.'

He shuddered internally as the possible repercussions of that particular statement sank into his brain.

Hyacinth smiled sweetly.

'Okay.'

'Okay.' Merc tried for a friendly, but uninvolved, smile. 'Well, I'd better be going.'

He walked at a reasonable pace towards the lift in the far corner of the open plan floor, then, once out of sight, put on speed, pressed the button for the tenth floor, where Flacker Winterbotham had his lair, and danced with impatience as the lift slowly made its way down towards him.

Here it came at last. He slid through the barely open doors, inched his way into a narrow space between three other people, and began frantically to manufacture conversations he might have been having with the unpleasant Chief Executive Brace Heatherspud of Planetary Banking and Insurance, one of the seven companies which currently ruled the planet. Which might be to the advantage of his own company, World-wide Productions, and of Flacker Winterbotham in particular.

Chapter Three

In his office on the tenth floor, Flacker Winterbotham, his hands writhing through his sparse black hair, was walking up and down the enormous floor space, dictating at speed to a girl from the typing pool, Esther Frantic. Esther had been the top student of her year, (which was how she had got her present job; in addition to her long blonde hair and comic book figure, that is). Nevertheless, she was currently in despair. No-one, but no-one, could take dictation at two hundred and fifty words a minute!

She considered pointing this out to her boss.

But she knew, without having to think about it, that not only would the argument fail to impress Flacker Winterbotham, but so would she if she relied on it.

Winterbotham wanted perfection plus. Perfection plus another one hundred percent, at least.

Esther was fully aware of her attractions. It was clear to her that this was the time to use them.

'Oh, Flacker!' she murmured, setting aside her notebook and pen. 'Oh, Flacker! I can't possibly concentrate on what you're saying, when you're here in front of me! Flacker, you're so amazing!'

(Although she was an excellent shorthand typist, Esther's dialogue skills clearly needed some work.)

Swaying forward voluptuously, she raised her arms and encircled her boss's neck, rubbing her body against him.

Flacker was not really surprised. He was used to women appearing to be wildly attracted to him.

And had no problem in believing that this was because of his sexual powers, rather than his sacking powers.

Esther had just succeeded in pushing him backwards over his desk, and writhing enthusiastically on top of him, while unfastening various buttons, when his personal assistant, Kyra Hotberthy, knocked briefly and walked in.

Flacker jumped. He was aware that Kyra had every right to expect not to see him involved with another woman.

It was particularly embarrassing because he had made certain promises just the previous night to Kyra, involving eternal fidelity and ever-lasting love.

'Merc Swingly to see you, sir,' barked Kyra, before turning on her heel and marching out, slamming the door behind her. The door, like Flacker Winterbotham, quivered uneasily.

'Flacker,' said Merc unhappily, only too aware of the situation.

'Merc.'

Flacker Winterbotham was also aware of something, that it might not now be appropriate for him to deal with Merc as he had intended to do.

Esther Frantic went out hurriedly, remembering to adjust her clothing before leaving the room.

Winterbotham walked over to his desk, rubbing furtively at his mouth as he went, and seated himself in his big, luxurious black leather chair.

Back in the trappings of authority, he felt slightly better.

Nevertheless.

'Good to see you, Merc,' he said. 'Ah.'

'Yes,' said Merc.

'I wanted to say ...'

Flacker paused.

'That is.' He paused unhappily.

'I've been watching your progress with interest, Merc,' said Flacker Winterbotham, drawing a deep breath. 'That is ... I wonder ...'

'Yes?' asked Merc, wondering exactly which bits the Chief Executive had been watching.

'Have a drink!' suggested Flacker suddenly, springing to his feet and heading for the drinks cabinet on the nearest wall.

'Oh. Thanks.'

Flacker poured two large whiskeys.

Downing his own, he filled the glass with the pale amber coloured liquid again, then went back to his desk and sat down.

He thrust the other glass at Merc, and sat sipping thirstily. Then he swallowed the rest of his drink. Banged the glass down on his desk. Sprang up again. And began to stride hastily about.

Finally he came to a halt behind his chair.

'It seems there's a vacancy in the Eastern Sales branch,' he said 'Er. Head of Fashion is being made redundant. General reshuffle. Room for a new man, assistant or something. Not settled yet exactly who's moving where. It would definitely be a step up for you, though, if you're interested?'

Merc gaped at him. Fashion was one of the more important branches of the Company.

'Sure thing, FW,' he managed.

'Might mean longer hours, naturally. And a fair bit of travel.'

Merc's face fell.

'Longer hours? Travel? I'm a family man, FW. Right now I –'

Merc knew what he wanted to say.

'Travel' nowadays normally meant long, sluggish boat journeys by sailing ship. Guaranteed to seem to last longer than a party political broadcast in Japanese, and in Merc's own case to make him sicker than a nineteen year old student on Saturday night.

No way was he taking on any job, promotion or not, which would take him away from Lucy and Seraphina even more.

However, for some reason the words seemed trapped uncomfortably in his mouth.

He noticed, uncomprehendingly, that Flacker Winterbotham appeared to have suddenly frozen, as if the pause button on the video had been activated by some automatic setting or by an impatient viewer.

Flacker stood with one hand on the back of his chair, and the other raised to his face. He had been in the act of picking at his nose, one of his many annoying little personal habits. The fingers were frozen in an unintentionally humorous attitude.

Silence poured into the room like thick vegetable soup (only not so hot and with less barley). The computers, the air conditioning, the rest of the office paraphernalia, all appeared to have switched themselves off. The sound of silence was deafening.

Merc, jumping to his feet, was aware that he himself seemed to be the only person outside the time-lock.

A moment later he realised that he was mistaken.

If 'person' was the right word, that is.

A faint delicate green light filled the office.

Merc looked behind him.

Gryphon Longfellow, Third Degree Representative, stood there, not exactly smiling, but peering at Merc in a reasonably friendly way.

An interested way, at least.

Which, Merc realised after a moment's thought, was not necessarily the same thing.

Chapter Four

'Hey,' Merc said. 'You're a dream! Am I still asleep?'

Gryphon looked puzzled.

'A dream?' he repeated. The frown on his long, battle scarred face – which reminded Merc quite unpleasantly of the ex boxer Nosher Boggs, with his marks and scars, the results of far too many fights – cleared as he worked out Merc's meaning. 'Ah! I understand you. You mean that when I spoke to you previously, you were in the condition known as sleeping. And now you are not.'

'Yeah,' said Merc. He felt dazed.

'I see. But humans have been receiving the messages we bring, both in dreams and in what, I believe, are called 'visions,' for several thousand years now. Surely the methodology must be fairly widely understood by this time?'

He sighed. And flapped one claw in a resigned fashion. Merc stepped back out of range just in case.

'But I had forgotten. This is the age of the new barbarism, is it not? When technology rules, and the wisdom of generations has been recycled via the rubbish bin. Yes, indeed. I now see the evidence of this state of affairs with my own eyes.'

'Hey!' said Merc, who thought of himself as an intellectual. 'I know stuff!'

'Well, know this,' said Gryphon Longfellow. He drew himself up impressively. 'You were not sent back to repeat the mistakes of your first attempt. Do not refuse the job your employer is offering you. It gives you an opportunity to make a difference.'

He frowned.

'Oh, dear! This is all much more complicated than I had expected. You seem to have no comprehension of what's needed. I can't keep appearing to you every time you're about to make a wrong decision.'

'No,' agreed Merc whole heartedly.

'I'll have to see – perhaps I should ask for some advice –' Gryphon broke off, and began to mutter to himself, while Merc watched in perplexity.

'Well! This'll not get the world saved!' the Third Degree Representative said after a moment in a more cheerful voice. 'Just leave that side of it to me. Meanwhile, I'm serious about this job! It's important that you accept it!'

Then Gryphon Longfellow, with a wave of one of his flappy, scaly wings, stepped back and began to dwindle, like a quicker than usual electrically powered vehicle disappearing into the distance.

Merc felt his head start to swirl. His knees gave way under him, and he collapsed into his chair.

As his vision cleared, he watched, with consternation, the fingers of Flacker Winterbotham's left hand resume their exploration of his left nostril.

Then he noticed that the office noises – computers, air conditioning, and the rest – had started up again.

The time lock was broken.

'So,' continued Winterbotham, as if there had been no break in continuity, 'the first thing will be for you to liaise with Han Lilong, the new Head of our Eastern Fashion section. I'll give him a ring and let him know the score.'

He pressed the intercom.

'Kyra.'

A frosty voice showered ice on him from the outer office.

'Yes.'

'Get me HL.'

Some music followed which must have been composed electronically by a tone deaf child seriously lacking in all technological skill.

Then Han Lilong's voice boomed over the hands free phone.

'FW?'

'Han. Good to talk to you. I'm making Merc Swingly your new assistant. Sending him along now, right? You can fill him in about the job. Bring him along to the board meeting next a.m., right? Great.'

Flacker Winterbotham pressed the cut off in the middle of Lilong's stuttered protests, but not before Merc had heard, 'Who? But FW! We haven't discussed this! I thought ...'

'Fine!' said Winterbotham, with his crocodile smile. 'Nothing like a promotion to increase loyalty, am I right, Swingly? Kyra will tell you which office is HL's, if you don't already know. Trot along, now!'

Merc trotted.

That is, he staggered out of the office, and came to a halt by Kyra Hotberthy's enormous light oak desk, with its load of electronic equipment, where he said, 'Wow!' and halted, clinging to the desk for moral, rather than simply physical, support.

Kyra Hotberthy was a tall, bosomy brunette with copper coloured skin which indicated her mixed racial origin.

Looking at her, Merc was aware of two things.

The first was Kyra's outstanding beauty.

The second was her blazing anger.

'So, he's buying you off, is he?' Kyra had a faint sing-song accent – probably a relic of her childhood, which he had vaguely heard had been on an island somewhere on the other side of the world – and it made her voice sound pretty strange when she was angry.

She saw Merc's look of astonishment.

'Oh, it's not second sight,' she added contemptuously. 'I keep the intercom turned on permanently at low volume out here. The fool doesn't realise I can do that. It keeps me properly informed. So much for anything there was between me and Flacker Winterbotham!'

Merc smiled weakly.

'He thinks he can buy anyone,' said Kyra. She ripped the top sheet from her notebook, where, Merc noticed vaguely, she had been doodling what seemed to be meant for a row of flowers, possibly roses, allowing for the inexpert drawing, with an enormous question mark beside them; crumpled it into a ball; and hurled it savagely at the wastepaper bin.

'But what does he think he's buying from me?'

'Your silence about his love life, right? Oh, it wouldn't matter normally. But he's decided to stand for election. Local to start with. Sees himself ending up as World President. But not if nasty rumours are circulating.' Kyra scowled horribly. 'In spite of all our advances, we still expect our politicians to keep to a high moral standard, sexually, don't we? It's okay for the rest of us, but not them. But you know all this.'

Merc nodded.

'I thought perhaps he was worried about his wife finding out,' he ventured.

'Much he cares about her! He's just finalised the divorce. By agreement. No blame. That's respectable enough these days, goodness knows. And she's gone off to marry Bilt Tong, the Chief Executive of Planetary Building and Construction. But Winterbotham needs to avoid any suggestion of sleaze. Huh! A regular sleazebag like him! How he dares! I'm through with him from now on, that's for sure!' she muttered vengefully, more to herself than Merc.

'Er – HL's office?' Merc asked. 'FW said you would tell me which it is?'

'Ninth floor. Number 904,' said the still scowling Kyra, banging files about on her desk. 'I'll let Personnel know about changing your title and pay scale.'

'I don't think it's quite decided which job I'll be given?'

'And it never will be if you don't grab it!' Kyra said. 'Look, I'm telling Personnel that you'll be Vice Executive of Eastern Fashion, right? Who's going to argue? Serve the fool right if he didn't mean to go as far as that!'

It was probably appropriate to say, 'Thank you,' so Merc did.

Then made a hasty exit, before she could change her mind.

Chapter Five

Merc, heading in some bewilderment towards his new job and undreamt of rapid acceleration upwards, of the nought to one hundred in two seconds variety, wondered vaguely if there was anything more behind Kyra's attitude to her boss than the recent episode with Esther Frantic.

He knew, in common with the rest of the staff, all about the rumoured relationship between Kyra and FW. But even to Merc, not the world champion when it came to understanding women, her vehemently expressed dislike seemed to have more to it than just jealousy.

He ran down the staircase to the floor below and found Han Lilong's office.

Lilong, like most people nowadays, was a mixture of races, but predominantly Eastern, Merc thought. His smooth round face and sleek dark hair gave a misleading impression of languor.

Bouncing up from behind his desk, he came to meet Merc with outstretched hand, as his secretary showed Merc in.

'Good to see you, MS!' he exclaimed loudly, a beaming but clearly synthetic smile spreading across his face. 'FW must think a lot of you, my friend! Sit down, sit down! What can I offer you? Something to pep you up? Or something to relax you? Ha, ha!'

He pulled out his pill case from the waistcoat of his dark blue designer suit. The small box was an elaborate affair of gold inlaid with his name written in silver, surrounded by various designs with the suggestion of eastern promise about them, but not, Merc knew, likely to contain Turkish Delight.

Merc, already feeling the effects of the large whiskey pressed on him by Flacker Winterbotham, to say nothing of the even stronger effects of his chat with Gryphon Longfellow, hastily refused.

'Well, well, bit early in the day for you, is it?' asked Han jovially.

'That's right,' confirmed Merc thankfully.

To tell the truth, he had never really got into the regular use of recreational drugs, in spite of the government posters on every hoarding and the regular TV ads encouraging the public to tone up their nerves and emotions by taking several every day.

Pop a pill three times a day

And worry just can't come your way!

the jingle went. There was a little, fluffy dog called Honey identified with the ad, who brought his master's pill box to him and sat up and begged with the box in his mouth. The pills were called Happy Honeys. Presumably this was meant to be cute and ingratiating. Not, Merc thought, to suggest that the dog should be given a spare pill as a treat.

And not that the pills were the equivalent of loo paper.

Merc had never told anyone but Seraphina, but actually he thought it was all rather silly.

Did anyone realise, he sometimes wondered, that in the dark ages, recreational drugs had been banned? And considered a bad thing?

He wouldn't go so far as that, of course, but he didn't really like being pressured to take them all the time. The world government made a fortune in taxes on the various drugs, okay, and that meant they had been able to cut income tax, right? But, still.

'Well, now, Merc, FW wants me to fill you in about the Fashion section, boy,' Han Lilong was continuing. 'What do you know as of now?'

Merc thought furiously. What was likely to be right? 'We want to keep cornering the market?' he offered at last. 'We need a cheaper source of finished products than we have currently?'

'Right!' beamed his new boss. 'I see FW was right on the ball, picking you, Merc! As he always is,' he added hastily. 'You've gone right to the heart of the problem.'

He jumped up and went over to his computer desk.

'Come and look at this,' he commanded, and Merc obediently went to look at the slimline screen over his shoulder. Spreadsheets packed with figures scrolled past his eyes, followed by pages of notes apparently giving options.

'What do you think of that, eh?'

Merc, who had completely failed to pick up a single word or figure as they flashed past, cleared his throat apprehensively and said, 'Amazing!'

It seemed to be the correct answer.

'Right!' said Han Lilong again. 'Amazing is right. Now, MS, what I'm going to do is, I'm going to send this info to your computer, and I want you to analyse it for me and come up with the top three options, in order of preference, okay? Tomorrow morning is the board meeting, and you can present your results there, right? Any questions?'

Merc's mouth opened and shut. Options for what? 'No questions, HL,' he managed finally.

'Good! Well, on you go, then.' Lilong stood up and headed back to his desk, while Merc slipped quietly out of the room.

Once outside, he stood holding his head in his hands, to prevent what seemed like a real risk of it falling off.

How on earth was he expected to analyse all those figures and plans before tomorrow morning? It was crazy. This was his night for giving Lucy her bath, too.

Merc groaned. What had he let himself in for?

He moved back to his own desk half in a dream.

Looking into his computer, he realised that the facts and figures had already been forwarded to him. With another groan, he sat staring at the screen.

'Problems?' asked a sweet voice in his ear.

Hyacinth Duckworthy.

'You bet,' said Merc absent mindedly, as he continued to stare at the screen, only half aware of who was speaking to him.

Hyacinth came much closer, and tried, not very successfully, to perch on the tiny half arm of Merc's chair, which was, unfortunately for her, already fully occupied by Merc's own arm. Then, giving that up as a bad job, she perched on the edge of his desk instead, rather too close to the computer screen and, even worse from Merc's point of view, far too close to Merc himself. .

'Maybe I could help?' she suggested in her soft coo.

Merc came abruptly back to reality. He stared at her speculatively.

'Maybe you could, at that,' he said slowly.

Building up a further debt to Hyacinth wasn't, probably, the wisest thing he could do, but on the other hand, if he wasn't going to stay here working all night – and there was no way he was doing that – then some help, in fact lots of help, was going to be essential.

'Listen,' he said hoarsely, 'if you really don't mind, then here's what I need.'

Chapter Six

Hyacinth, as he had expected, proved to be very adept at manoeuvring figures.

Including, unfortunately, her own.

Still, by late afternoon, an amazing, to Merc, amount of work had been done.

And owing to Merc's strenuous efforts, nothing except work.

Between them, they had gone through all the spreadsheets and reduced the unwieldy mass of figures to a number of simple results which, as Hyacinth remarked, even Board members ought to be able to take in.

'Thanks a bunch, Hya,' said Merc gratefully. 'I don't know what I'd have done without you.'

'No problem, sexy,' smiled the junior analyst. 'But we still have to work out the options.'

'Yeah, well, I'll be okay to do that myself,' mumbled the blushing Merc. 'No need to keep you any longer.'

'I can probably give you a few tips there, sweetie,' said Hyacinth, smiling happily. Things were definitely going her way. 'All you need to do is pick out the three cheapest options. The board isn't going to look at any other reasons, so you can put in any rubbish you like. Just highlight the money – they won't even read the rest, or listen to you presenting it, see?'

It sounded dishonest to Merc, but he knew she was right.

Nevertheless.

'Thanks, Hya,' he said reluctantly, 'but I think I'd rather put a bit of work into the reasons, too. It won't take that long, though. You should run on, okay?'

'I thought,' said Hyacinth in her most sexy voice, 'that you might like to reward me for my help? Dinner this evening, for instance?'

'I can't do this evening,' said Merc quickly. 'But, yeah, maybe we could set up a date some other time?'

He groaned inwardly as he visualised Seraphina's reaction. To say nothing of his own dread of spending time alone with Hyacinth Duck-worthy, in quasi-romantic circumstances.

Perhaps he could keep putting it off till she got the message?

Making his slow way home through the electric traffic, Merc reflected on some of the things which had happened to him since he woke up that morning. Or possibly from before he woke up. The weight of work he had ploughed his way through that afternoon, with Hyacinth's help, had prevented him from thinking much about anything else until now.

Had he really had two interviews with a being from another world? Had he really been given promotion beyond his wildest dreams for no real reason? Had he really promised to take Hyacinth Duckworthy out to dinner?

And tomorrow was the Board meeting. How on earth was he going to get through that?

At this stage in his thoughts, he was suddenly aware that someone was running alongside the car, keeping pace easily enough with the crawling thousand wheeled worm of traffic.

A hand was raised and a fist knocked lightly on his window.

Merc stared.

It was a small elderly man, dressed in rather shabby, old fashioned clothes. As he saw that he had caught Merc's attention, he beamed, and raised his red baseball cap in an out of date gesture of politeness.

'Merc Swingly?' he bawled, at the top of his voice, so as to be heard through the closed window.

Merc nodded, his surprise showing on his face.

'Can I come in?' bawled the little man. 'Gryphon Longfellow sent me.'

Merc gaped at him.

Then, moved by a compulsion he only half understood, he found himself pressing the electronic switch to swing the door open.

'Thanks,' said the little man, climbing gratefully in. 'All this running takes it out of you, at my age. Still, look on the bright side, all good exercise, right?'

He saw that Merc was still staring at him in amazement.

'Better watch the road, sonny,' he said genially. 'Now, let me start by introducing myself. I'm Mr. Brown.'

'Mr. Brown?'

'Yep. I'm here, right, to help you.'

Seeing Merc's blank expression, Mr. Brown explained further.

'See, Gryphon isn't too used to human beings. He was at a bit of a loss as to how to communicate with you on a regular basis. Keep you from making the wrong decisions, okay?'

'Yeah,' Merc remembered slowly. 'He said something like that.'

'So he used his wisdom, and asked for help and advice. Result, me!' Mr. Brown beamed.

'You?' Merc's tone, he realised a moment later, was hardly flattering.

'See, Gryphon, right, is more into the message delivery side of things. But your actual day to day protection, that's more our branch. Looking after special individuals – sort of bodyguard work, you might say. And I drew you, sonny.'

Seeing Merc's face, he added hastily, 'Oh, it's all been cleared higher up, natch. We don't do anything without his say so, I can tell you!'

'But,' Merc asked with unconscious rudeness, 'what exactly can you do to look after me?'

'We – ell,' drawled Mr. Brown, 'it's all a matter of stopping you in time, sort of thing. Giving you a bit of a nudge onto the right track, when you start wandering off the edge, right? See what I mean?'

'And what makes you think you would know better than me what I should do?' asked Merc in some indignation.

'Comes with the job, sonny,' Mr. Brown said. 'Part of the equipment. Wisdom, that sort of thing, right? Take it from me, I'll just know.'

'And another thing,' Merc added, 'you can't always be on the spot, how could you, when I'm making important decisions? I don't see how you're going to be much practical use, to be honest.'

'I can go anywhere you can go,' said Mr. Brown seriously. 'Thing is, you won't always see me unless you want to. But you can ask me anything you want anytime.

'A bit of advice, sonny,' he added with his usual beam. 'Explain all this to your wife. You're going to need her support before long. Things can only get more complicated, the way they're heading.'

'Explain to Seraphina?' Merc said in horrified tones. 'She'd think I'd gone mad!'

'She might or she might not,' said Mr. Brown mysteriously. 'Anyway, that's my advice to you.'

He pressed the button on the door which made it swing open again.

'Right,' he said. 'This is where I get off. Have to call in at the super-market before suppertime. So long, sonny!'

He stepped out into the once more halted traffic.

'Hey, wait!' protested Merc. 'You haven't explained anything! I want to ask you –'

But Mr. Brown had gone.

Chapter Seven

The house where Merc lived with his family was pleasant enough. True, it was practically identical to every other house in Nexus Luxuria, which were all two stories, made of concrete, and painted in a one of a small range of pastel colours. This one was a pale blue. The houses fronted directly unto the street, although there were small gardens to the rear, consisting mainly of grass.

The only things which distinguished Merc's house from the rest of the row of houses were the flowers which Seraphina had insisted, at great expense, in planting in two small tubs beside the door. And it belonged to the Company, went with Merc's job, and would be promptly taken off them if ever Merc was made redundant. But, hey, Merc thought, it was warm and comfortable and there was room for all three of them, and possibly for one more in another year or so. He smiled happily at the thought. Things could be a lot worse.

As he walked through the door, Merc could hear Seraphina's voice

Then he heard Lucy wailing.

What was Seraphina doing to her? he wondered indignantly.

He went into the kitchen, and saw his wife rocking their daughter in her arms, trying unsuccessfully to comfort her.

Seraphina looked round at him, and he saw her tear stained face.

'Oh, Merc!' she exclaimed thankfully, thrusting Lucy towards him. 'See what you can do with her.'

'What's the problem?' asked the father of the family, dropping his briefcase, and taking on his responsibilities in the form of a weeping wife and a howling baby.

'I don't know!' wailed Seraphina. 'I've never seen her like this before! She's been crawling round all day, looking for something, and finally she seemed to give up, and started howling instead. I can't do anything with her.'

'But what's she been looking for?'

Seraphina didn't know.

But Lucy, distracted from her crying by the appearance of that wonderful person, Daddy, managed to enlighten them. Making history by speaking her second ever real word, she brought out, 'Dinso!'

Then, as Merc and Seraphina gazed admiringly at her, she crowned her triumph by adding, happily, 'Big!'

'Big Dinosaur?' guessed Seraphina. 'What – ?'

Merc gasped.

Seraphina gulped.

Seraphina said slowly, 'Does she mean – ?'

Then she looked at Merc.

'I – I remember something about a big creature a bit like a dinosaur – but – ? That was a dream? Wasn't it?'

Merc gulped.

'Well –' he began.

'You know something about this, Merc Swingly, don't you?' said his wife accusingly.

'I think –' Merc said slowly. 'Well, I don't know – but it sounds like – Seraphina, did you possibly have the same dream I did last night?'

'The end of the world?' Seraphina asked.

'Rocks everywhere?' Merc added.

'Flying dishwashers?'

'A sort of cave?'

'A 'big dinosaur'?'

'A message?'

'Being sent back?'

'Right!'

They stared at each other.

'And Lucy was there, too,' Merc said. 'She dreamt it, too.'

Seraphina looked at him. She sat down slowly on the nearest chair.

'So, what you're saying is,' she said carefully, 'that it wasn't so much a dream as a real experience?'

'I'm not sure,' admitted Merc. 'Perhaps not exactly real yet. A sort of glimpse of a possible future, maybe? The future if we don't make the right choices now?'

Seraphina sat rock still, looking at him, her face a study.

Then came dawning realisation. 'So, Merc Swingly! This word Lucy's been saying all day! I remember what you said in front of the child! It isn't 'Duck' she's saying, is it?'

Merc hastily changed the subject.

'You won't believe the day I've had, honey!' he began.

Half an hour later, sitting round the kitchen table, with Lucy now crowing happily in her high chair, Merc and Seraphina ate mock chicken curry made from soya beans and considered their position.

'You're in this just as much as me, Seraphina,' Merc pointed out eventually. 'You had the dream, too.'

'But the message was for you, Merc,' his wife said. She seemed indignant about that.

'I don't think that means much,' said Merc, with the diplomatic approach learnt over three years of marriage. He and Seraphina had married early, straight from university in fact, as soon as they knew that Merc had landed the great job with Nexus Productions management. Just before Worldwide Productions took it over. 'We work as a team, right? We need to tackle this business together.'

'Fair enough,' agreed Seraphina suspiciously. She was familiar with Merc's attempts at diplomacy, and knew when to be on her guard for what was coming next.

'So – what should I do about this Hyacinth Duckworthy business?' asked Merc. 'How am I going to get out of taking her to dinner? Without annoying her so much that she makes trouble for me?'

'Really, Merc!' snapped Seraphina. 'That's the least of your worries, I should think. What are you supposed to do at the board meeting? That's more important, right? And why are you in this new job? What's it supposed to lead to?'

'But you don't know this Hyacinth pest, honey! She's a real –'

'Um?' warned Seraphina, her finger to her mouth, and her eyes on Lucy.

'Oh – sorry. A real mean one. She wouldn't think twice about shopping me to the boss. Claiming she did all the work. She'd have the computer records to prove it, too. And then, goodbye new job and whatever it was meant to lead to!'

'Oh, take her out, then!' said Seraphina impatiently. 'But make it straight after work, and get called home by an emergency phone call as soon as you've finished eating, okay?'

'Yeah, that would work,' agreed Merc. 'Great idea.'

'Now,' said Seraphina briskly, 'it's time for Lucy's bath. We can talk some more about all this when someone's safely in beddy-byes, okay?'

Lucy's bath, when it was his turn to supervise, was one of the highlights of Merc's week.

When the splashing and laughing were over, and he held her wrapped in a soft, fluffy white bath towel, warm and solid and sweet smelling, Merc felt a deep satisfaction unequalled by anything else in his current life. It came home to him that he would take any risks necessary to keep Lucy safe.

'What about this Mr. Brown?' asked Seraphina presently when they were both downstairs, and Lucy was tucked up in bed with her favourite teddy, her long lashes angelically resting on her soft, warm cheeks. Hopefully, settled to sleep for the night.

'What about him?' asked Merc sleepily. It had been a long day.

'Well, maybe you should go and have a look for him. Ask him what you're supposed to do next. He seems to know all about it.'

'But how am I going to find him?' objected Merc. He lay back in his easy chair, and watched Seraphina lying in the chair opposite him, her long, dark hair brushing her shoulders, breathing in and out in an exciting way.

Seraphina sat up straight, spoiling the effect.

'Why not start where you saw him last?' she suggested practically. 'At the supermarket, wasn't it? Maybe someone there could point you in the right direction.'

Merc stood up reluctantly. 'You don't think it would be easier, quicker, right, if we both go?'

'And what about Lucy?' Seraphina protested indignantly. 'There's no way we can get a baby sitter at this hour. No, I'll stay and look after her, and you go on.'

'Okay,' said Merc, who had learned by now when not to argue.

He shrugged on his coat and went back out to the car.

Chapter Eight

There was no sign of Mr. Brown in the supermarket, which like all the other shops was open twenty four hours and crowded for most of them. Like every other retail outlet in the city, it was run by the Company. Most things were. The actual buildings, of course, were leased from Planetary Building and Construction.

Merc wandered through the busily shopping crowds, sighing softly to himself.

There was nothing he specially wanted to buy, although he felt rather guilty about this, for it was a clear breach of government policy. Government policy laid it down firmly that it was every citizen's duty to buy as much as possible, as often as possible, every day, so as to keep the wheels of commerce and industry not just turning but revolving as furiously as the wheels of an out of control lorry heading down the nearest 1 in 10 gradient with the brakes off.

Horror! There was Hyacinth Duckworthy, down the next aisle!

Fortunately she hadn't noticed him yet. Merc dodged down the neighbouring aisle in the opposite direction.

He turned a corner, and there was Hyacinth again, bending over to take something from the lower shelf to put into her trolley.

For the next five minutes, Merc tried in vain to escape. But in accordnce with the laws of supermarket shopping, it was, as always, impossible to avoid anyone you didn't want to speak to.

Every fresh aisle he tried seemed to have Hyacinth Duckworthy at the far end of it.

Merc looked round desperately.

Ah.

There was an open door just behind him.

He had no idea where it led, but surely he could dodge in there for a few minutes, and come out again when the dreaded Duckworthy was well away.

He went through the doorway.

To his vague surprise, he was now in the open air.

A number of people were sitting or lying in the shelter of the back wall of the building. It made Merc shiver to look at them, although they mostly seemed to be wrapped up in many layers of clothing.

A back whose head was topped by a red baseball cap seemed familiar.

The man turned round.

Yes, it was Mr. Brown.

Merc hurried forward.

'Mr. Brown! Mr. Brown!'

'Just a minute, sonny Jim!' said the little man. 'I'm in the middle of something important here. Unless you'd like to give me a hand?'

In front of Mr. Brown was a large pile of wood. Some of it was sticks, some of it was logs. All of it was apparently very damp.

'Got a match?' asked Mr. Brown briskly. 'Or even a gas lighter?'

'Um – I don't actually smoke, sorry,' Merc mumbled. He always felt apologetic when explaining his failure to conform to the norm. Everybody smoked now, since the scientists in World Health and Chemicals, researching the uses of tobacco, had reversed the old, obsolete ideas by discovering how good for your health smoking actually was.

'Good!' said Mr. Brown. 'Not good that you don't have a lighter, though. Oh, well, have to do the best we can, then.'

He advanced nearer to the woodpile and stretched out his hands, slightly raised, so that their shadow, cast by the light from the open doorway, fell across the logs.

Merc heard him speak, but couldn't pick up the words.

Immediately a bright flame burst from the heart of the wood, and a moment later it was a roaring, crackling mass, throwing out a fierce heat.

The nearby people gathered round, rubbing their hands together and grinning.

'Why on earth did you ask me for a match or a lighter when you could do that all the time?' asked Merc in bewilderment. For some reason, he found himself accepting Mr. Brown's ability to produce fire as if it was the most natural thing in the world.

'It's always better if you people do what you can to help,' Mr. Brown explained patiently. He sounded as if he were telling a six year old an elementary fact which everyone a little older knew.

'You don't actually need that coat you're wearing, do you?' he added. 'You'll be going home in a nice warm car, and you have several more at home, right?'

'Right,' Merc agreed.

'Well, don't you want to take it off and give it to Leandra here?'

Merc saw that one of the figures currently warming their hands round the now blazing fire was a thin girl of around Seraphina's age. Unlike most of the group, she was lightly clad in a skimpy summer weight dress.

Hurriedly he took his coat off and offered it to her.

'Ta,' the girl said, taking the coat and wrapping it round her shoulders. She smiled at him.

Merc felt upset.

'Where will these people sleep, tonight?' he asked Mr. Brown in a low voice.

'Probably just inside the door here,' Mr. Brown explained. 'If they can keep out of sight of the manager, some of the staff are happy enough to turn a blind eye. Several of these fellows used to work in the supermarket here, before they were made redundant at the last takeover. They like to hang out where people know them.'

Merc, who had certainly known that the town was full of homeless people, had never come in such close contact with any of them before.

'This is awful!'

'Yeah, you've got it in one,' Mr. Brown agreed.

'But surely something can be done about these people?' Merc asked Mr. Brown desperately. 'A hostel, or affordable housing with a cash advance to start them off, or something? Why do they have to sleep outside like this? And I suppose they aren't the only ones?'

'You suppose right, Sonny Jim,' said Mr. Brown evenly. 'This is only a representative sample. Something to give you a bit of a scare and maybe make you think, see? As for doing something about them, we're hoping that you'll be the one to do something about them before too long. That's one of the things you might be able to help out with if you pay attention and end up where you're meant to be, with a bit of influence, get me?'

Merc gaped at him. Did Mr. Brown really think that a middle of the road computer programmer like him could make that amount of difference?

But, hey, it seemed as if he did.

Looking at the man nearest to him, Merc thought he recognised, behind the stubble, a fairly familiar face coming and going in the flickering firelight.

'Clotson? Silo Clotson?' he ventured. 'Is that you?'

Silo Clotson had worked two desks away from Merc until Flacker Winterbotham's recent clean sweep of half the work force. He was a tall, heavily built, rather overweight young man, with a chubby red face which Merc remembered as usually wearing a perpetual grin. The grin seemed to have disappeared for now and been replaced by a worried scowl.

More recently, Merc had seen his head disintegrate. Just last night.

It was a shock to see it in its old shape again.

'Merc,' said Silo briefly. He didn't seem inclined to be very friendly.

Well, Merc reflected, they had never been exactly friends. And he hadn't even wondered what had happened to Clotson when he lost his job. He'd just assumed that Clotson would be all right, he supposed. He'd been too busy instead being thankful that he hadn't lost his own.

'Look –' Merc said awkwardly, 'why don't you come round to my place for a meal? Seraphina's a good cook. And we could probably put you up for the night, okay? If you don't mind it being a bit basic?'

Silo looked reluctant.

'Come on!' urged Merc. 'Look, I'm sorry I didn't think of it before. Really!'

The thought passed hurriedly through his mind that Seraphina would kill him.

Nevertheless.

'Well. Okay,' said Silo Clotson eventually. 'Thanks,' he added, obviously with some difficulty.

Merc turned back to Mr. Brown, who was helping Leandra into Merc's coat.

'Thank goodness I found you,' he began. 'Look, you really need to explain things to me better, right?'

'Explain what?' asked Mr. Brown, apparently puzzled. His crinkled face wrinkled up even more, and his bushy eyebrows shot up high into his forehead where they almost disappeared under the brim of the red baseball cap.

'Hello?' Merc said. 'End of the world, sent back on a job, new promotion, Board Meeting tomorrow – is there anything else? Oh, yes, apparently someone was able to put Silo Clotson's head back on after all. Nothing much, right?'

Chapter Nine

'No need for sarcasm, sonny,' said Mr. Brown evenly. 'I can't tell you much more than you already know. The main thing is this Board Meeting, I guess?'

'Right!' said Merc fervently.

'Just follow your instincts, Merc,' said Mr. Brown. 'You have quite good instincts, as it happens. Reason you were picked for this job, okay?'

'Oh.'

'But one word of advice. Don't turn down anything you're offered just yet. The time for that will come. But right now, the main thing is to get you into a position where you can make a difference in a way that matters, like we've just been saying.'

Mr. Brown grinned happily.

'Don't worry, sonny, it's not all up to you, right. Even among you humans, there are people on your side, if you look out for them. Just keep on trucking.'

'Trucking?' Merc asked. The expression seemed vaguely familiar. Maybe he'd heard it in an old film?

Mr Brown looked annoyed. 'Yeah,' he said evenly. 'Continue to do what seems obvious, if you prefer that. Would you rather I talked like Gryphon Longfellow? Hey, I talk to you in your own lingo don't I? Makes it easier to relate, right?'

None of this seemed particularly enlightening to Merc, but it seemed to be all he was getting.

'Oh and hey, next time you want to ask me anything, you don't need to come out in the cold to do it!' Mr. Brown added. 'Not that it did you any harm to open your eyes and see a bit of what's going on round you.'

'Yeah,' mumbled Merc.

'I told you earlier, I can go anywhere you go. So next time, just speak to me and I'll come right back to you.'

'What, speak to you in front of everybody at the Board Meeting, like? They'd have me in the nut house!'

'See what you mean.' Mr. Brown looked thoughtful. 'Tell you what, I'll give you my mobile number, and you can message me whenever it's easier that way. Don't want to go on freezing time, just so's I can appear to you, too often. Mucks up the works something chronic, that does. In emergencies, right, but not just as a regular thing.'

Mr. Brown fished in his pocket and produced a rather dog-eared card. 'My number.'

He winked.

'And, hey, you can call me MB, if you want, now we're getting so pally. Okay?'

'Right,' responded Merc, taking the card. Then he couldn't help asking. 'Er – ? What does the 'M' stand for?'

' 'Mr.', of course,' said Mr. Brown.

'Gotta run, now,' he added. 'Things to do, people to see! Be seeing you, MS. Ciao!'

'Nobody says 'Ciao' now, MB!' began Merc. Too late. Mr. Brown was gone.

Merc looked round him. Everything was just the same. The blazing fire, the crowd of much warmer people round it.

But of Mr. Brown, no sign.

He suddenly became aware of Silo Clotson at his side, obviously trying not to look too expectant.

'Silo,' Merc said.

What had he let himself in for? Seraphina would hit the roof.

Nothing else he could have done, though.

'Um – got anything to bring with you? Bags or like that?'

'Just what I have in my pockets,' Silo Clotson said, looking embarrassed.

'Let's go, then.'

They went in through the supermarket door, and out to the front where Merc had parked his car. Lots of space, and free parking, for motorists who were going shopping. Not much chance of parking, anywhere else.

As they drove through the marginally smaller amount of traffic, Merc ventured to ask Silo why he was in his present position.

No home, no apparent money.

'I lost my job. End of story,' Clotson said briefly.

'You were made redundant,' Merc agreed.

'Ah, you're thinking of the redundancy package the company talks so much about when you begin working for them? About as much use as an ashtray on a motor bike, right? Doesn't exist. That is, there are so many loopholes and conditions – did you ever read the small print? –'

'– No way,' admitted Merc –

'– you should go home and do that – it's not humanly possible to qualify for any money. So – they did away with support for out of work people years ago, right? Bad for people's morale to rely on the state to support them, etc. So, that's about it, then.'

Merc listened in horror as Silo ran the steamroller of reality over the ideas he had been brought up to believe were fair and right. Surely there was some mistake?

It couldn't really be that all his basic beliefs led to this sort of thing?

Well, when he said 'his beliefs', maybe not exactly his. He couldn't remember ever really thinking about them.

They were just there, in the background.

The things everybody knew were right and normal.

He'd learnt them at school.

Then there was the horrible realization that if this could happen to Silo, maybe it could happen to him?

Merc shuddered.

He was almost glad to see that they were nearly home.

True, he now had to face Seraphina's reaction to the unannounced arrival of a guest for the night, and to crown it, a guest in Silo's condition.

But at least, he thought at some unconscious level, she couldn't say much until she got him alone, and then it would act as a sort of counter irritant, which would help him to ignore the floods of guilt welling up inside him when he thought about Silo Clotson.

He drew the car to a halt and pressed the button to open the doors.

At least, Merc thought, Silo had his head back on in one piece, anyway.

Chapter Ten

The Board meeting was held in a very flash room in the penthouse suite of the Company Headquarters building. The views were stunning.

Merc, nervously clutching a sheaf of notes, sat on the edge of his luxurious leather chair at the beautifully polished rosewood table, and waited for the initial chit chat to subside.

There were eleven other people standing around the room, the Executives of the various branches of Worldwide Productions, and in front of each Board member was the outline of Merc's proposal, which Kyra Hotberthy had helped him to copy and distribute early that morning.

HL from the Eastern Fashion section was there, and a huge, even gross woman. ('I shouldn't call her that,' thought Merc. 'It's not very kind.' But his inner critic rejected this and insisted that, yes, gross was the exact word.) He remembered that her name was Reta Glutt, and that she had an amazing amount of influence in the Company for someone who was, after all, a woman.

He accidentally caught Ms. Glutt's eye. Before he could hurl it back again, she was bounding over to him with the wide grin of a tiger in search of fresh meat. Sabre toothed, wasn't that it? Merc thought.

'So, who's the new talent, sweetie pie?' boomed Reta Glutt. She beamed at him, her enormous teeth showing between thick heavily glossed lips. Her bright blonde hair hung in loose artificial curls on either side of her plump red cheeks. 'Coming to give us all a bit of a lift this miserable morning?'

She flung one arm expansively round Merc's shoulders.

'Um. Merc Swingly,' Merc muttered unhappily.

To his horror, Reta Glutt seemed inclined to keep her arm in place, but just then, her attention was distracted by a man wearing an orange bow tie and an air of importance who called her imperiously away for a consultation.

'Reta! We need to talk! These expansion plans, can we agree a policy before it gets set in concrete?'

Merc vaguely remembered this man from ceremonial meetings of all the Company staff, when the leader, Flacker Winterbotham or his current equivalent, would address them about the hopes and aspirations of the Company. Beaver Sturge, he thought.

Beaver had been expected to be the next Chief Executive. If the Company hadn't had that takeover, with consequent reduction of all senior staff, as well as the fifty per cent cut in ordinary staff, and the introduction of Flacker Winterbotham as the new whiz kid who was going to set everything back on its feet and save untold amounts of money, then Beaver Sturge might have been Chief Executive by now.

He had clearly no reason to like Flacker Winterbotham. But as Winterbotham came bustling into the Conference Room at that moment, followed by Kyra Hotberthy equipped with notebook and pen, clearly ready to take minutes for Winterbotham to tear up later, Merc noticed that Beaver Sturge hastily broke away from Reta Glutt.

And, he noticed, began to suck round FW in a rather annoying way, pulling back a chair for Winterbotham to sit down, rushing to bring him coffee, and, when that was impatiently rejected, offering a large whiskey.

Reta Glutt said commandingly, in her great, booming voice, 'Well, come on, let's get started, man! We're running ten minutes late already.'

Merc noticed Flacker Winterbotham flash her a glance of dislike.

Off to one side, clearly a less important personage than anyone else in the room, even Merc, was a younger, better looking woman, with brown eyes, fair curly hair, and a clipboard; who he vaguely recognised as the Press Representative stroke Public Relations person; the liaison with World News and Recreation.

She must be there, he thought, to take some notes and possibly to come up with an interesting point to use for the daily television news bulletin, boosting the Company's kindness and generosity to all its employees.

Seeing Merc watching her, she smiled in an ingratiating way, fixing her big brown eyes on Merc's face.

Then she sidled over towards him, and sat cautiously in the next seat.

'Hi!' she more or less whispered. 'Okay if I sit here?'

'No problem.'

The girl brightened up.

'Hi!' she said again, in a more audible voice. 'I'm Fancy Linnet. I'm here to take notes of what happens. I should really know your name, of course, but I'm afraid – ?'

'Oh. Merc Swingly,' Merc mumbled. 'What an interesting job,' he added.

'Well, no, it isn't really,' said Fancy Linnet sadly. 'But if anything gets mentioned that would do for the news, and I make notes about it, then I maybe get to interview some people. That's more interesting. Well, sometimes. Well, not often, to tell you the truth.'

Merc blinked.

'So, are you here to report on anything in particular?' she asked him, with a winning smile.

'Yeah, on our new factory extension in the Tiny Isles – ' Merc began. Then it occurred to him that this might be private information, not meant for the Press as yet. His report to the Board might be a 'For your ears only' document.

An icy qualm shuddered its way through Merc's stomach as he realised that any minute now he would be speaking to all these people.

Flacker Winterbotham swallowed a pill (pink – a calmer, Merc noted) and tapped lightly on the table with his now empty whiskey glass.

Conversations came to an end. People took their seats and tried to look bright and alert and interested.

Flacker cleared his throat.

'Okay, folks. Let's work through the first three items on the Agenda quickly. Apologies – okay, everybody's here. Minutes of last meeting? Everyone's seen a copy, right? Passed? Good. Matters arising?'

A pale, thin man with a sharp face who was sitting on Merc's left, raised one hand slightly and attempted to speak, with the obvious intention of drawing attention to himself in order to increase his importance, but Winterbotham rushed over him.

'Nothing that can't wait, Darwin, right? So. Item 4, Options in the Far East Fashion Department. That's you, Merc. On you go.'

He gave Merc a version of his crocodile smile which enhanced Merc's qualms to an all out shudder.

Merc opened his mouth, but Flacker was still talking.

'Three main options, right, guys? But the outstanding one is the one at the top. Expand the factory in the Tiny Isles. We've been going a bomb there. Profits gigantic compared to anywhere else. And we already own the land beside the present building, right?'

'Er – not as such, FW –' began his second in command, a thin, weedy man with accountant written all over him – especially on the backs of his hands where he had a habit of noting down numbers. His name was Hedley Barton.

Flacker paused and glared.

'The lease needs to be renewed in six months time, FW,' quavered the little man bravely.

'Hedley, I surely appreciate your helpful comments,' said Flacker. His frown made it clear that he was lying in his teeth. 'But, hey, own, lease, so what? The profits over the next six months will more than cover any new lease. They'd better, ha ha!'

'Ha ha!' echoed dutifully round the table.

'So, Merc! Excellent job! Next thing is, we need someone to go out there and set things up, right?' boomed Flacker. 'Suggestions, anyone?'

Han Lilong cleared his throat and looked modestly round.

'I suppose, really. We need the man with the know-how –' he began.

Flacker swept loudly on.

'Right, HL! And that means, the guy who worked all this out. Merc! MS! How's about it, pal? Fancy a trip to the Tiny Isles?'

Chapter Eleven

Merc gulped.

'Well, FW,' he began weakly.

Flacker Winterbotham swept on.

'When we have the advantage of a bright young guy like Merc on our team –'

Beneath the rim of the table, Merc fumbled rapidly with his mobile phone.

Switch on – right.

Mr. Brown's number – right.

Message.

'What the flip am I to do?'

Looking down, he saw an answer flash up on the display.

'Accept, of course! What did I tell you?'

The photo option showed, for a brief moment, the usually kindly face of Mr. Brown exhibiting extreme annoyance.

'Get on with it!' the message continued.

Then the screen went blank.

Merc raised his head and smiled weakly.

'Er – great, FW!' he managed to say in the next short break in Winterbotham's flow. 'That sounds great!'

'We'll send you by air, how about that?' went on Flacker expansively. 'Fly all the way, ha ha! Bit of an experience for you, MS, right?'

Merc gaped at him.

He had heard of flying, of course. Who hadn't?

Back in the olden days, it was said, everyone had flown in the great clumsy objects known as aeroplanes.

But for so long now aeroplanes had been grounded for lack of fuel.

Merc knew, of course, that a few of the very rich still kept their small private aircraft, and a secret supply of the last air fuel in the world, but he hadn't realised that Flacker Winterbotham was one of these.

He particularly hadn't expected that Flacker would be prepared to use a portion of his precious fuel up on Merc.

He must really want Merc on his side! It seemed that it was worth almost anything to Flacker to keep Merc from spoiling Flacker's chance to end up as World President.

Something worth remembering, perhaps? A sort of bargaining tool if things got too tough?

'So, MS,' continued Flacker jovially, 'I think that about wraps up the Board Meeting for today, right? How's about some lunch, guys?'

He stood up. So did the rest of the Board, hastily shuffling to their feet.

Flacker Winterbotham put one arm around Merc's shoulder in a friendly way, and ushered him out of the room, followed by the dropped jaws of the dumbfounded Board Members.

Merc, clumsily gathering up his papers, allowed the boss man to take him as far as the corridor, where it became apparent that the suggestion of lunch did not include an invitation to Merc to join him.

'See you later, MS. Kyra will take care of you for now.'

Winterbotham disappeared into his office, where almost at once his voice could be heard booming from the room, and out into the corridor. He had forgotten to switch his phone from hands free voice over.

'Sandy? Still on for lunch? Be with you in ten, big guy!'

Sandy McPherson. The current Local Vice President. Possibly due to retire soon. Merc deduced without much trouble that Winterbotham was cultivating him with a view to being nominated as his successor.

McPherson. Who with his Scottish background and big, dour, serious face had the reputation of being the one honest politician (there always has to be one, or the public would get suspicious). Merc seriously hoped McPherson had enough common sense, in addition to his honesty, to see through Winterbotham.

But he really doubted it.

Meanwhile, Kyra Hotberthy was waiting by his side, her arms, like Merc's, filled to overflowing with a bunch of papers.

'Okay, Swingly?' Kyra said 'Let's go, then.'

They headed for the nearest bank of lifts.

Merc attempted, as he walked, to sort his papers into some sort of order.

He had grabbed at them too hastily when Winterbotham's arm had been flung round his shoulders.

Options – yes.

Back-up figures – yes.

Notes for proposal to the Board – unnecessary as it turned out.

Hullo. What was this?

He had apparently lifted someone else's letter or something by mistake.

But it was addressed to him.

Merc Swingly.

They had reached the lift.

Look at it later, Merc decided.

If it was from, say, Mr. Brown, he didn't really want Kyra to get a glimpse of it.

'Hey!' he said brightly. 'So what now?'

Kyra looked at him coolly as the lift doors slid smoothly open.

'You heard the man,' she said, with a hint of sarcasm in her velvet tones. 'Lunch, wasn't it? Come on! I'm taking you to the New Ritz Go-Go Room.'

Merc, who had just about heard of this haunt of the very, very rich, felt his mouth drop open.

'Right,' he managed to say. 'Lead on, MacDuff.'

'Who?' said Kyra. And they stepped into the lift.

The New Ritz, which was some distance away from the company offices, in the plushest part of town, was amazing. (It belonged to World News and Recreation, like all restaurant and entertainment centres, of course.)

In the Go-Go Room, Merc sat looking round him instead of studying the menu.

Subdued lighting.

Gilt and black velvet everywhere.

Or make that guilt.

Tables draped in white linen laid with sparkling cut glass goblets and flutes, and shining silver cutlery.

Large heavy men in business suits. With, occasionally, well-dressed, good-looking women.

And two menus.

Healthy, and Normal.

Did that mean that Normal was unhealthy?

Yes, it probably did, he reflected as he finally lowered his gaze to the 'Normal' menu in front of him.

Kyra was ordering briskly from the healthy menu.

Her meal, when it came, consisted of two tiny lettuce leaves arranged artistically with six very julienne slices of carrot, a few pitted black olives and some minute cubes of cheese.

Oh, and a cherry tomato, carved into the vague shape of a water lily, placed cunningly off centre, to add a touch of diversity.

It looked pretty, but, to Merc, it didn't suggest an adequate meal for a mouse.

He wasn't going to fall for that one. Defiantly, Merc ordered a large steak with fried potatoes and chef's selection of vegetables from what was called the Normal menu. Normal for the very rich, he supposed.

After all, it wasn't every day that someone in his position got a chance to try out the taste of real meat.

It might never happen again.

'Now,' said Kyra when the food had finally arrived, and they had started to eat.

'Yes?' Merc mumbled through a mouthful of steak. Yeah. This was really good.

Chapter 11

'Do you,' asked Kyra, 'know anything about this place you're going to? The Tiny Isles?'

'Well – not as such –'

'Okay. I need to fill you in.'

Chapter Twelve

Kyra took a brisk snap at her lettuce, which refrained from snapping back at her.

'The Tiny Isles is probably the poorest place in the universe. At a guess.

'The inhabitants regularly die of starvation, because the ground isn't too fertile since the Worldwide Weapons Tests there, about twenty years ago. The sea round the Isles, likewise, doesn't have much in the way of fish, or at least what we would recognise as fish, since the attempt, ten years ago, by World Health and Chemicals, to raise oil from the ocean beds in that area.

'Unsuccessful, as I'm sure you know.

'The only thing that has kept the population in existence, at one percent of their former level, is the Company's factory. We pay more or less in kind – really kind of us, huh? – enough to buy a day's food, clothing, Happy Honey pills and shelter, for a day's work. All of which are sold to them by the Company.

'Nowadays, the whole population works for us, from the age of five upwards. Mothers of younger children get a small increase, to cover up to two kids per family. We may want to increase this to three or four if we plan to extend the factory and take on new workers.'

Merc listened.

Surely there was something wrong about this set-up?

Of course, the Company was okay. Had to be. That was basic.

But all the same.

Kyra was still speaking.

'So I imagine the news of the plans for expansion will be greeted with enthusiasm by the present workers.'

'But don't any of them want to leave?' it occurred to Merc to ask. 'Couldn't they do a lot better somewhere else?'

'Most of them hardly know there is somewhere else,' said Kyra, still speaking crisply. 'So far, no-one's told them much. And, hey, where would be so much better? Here, you think?'

Her large, slanting green eyes met Merc's for a duration so short that he couldn't be completely certain it had happened.

'Maybe not,' he said slowly.

Kyra glanced round.

'See the big guy over there?'

Merc's glance followed hers.

At a table across the restaurant, an over dressed, overweight, over-loud man in an over bright checked suit was laughing at something that had just been said by his companion. Who matched him in every annoying particular.

'That's Herbie Shuffle. Head of World Health and Chemicals.'

'And the fat man lunching with him?'

'Garnie Porker – head of Worldwide Weapons.'

'Yeah?'

'The two guys actually responsible for the tests I mentioned.'

Merc gazed at the two enormous people at the table across from him.

'Don't they care about anyone?'

He wasn't sure if he had said it aloud.

He was rather frightened that he might have done.

Then he noticed that Kyra was giving him a look that almost seemed approving.

He met her gaze.

But the look, if it had ever been there, had gone.

'I'm tied up this afternoon, Merc,' Kyra said. 'But I'm free tonight. We'll meet about eight thirty, and I'll fill you in some more about the Company's development plans. Until then, feel free to do what you want. Go down and have a look at the plane, why don't you?'

'O-kaay!' Merc agreed. 'Like where?'

'Joe'll take you.'

'So.'

Chapter 12

Merc looked across the table at Kyra. 'So, Kyra. Tell me about yourself. How did you come to join the Company?'

Kyra looked at him for a moment. Then she seemed to make a decision.

'I grew up on an island far away from Nexus Luxuria,' she said. 'But I heard about it all my life, ever since I understood anything. I always wanted to come here. So I worked hard in school, and got first class grades all along the way.

'My father died just after my eighth birthday.

'It was a bit of a mystery how it happened. He was always a faithful follower of the companies. World Health and Chemicals, he worked for. Did what he was told all along the line. Obeyed orders, said, 'Yes, sir!', jumped when the boss said, 'Jump!', etc. I never heard a bad word from him about the Seven Companies all my life.

'Until I was eight, that is. Then, one evening after supper, instead of giving me my usual pill before bedtime, he suddenly turned round and threw it down on the floor, and jumped on it with both feet. It made a real mess on the polished wood, and I wondered what Mum would think. So then he said, 'I don't want you ever to take those things again, Kyra! Think for yourself!'

' 'Yes, Daddy,' I said. Though I wasn't really sure what he meant.

' 'Promise me you won't ever take those pills again!' he said.

''I promise, Daddy,' I said.

'And I kept my promise.

'The very next day, he was killed in a road crash.

'It was really weird, because by then traffic was so slow, with the new electric cars, that fatal accidents hardly ever happened.

'But no-one except me seemed to think there was anything funny about it, and life went on. Only I was determined to keep my promise to my father, and I managed after that never to take the Happy Honey pills. My mum didn't bother much. She just expected, I suppose, that she could leave it up to me to take them. I always acted it out, natch, in case the security cameras were turned on. (We had the security cameras in our house, although most people don't, because my Dad had a pretty senior job, so the bosses wanted to keep an eye on him, right. Wanted to be sure they could trust him.) But I guess they mostly weren't on.

'Though when I thought it out, I sort of guessed that the cameras must have been on that day, and they had seen Dad jumping on the pills, and I had an idea that maybe there was some connection between that and his accident.

'My mum married again, but she died when I was not quite nine. Natural causes. Heart, like most people who keep on taking the pills. I suppose she was happy enough. That's what the pills are for after all. I wasn't too happy, myself, for the first few months after I stopped. But people put that down to my Dad's death, and just encouraged me to take extra doses. It was funny. Life didn't seem so lit up, somehow. But when I got used to it, things were actually better in a way. I had a better idea of what was going on, for one thing. So then I moved to Nexus Luxuria, with my new Dad.

'When I was eighteen, I was head hunted for Worldwide Productions. The Company. I'd been brighter, apparently, than most of my year. Maybe because my head wasn't always in a mish-mash. Anyway, they sent me to university, and from then on it was all onwards and upwards.'

The universities, run by Cultural Education and Indoctrination, were all sited in Land Mass 2, although there were local schools everywhere, staffed entirely by employees of CEI. Merc had thought at one time of working with CEI, but when he got the job with Nexus Luxuria Productions, he had promptly abandoned that idea. Nexus Luxuria Productions, even then, before the last takeover, was so powerful. And anyone could see it would soon be part of the one big Worldwide Productions.

Like, Merc thought, World News and Recreation, and Planetary Building and Construction. Both of them, rumour had it, were next in line for takeover any time now.

'I don't know why I've told you all this,' Kyra said.

Merc smiled.

'Cheer up, Kyra,' he said. 'I guess you weren't the only one cheating the system. Neither Seraphina nor I have been taking the happy pills since we were so high. Our parents were like your Dad. They didn't like to see us taking them.'

'I knew it! I could sort of tell – that's how I knew I could trust you!' Kyra exclaimed. 'Merc, we really need to talk. About the details of this mission you're being sent on, right. But other stuff.'

'Go ahead.'

'Not here,' Kyra said. 'Too many bugs. We'll get together somewhere safe, like a private house, where they don't have scanners for our identity chips, or security cameras. Or,' she paused, and grinned mischievously, 'I know! Somewhere that hasn't installed scanners or cameras yet, because the bosses think they're above that sort of thing – the Company offices! They haven't realised yet that they could use the chips to keep track of us all, all the time, if they put in more scanners. But no doubt the day will come! Meanwhile – let's take advantage of the way things are! We'll meet there tonight.'

Chapter Thirteen

Outside the Ritz, Joe, the Company driver, had pulled up to the kerb.

The car wasn't any bigger than Merc's own. No cars were, nowadays. But there was something sleek about it, something to do with the smooth black paintwork and the silver trimmings and silver lion on the bonnet, which made it rather special.

Kyra waved goodbye and got into her own feminine looking midget car, bright scarlet with gold trimmings.

'Wow!' said Merc. 'Well, Joe! How's about it?'

They drove for miles.

At the normal pace of electric cars, it took quite a while.

Presently, Merc remembered the letter or something he had picked up at the board meeting.

Joe, a small, thin, silent, coffee-coloured young man with a brush of crimson dyed hair, was concentrating on his driving.

Merc pulled the letter out of his file, smoothed it out, and looked at it.

It didn't say much.

Most of the single page was taken up by a not very good drawing of a flower. A rosebud, probably. But so badly drawn that it seemed twisted and hard to recognise.

'Look out for us,' was printed in big letters below. *'You'll be hearing from us soon.*

The Twisted Rosebud.'

It didn't seem to be Mr. Brown's style, somehow.

Anyway, wouldn't he just have messaged Merc on his mobile?

Merc folded the sheet in half, and hastily tucked it back inside his file, before Joe could notice it.

Just in time.

'Nearly there now,' Joe said, turning his head to grin at Merc.

They were turning into a small lane which meandered along for a few miles before ending up at the entrance to a large complex, buried in the heart of one of the few remaining woods.

There was a large, old-fashioned wrought iron gate – obviously very old, an antique. A new one would have been impossibly expensive these days – and a high barbed wire fence which stretched along each side of the grounds until it was nearly out of sight.

Joe spoke for the second time.

'This is it.'

Then he got out of the car, pushed the buzzer on one side of the gate, and whispered into it, in a low voice which Merc found it impossible to hear.

A moment later, the gates slid silently open, and the car made its way inside.

Seraphina was very nearly at her wits' end by the time Merc got home.

She hadn't put herself out too much to entertain Silo Clotson, but all the same – !

Silo, give him his due, had been good about playing with Lucy, and had proved to be very successful at the role of Big Paddy Bear (usually Merc's job). But when Lucy went down for her nap, there was Silo, grinning apologetically, and apparently without very much to say for himself.

Seraphina had employed him to empty the dishwasher and to bring in the washing, but after that she had been obliged to offer him a cup of coffee and to sit down and chat with him.

It appeared that Silo didn't know how to chat.

Seraphina had been reduced to leaving the room on the pretext of going to have a shower, and had actually, a first, been relieved to hear Lucy waking up again, and putting in her demand to be lifted.

When she heard Merc's key in the door, Seraphina burst out into the hall and seized him angrily by the coat collar, hissing in his ear, 'Never again! Don't do this to me ever again, Merc Swingly!'

Merc stared at her in bewilderment.

'What – ? But I'm home early – ?'

After his trip to see the plane he had called only briefly at the office, where, to his relief, he had realised that he had a valid excuse for putting off his promised dinner with Hyacinth Duckworthy again – 'A really important late meeting here at the office, Hya. With Kyra Hotberthy, you know – FW's PA. V. Important!' – and, ignoring Hyacinth's disappointed face, had hurried straight home.

From the sitting room came sounds of Lucy screaming with glee, and Silo screaming for quite different reasons as chubby infant hands grabbed determinedly at his hair.

'Silo seems to be getting on well with Lucy, right?' Merc said as he identified the noises. 'Great! I knew he'd be worth his keep in child minding, yeah?'

Seraphina spluttered helplessly.

'Get him out of here before tomorrow, Merc!' she demanded. 'I can't take another day like today. This is my house – my space, see?'

'No problem,' Merc said. 'I have to go out tonight. But I'll sort something out, no probs, okay, honey?'

He grinned hopefully at Seraphina's angry face, and added, 'I've been given a really important job, sweetheart. Wait till I tell you about it!'

It turned out that Silo also had to go out. He hesitantly asked Merc if he could scrounge a lift, and beamed gratefully when Merc said, 'Sure!'

Lucy had been as sweet and warm and cuddly as usual after her bath. Merc held her close to him and for some reason felt near to tears.

Then it was time to go, hugging Seraphina briefly and gathering up Silo as he went.

'Where do you want me to drop you?'

'Oh, just take me the whole way to the Company office, and I'll be fine. I'll get out when you do.'

Merc didn't see why, but was too preoccupied to ask questions.

At just about twenty past eight, he pulled into the Company car park and switched off the engine.

'I'll probably be at least an hour,' he said. 'When do you want me to meet up with you?'

'Oh, that'll be okay,' said Silo vaguely. 'I'll be back here when you are.'

Merc wondered briefly how he could know that, then gave a mental shrug and went towards the Company building.

He used his electronic pass to open the main door.

Everything was dark. He wondered if Kyra was here yet. He didn't remember seeing her car in the car park, but maybe it was round the back. Should he just wait in his own car until she arrived?

Perhaps it would be better if he checked to see if she was upstairs, first.

He pressed the switch beside the lifts, and light sprang into being from all directions. Merc called up the lift, got in, and pressed the button for the tenth floor, the floor where Kyra had her office.

There was something eerie about the silence as the lift skimmed swiftly upwards.

Merc couldn't remember ever being in the office before on his own.

The light turned to a large red letter ten. His destination.

Merc waited while the doors slid silently open, and stepped out.

The lights shone brightly for all of two seconds.

Then with uncanny speed they went out and everything was darkness.

Merc began to say, 'Wh – a – a – ?'

But before he could complete the word, something soft enveloped his face and head, and he dropped to the ground in total unconsciousness.

Chapter Fourteen

Merc came slowly back to reality, wondering why it was still so dark.

His head and mouth were closely covered, and this was making it difficult to breathe.

Scrabbling frantically at the soft material smothering his face, he managed to create a little breathing space, and used it to shout as well as breathe.

'What's going on? Who are you?' He spun round, looking for light, but failed to find any.

'I know! This is a test, isn't it? The company wants to know if I'm up to the new job! Well, I'm not buying it! You let me out of here, Flacker Winterbotham! I know you hang around the office all night, you haven't caught me by surprise! I don't care about your rotten promotion any more! Let me out!'

A little, quite sweet laugh sounded in his ear.

It didn't sound like Flacker Winterbotham.

It didn't sound like a threat.

'Right. What's going on?' asked Merc more slowly. He stopped trying to turn round.

No-one answered.

Instead, he felt several pairs of hands grasping him, and then he was being propelled, in a don't argue, no sense in resisting sort of way, along what might have been a pretty long corridor.

There was something soft, presumably carpet, under his feet.

Merc, who had no previous experience of walking blindfold since far off childhood games, stumbled with boring regularity, and once managed accidentally to trip up the person on his left. This caused a moment of panic, and someone exclaimed sharply in a frustratingly familiar voice which he could not quite identify.

As he walked, or rather stumbled, along, Merc tried to make some sense out of what was happening.

He had almost, though not quite, given up the idea of some fiendish plan by Flacker Winterbotham to test his suitability. Some type of management training, right? He had heard some horror stories of things that had happened on those courses.

But the gentle laugh he had heard – more of a giggle, really – wasn't something he could remotely associate with Winterbotham.

The other obvious explanation was the weird Third Degree Representative, capturing him inappropriately in order to pass on some more information or instructions. Probably, if Merc protested afterwards about his methods, Gryphon would simply look uncomprehending, and say that it had seemed the simplest way, or something unhelpful like that.

But, no.

Wasn't Mr. Brown there to act as liaison, instead?

And in that case, what was wrong with a simple mobile phone call?

Merc's confused thoughts came to an abrupt end as his legs were hooked from under him, someone pushed him firmly backwards, and he found himself sitting in what seemed, to those parts best suited to judge, to be quite a soft, comfortable armchair.

Fizzling noises and low mutters in the background suggested some ongoing activity.

Merc tried to protest again.

'Listen, this is stupid! What's going on? And who are you anyway?'

No answer.

'Mr. Brown – MB – is that you?'

This time a gruff voice, obviously disguised, replied, giving Merc some orientation for the first time.

'There is no-one called Mr. Brown here. We are the Twisted Rosebud. Merc Swingly, there is no need to fear. You are simply about to undergo a truth test.'

'What? No need to fear? I hate those things! And aren't they illegal except for the government? And the police? Oh, and big business? And anyone really friendly with the World President?'

'Be quiet!'

A hand seized Merc's arm.

Someone else was rolling up his sleeve.

Then the cold pain of the needle.

Merc ceased to struggle, and, sliding down in the chair, he passed out.

Eons went by.

Merc, cushioned in a comfortable dream of himself and Seraphina teaching Lucy to swim, on their last Company sponsored holiday, resisted at first the urge to float back to the present.

Then the pull became too strong.

Leaving behind him the sound of Lucy's laughter, the salty splashes from her chubby kicking legs, and the happy relaxed expression on Seraphina's face, he allowed himself to be dragged back to the voice speaking persistently in his ear.

'Merc! Merc Swingly!'

It felt like a hard punch right in his face.

Hating what was happening, Merc sat up a little in his soft chair.

He kept his eyes firmly closed. In fact, he realised, he didn't seem to have the option of opening them. They felt as if they were glued shut.

'Merc Swingly!'

'Yes?' Merc heard his voice reply.

'Merc, you will answer these questions truthfully. You will not attempt to dodge or twist. You will be honest and frank, to the best of your ability and the limits of your knowledge.'

The voice seemed familiar, but Merc was in no state to put a name to it.

'Do you understand?'

'I understand,' said Merc.

There was no effort or willpower involved in the words. They came, in a sense, automatically.

But deep down, something in Merc wriggled furiously and said, 'I told you I hated this! I hate this!'

'Merc Swingly. What do you think of the Company?'

The answer came haltingly.

'What? ... I don't know.'

'Do you like the Company?'

'Well ... sometimes ...'

'Do you think the Company is good?'

No question about it this time.

'No way!'

A sigh, somewhere.

A pause.

Then, it seemed, a different tack in the questioning.

'Merc Swingly. Does the Company rule your life?'

Merc paused for thought.

Then. Dredged up from deep inside him,

'Too much!' Merc said.

Another sigh.

'Are you happy about this?'

No hesitation this time.

'No!'

'Would you like to change this?'

'Yes!'

Merc felt himself floating on the Lake of Limbo. Nothing seemed to matter much. He had no idea where he was going, or if it even mattered.

All that mattered was that he should speak the truth.

That might be important, ultimately.

Or perhaps not.

Another question.

'Would you help to change this situation?'

Merc was not totally aware of it, deep down in his drug induced daze, but something dimly told him that his answer to this question needed to be many decibels greater than his previous muttered responses.

'YES!'

Chapter Fifteen

It seemed from the murmured reactions to be the right answer.

Or at least, the expected one.

Merc wasn't too sure about 'right', in the more epistemological sense.

And he wasn't too sure how come he knew a word like epistemological.

Was someone messing with his brain?

'Merc Swingly!'

'Yes?'

'What is it that matters most to you?'

Merc didn't speak.

Dimly, thorough his brain, floated the image of Lucy, laughing and splashing in the salty waves, of Seraphina laughing in turn, of both members of his family smiling at Merc as if he was the most important person in their world.

No words seemed to be coming.

Then the question came again.

'What matters most to you, Merc Swingly?'

All of a sudden, the words rushed out.

'Lucy – and – Seraphina!'

'Right answer!'

A collective sigh.

There were far more people listening than Merc would have chosen to have, for this baring of his soul.

'We need your help to do this, Merc!'

'Yeah?'

'Look out for the sign of the Twisted Rosebud!'

'Right!'

Then everything went hazy again, and Merc found himself sinking again into the wonderful, salty, splashy, funny experience of teaching Lucy to swim.

Where was he?

'Where am I?' said Merc.

'Merc! Are you okay?'

He knew that voice!

It was Kyra Hotberthy.

'Merc!' He felt Kyra shaking him. Cautiously he opened his eyes.

'Hi, Kyra. Sorry if I'm a bit late. I – sorta – got held up. I think.'

'No problem, MS. But you seem to be a bit out of it. What happened?'

'Oh. I'm not too sure. I guess I got clobbered. Like. Muggers. I guess.'

'Heavens! Well, are you okay, Merc? Like, do you need medical aid?'

'Oh, no way, Kyra!' lied Merc. 'I feel fine! Dunno exactly what happened to me, right? But I'm okay!'

'Have you got your wallet, big guy?' asked Kyra, radiating anxiety.

Merc patted his pockets carefully.

'Yeah, right here!'

He pulled out his wallet and examined it. 'Nothing missing!'

'Great!' Kyra sighed.

Merc looked round him.

He was sitting in his own chair, at his own desk.

The desk he had claimed ownership of for the past number of years, that is.

Like everything else in his life, it occurred to him, it belonged to the Company.

But that was okay, wasn't it?

The Company was okay.

Why was there something deep down which seemed to be struggling to tell him that he didn't really believe that?

'So.' Kyra smiled at him. 'And you don't remember anything else? No way you could give some sort of description of these muggers?'

'No.'

As he spoke, Merc was conscious, somewhere at the back of his brain, that that wasn't entirely true.

But as he tried, fuzzily, to chase after the elusive memory, he found it flicking up its tail and darting away from the shallows of recollection into the murky depths of oblivion.

'No,' he said again.

'Oh, well,' said Kyra Hotberthy cheerfully, 'never mind. You seem to be all in one piece, anyway.'

She looked at Merc sharply.

'Well, Merc,' she said. 'We arranged to meet tonight so that I could outline to you some of what the company expects of you out in the Tiny Isles. Maybe we should get down to it.'

'And you were going to tell me some other stuff,' Merc said. 'More, like, personal, right?'

'Yeah. Well, look, maybe this isn't the right time. I don't know if your head's up to it?'

Merc wasn't exactly sure either.

And he couldn't help wondering.

The voice which had sounded so familiar. Could it have been Kyra's? The things she had already told him, didn't they mean that she was a bit of a rebel? Just the type to be mixed up with these weird people? Whoever they were? Pretty well opposed to the Company, anyway. They had certainly made that clear.

But the voice he had thought he recognised? Surely Kyra's voice wasn't just like that? Maybe he should let it go for now, talk to Kyra some other time, when his head felt normal?

'You could be right, Kyra,' he said eventually. 'Suppose you just fill me in on the trip, anything else I need to know, and we'll talk again.'

'Fine,' Kyra Hotberthy said briskly. 'Come along to my office. I have a pack there that I've put together for you. Maps, history of the Company's role in the Isles, future aims and objectives, that sort of stuff. I'll zip through it quickly and then you can take it home and read it when your head stops spinning.'

'Okay,' Merc agreed. 'And I need to pick up Silo Clotson, before I make for home.'

He was aware of a sudden silence.

'Silo Clotson?' Kyra said eventually. 'Isn't that the guy whose head – ?' She stopped.

Merc, who still wasn't thinking too clearly, said absently. 'Oh, his head's okay now.' Then it dawned on him what Kyra had said.

His jaw dropped. 'Kyra – ?' he began.

But Kyra Hotberthy had already begun to talk again. 'I always thought Silo's head was far too far up in the clouds for him to do any real work. And, hey, the Company must have thought so, too. Wasn't he made redundant?'

Merc realised that he must have misunderstood Kyra. He had nearly made a major mistake! He didn't want to tell anyone else about his dream! If he had said any more, Kyra would have put him down as a lunatic! 'Yeah, that's right,' he mumbled hastily instead. 'I happened to bump into him the other day, and I thought maybe he wasn't so bad.'

'Oh?' said Kyra doubtfully. 'Well, let's just go over this stuff, quickly, then, MS.'

Merc thought carefully over Kyra's information as he drove home with Silo Clotson some time later. It seemed that the Company was expecting a lot from him.

To be honest, he wasn't quite sure what he thought about it.

The Company was certainty providing food and shelter for a considerable number of people, and if he worked this deal out properly, they would be providing for even more people.

On the other hand, surely someone should have compensated these people for destroying their land and the surrounding sea?

And if they had been properly compensated, then wouldn't they have been able to make better lives for themselves?

With a better overall deal than the one that the Company was allowing them?

Merc found it hard to work it out.

A much larger problem loomed before him.

'Silo?' he ventured at last.

'Yeah?'

'Em – I was wondering – '

'Yeah?'

'It maybe isn't the best arrangement for you to be staying with Seraphina when I'm not around –'

'Oh?'

'I mean – it must be awkward for you – ?'

'Hey, no, no worries!' said Silo enthusiastically. 'I love helping out! And the kid – ! Wow, she's magic!'

Merc found himself beaming.

'Right, she's something special, okay?'

He cleared his throat hastily.

'But – well – ?'

'Yeah?'

'I just thought –'

Merc trailed off miserably.

Suddenly inspiration flooded in.

'I wondered –? I'm heading off on this special mission tomorrow. I wondered if you'd like to join me? I'll certainly need an IT stroke numbers expert. I guess you'd be the right guy for the job?'

He looked round hopefully and saw that Silo's jaw had dropped spectacularly.

'So – how about it?'

Silo breathed deeply. His face had gone red.

'You're offering me the chance to work for the Company again?'

Merc nodded.

'Well, you can take your Company and –'

Silo stopped suddenly. He breathed deeply. Then he spoke.

'Er – yeah, great idea, Merc. Thanks. Er – right, then. Right.'

Merc was momentarily puzzled.

Then he paused for reflection. Silo had probably been really choked up with gratitude at the prospect of working in a decent job again.

Meanwhile, his thoughts drifted back to another worry.

Right, Seraphina would be rid of Silo by tomorrow. Good.

Meanwhile, where was Mr. Brown?

And why hadn't he been in touch all day?

Was Merc making the right decisions? Left to himself, he just had no idea.

Right on cue, his mobile vibrated.

Chapter Sixteen

An incoming message.

Hi, MS! It's MB here!

Merc punched in, with one hand,

Where are you? I can't talk to you and drive! I'll pull in. Ring me back!

It looked as if there might be room for the electric car to pull in a few yards further on.

Merc found a space, parked, and took out his mobile phone.

A moment later he was speaking to Mr. Brown.

'I have Silo Clotson with me! You know Silo, right? Just mentioning before you start telling me anything.'

Mr. Brown apparently understood the point. He spoke quietly and carefully.

'I'll meet you later, MS. Need to confirm a few things. How about we do lunch tomorrow?'

Merc almost yelled in his frustration.

'I won't be here tomorrow! I need to talk to you now! I don't know what's going on!'

'Okay, okay!' There was a pause while Mr. Brown considered.

'Right. Send Silo for a walk. And wait where you are. I'll join you shortly.'

Merc felt rather embarrassed at asking Silo to go for a walk.

'Just twenty minutes or so, right?'

But Silo seemed quite happy about it.

And Merc really, really needed time alone with his mysterious advisor.

And when Mr. Brown arrived beside the car quite suddenly, Merc felt nothing but thankfulness.

It took Merc a moment to recognise him.

The old fashioned clothes had gone.

Dressed for jogging in tracksuit bottoms and vest, complete with water bottle, Mr. Brown arrived at a brisk trot, and continued jogging on the spot as he drank a mouthful of water, and nodded to Merc politely.

He seemed to have shed about thirty years. No longer a small, wiry, elde ly gentleman, he was now not too much older than Merc, quite a bit larger, and much better equipped in the way of muscular development.

Merc wasn't even sure how it was that, after the first surprise, he had recognised this as the same person.

The eyes, maybe.

They hadn't changed at all.

Small, bright, and twinkling.

And possibly the ever present bright red baseball cap?

'Well?' asked Mr. Brown. 'You wanted to speak to me?'

'Yeah – ' gasped Merc. He pulled himself together. 'Look, you were supposed to be helping me. Things are happening, and I don't know what's going on!'

Mr. Brown listened politely.

'I'm being sent to the other side of the world! I'm supposed to set up a factory, and it sounds completely awful to me! And now I've been kidnapped – well, captured, anyway – and given a truth test, and I've no idea what I said or who I said it to – !'

'Don't worry,' said Mr. Brown.

'Don't worry! Oh, right, nothing to worry about! Well, suppose I told these guys about you, how do you feel about that? Suppose they're after you now? Is it still, 'Don't worry,' or what?'

'You couldn't have told anyone about me,' Mr. Brown pointed out calmly, still jogging on the spot, 'because I naturally put a basic lock on your tongue as far as your meeting with me went. You can't talk about me to anyone, apart from your wife, unless I allow it.'

'Oh, right! Great! So you're okay, then! But what am I supposed to do? All these decisions I've been making – taking Silo Clotson with me, e.g.! I don't even know if that's right!'

'Oh, no problem about Silo,' Mr. Brown assured him. 'Silo'll be okay. Quite helpful, probably.'

Chapter 16

'And how am I supposed to set up a factory? I don't know anything about it! Or even if it would be a good thing to do! And please stop jogging on the spot like that!'

'Don't worry,' said Mr. Brown again. 'Just follow your best instincts. And keep in touch. I'll soon let you know if you're going wrong.'

Suddenly Mr. Brown began to jog off into the distance.

A few words came floating back.

'And try not to use so many exclamation marks, right?'

Merc breathed deeply.

That seemed to be all he was getting.

Right!

He noticed that Silo Clotson had now appeared beside him.

'Can I get back in the car, Merc? I've had a good walk?'

'Oh – yeah, right, Silo.' Merc spoke absently.

Time he was getting back to Seraphina.

He wasn't quite sure what he should be saying to her. Or what she would be saying back, for that matter.

At least he wouldn't be leaving Silo with her all day tomorrow.

He needed some space. A chance to think out what he was going to do, regardless of Mr. Brown and his, 'Don't worry!'

He hadn't asked Mr. Brown, he realised, about the 'Twisted Rosebud', whatever that was. Or if Mr. Brown himself had had anything to do with the truth test people.

Somehow, he felt fairly clear that the answer to that was, 'No.'

The people who had seized him as he got out of the elevator at work a few hours earlier had a different feel to them, he was pretty sure. Mr. Brown might be weird, but for some reason, Merc trusted him.

Whereas, these 'Twisted Rosebud' people –!

Merc wasn't prepared to trust anyone who forcibly gave him a truth test.

Ugh! He'd always hated the things. He remembered his first one, the routine test carried out on all eleven year olds. Some of the things he had been vaguely aware of being asked –!

It just wasn't fair to any boy on the verge of puberty!

How could they expect him to always remember to change his socks every day?

Meanwhile, he had a lot of explaining to do to Seraphina when he got home.

The car drew up at Merc's front door.

He went forward and unlocked it.

Seraphina burst out of nowhere towards him.

She flung herself into his arms.

'Oh, Merc!' she wailed. 'Thank goodness you're back!'

Merc gaped.

'Help me, help me!' Seraphina wailed.

She collapsed against him.

'We've just been burgled, Merc! I've been attacked and tied up! Help me, Merc!'

Chapter Seventeen

Merc sat, well strapped into his seat, in the little bi-plane, and raced at an unbelievable speed through the clouds.

Behind him, Silo Clotson, Kyra Hotberthy, and, to his reasonably well concealed horror, Hyacinth Duckworthy, were also carefully strapped in.

His attention was fairly evenly divided between wonder and amazement at the sights flashing by beneath his eyes – how tiny the occasional cities were. How blue the sea. How white and shining and fluffy the clouds as the plane soared above them – and, on the other hand, his memory of Seraphina's behaviour the previous night.

'Darling!' he had called, rather nervously, as he unlocked the front door and went in.

A soft, tremulous warm ball of affection had burst out of the hallway and hurled itself into Merc's arms.

'Oh, Merc! You're home! You're home!' had sobbed Seraphina. A strange, new, unsettlingly dependent Seraphina.

'Thank goodness you're back!'

Silo Clotson, with more tact than Merc would have given him credit for, had slunk quietly away to the spare room where he had slept the night before.

Seraphina apparently didn't even notice him, as she babbled on.

Merc, his arms holding his wife close, attempted a few remarks of the, 'There, there!" type, and drew Seraphina into the living room, where they collapsed in a tangled heap onto the sofa.

After that, one thing led to another, and it was some time later that Merc found an opportunity to ask for some explanation of the problem.

Cuddling close against him, Seraphina at last whispered a confused account of her story.

Someone had broken into the house. She had no idea who. She had been tidying up in the kitchen, her hands sloshing the hot dish water noisily in the sink, and her thoughts sloshing round noisily in her mind, and had noticed nothing. Until she had been seized from behind, someone's hand clamped over her mouth – she had managed at least one good bite, and was pretty confident that his shins would be quite painful for some days as a result of her frantic backward kicks – tied up, and pushed into a cupboard.

Thank Heavens, Lucy had slept safely through it all.

Eventually, Seraphina had managed to struggle free from her ropes. Her first thought had been to check on the safely sleeping Lucy. Then she had crept shiveringly to the door, to wait for Merc's return. By that time there had been no sign of any intruders, and Seraphina had no idea who they had been, or what they had wanted.

Nothing seemed to have been stolen.

But a terrible mess had been made by people searching through various drawers, mostly in the living room.

The whole experience had made an unbelievable impression on Seraphina.

All the more so when they made their way to the bedroom, and found a note placed carefully on Merc's pillow.

Clean bill of health awarded.

Good! So far, you qualify as a very suitable candidate for senior membership!

> *You'll hear from us shortly.*
>
> *The Twisted Rosebud.*

And below that, apparently as signature, a badly drawn flower which might have been intended to be a rose.

Merc had been angry. Very angry.

How dare these Twisted Rosebud people check up on him like this?

What had they expected to find?

And how dare they terrify his wife like this?

On the plus side, he had to admit, he couldn't remember ever seeing Seraphina so soft and loving before.

And so inclined to respect his opinion.

Or was that a plus?

Chapter 17

Something in Merc rejected the idea that he preferred this scared, dependent Seraphina to the self-sufficient, forth-right person he had fallen in love with.

He wanted the old Seraphina back.

And he was glad to see, as he recounted to her his own experiences that evening, that the old self-confident Seraphina was beginning to return.

Until at last, when Merc explained that he would be taking Silo Clotson with him, Seraphina had remarked tartly, 'Well, thank goodness for that, anyway! At least I won't have him under my feet all day!'

Merc grinned happily at the memory.

Lucy had been okay.

They had crept quietly into her bedroom together, and watched her breathing gently in the soft moonlight, her warm cheek against the pillow, her baby curls a tangled mess.

Merc had stretched out one hand to touch Lucy's hand, which clutched as always at her left ear, and had felt the overwhelming love which the sight of his daughter sleeping always invoked.

A hand touched his shoulder. He looked round.

Kyra Hotberthy, unable to make herself heard over the engine noise, was pointing down. He was just about able to follow the words she was mouthing.

'The Tiny Isles! Look down!'

Directly below them, spots of green in a blue, blue ocean. Their destination.

Chapter Eighteen

As they came nearer, Merc looked with interest at what could be seen of the Tiny Isles from the air.

There were several islands, but only one, the one they were approaching, was of any size.

What had seemed at first to be flourishing vegetation turned out to be widely interspersed with huge barren spaces apparently covered in concrete. Three of these open places contained buildings. Apart from the airport building just beneath them, Merc managed to take in a long, low, ugly building with a corrugated iron roof – the factory? – and a much more up market building with a swimming pool and attractive gardens – the hotel, he hoped, where they would be staying?

There was little else to be seen, except for patches of thick vegetation, mostly tangles of trees and undergrowth, creepers and stuff like that, Merc decided. More or less in the middle of the island, the ground rose to a peak which could be better described, Merc thought, as a hill than a mountain. Tall cliffs fell away on every side of the island, with only the occasional break where it might be possible to bring a boat ashore, and there seemed to be little or nothing in the way of beaches.

Close up, it was a lot less attractive than the first, more distant, view.

The plane circled, lost height.

The runway appeared before them, rushing closer and closer.

There was a bump. The wheels had touched land.

Merc held on tightly as the plane roared at breakneck speed along the runway, then slowed gradually until at last it came to a halt. The passengers, grinning with relief, stretched, and staggered to their feet and down the low flight of stairs to the hot tarmac.

A portly, beaming figure in a white silk business suit, wiping his brow with a large handkerchief, came hurrying forward to meet them.

'Hi, guys! I'm Ully Beers, your local company manager. You must be MS, right?' he said to Merc. 'I've heard lots about you! Great to see you! And all you other guys!'

Merc, realising that it fell to him, hastily introduced his companions to the beaming Ully.

'Now,' Beers went on, 'how's about I drive you out to your hotel, and then we all go for a drink and some lunch, you'll be wanting to relax for a few hours, I guess. Not being used to this heat, right? And after that I'll come and collect you and show you round the works, how's about that?'

'I think Merc Swingly and the rest of us would value a rest room and a chance to freshen up, first out of the hat, UB, if it's okay by you?' Kyra said in crisp tones which belied the polite form of words, and Ully Beers began to fall over himself in apologies.

'Yeah, right, course, course, what was I thinking of? Chance to freshen up, yeah, right. Thing is,' – he became confidential, leaning closer and lowering his voice, although who else could have heard him, Merc was at a loss to understand – 'thing is, this airport isn't at all well equipped. Toilets, sure, but not what you would call a proper rest room. I've felt bad about it for years, whenever we have important guests like yourselves, but it's as much as my job's worth to complain, maybe if you would put in a word yourself when you get back, I've asked all the VIPs but they never bother, I suppose it's out of sight out of mind and no-one ever comes here twice. I guess if Flacker Winterbotham himself ever came it would be a different matter, all the facilities you could dream of set up in advance, but there, I don't expect he'd ever want to –'

Kyra succeeded in cutting short the flow by setting off firmly in the direction of the only building in sight, leaving the car driver to stow away the luggage, in a covered trailer attached to the rear of the little electric car.

Ully Beers had spoken the truth.

The only facilities offered in the airport building shocked Merc badly. He wondered what Kyra thought of the female version.

Better not ask, perhaps. He didn't think he wanted to know.

No-one wanted to linger.

Shortly afterwards, they were rolling along a bumpy road in an electric car which just about held their party.

It was the dry season.

A good thing, as Ully cheerfully pointed out.

'Come the rains, we'd be stuck halfway there, guys!' he explained happily. 'Good thing they're not due for a couple of weeks yet, right?'

No-one bothered to answer.

There was no air conditioning in the little electric buggy.

An hour later, as they staggered out at the so called hotel, to lunch as promised, Merc realised that he was dripping with sweat.

Collapsing on his bed, some time later, he experienced great relief. The interior of the hotel had at least some air conditioning, if of a primitive variety.

Ten minutes later, stripped and showered, he was deeply asleep.

A soft knocking on the door of his room disturbed him after about an hour.

'Wha – what?'

Merc stood up reluctantly, realised that he was mostly naked, and whisked the bed cover round him.

Someone was gently pushing the door open.

A pretty blonde head peered cautiously round the partly open door.

Hyacinth Duckworthy.

Merc took time to wonder if he was dozing through some horrific nightmare, but, no, he was awake enough to be clear that he wasn't asleep.

'Sorry, Hya!' he managed. ''Fraid I'm not decent. Come back shortly, okay?'

Hyacinth, instead of taking the hint, came further into the room, closing the door quietly behind her.

'Merc, we're close enough friends not to bother about that, honey,' she murmured.

She approached alarmingly near to him. Merc, feeling like someone in an old fashioned comedy sketch, retreated to the far side of the bed.

'We need to talk, baby,' Hyacinth continued in the same low, sexy voice. Merc noticed that like himself, she had stripped off to rest, and hadn't put much back on. A flimsy wrap about covered it, or rather didn't. He began to panic.

'Maybe later, Hyacinth,' he said feebly, backing away.

There was a low table containing writing paper, postcards, and a coloured brochure of the Tiny Isles' attractions, mostly consisting of the warm, polluted, shark-infested waters (our sharks are different from the sharks you'll see anywhere else! They have at least two heads!) and the night life, i.e. the floorshow in the hotel.

Merc chose this moment to trip backwards over this table.

Everything went flying, including Merc. And his bed cover.

He ended up on the floor gazing at close quarters at a large coloured photograph of one of the two headed sharks.

Which was preferable to, a moment later, gazing closely at the face of Hyacinth Duckworthy, who had followed him down, and was gently stroking his left arm.

At least it was only his arm.

Panic accelerated, lapping all previous contenders.

He tried not too successfully to scramble backwards out of Duckworthy range.

Another low knock sounded on the door.

Hyacinth hastily stopped stroking Merc's arm and scrambled to her feet.

'Merc? Are you awake?'

It was Kyra Hotberthy.

Like Hyacinth, she pushed the door open without waiting for a reply.

'I came to tell you,' she began, and then noticed her fellow visitor.

'Oh.'

'Good of you to call, Kyra,' babbled Merc feverishly. He made a not very successful grab for the bed cover. 'Hyacinth came to tell me it was time to get ready ... I was just heading for the shower ...'

This was degenerating from comedy to farce, he reflected.

'And that's just why I came,' Kyra said sweetly. 'We're heading off to the factory in about twenty minutes. Talk to you later, Merc.' She flashed him a cold glance which clashed badly with her tone of voice. 'Come on, Hyacinth, we'd better give Merc a chance to get ready.'

Efficiently gathering up Hyacinth Duckworthy, she left.

Merc wondered.

He was pretty clear on why Hyacinth had come.

He just wasn't quite so sure about Kyra Hotberthy. Tell him what? Just to get ready?

He wondered.

Chapter Nineteen

Half an hour later, they had piled back into the electric car and were bouncing over another rough road towards the factory building.

Merc, once more dripping with sweat, decided that his recent shower had probably been a waste of time.

The factory was a long, low building made of rusty metal with a corrugated iron roof, the building Merc had noticed from the air. The heat inside, when they entered the ugly front door, was horrific.

'We needn't stay long,' Ully Beers apologized anxiously. 'Just thought you'd want to see it for yourselves. This way.'

He shepherded them down the short entrance passage, circling round the small group like a large, not very well trained sheepdog, eager to do everything expected of him and at the same time make a good impression.

Merc had begun to feel slightly sorry for Beers.

Then they entered the main floor of the factory, and all inclination to sympathise with the man abruptly disappeared.

Crammed into the hot, fetid room were several hundred people of both sexes and every age group.

Many of them were clearly children, but their faces were so worn and lined that it would have been easy to mistake them for wrinkled old men and women – their size was the only giveaway.

Every person in the room looked up as Merc and his party entered, then listlessly returned to their work, sewing either by hand or by the type of old-fashioned treadle machine Merc remembered seeing in his granny's lumber room as a child.

Horror swamped Merc's face.

He began to speak, hesitated as to what to say, looked all round him in despair.

One of the women, a less exhausted, prettier one, whispered something to her neighbour.

Ully Beers was transformed.

'You!' he screamed. 'You, women! Why are you speaking? You have work to do!'

The first woman cast down her eyes and returned immediately to her sewing, but Beers continued to thunder at her, until a distraction across the room silenced him.

Another of the women had slumped quietly over her work, and now slid slowly to the floor.

Her neighbour sprang to her feet, calling loudly for water, anything, help of some sort.

'Ailia has fainted from the heat!' she insisted. 'She needs water!'

'Oh, very well, then,' Beers said crossly. 'You, Samda, you know where it's kept. Here, take my key and bring the woman a small glassful. Be careful not to spill any, now!'

He handed over the key to a tall, surly looking man, and turned apologetically to Merc.

'Water is like gold dust out here,' he explained. 'But sometimes they have to be given it. Mind, I wouldn't be surprised if she was faking it! Still, wouldn't do to let her pass out completely. Trained workers have some value, see? They can't be replaced as easily as the run of the mill labourers, and this Ailia is semi-trained, at least.' He smiled at Merc in an effort to seem pleasant, conscious that there seemed to be some aversion to the way he had spoken to the women.

Merc wanted badly to speak. He thought desperately what he should say. Surely this couldn't be normal?

Did the company really live off the pain and labour of these people?

Was his own modestly luxurious lifestyle really funded by this misery?

He found it hard to take in.

Should he message Mr. Brown?

Yes.

He took out his mobile, turned politely to one side, and sent a message.

'What should I do? This is awful!'

Moments later, the answer came.

'What do you think yourself?'

'I don't know!'

'Yeah, you do know!'

Merc gulped.

Yeah, he did.

Even the people camping behind the supermarket hadn't affected him like this.

He cleared his throat.

'Er. Shouldn't there be a supply of water available for them whenever they need it?' he suggested. 'And what about air-conditioning? It seems like a basic essential in this heat?'

'Ah.' Ully Beers cleared his throat. 'Well, at first sight, yes. But if you'd like to come into my office, I can show you the figures. We can produce clothes here for fifty per cent less than our previous best, but only by keeping costs to a minimum, you see? Any extra cost blows the whole system sky high, right? I can show you all the figures, MS.'

Rage mounted up in Merc's head.

'So this is all because of the bottom line?' he said. The word seemed an appropriate description of the current Company policy.

Samda came back in, with a minute container of water.

Merc could remember his granny telling him about the widespread use of plastic cups in her own childhood, but of course those days were long gone. The availability of plastic was a thing of the past. This was a rather rusty tin mug, converted from an old food can and retained for maybe fifty years.

The woman's friends propped her up, held the mug to her lips, and helped her to sip. She took the water gratefully.

A noise erupted in the far corner of the factory floor.

A child, a girl of maybe twelve, had sneaked quietly in from the back entrance, hoping to avoid notice.

She might have succeeded, if her attention had not been drawn to the woman Ailia, sitting up on the floor with her friend's arm round her neck and sipping slowly and carefully at the precious water.

The girl gave an uninhibited shriek and rushed forward.

'Mum! Mum! What's wrong? What is it?'

Ully Beers strode towards her.

'Alexa Darnhurst! I might have known! Anywhere there's trouble, there's Alexa! And where did you suddenly appear from? Have you been mitching off from work again? You'll know all about it if I find out that that's the story.'

He attempted to seize hold of the child, who wriggled free from his outstretched hand with ease and said contemptuously, 'Oh, leave it out, Ully! Tell me what's wrong with my Mum, you big fool!'

Beers gasped speechlessly, but the woman who was supporting Ailia said quickly, 'Your Mum's okay, Alexa. She fainted from the heat. Mr. Beers sent for water for her.'

'So I should hope!' Alexa said. 'This place is far too hot for people to work in. Time something was done about it.' She glared at Ully Beers.

'You never liked me, Ully, did you? I don't know what your problem is! You even stopped me bringing my machete to work with me!'

Her gaze swept challengingly round the room, and rested on Merc.

'You,' she said. 'A visitor, are you? Well, now you've seen this place for yourself. Are you going to do anything about it?'

Merc looked at the bright, challenging eyes.

For a moment he was silent.

Then he spoke.

Yes,' said Merc slowly. 'Yes, I believe I am.'

Chapter Twenty

For a moment there was silence on the factory floor.

Merc looked around him.

Kyra, Silo, and Hyacinth were behind him. He couldn't see their faces. He had no idea what they were thinking.

Most of the workers in the room were too far off to have heard him. Alexa alone seemed to have taken in what he had said.

A cowardly streak in Merc realised that maybe he hadn't fully committed himself after all.

Then a howl of rage from Ully Beers disillusioned him.

'What! MS, you don't know the situation!'

'Don't I?' Merc asked coldly.

Ully gaped at him.

'If you try to change things you'll end up by getting the factory closed down. How's that going to help anyone here?'

Most of all, me, Ully Beers, Merc saw in his eyes.

Ully sprang up on a nearby bench.

'Listen, you guys!'

Merc stared at him.

'The Company runs this place because it has a healthy bottom line. Because it brings in a worthwhile profit! Increase the costs and the whole thing becomes pointless! Do you want to see this place closed down, just so's you can have free water available? Well?'

All round the factory floor the cry went up.

'No way! How're we going to live?'

'Don't risk it!'

'Keep it going!'

Only one voice protested, the girl Alexa.

'We have to make changes! We can't just carry on like this!'

Merc took a good look at her.

She stood, flushed and clearly very angry, beside her mother, hands on her hips, dark eyes flashing. Twelve, going on twenty, he thought. Forced to grow up early by the terrible conditions of life in the factory in the Tiny Isles. And, probably, by having to look after her mother, instead of being looked after by her, if Ailia's present state of health had been on-going for any length of time. This girl was a fighter. A strong willed person, with her own ideas about life. Used to struggling for her own way, in the face of a dreadful system.

In some strange way, she reminded him of Seraphina, and even more of Lucy.

Lucy as she might be in ten or twelve years' time.

She had a cute, appealing, but very determined face, with a strong jaw-line, eyes either dark brown or black, it was hard to tell which at this distance, a small snub nose, and light brown hair straggling over her shoulders, and cut in an untidy fringe which she shook back from her eyes impatiently every few minutes, only to have to fall forward over her face again. She was slim and slight, but wiry, and clearly lithe and agile.

As he watched, she stooped, gathered up a handful of wooden bobbins, and hurled them with amazing aim and a full head of anger at Ully Beers' face.

Followed by the dregs of the mug of water.

The mug cut Ully across his forehead. Merc couldn't help applauding.

Ully Beers, now equally angry, stood for a moment wiping his face. Then he jumped down from the bench, lunged forward, arms out-stretched, and made a grab for Alexa.

Alexa squealed, and ran for it. Round and round the factory floor, darting behind the frozen workers, dodging round the sewing machines, leaving the round bodied Ully Beers out of breath and panting in her wake, until she came safely to harbour behind Merc Swingly, clinging hard to the tail of his T shirt.

'Stop!' thundered Merc. 'Stop!'

Ully Beers, catching his breath, suddenly realised that he was reacting in a way unacceptable to his immediate boss.

He pulled up to a halt, glared at what he could see of Alexa, and began to stammer apologies to Merc.

'Hey, sorry, MS, these people can get out of control so easy, I didn't intend for you guys to get involved in this sort of deal, maybe we should go into my office and have a drink or something, right? And cool it, okay?'

Merc glared at him.

'So, let's do that, then, Ully,' he said. 'And Alexa here should come with us. I want to hear her side of things, okay?'

The question which was not a question left no room for disagreement.

They went into Ully's office.

Not altogether to Merc's surprise, this was a cool, air conditioned room, pleasantly furnished with an attractive rosewood desk, a number of comfortable chairs, and a large cabinet containing a good range of drinks.

'Drink, everyone?' said Beers hospitably. He seemed to have recovered his earlier, eager to please, approach. 'Or a pill? Time for a pink one, isn't it?'

'No, thank you,' said Merc coldly.

'Hey, I'll have something,' broke in Kyra Hotberthy, who had been uncharacteristically silent until now. 'White wine, please, UB. I prefer my own pills, thanks,' she added, waving aside Ully's offered box.

'Same for me,' murmured Hyacinth Duckworthy, perking up a little. Merc, glancing round at her, caught the tail-end of an expression of horror, hastily wiped from her face as she caught his eye.

'Give the kid something,' he ordered. 'Cool orange or like that, okay? And Silo, feel free.'

So Silo Clotson asked for a beer.

Ully Beers seemed grateful for the relief. Putting a pink pill in his own mouth, and washing it down with a large whiskey, he beamed round.

'Sit down, everybody,' he suggested. 'I'll just fix the drinks.'

'Now, then,' he added, when they were all sitting, 'I'm sure we can work this out.'

He bustled over to the large, luxurious looking drinks cabinet.

Merc looked round idly.

His attention was caught by a sheet of paper half hidden under a file on Beers' desk.

He could read what was visible quite easily.

'This can't go on. You have been warned. Unless ...
we will take action to change things if you ...
The Company needs to realise that ...
Beware! ...

Merc gasped.

What was going on?

Chapter Twenty One

'We can work this out, I'm sure,' repeated Ully Beers, handing out the drinks and sitting down behind his desk.

As his eye fell on the sheet of paper, he hastily tidied the rest of it away beneath the file.

'Work what out?' asked Merc.

He glared at Ully Beers, who hastily gulped down the remainder of his drink, and attempted a placatory grin.

'The situation here doesn't bear thinking about,' Merc said. He was very angry, and finding it difficult to keep his reactions under control. The urge to lift the fancy marble paperweight sitting on Ully Beers' desk and hurl it at him was almost too strong. He clenched his hands together forcefully, making sure he didn't act on the impulse. 'People can't be expected to work in conditions like these. I don't want to undermine anyone's job, but there have to be changes, as long as I'm in charge round here.'

Merc looked angrily round him.

He met a weak smile from Hyacinth Duckworthy, a look of amazement from Silo Clotson, and, to his surprise, a glance which seemed to carry at lot of approval from Kyra Hotberthy.

'And how long will that be?' he thought he heard Beers mutter under his breath.

He wondered, himself.

Meanwhile, however.

'First thing is, we need a water cooler. In the main factory. Available to everyone.'

'Well. I guess we could set up a system,' said Beers doubtfully. 'Deduct the cost from people's wages. Break even. Hey,' he added more cheerfully, 'might even make a profit, right?'

'Free,' said Merc firmly. 'No deductions from wages. Next, air conditioning. You have a really nice system going here, Ully, right in your office. Couldn't be too hard to extend it to the working quarters.'

Ully Beers gaped at him. But kept his mouth shut when he saw the look in Merc's eye.

'Then, hours and wages,' Merc went on. 'You can fill me in on that, Alexa.'

'We work fourteen hours a day,' said Alexa promptly. 'And we get two dollars a week, less deductions.'

'Deductions?' asked Merc softly.

'Food, uniforms, stuff like that. I made 80 cents last week,' she added proudly. 'That was with overtime, okay?'

Merc's anger was by now fiercely bubbling in a tightly contained percolator whose lid jerked and thrust upwards in an effort to explode. He held the anger bottled down firmly in the cause of asking yet more questions. 'And what do you do with your eighty cents, Alexa?'

'I help Mum pay the rent,' Alexa said. 'And I'm saving up for a trip to the Company headquarters, in Nexus Luxuria, right? I want to see the whole of the world as soon as I can.'

Merc felt like saying, 'It's just more of the same, Alexa. But with a bit of sugar coating.' But he didn't. Instead he said, 'Get moving, Ully. I want to see your plans for the air conditioning by tomorrow p.m. And the water cooler needs to be in place by tonight. If necessary, buy one from the hotel. They seem to have plenty. Then I want to sit down and talk to you about revised hours and wages, so if you have any figures you want to show me, figures that you think might make a difference to how I think about this business, you'd better look them out now.'

Ully's anger had resurrected.

'I'll do just that little thing, MS,' he said. 'And I'll show you the written instructions from Flacker Winterbotham himself, while I'm at it.'

'FW and I have talked about this, Ully,' Merc said easily. He didn't add that the talks had consisted of Flacker Winterbotham reiterating the importance of the bottom line. 'You get your figures out and we'll look at them.'

A full bottle of gin rolled off the top shelf of Ully Beers' drinks cabinet, crashed through the door which had been left half open, and landed on the floor at Kyra Hotberthy's feet, where it continued to roll about.

A picture of the Company headquarters in Nexus Luxuria which had been hanging on the opposite wall of the office fell to the floor with a crash.

Alexa rose composedly to her feet.

'Come on,' she said. ''Quake. We need to get out of here, like quickly, right?'

Seizing Merc by the hand, she half dragged, half pushed him out of the doorway.

A loud buzzer went off in the factory as they spoke.

Men, women, and children began to pour out of the room in ever increasing floods.

Ully Beers recovered his wits and started to bundle his distinguished visitors to safety.

'Earthquake!' he tried to explain. 'We get lots of them. Everybody into the quake shelter! Come on, let's get moving!'

Merc looked round at the rest of the people from Nexus Luxuria.

Hyacinth Duckworthy seemed dazed by the sudden event, but ready to escape if only someone would show her where to escape to.

Silo Clotson moved unsteadily towards the exit, his mouth still open, his arms outstretched as a means of holding off the danger that threatened from all directions.

Merc had time to wonder why he had decided to bring him.

Then he remembered Seraphina, who had wanted rid of him, but not, Merc thought, at the cost of sending him to his death.

At least, he didn't think so.

The only one of his companions who seemed to be on top of things was Kyra Hotberthy, who said crisply, 'Okay, which way? And what about the factory workers?'

'Just follow me!' said Ully Beers. 'Never mind about the workers. They know where to go!'

Merc ignored him.

Instead, he stumbled after Alexa, who still had hold of his arm and was running in the opposite direction from Beers.

'My Mum! My Mum!' she called out in an insistent voice. 'You've got to help me find her!'

They burst through the door leading to the main factory floor.

Alexa was looking round eagerly for her mother. There she was, in the middle of the crowd of workers.

They struggled towards her.

Then the rumblings got worse. Merc found himself suddenly unable to see.

It took him a minute to realise that he was in the process of being buried alive beneath a pile of rubble.

Chapter Twenty Two

He shook his head frantically, trying to get the dust out of his eyes and ears, pushing the rubble aside, to get free of the worst of it.

And was able to see around him again.

In every direction were people, both frightened and angry, trapped under the same rubble, the remains of the cheap quality huts.

Alexa let go of Merc's hand and began to scrabble frantically in the collapsed wreckage of the main factory building, tugging at broken pieces of wall and mortar.

She turned fiercely on Merc, tears flooding down her face and leaving streaks of comparative cleanliness on her dust covered cheeks.

'Help me!' she ordered. 'You said you wanted to help. Start doing it, then, why can't you?'

Merc recovered his senses. He began to dig in the piles of smashed wooden supports and walls around him. Alexa, tight mouthed, worked beside him.

Something.

No.

Someone.

An arm emerging, then a head.

'Mum,' Alexa said.

Merc dug more frantically.

Then she was out, and they were able to pull her, gasping and choking, clear of the wreckage. Merc stood up, wobbling slightly, put his arm under Ailia's and raised her carefully to her feet.

Ailia looked even paler than she had done when Merc first saw her. She stood between Merc and her daughter and swayed from side to side as she tried to stay upright. Merc held on to her arm tightly. Alexa gave what support she could on the other side.

Together they staggered in the direction of the earthquake shelter. Howling winds hurled flying debris past their heads, scored several near misses, and landed one successful shot on Merc's right cheek.

They needed to get undercover, and fast.

The shelter, or bunker, when they reached it, had nothing much going for it except that it was made out of strong concrete, unlikely to collapse in a hurry.

Otherwise it was one of the ugliest buildings Merc had ever seen.

And not at all to his surprise, he found, when he finally reached the doorway, half carrying the fainting Ailia with what help a small but determined Alexa could give, that it was already crowded to bursting point with Ully Beers, his senior staff, and the party from Nexus Luxuria.

Pushing his way without scruple past the people blocking his way, and realising with satisfaction that he had trodden quite heavily on Ully Beers' right big toe, Merc deposited Ailia against the far wall, and took a deep breath.

'Get her some water,' he demanded.

Kyra Hotberthy, looking paler in spite of her copper coloured skin than Merc had ever seen her, scurried to obey.

There was a water container attached to one wall. Kyra filled a tin cup, and held it carefully to Ailia's lips.

'Now,' Merc said, turning to the hopping Beers, who, his face screwed up in agony, was nursing his toe tenderly, 'now.' He glared at Beers. 'I want to know, and I want to know as soon as we have time to talk about it, who is responsible for the disgraceful state of Health and Safety round here? One tiny shelter for several hundred people? And a factory building which collapses at the smallest sign of an earthquake? What happens when you get something a bit higher up the Richter scale? But above all –' He paused and glared again. 'I want to know why you people are huddling in here instead of helping to get some of your staff out from under the rubble? Now, get out there and start doing something!'

They moved slowly out from the shelter, driven both by the note in Merc's voice and by his pushing hands.

No-one seemed particularly keen.

But they moved into action presently.

Helped by Alexa, Merc began energetically to shift rubble, and to release trapped factory workers. This was okay at first. They found about a dozen people who were quite near the surface and still breathing, and were able to drag them out. But the deeper they went, the harder it got. Nobody could be buried under so much dust and rubble and still be alive.

They worked on, anyway.

Then there were only bodies.

One by one, the rescuers gave up and drifted away, until only Merc and Alexa, with Silo Clotson and Kyra Hotberthy, were still digging frantically.

Then there were only Merc and Alexa.

So then Merc gave up, and took Alexa by the hand to lead her gently back to the earthquake shelter.

Kyra Hotberthy looked up as they came in. 'It's no use,' she said flatly. 'We've done what we could. That's it.'

Merc looked at her blankly. He knew she was right. He just didn't want to hear it said.

'How's Ailia?' he asked.

'Not good.'

'Oh.'

Merc was conscious of a bad feeling in the pit of his stomach.

This wasn't how it was meant to happen.

The people you rescued ought to be okay. They ought to stay rescued.

But he knew, as he looked more closely at Ailia, that that wasn't how it was going to be.

He bent over the pale, sad faced woman.

'Ailia.'

She looked up and smiled at him. She knew it was too late.

'Hi.' He smiled back.

Ailia was past caring. There was nothing to be done. He saw her eyes slowly closing.

Then he looked round.

Alexa was standing by his shoulder.

He couldn't look at her face.

Ailia gave one final, gasping breath.

Then stopped.

Merc heard Alexa give a cry of anguish.

He turned to her and put his arms round her without thinking.

There was nothing to say, but he heard himself saying the meaningless words one offers to a hurt child.

'There, there. It's all right. Don't cry. It's okay, pet.'

Alexa sobbed into his T shirt. For some reason, Merc drew comfort from the warm wet tears soaking into his chest. He patted her back helplessly.

Presently the sobbing stopped.

Alexa looked up at him fiercely.

Merc found himself unable to meet her eyes.

'This is never going to happen again,' he said grimly. 'The factory will be rebuilt to the highest safety standards. No more flimsy lightweight roofs or walls. No more lack of earthquake shelters. I'll talk to Planetary Building and Construction myself. We need to be able to rely on the buildings we put up, okay?'

The factory workers looked at him. So did the supervisors.

'Okay. That's right. We need to make sure everything's safe,' said one of supervisors. 'We can't afford a repeat of this sort of thing.'

Ully Beers opened his mouth to protest, but all that came out was a high pitched squeal.

'What about the bottom line?' he managed after a moment of maximum effort.

'What about it?' asked Merc softly.

Something in his eye made Ully Beers shut up.

'I will take full responsibility for the cost of rebuilding,' Merc announced. 'In a few days I will be returning to Nexus Luxuria to make a report to Flacker Winterbotham. Before I leave, I want to see serious plans made for rebuilding this place in earthquake proof materials, with the air conditioning and water facilities previously discussed. Ully, you and I need to get together to have that discussion about hours and wages that we talked about before all this.' He glared at Ully Beers. 'Understood?'

'Understood, MS!' stuttered Beers, wiping the sweat from his forehead 'But – but –'

'But what?'

'I don't know. Was it an earthquake? Or was it – ?'

Ully Beers shut up abruptly.

Merc stared at him.

Beers was clearly very worried. About the Twisted Rosebud? Did he really think they might have been behind the collapse of the factory? But who would do such a thing? Not people who seemed to be against the Company, and pro the Company workers, surely? It wouldn't make sense!

Anyway, it had clearly been a genuine earthquake.

'Suppose something like this happens again?' Beers asked eventually. 'Only worse? You can't blame me for it, if the new building still isn't strong enough!'

'I'll see to it that it is!' Merc said grimly. 'We'll go over the plans together, now.'

'Good!' And then you'll be responsible, Beers carefully didn't add. But Merc understood him anyway.

Merc looked down at Alexa, still clinging to his T shirt tail.

'And what on earth are we going to do about you?' he added softly, mostly to himself.

Alexa beamed up at him. 'You're going back to Nexus Luxuria?' she asked.

'Yes.'

'That's okay, then. I'll go along with you!'

Chapter Twenty Three

The plane touched down at the runway near Nexus Luxuria, late on the morning that they left the Tiny Isles.

Behind him, Merc was aware of worried stroke angry whispering from time to time.

Beside him, Alexa was silent. Whenever Merc stole a glance at her, he could see that her eyes had apparently grown even larger since his last look. Also shinier.

This helped him to deal with his frequent visualisation of Seraphina's face when he explained matters to her. And her reactions.

At least to a minor extent.

Bringing Silo for a night was one thing.

Bringing Alexa, presumably permanently, was, Merc was gloomily aware, almost certainly quite another.

However, he remained firm in the knowledge that there was absolutely nothing else he could have done.

There was also Flacker Winterbotham to think of.

Merc felt almost lighthearted about Flacker. If he could succeed in explaining his course of conduct convincingly to Seraphina, then talking to FW would be a walkover with no extra time or penalty shoot out necessary.

They got out of the plane and headed for the cars.

It was clear to Merc that his companions were carefully keeping their distance from him.

No-one was quite sure what Merc was getting himself into, and no-one particularly wanted to be more involved than necessary.

Especially Hyacinth Duckworthy, he noticed.

So, there was definitely an up side, then. He could probably forget about that promised dinner date.

As soon as they had been driven back to the company car park, Merc bundled Alexa out of the car and went straight for his own small machine.

He put Alexa in the back seat, and hurriedly took out his mobile.

'Mr. Brown?'

'Yip?'

'What do I do now?'

'Stop worrying and get a good rest, sonny boy.'

'What? I mean – What should I tell Seraphina?'

'Ah, now, MS, that's between you and your missus,' replied Mr. Brown infuriatingly.

'So, no suggestions?'

'Tell her you had no alternative. You hadn't, had you?'

And on this note of practical common sense, Mr. Brown switched off.

A painful version of 'The sunny side of the street' tinkled in Merc's ear, until he flung the mobile down and started up the car.

'What!?' said Seraphina. 'What!!??'

Then she caught Alexa's eye, stopped in mid scold, and said instead, 'Well, come on in, you must all be shattered with the travelling. I'll make some coffee. And Alexa had better have a sleep. You and I, Merc Swingly,' she added quietly, behind Alexa's back, as she ushered the still silent girl into the house, 'have some things to talk about while Alexa's resting.'

But in the end it wasn't so difficult. Taking Mr. Brown's advice, such as it was, Merc described the whole situation to Seraphina, and found her equally horrified at the Tiny Isles factory set-up.

He couldn't, she agreed, have left Alexa to the tender mercies of Ully Beers, especially now her mother had died.

'But I don't quite see what we do now,' she added firmly. 'I don't think Flacker Winterbotham is going to like all this, Merc. And if that's so, then we probably won't have a house for ourselves and Lucy, let alone Alexa. After Winterbotham sacks you, I mean.'

Merc, who felt remarkably cheered by his wife's unexpected reaction, especially at her amazing calm in the light of his possible sacking, smiled.

'Well, we'll just have to see, honey. It may not come to that. I think Mr. Brown may have a plan.'

Chapter 23

'I thought he didn't say anything much when you spoke to him?'

'No. But he likes to keep his little secrets, have you noticed? I'd be surprised if something isn't brewing.'

Merc was expected at the office later that afternoon.

In spite of his words to Seraphina, he felt apprehension leaping enthusiastically from his throat to his mouth and struggling to take control of his stomach, as he approached the familiar thick oak door with its iron bands as strong as the blacksmith's arms in the song. As usual, it reminded Merc of the bank it had once led into, and an automatic reaction of fear mixed with repulsion rumbled round in his stomach. Banks were the enemy, he knew that.

For whatever reason, the door was sagging open.

Inside, for a moment he thought he must have somehow managed to come to the wrong place.

Rubble and dust on all sides, reminiscent of the mess left by the earthquake in the main factory building in the Tiny Isles. Clouds of dust floating through the air.

People, confused and upset, covered in dust and dirt, were exchanging loud comments and questions, and looking for some sort of help and support, as they ran distractedly to and fro like mice hoping to escape from an angry prowling cat – an enormous ginger Tom, probably – and wondering what they should do and where they should go.

Kyra Hotberthy, a clipboard in her hand, was talking rapidly to a small stout man wearing thick rimmed glasses and with a short pencil stuck behind his right ear.

Kyra, Merc saw in astonishment, was looking disheveled. There were streaks of dust on her face, and her hair, normally perfect, was tangled and messy. He watched as she poked about among the rubble, wiped the back of her dirty hand across her forehead, then ran her hand through her hair, adding to the dishevelment.

Merc, who had never before seen her anything but tidy and well groomed, even in the aftermath of the earthquake, gaped in astonishment.

In the background, hovering, was Fancy Linnet, the quite pretty Public Relations officer stroke Press Representative who had been taking notes for the News at the Board Meeting. On her face was a strange expression, a mixture of horror and excitement.

Merc wandered over uncertainly, towards Kyra.

'Um. Kyra.'

'Yes, MS?'

'Is anything wrong?'

For a moment Kyra Hotberthy's copper coloured face grew redder and redder until it seemed possible that she might produce an explosion of her own. Then she recovered partial control.

'Yes, MS, there is something wrong,' she managed to say. 'Look around you.'

Merc looked around him blankly.

'The Company's reception area has been blown up, Merc,' said Kyra Hotberthy slowly and clearly. 'Do you understand?'

Merc's face must have told her that the answer was still no.

'A bomb exploded about two hours before we got back from the Tiny Isles. It was the first thing they told me when I walked in the door half an hour ago. I'm still trying to find out how it could have happened.'

She saw that Merc was looking at the small stout man with the pencil behind his ear.

'This is Jo Hubbard from Maintenance,' she said impatiently. 'He's going to examine the area and make a quick report – aren't you, Mr. Hubbard?' She turned swiftly on the hapless little man hovering beside her, and smiled ferociously. 'Now I need to speak to the security staff and find out how this could possibly have happened.'

'I'll come with you,' offered Merc weakly.

'Thanks, but I'm not going anywhere. That's Grel Onions, the Head of Security, over there.'

Kyra indicated a burly six footer in cap and uniform, hovering disconsolately near the site of the former reception counter.

Seeing Kyra gesturing towards him, Onions came forward cautiously.

'But – was anyone hurt?' Merc asked. He realised that this was something he should probably have asked much sooner.

'No. Although we think they were aiming at Flacker Winterbotham.'

Chapter Twenty Four

Merc stared at her in surprise.

Then recovered himself enough to ask, 'But he's okay?'

'Yes.' Merc identified a distinct note of regret in Kyra Hotberthy's voice. She went on hastily, 'He's lying down right now. Trying to get over the effects. He was meant to be down at Reception, giving a team talk to the clerical staff, at ten a.m., when it happened. The talk had been scheduled since last week, and announced widely. Anyone could have known he would be there. FW was meant to be standing on the rostrum. Right where the bomb went off. With the staff grouped round him at a respectful distance.'

'So. You think it was one of the staff?'

'Not necessarily. That rather depends on what Mr. Onions here has to tell us,' said Kyra grimly.

Grel Onions, cap in hand, offered her a weak smile.

'Well, Grel, what can you tell us?'

Fancy Linnet approached them, smiling ingratiatingly.

'Is this likely to be anything for me?'

'No!' snapped Kyra. 'The last thing we want is to see this story on tonight's news! Go away and cover a local flower show!'

Fancy smiled weakly, and said, 'Oh. Sorry. I just thought –'

Then, catching Kyra's eye, she retreated.

Grel Onions pulled himself together.

'For a start, the explosion is timed at ten oh ten Nexus Luxuria time,' he started. 'We have that from most of the witnesses. Bad planning, if they hoped to get Winterbotham, because he was running twenty minutes late, and was still in the lift coming down when the event occurred. The lifts, as you can see,' he said, indicating the bank of lifts at the further end of the Reception area, 'are undamaged, being outside the range of the explosion and thus remaining intact, even at the time of the occurrence –'

'When the bomb went off,' corrected Kyra Hotberthy.

'It hasn't yet been confirmed that the cause of the explosion was a bomb,' corrected Onions pedantically in his turn. 'My men are currently examining the area in order to retrieve as many pieces of wreckage as possible. The next step will be to analyse these. Then we can make a report suggesting alternative solutions. However,' he went on hastily, seeing the growing thunderclouds on Kyra's face, 'I agree that a bomb seems to be the most likely root of the trouble.'

'Fine,' said Kyra briskly. 'What I really want to know is how a bomb could have been brought into this building under the noses of your security men? And who brought it?'

Grel Onions' red face was slowly growing redder.

'I can assure you,' he said stiffly, 'that a full enquiry is being conducted to ascertain the facts. The ingredients of the bomb may have been smuggled in over the past week in small bundles and hidden in a locker –'

'So. Are you claiming a member of staff is responsible?'

'– probably by more than one person,' continued Onions, ignoring the interruption, 'and clearly at least one member of staff must have been involved to supply the locker and its key. However, outside visitors may also have smuggled in some of the ingredients. All visitors are searched, as you are aware, Miss, but some of the ingredients would have looked harmless enough, e.g. fertilizer, which could have been disguised as a sample. Alternatively, some items could have been concealed among normal deliveries, such as stock for the canteen, with, that is, the collusion of the canteen staff, etc., or –'

'Oh, put it – in a written report,' interrupted Kyra impatiently. 'Haven't you found anything useful yet?'

'Not as such,' Grel Onions was beginning again, but thankfully was stopped by the approach of one of his uniformed staff.

The man, a cheerful freckled youngster with ginger hair, saluted briskly and waited for permission to speak.

'Well?'

'Sir, we've found what's likely the detonator. A simple timing device, sir.'

'Good.'

'And, sir, there's this letter. Just found it attached inside the lift, sir. Undamaged, sir. Since, as you are aware, the lifts were unharmed, sir.'

'Heavens, another one!' muttered Kyra Hotberthy. 'Stop talking about it and open the letter,' she ordered. 'Or better still, give it to me.'

'Can't do that, Miss,' Onions took pleasure in saying reprovingly. 'Might be traces of the writer to be identified. Fingerprints, DNA, etc. Give it to me, Ricicles.'

He took the letter carefully in his gloved hand, and pulled it open.

'Read it out,' Kyra said.

Onions read,

Greetings and commiserations on the loss of your Boss.

Or should it be congratulations?

We can all do with fewer people like him around.

From your friends,

> *The Twisted Rosebud.*

'They wrote this in advance,' Grel Onions pointed out unnecessarily. 'They expected that when we read this, Mr. Winterbotham would be dead! But who are they? The Twisted Rosebud? They aren't one of the known terrorist organizations!'

Merc swallowed hard.

'The Twisted Rosebud!' he found himself saying. 'Do you mean to tell me the Twisted Rosebud is capable of something like this?'

He remembered that the Twisted Rosebud had been in his house, had been under the same roof as Lucy, had tied Seraphina up and had been into their bedroom to leave a note on the pillow. He felt his stomach churning, but managed not to be actually sick.

'What do you know about the Twisted Rosebud?' snapped Grel Onions, sticking his face forward threateningly into Merc's.

'Not a lot,' admitted Merc. 'Are they some sort of terrorists, then? Or what?'

'This is Merc Swingly, a senior member of the Board,' Kyra Hotberthy intervened sternly.

Grel Onions, a man who had just spoken to his boss in an unacceptable way, took a pace back and smiled weakly.

'So, sir. You've heard of these Twisted Rosebud guys?'

'I've heard the name,' Merc replied cautiously.

'And?'

'Er. Nothing else.'

Grel Onions shrugged. 'Doesn't really help us, then.'

Kyra said, 'You'd better carry on, Grel. Let me know when you have something worth hearing, right?'

She turned to Merc.

'You'd better come and speak to FW. He was asking for you earlier, I'm told.'

'How did he seem?'

'I haven't seen him yet. I didn't get here much before yourself, MS.'

Flacker Winterbotham was stretched out on a leather couch in his own office. Esther Frantic hovered over him anxiously, offering brandy and pink pills. Any moment now, Merc reflected, she would start to fan his forehead with palm leaves or peel grapes for him.

When Merc knocked and went into the office, followed by Kyra Hotberthy, Winterbotham raised his head and regarded them with bleary eyes.

Merc was shocked to see the change in him.

Where was the confident crocodile of their last meeting?

'MS! Thank goodness! Great to see you back. I really need you, MS! You've got to do something! You've got to save my life!'

Chapter Twenty Five

Merc gaped at Winterbotham.

Then he hurriedly swallowed the mouthful of apologies and explanations about the Tiny Isles which he had been holding back with great difficulty, like an unnecessarily hot curry stupidly eaten late on a Saturday night already too full of experimentation in the area of alcoholic refreshment. And now ready to overflow.

If no-one was asking, better say nothing.

'You've heard about this terrible thing that's happened?' Flacker Winterbotham went on. 'An attempt on my life, no less! We need to take action immediately! Increase security! Bring in bodyguards! Track down these villains at once! Give them what they deserve!' He sank back, panting. He was running out of exclamation marks.

But a moment later he was up again.

'It's all this involvement in politics. Must be,' he muttered. 'But nobody really knew anything about that as yet, did they? I haven't really taken any open action. Spoken to a couple of old friends.'

He looked distraught.

Esther Frantic approached him, and offered more brandy in a cooing voice. Flacker seized the glass from her and gulped it down.

'What are you doing still here?' he suddenly shouted at Esther. 'This is a private conversation! Get out!'

Esther hastily departed. So much, it dawned on her, for her hoped for affair with the boss.

'Never liked that girl!' muttered Winterbotham. 'Nothing but a pest.'

Looking up, his eye fell on Merc.

'I don't know who to trust!' he said. 'It could be people close to me! That's why I need to speak to you, MS! I can trust you! You didn't know anything about me and politics. You're new to the Board. You don't have anything against me – do you?' he asked almost pathetically.

Merc found himself saying, 'I certainly don't want to assassinate you, FW, that's for sure.'

Flacker Winterbotham shuddered at the word.

'You're a good boy, MS. So I want you to take charge of this whole business. Head up a team. Pick your own people. Find out who's responsible for this and deal with them! You've got a free hand, okay? Just don't let them get me!'

Merc gasped.

He wondered if he had heard properly. While he had no desire to murder FW or anyone else, there was no way he considered him his best buddy. And what did Winterbotham expect from him? Merc wasn't a trained investigator. He didn't even know if he wanted to track down these people. He didn't know enough about them, their aims and motivation.

And intuition told him that this would be one of the few examples of team action which would be expected to produce something more, as its outcome, than a long and impressive looking report with an easy to read points summary.

Flacker Winterbotham was still speaking.

'You can take Kyra, here,' he said. 'Kyra will keep you on the right track. And if I can trust anyone else, it has to be Kyra. She's always had my best interests at heart.'

Merc stopped himself from laughing with difficulty.

How could a man in Flacker Winterbotham's position be so blind?

Even Merc was quite clear that Kyra Hotberthy, close as she was to Winterbotham, and whatever she may or may not have felt in the past, was currently far from being his biggest fan. In fact Merc, if asked for a candid opinion, would have felt safe in saying that she hated Flacker Winterbotham's guts. And how!

'And neither you nor Kyra were here when the bomb went off! You were still in the air at the time! So I know you had nothing to do with it!'

Merc gasped again. Surely Winterbotham could see the flawed logic in this? Not all the members of a conspiracy needed to be on the spot to trigger an explosion.

Still.

Better not point that out just now, perhaps.

'Em – so, FW, I should get a team together now, right?'

'A man of action, MS. That's what I like to see! No, no, sit down for a moment. Fix yourselves both a drink, why don't you?' He gestured at the tray on the nearby table. 'And let me tell you about my experience. It will help you sort out your plan of campaign, right?'

Merc sat down cautiously, hoping that he was not just imagining that he was off the hook as far as his actions in the Tiny Isles went. Flacker Winterbotham seemed to have completely lost interest in the outcome of his recent trip.

It appeared that when it was a question of his own safety, everything else disappeared into the discard, and was already being pulped in preparation for oblivion in the nearest landfill.

This, Merc knew, was not an unusual human reaction.

Possibly Merc might get some idea of what the investigating team was supposed to do next, by listening to Flacker Winterbotham talk about his ordeal?

Which seemed to have consisted of traveling downwards in his luxuriously fitted personal lift; hearing a muffled banging noise; and being hustled back up to safety almost as soon as the lift door had opened on the view of the reception area.

And then being fussed over and pampered by numerous assistants including his own doctor and, of course, various attractive young women and Senior Board members. The last of whom had been firmly but politely escorted to the door by Esther Frantic only a few minutes before Merc and Kyra Hotberthy had arrived.

No, not a lot to be learnt there.

Nor were Winterbotham's ideas about the motivation of the terrorists more helpful.

Merc, remembering his recent late night experience in the company buildings, felt pretty sure that Flacker was barking up entirely the wrong tree.

He hadn't even begun to get involved in politics yet, by his own account. He didn't stand for any political action that the terrorists might want him to change.

Why should anyone expect political profit from Flacker Winterbotham's assassination?

It didn't make sense.

No.

The thing which did make sense, Merc thought, was something which he found unsurprising. It was only strange that no-one had attempted it before now.

The terrorists, he was pretty sure had one aim only.

To destroy the Company.

And probably the six other multi-national companies as well.

The people who, much more than any politicians, really ran the world these days, and who had reduced it to its present very bad condition.

Chapter Twenty Six

Merc wanted some coffee badly.

Shaking off Kyra Hotberthy easily enough as they left Flacker Winterbotham's room – she wanted to get back to the reception area to harry the Maintenance and the Security people some more – he headed for the staff canteen.

He was glad to see that it was nearly empty. The company staff as a body had gone home early. Except for those still hanging round the scene of the explosion, hoping for more excitement.

Sitting in a far corner with a large coffee in front of him, Merc cautiously took out his mobile and rang Mr. Brown.

'Hi! How's it going?' came the chirpy response.

'Okay,' said Merc cautiously. 'You were right about not worrying. About the Tiny Isles, and Alexa, and that. But what about this Twisted Rosebud gang?'

'What about them?'

'Em. How am I supposed to catch them? And should I even be trying to, right? I need you to give me some answers here, MB.'

He heard Mr. Brown laughing. Pleased at being addressed as MB, apparently.

'All will become clear, sonny. Meantime, why not set up your team and chat to the team members? Could be they can tell you something. Talk to me when you've done it!'

Then came the annoying little tinkle of *'The Sunny Side of the Street.'* Mr. Brown had rung off.

Merc finished his coffee.

Time to find himself a team.

Well, there was Silo Clotson for one.

He had been putting Silo to the back of his mind, recently. He had taken him on the trip to the Tiny Isles. At least that had kept him off the streets, and out of Seraphina's hair. Not that the conditions there had proved to be a much better option. But now they were home again, and the weight of Silo, a big man, too, hung heavy upon him.

Put him on this team, thought Merc, and at least he'll have a job again for a while. Think again after that.

Kyra Hotberthy, of course. Flacker Winterbotham had suggested her in tones which made it rather more than a suggestion.

Well, that was okay. Kyra could probably help him.

But not – Merc shuddered – not Hyacinth Duckworthy. No way.

That was three, including himself.

Merc felt that a team was supposed to consist of a few more than three members.

However, it would do to start with.

He went down to Reception and tracked Kyra down by following the sounds of the loud voices.

She was busily sorting Jo Hubbard and his staff into order, in her usual cool and competent manner. To judge from their faces none of them were particularly happy about this, although Kyra seemed to be enjoying herself.

'Um. Can I have a word, Kyra?' Merc asked, ready to jump backwards from her response if necessary. But Kyra Hotberthy seemed pleased enough to see him.

He said, 'It's about the team, right? We need to arrange a meeting to talk out some stuff, okay?'

'Fine!' said Kyra. 'So when should we meet?'

'Now?' suggested Merc. 'And do you know how I could get hold of Silo Clotson, maybe?'

'Sure! I'll send one of the staff to find him. If there are any of them still around, that is. So, would you like to meet in the Board Room?'

'Em. Maybe somewhere smaller? Like, my office, maybe?' He suddenly remembered Hyacinth Duckworthy, who would be there if she hadn't, like most of the staff, gone home, and hastily changed his mind. 'No, I guess the Board Room would be just fine.'

'It's normally empty between Board meetings,' explained Kyra Hotberthy briskly, 'and it has a drinks dispenser and comfortable chairs.'

She paused to call over one of the happily spectating staff, and sent him to find Silo, with instructions to bring him to the Board Room straight away.

Then she ushered Merc over to the lifts.

The Board Room was, as Kyra had predicted, empty.

'Now,' said Kyra, when Silo had joined them and they were all settled in the big comfortable chairs with drinks, from the machine, at their elbows, 'what did you want to discuss, Merc?'

Merc, though glad to see that she was not taking any further control, at least temporarily, over what was, after all, his team meeting, felt slightly flustered at this direct attack.

'I want to begin by pooling information,' he said after rather too long a pause. 'I get the impression that this Twisted Rosebud isn't so entirely unknown as the Security man thought?'

No-one said anything.

'Well, come on, guys,' Merc protested after a moment or two of heavy silence, 'even I had heard of them, and my record doesn't put me too high up the gossip reception scale!'

'Okay, MS,' Kyra Hotberthy said eventually. 'You're right. The bosses still don't know, but most of us working people have heard something about the Twisted Rosebud, okay. Not necessarily good.'

'You, too, Silo?' Merc asked.

'I guess so,' came a mumble from Silo Clotson's direction.

'Okay. Then spill it!'

Kyra Hotberthy took a deep breath.

'Where do you want me to start?' she asked simply.

'There's a lot?'

Kyra Hotberthy looked at him.

'Do you really mean to tell me, Merc Swingly, that you've never heard of the assassination of Buster Panter, the last head of the Company?'

'Or,' said Silo Clotson, 'the explosion that wiped out the Board of Planetary Banking and Insurance?'

'Or the bomb in the new World Parliament building?'

'Or the assassination of Snider Cummings, the boss of World News and Recreation?'

They looked at him.

'Um. Well. Been a lot happening in my life this year, right?' Merc mumbled. 'Lucy. Family things. I don't seem to have heard –'

He trailed off.

'Listen,' said Kyra.

She drew another deep breath and began.

Chapter Twenty Seven

It seemed, Merc learned, that the Twisted Rosebud had been operating for over a year now. No-one was quite sure who they were, although there were a lot of guesses floating round.

But it seemed clear that they had an agenda. To demolish the seven large multi national companies which were currently running the world, and to do it by any means that worked. They didn't just want to destroy buildings, which could be erected again. They wanted to destroy the people concerned, the leaders of the current world economy.

'And while no-one would want to say that that's a bad thing,' said Kyra fair mindedly, 'they don't seem to care too much about anyone else who gets in their way.'

The death toll from their various bombs and murder attempts was, so far, in the region of several hundred.

'And that's only as far as I can work it out from the stuff I know,' Kyra said. 'It's not the sort of thing that gets onto the news, right, under our current government. Wouldn't sit well between 'Congratulations to Flacker Winterbotham for supplying new jobs in the Tiny Isles' and 'President of the World opens flower show.' Keep the people happy, that's the motto. Lots of consumer goods, lots of debt, lots of little pills.'

She sounded angry.

'But killing hundreds of innocent people isn't the way to do it,' Merc said.

'Maybe they didn't actually mean to?' suggested Silo Clotson tentatively. 'Accidents can happen.'

'Look at today!' retorted Kyra. 'A bomb exploded with all those staff around. Any of them could have been wiped out. And they didn't even get Winterbotham!'

Merc felt suddenly tired. He just wanted to go home to his family.

'So, what you're saying is,' he began slowly, 'that while these Twisted Rosebud people may have good motivation, they can't be trusted not to hurt too many people, using the methods they're using? And so we ought to try to stop them?'

'Right!' said Kyra Hotberthy briskly.

Silo just nodded, looking rather unhappy.

I don't like people who go round assassinating people, even if they manage not to kill anyone else, thought Merc suddenly. I just don't like it, however good the reasons seem to be.

'So. Ideas?' he said, sitting up straighter. That was the good thing about being a team leader, as he'd already discovered in his short time in business. You didn't have to think of anything yourself, just let your team come up with the suggestions.

Unfortunately, that only worked if the team thought of things.

Silo looked at him blankly.

Kyra fidgeted with her clipboard and pen.

'So,' said Merc eventually. 'You mentioned that rumours were flying round about these guys. Guesses about who was part of it? Maybe if you could throw out a few names and we could think about how to follow them up?'

This suggestion was received with gratitude.

'Mind you,' said Silo Clotson carefully, 'it will only be guesses.' He hesitated. 'I have heard that Flacker Winterbotham could be behind it all. Heavily undercover, right?'

Merc politely managed not to laugh.

'What do you think, Kyra?' he asked.

'FW? I don't think so! Apart from the obvious objection that he's half witted, he's making far too much out of the company to want to destroy it.'

'But that would be his deep cunning!' urged Silo Clotson eagerly. 'He'd be the last person anyone could ever suspect!'

It was borne in on Merc that Flacker Winterbotham wasn't the only person around that Kyra could accurately describe as half witted.

'Well, thanks for the suggestion, Silo,' he said as kindly as possible. 'Maybe we should leave that one on the back burner and see if any more evidence turns up, okay? Meanwhile, Kyra, any more possibilities?'

'Oh, yes,' Kyra answered promptly. 'But only a couple that I think might really have a grain of truth in them. You remember Reta Glutt?'

'Reta Glutt?'

'Yeah, you must remember her, she's on the Board. Big woman.'

Merc called back a vague memory of a huge hovering presence over to his right, who had at one point put a massive arm like a tree trunk round his shoulders. He shuddered.

'Yeah, I guess I remember.'

'Reta Glutt has come up out of nowhere in the past couple of years. I have the impression, maybe wrong, maybe right, that she isn't too sincere in the support she gives the Company. Like, mostly she's well covered up, but every now and then the covering drops, and you get the naked person showing through.'

Merc's shudder intensified. Not a good metaphor, he thought. Some things were too much for the imagination to cope with. Especially his.

'So. Reta Glutt. Someone we might take a look at.'

'Yeah. If you can get past the outer covering.'

Merc broke in desperately. Time to derail this conversation before it took him further into realms of unknown horror.

'And the other one you mentioned?'

'Yeah, Beaver Sturge. You saw him at the Board Meeting, too. In the orange bow-tie? He has a major grudge against FW for getting what Sturge thought would be his job. I guess he'd do a lot to damage FW. But not the Company as such, maybe. He wants to take it over, not smash it. Or the other companies. I guess.'

'Hm. Okay, still, worth remembering. So, any other ideas? Silo?'

Silo thought hard.

Then his face brightened. He remembered some recent gossip which really did seem to give him something good to suggest.

'Tonky Spoutforth!'

'Tonky Spoutforth?'

'Used to edit the Global Recorder before the Company had it closed down? Made a lot of money, but was supposed to be honest with it? Disappeared from public life, said to be living in luxury on a remote island on his fortune, but it's my bet that he went underground not too far from here and started up the Twisted Rosebud. No-one had heard of it until a few months after he lost his job. Not a bad guy, but ready to cut a few corners when he thought he could get away with it. He's always sounded to me like a real possibility.'

'H'm, yes,' Merc said thoughtfully. 'He used to run crusades in the Globe, didn't he? Took the moral high ground, sort of thing? Maybe he hasn't been able to get out of the habit.'

'Yes, and he'd have plenty of contacts to set up an organisation like this,' Silo continued enthusiastically. 'And moral high ground or not, he wasn't always too scrupulous about how he got his stories. I've heard things.'

'But isn't he quite an old man by now?' asked Kyra Hotberthy. 'Would he be up to all this stuff?'

'Why not?' Silo said. 'All he needs to do is to organise other people. He wouldn't need to do much active stuff himself.'

'Well,' said Merc judiciously, 'this Tonky Spoutforth sounds like a likely prospect. Maybe we could begin by checking into him a bit. See if we can track him down for a start. Identify this island he's supposed to have retired to, see if he's really there or what. What do you guys think?'

'No problem,' said Kyra Hotberthy briskly. 'I'll look him up on the Web. Get back to you in an hour or so.'

'Um. Great.'

Merc cleared his throat.

'How's about we have a break for now?' he said. 'We can each follow up anything we think looks good. Um. Kyra. I'm just going out for some air, right? I'll be back by the time you've got the info. Maybe we could touch base here in a couple of hours, then, okay?'

Kyra looked annoyed. Then her face cleared.

'Fine, MS. Frankly, apart from this, I've got a lot of other stuff to sort out meanwhile. See the Maintenance people. And the Security guys, right. See you in a few hours, then.'

Merc smiled weakly at his fellow team members. Then he went out.

He needed to see Mr. Brown. And ask him some questions. He needed to assure himself that the things that were happening were what Mr. Brown and his boss intended. And weren't just random nonsense kicking in.

And he needed to think a little.

Chapter Twenty Eight

It was nice to be out in – well, it wasn't exactly fresh air. Even since Merc's own childhood, the air had deteriorated noticeably.

Still, it was better than the artificial stuff inside the Company buildings.

Merc rounded a corner, walked on briskly for several minutes, rounded another corner, and arrived at the familiar coffee shop.

He would have hesitated to describe it as his favourite. A favourite anything should be something you liked, and thought was nice, right?

Glooper's coffee shop couldn't come under that heading by any stretch of the imagination.

But it was familiar.

And there were chairs and tables of sorts. And coffee.

If you could call it that. It tasted, Merc thought, rather like washing up liquid.

And at the very least, it wasn't the Company canteen. It didn't even, as far as he knew, belong to any of the Companies. Which made it fairly unique, as far as Merc's information went.

'Glooper.' Merc looked round nervously, but the coffee shop seemed to be empty He smiled ingratiatingly at the thin, sad, little man with the drooping moustache, who stood wiping his spotlessly clean hands on his whiter than white apron and waiting to take an order. 'Er. Coffee, please.'

Glooper smiled. With some difficulty.

No problem, Mr. S.' he said mournfully. His big, sad, brown eyes gazed at Merc. 'Good that somebody wants it, Mr. S.' His head drooped.

'What a day, Mr. S. I'm always ready to serve, Mr. S. Always waiting till somebody wants me, Mr. S.'

To Merc's horror, Glooper's face grew even sadder.

'But nobody seems to want me, Mr. S.'

His mournful brown eyes filled with tears.

'Why would that be, Mr. S.? I've always got a smile for my customers, you know. Always trying to be cheerful. Although it's hard to say what I have to be cheerful about, when nobody seems to want to come here.' He sighed deeply. 'Well, I suppose that's life. Why should anyone care, after all?'

Merc attempted an encouraging smile, then looked hastily away as Glooper's mournful moustache drooped ever more closely over him.

Glooper moved slowly over to the back of the shop, wiped an already clean cup and saucer on an incredibly clean dish cloth, and began to pour coffee from the sparkling coffee urn set up against the rear counter.

Merc, trying to keep up the smile, sipped cautiously at his coffee while waiting for Glooper to take himself off to a safe distance. One that would allow Merc to extract his mobile phone and ring for the urgently needed information stroke advice.

But Glooper showed no signs of moving.

'Hear you had some trouble up at the Company office today, Mr. Swingly?' he questioned, absent-mindedly wiping another perfectly clean coffee cup on his spotless apron, as he hovered around Merc. His gloomy brown eyes peered anxiously out of his long face, his drooping moustache hung mournfully around his unhappy mouth.

The sun, which had been beaming happily into the coffee shop and lighting up the white table clothes and the brightly coloured flowers in the table vases, grew dimmer.

'Um. Yes.'

Suddenly it struck Merc that here was a possible source of information, or at any rate gossip.

He had never encouraged Glooper to talk before, being only concerned to get rid of him and drink his coffee in peace.

But maybe he should take a different approach today? After all, here was a man who owed no allegiance to the Company. Probably because the Company had considered him not worth taking over.

But, still.

'Yeah, we did. Trouble describes it.'

'A bomb, I heard?' Glooper, encouraged by the first ever sign of Mr. Swingly apparently being willing to talk, attempted another smile. The result, Merc considered, was even more depressing than his normal expression of confirmed gloom.

'So they seem to think.'

Glooper gave the coffee cup another wipe.

'Too many bombs around these days.'

'Yeah.'

'So. Do they know who did it? I mean. Who claims responsibility for this act of po–lit–ic–al self ex–press–ion?'

'It seems to be a crew called 'The Twisted Rosebud," Merc said. 'Have you ever heard of them?'

Glooper gave his attempt at a smile again. 'Well, yes, I've heard of them,' he said cautiously.

'And, if you wouldn't mind saying – what exactly have you heard?'

Glooper looked round carefully.

'Quite a lot.'

'Yes?' Merc smiled encouragingly.

'They hates the bosses, see?' hissed Glooper in what was presumably meant to be an undertone, but to Merc's ultra sensitive ears echoed not only round the shop, but far and wide beyond it. 'They hates the bosses and what the big companies are doing to the world, and they wants to destroy them!'

'Shout a bit louder, why don't you, there may have been one or two people in the Tiny Isles didn't hear you,' Merc murmured, then caught himself up as he saw, to his horror, that Glooper's under lip was starting to tremble tearfully. 'Just joking, Glooper!' he added hastily.

'I'm sensitive to sarcasm, Mr. S.' Glooper said through his tears. 'I suffered from sarcasm when I was at school, right. Some of those teachers were evil bastards, see? Don't do sarcasm on me, Mr. S.'

'Goodness, sorry, Glooper!' Merc stammered. 'Sorry!'

'All right, Mr. S. I know you doesn't mean any harm. I know I don't really matter,' Glooper said. 'Some of us has to put up with the way life treats us without complaining, Mr. S. You'll never see me complaining. Always wear a smile on my face, even when I'm aching inside, Mr. S. I knows you don't mean to stab me to the heart, Mr. S.'

'No, not at all!' Merc stammered. 'Um. I just wondered if you know anything more about the Twisted Rosebud?'

'Ah!' Glooper raised the coffee cup in a gesture indicating important knowledge. 'Now you're talking, Mr. S.!'

He stared mournfully at Merc.

'Rumour has it they have a base not far from here, Mr. S!' he confided in his hissing whisper. Merc, although unable to refrain from wincing as the thin miserable face came closer to his right ear, and the drooping moustache began to tickle his cheek, at least managed to make no comment this time. 'I hear Tonky Spoutforth has a secret underground headquarters, where he plans everything! Height of luxury it is too, they tell me.'

'They?' inquired Merc.

'Oh. People. Customers. They come in and out, and they talk to each other, not to me, of course, but I can't help hearing, right. And sometimes they tells me things when nobody else more interesting is about, see?'

Merc nodded. 'And has anyone given you any idea where this secret headquarters might be?' he inquired.

'Ah. Well, no, not as such,' admitted Glooper. 'But it's pretty clear it's somewhere local. Right here in Nexus Luxuria, see?'

Merc sighed. 'Glooper,' he said, 'Nexus Luxuria, as you know, covers about fifty miles of intensive building. Housing, shopping malls, businesses. Branches of the Companies, that is. A bit more narrowing down would seem to be necessary.'

Glooper looked interested. 'So, you want me to ask around? Let you know if I hear anything useful?'

'That would be great, Glooper.' Merc smiled encouragingly, though without the slightest expectation of any useful response. 'Just make sure you don't get into trouble asking around!'

'Sure thing, Mr. S!'

'And now, Glooper,' said Merc firmly, 'I'm very grateful for your input, but, hey, I've just realised that there's a majorly important call I need to make, so if you'll excuse me –?'

He took his mobile phone from the case fastened to his belt, and flourished it meaningly.

'Oh, go right ahead, don't mind me. I don't matter,' Glooper said pessimistically. Continuing to hover.

'Top secret. Highly confidential. V. private,' Merc said, his voice growing louder.

Glooper continued to hover, looking ill-used and ignored again.

'Go away, please, Glooper!' said Merc at last, risking a further out-break of tears. 'I don't want you to hear this!'

Chapter 28

Glooper, finally realising what Merc was saying, backed away, and settled himself safely out of earshot. And Merc dialed Mr. Brown's number.

Chapter Twenty Nine

Mr. Brown's phone gave its usual annoying tinkle. It was still set to play, *'The Sunny Side of the Street.'*

Mr. Brown's voice came on presently.

'MS?'

'Yeah.'

'Why keep ringing me, MS? You're doing great!'

'Oh.' Merc, although not sure how this applied, felt better.

'But how am I going to find these Twisted Rosebuds, um, MB?' he asked, remembering just in time not to say Mr. Brown. 'No-one seems to know any details. Just that they're around somewhere near!'

'Don't worry! It'll all work out!'

'Yes?'

'Look, you've got people working on it, haven't you? Soon be time to go back and see what they've found out!'

'And you think they'll have something?'

'You can only hope!'

'Yeah.'

'You're doing great, MS! Just keep following your instincts!'

'But why can't you spell it out a bit more?' Merc asked urgently. 'I could really do with some actual instructions, right? Like, do this, but be sure you don't do that. And such!'

'The whole point is, you're supposed to decide that stuff yourself. As you go along. We aren't allowed to run your life for you, like some robot creature. You're a free man, MS!'

'Free? With the Company running my life? All our lives?'

'That's the whole point, MS! I thought you'd got that. You, and a few others, haven't allowed the Company to run your lives. At least not all the time. That's why you can work out some stuff for yourself. Instead

127

of going along with all the rules and regulations. Falling in with how the Company sees things. You just need to go on acting as a free agent, right? It'll all work out!'

'But –'

Too late.

There came the tinkly tone again.

Once more, Mr. Brown was gone

Merc switched off his mobile, paid Glooper for the coffee, or whatever it was, and made his way back to the office.

Kyra and Silo were waiting for him in the Conference room.

'Ah, here you are, MS,' began Kyra, in the brisk tones which indicated that she was on top of things and the person she was speaking to probably wasn't.

'Kyra. Good.'

'I've been tracking stuff down on the Internet,' Kyra said. 'I've got some useful printouts here.'

She handed Merc an enormous sheaf of papers, then as an afterthought, kindly thrust a similar bunch at Silo Clotson.

Who looked more bewildered than ever.

'The important one is on top,' said Kyra Hotberthy in her briefing the half witted boss tone. 'I've typed up a summary there of the main points.'

'Oh.

'Thanks, Kyra,' added Merc belatedly.

He began to read the summary sheet. But Kyra had other ideas.

'Perhaps it would be best if I just run through it,' she suggested, in a voice which allowed no argument.

'Um. Right.'

'First of all, I've put the main effort into tracking down Tonky Spoutforth, as we agreed,' Kyra began.

She glanced at her two auditors, noting the open mouths and the already glazed eyes.

'Tonky Spoutforth retired from his post as editor of the Global Recorder, popularly known as the Globe, two years ago, as we said. He was supposed to have retired to a remote island which he bought long before that as a possible retirement base, but in fact he didn't stay there for long – he went somewhere quite different.'

'Nexus Luxuria,' nodded Merc absently.

'What?' Kyra's reaction could only have been described as a yelp. 'How do you know that?'

'Oh.' Merc's face reddened. 'Well. I have my sources.'

'Gossip, I suppose?'

'Um. Sort of.'

'Gossip has been saying that for some time,' said Kyra smoothly. She had recovered her poise. 'Gossip is all very well, but we need something more definite if we intend to work on the information.' She paused impressively.

'What I have been doing is confirming the accuracy or otherwise of the rumour. And I have, in fact, confirmed it.'

Chapter Thirty

'Great!' said Merc enthusiastically, feeling that something like this was definitely required. 'So. What, exactly –?' His voice trailed off.

'I first of all looked up the records of travel to the island, known as 'Wildfowl Island', incidentally, because there are a few wild ducks still remaining there, in spite of the general extinction of the wild variety some time ago –'

'Great!' murmured Merc again, then, as a cool look from Kyra Hotberthy informed him that his encouragement wasn't really necessary, he decided to shut up.

'Clearly, Tonky Spoutforth sailed over to Wildfowl Island two years ago. However, recent sailings show that he returned to Nexus Luxuria a year later. I naturally followed this up by an examination of the street map and address listings. However, there is no record of a T. Spoutforth anywhere in the city.'

She paused.

'This might,' she acknowledged, 'have meant that he was living somewhere in the wilds, outside the city boundaries, or else in one of our smaller neighbouring cities. I checked that there was no sign that he had sailed for another Land Mass. Which, in any case, would have been difficult to do these days when so much travel, especially so far afield, is reserved for Company heads and politicians. There was no sign, either, of the name in any of the street listings of our neighbouring cities.'

'Couldn't he have changed his name?' Merc ventured.

'My dear MS,' Kyra smiled in her irritatingly superior way, 'aren't you forgetting that we all have a chip inserted at birth to prevent anything like that? If Tonky Spoutforth was trying to go around with a name which didn't correspond with his chip, it would flash up on the screen every time he tried to buy something, every time he went into a supermarket, every time he needed a doctor, etc, etc, etc.! Of course, only the important public buildings have scanners. Our bosses are mainly concerned to make sure that everyone is spending lots of money, in this commercial tyranny we live in. But there are enough of them to make sure no-one can buy or sell, which means, in practice, survive, without being identified by their chip. You can be quite certain that whatever Tonky Spoutforth is doing, he isn't doing it under another name!'

Merc wisely kept quiet.

'So. What does that leave us?' inquired Kyra Hotberthy triumphantly. 'Only one possibility.'

Neither Merc nor Silo made any suggestion.

'Why, that Tonky Spoutforth is hiding out with friends, who are feeding and supporting him. Probably not supporting him as such, because he's said to have enormous sums of money, but doing all his shopping for him in their own name. What about that?'

'Brilliant, Kyra!' enthused Merc. 'So now all we have to do is find out who these friends are!'

'That is,' added Silo Clotson heavily, 'if you're sure he's definitely here?'

'Didn't I explain that I tracked him down on the list of passengers from Wildfowl Island a year ago?' snapped Kyra. 'The list's there in your hand. See for yourself! And he doesn't appear on any other sailing since! Use your brain, Silo!'

'Oh. Ah,' said Silo Clotson. Not, Merc thought, entirely convinced, not fully understanding the logic, but reluctant to expose himself to more criticism from Kyra.

'So, Kyra,' Merc said hastily, 'have you any thoughts about how to track down these friends who seem to be shielding Spoutforth?'

'In a way,' said Kyra Hotberthy. 'I began with the obvious.'

Merc, like Silo, preferred to remain silent.

'I've been trying,' said Kyra, 'to hack into the internet mail service. Into Tonky Spoutforth's account, naturally. To see if there's anyone he's keeping in touch with.'

Merc gasped. Partly in amazement, but mostly, it has to be confessed, in admiration.

'But, Kyra! If anyone finds out you're doing that, you'll be in deep sh – er – trouble! It's the death sentence, right?'

'Not when we've been given a free hand by the boss of the Company!' retorted Kyra. 'Flacker Winterbotham himself told you to use any means to track down the Twisted Rosebud, right? So all I'm doing is use one of the most obvious means, right?'

'Well, I don't know –' Merc said dubiously. 'FW isn't the biggest noise, is he? And I don't know that I'd trust him to support us if someone even higher up, like the President of the World, decided to make a stink about it –'

'Nonsense!' snapped Kyra. 'They're all just as scared for their own skin as FW! They won't do anything to get in our way, when we're trying to catch the people who want to assassinate them.'

'You could be right,' Merc said, uncertainly. 'So, have you got anywhere with this hacking?'

'Not yet,' admitted Kyra reluctantly. 'But I might do any minute. I'm going to go on trying, anyway.'

'Do that,' Merc said. 'Let me know when you have any joy.'

He turned to Silo.

'So, Silo. How about your investigations? Get anywhere?'

'I talked to some of the guys,' Silo began. 'They all think Flacker Winterbotham knows more about the Twisted Rosebud than he's saying, okay? Why did he think straightaway that the bomb was aimed at him, if he didn't know something?'

'Because he's the boss, Silo. The main man,' Kyra Hotberthy said impatiently. 'He just naturally thinks anything that happens round here is about him, right? He thinks the whole universe centres round him, for goodness sake. It doesn't mean he knows anything. Why would he put us on to find the Twisted Rosebud, if he knows who they are already, or if he's part of it? It doesn't make sense.'

'But that's his clever double bluff,' Silo began to explain eagerly. 'Anyway, even if he isn't the leader himself, the guys think he knows who it is, has some connection, see?'

'Keep up, Silo!' Kyra said in exasperation. 'If he wants us to catch them, put us on to catch them, he'd have told us everything he knows, wouldn't he?'

'That would seem to make sense,' Merc agreed.

'Well, anyway,' said Silo stubbornly, 'I looked up FW on the internet, see what his background is, that sort of thing. And guess what? I found out he doesn't even come from Nexus Luxuria or anything!'

'Of course he doesn't, Silo.' Kyra spoke this time with exaggerated patience. 'He came over here from Land Mass 1 when they needed a new boss, when the Worldwide Productions Company took you over last year. By 'you' I mean what used to be the Nexus Luxuria Independent Production Business, right? You remember the takeover, Silo? That was when you –' she hesitated on the verge of saying the wrong thing, and corrected herself, '– when you and half the rest of the staff were made redundant.'

'Oh, yes.'

'That's when FW came over here.'

'Oh.'

'So it's not really relevant, is it Silo?'

'No. I suppose not.'

Silo looked so miserable that Merc cut in hastily.

'Hey, still, good thinking, Silo. Keep on coming up with stuff. We'll get there sooner or later.'

He glanced round.

'So, is that as far as we've got to date, team?'

'Not quite,' Kyra Hotberthy said crisply. 'Just one other thing, MS.'

'Fire ahead, Kyra.'

'I've noticed some strange things lately.' Kyra Hotberthy frowned thoughtfully, making creases on her attractive copper coloured forehead. 'There's been something going on in the Company office. I don't want to start going into details right now. But if I'm right –' She broke off. 'Well, let's just say, I have a few ideas about things, and if I follow them up, we might be on to something useful, okay?'

Merc wondered. Did Kyra mean things going on at night in the Company building? If that was what she meant, thought Merc, remembering his own experiences with the Twisted Rosebud, then Kyra was definitely right. And how!

'Sounds hopeful, Kyra,' he mumbled. 'Make sure you don't take any risks, mind.'

He stood up.

'Okay, people,' he said. 'We've done a good day's work. I would say the team has got off to a flying start. So let's call it a day, then. Time we all went home. See you both tomorrow!'

And Merc picked up his heavy bundle of papers, and went home.

Chapter Thirty One

Seraphina and Alexa were busy making supper. They were giggling together about something which Merc knew he would be better not to ask about. The things girls stroke women found funny remained a profound mystery better not explored.

They looked up when Merc came in, and both smiled.

Seraphina came forward, a ladle in one hand and the salt in the other, and held up her face to him for a kiss.

'Hi, honey,' said Merc, thankful to see that this was not the Seraphina who had greeted him after a day spent with Silo Clotson.

'Alexa's teaching me to make a Tiny Isles' specialty for supper, the usual soya, but putting in lots of spicy herbs from the garden, things we would call weeds, that we would never have thought of using,' Seraphina smiled.

'And you're really going to enjoy it!' Alexa promised enthusiastically.

Lucy, sitting on a cushion on the floor, looked up from her toys and gurgled happily at the sound of her father's voice.

'Uck!' she unfortunately said again.

Then she held up a fluffy, yellow, beaked object.

Merc saw that Seraphina had re-invented the meaning of Lucy's first word.

'Uck!' said his daughter again, holding the fluffy duck type creature up to Merc.

Bending down, he picked up both Lucy and her friend and hugged her enthusiastically.

'Why don't you go in the other room, Merc,' suggested Seraphina, 'and play with Lucy until Alexa and I have finished here?'

'Great idea!' said Merc.

Gathering up Lucy and his belongings, he retreated.

Supper was as good as promised, much more spicy than Seraphina's usual cooking, but all the better for that.

Over the meal, as Lucy gurgled happily in her high chair, seizing her specially cut up baby food with both hands, and stuffing it happily into her mouth (a messy process which should, her parents hoped, lead eventually to Lucy learning to feed herself), Merc began to explain to Seraphina and Alexa what he now knew about the Twisted Rosebud.

To his surprise, Alexa seemed to be quite familiar with the whole set up.

And even with the rumour that Tonky Spoutforth might be the power behind the terrorists.

Apparently, Merc learned, there was an underground network of gossip and information, even as far afield as Alexa's native Isles.

Alexa, Merc discovered, knew more than he did himself about some of the terrorist episodes mentioned by Kyra Hotberthy and Silo Clotson.

Even Seraphina had picked up some gossip from her neighbour, Mrs. Bertha Kitt; although until now she had not associated the stories about terrorists with the burglars who had broken into their house and tied her up a few nights ago.

Alexa seemed inclined at first to resist the idea that the Twisted Rosebud was a bad thing, and should be put a stop to. Clearly, she knew nothing about Ully Beers' suspicions that the Twisted Rosebud might have engineered the earthquake, and that it might actually have been not an earthquake, but a bomb in the factory. Which, Merc was now sure, was not the case. The bomb in the Company Reception Area, he had noticed, had produced quite different results.

However, Alexa allowed herself to be persuaded, after some argument, that people who blew up other people at random shouldn't be encouraged, however good their initial motivation might be.

'And Flacker Winterbotham expects you to catch these people yourself? You, Merc?' Seraphina asked incredulously. Merc, who had experienced a similar incredulity when Winterbotham had selected him for the job, was unreasonably annoyed that Seraphina should feel the same way about it.

But before he could protest, Alexa cut in stoutly. 'The best possible person! If anyone can catch them, Merc can!'

Merc grinned weakly, his momentary annoyance swallowed up in alarm. Alexa seemed to have an utterly unrealistic idea of his capabilities.

'Yes,' said Seraphina. She seemed to be thinking. 'Well,' she said finally, 'why not you, Merc, as much as anyone else? You've got one advantage at least. You've met these people at first hand. You have some idea of their methods.'

'Yeah, they like using truth drugs,' Merc put in gloomily. 'That limits it to a few hundred thousand, right?'

'It limits it to people who could get hold of truth drugs!' Seraphina retorted.

She swept on. 'And –' she paused impressively, '– you've heard some of their voices. In fact, you thought you half recognised one!'

'Yeah, but I couldn't remember – '

'It will come back to you. In the middle of the night, probably.'

'Maybe.'

'So we know there must be someone involved in it that you've already met. Probably someone you know quite well?'

Merc, about to argue, paused as the truth of Seraphina's words struck home.

'What's more,' went on his wife triumphantly, 'don't forget we have Mr. Brown on our side. So far he hasn't done too much,' she added reverting to her usual critical self, 'but I should think he'll give us a few nudges from time to time to keep us on the right track, what do you think?'

'Um. Right.'

'And –' Seraphina finished, 'You'll have Alexa and me to help you! I don't see,' she added reflectively, 'how you can fail, Merc.'

Merc, giving Seraphina a quick hug, felt unaccountably cheered.

'So, what should be our plan of campaign?' he asked.

Alexa spoke quietly.

'Shush!'

Seraphina and Merc looked at her. Even Lucy stopped trying to put a bread stick into Merc's ear and looked interested.

'Goo!' she said.

'I can hear something!' whispered Alexa.

Merc, listening now, heard it too.

Seraphina spoke for all of them.

'Someone moving about upstairs.'

'We've got burglars again!' Merc whispered.

'Or,' said Seraphina, taking the fork, which Lucy had managed to snatch from Merc's hand in his momentary abstraction, from her daughter, and putting it safely out of reach, 'more than likely, we've got another annoying infestation of Twisted Rosebuds.'

Chapter Thirty Two

They looked at each other.

'Stay here, both of you,' said Merc after a pause. 'I'll go and see what it is.'

'Wait, Merc,' Seraphina said sharply. 'I just want to go next door for a moment. Don't you or Alexa move yet. '

Not waiting for Merc to answer, she slipped quickly out of the back door.

'Seraphina –' began Merc urgently. But it was too late. She had gone.

'Of all the stupid behaviour –'

'Just give her a minute,' Alexa said calmly. 'She has an idea.'

Then Seraphina was back.

She was carrying a small but potentially fierce animal, which Merc recognised as the fearsome Pekinese miniature dog which belonged to Mrs. Bertha Kitt, the middle aged widow who lived next door. The dog which regularly nipped at Merc's ankles when he entered his neighbour's garden for the most harmless of reasons. For instance, to pass on wrongly delivered post – most days – or to return the hedge clippers – at least once a year.

He glared at the animal.

'What's that pest doing here –?' he started to ask, but was interrupted by Seraphina laughing.

'Pootles is very good with burglars or intruders of all sorts,' she gurgled. 'That is, very bad, from their point of view. I've borrowed him from Bertha. Now we'll see how those Twisted Rosebud creatures enjoy meeting him!'

Merc was forced to acknowledge the brilliance of the idea.

Pootles, he knew from vast personal experience, was capable, in spite of his size, of dealing severely with any number of intruders. Who would probably resolve in no time at all to stop intruding right now, and never to intrude again.

Seraphina set Pootles down on the floor.

'Now, boy!' she encouraged him. 'Go get 'em! Burglars!'

'He knows what that means,' she explained to her admiring audience. 'Apparently Bertha has taught him more than twelve words.'

A pity she never taught him 'friend,' Merc thought. But said nothing and watched as Pootles waddled out of the kitchen and up the stairs. Barking shrilly as he went.

Lucy, who had been reaching out eagerly for this new fluffy toy, added to the uproar by screaming at the top of her lungs as she saw the dog disappear from view.

Merc, with Seraphina and Alexa, followed cautiously.

As they approached Merc's study, which seemed to be the source of the noise, they heard a series of alarmed yells, then a scrambling sound, as of someone taking a flying leap for safety, then hoarse cries, which mingled unpleasantly with the shrill barks of Pootles and the continued wails of Lucy from downstairs.

Merc pushed open the door.

Inside, he caught a glimpse of a leg hanging down from the tall set of bookshelves against the far wall. In the foreground, Pootles bounded enthusiastically backward and forward, jumping repeatedly into the air and making snapping motions within inches of the dangling foot.

Peering up, Merc saw that a figure was crouched precariously on top of the bookcase.

Which was starting to rock a little.

It seemed to be a man. A large, heavily built man. The last type of man to try to balance on a piece of furniture which, while sturdy of its kind, was made to support books rather than fugitives. A man wearing an animal mask – possibly meant to represent a wolf? – which covered his whole face and head.

As he watched, the man attempted to kick out desperately at Pootles' bared teeth. Foolishly.

The bookcase, not in fact very securely attached to the wall – Merc knew this, he had attached it – swayed dangerously.

'Stop!' ordered Seraphina furiously. 'How dare you kick the poor, harmless little dog!'

Merc gaped in surprise. Did she mean Pootles?

There seemed to be only the one unwelcome visitor in the room.

Merc wondered if there were more. In any of the other rooms upstairs.

Leaving the intruder safely treed for a moment, he backed out and took a quick scurry round.

No, no one else. Good.

Hurrying back into the study, he saw that matters had moved on during his brief absence.

From somewhere or other Seraphina had acquired a long handled broom, and with this she was poking vigorously at the stranger on the book-case, saying between pokes, 'Come down, you scum bag! Come down and explain yourself!'

Pootles, meanwhile, continued to leap as high as he could, barking shrilly and still snapping ferociously.

Alexa, he noticed, had collapsed into a chair and was holding her sides. For a second Merc wondered if she had been hurt. Then he realised that she was laughing helplessly.

As he watched, Pootles managed to catch the wildly flailing foot, and ripped a great tear in the intruder's sock.

'Look out!' yelled Merc.

Seraphina leapt back, managing to seize the still frantically barking Pootles as she did so.

The inevitable was happening.

The bookcase swayed further and further from an upright position.

The man clinging to its top let out a terrified scream.

Then, almost in slow motion, as the books slid forwards in an uneven stream, the bookcase finally toppled over, hurling the heavy man, mask and all, to the ground.

Chapter Thirty Three

All the breath knocked out of him, the intruder lay helpless at their feet.

Seraphina laid her broom down carefully, retaining her hold, however, on Pootles.

Alexa sat up and wiped the tears of laughter from her eyes.

And Merc took a few cautious steps forward to explore the situation.

The intruder, he was relieved to find, was still breathing.

Merc bent over him and attempted, without much expertise, to feel his pulse.

Seeing what he was doing, Alexa came over and pushed him out of the way.

'Here, let me!' she ordered. 'I think I know a bit more about first aid and nursing than you seem to do.'

'You do?' Merc asked in surprise.

'Anyone who wants to survive in the Tiny Isles these days needs to know more than a bit about medicine.'

'Oh.'

'Lucy!' exclaimed Seraphina suddenly. 'I must fetch her!'

Setting Pootles down, she rushed out of the study.

Pootles approached his unconscious victim. Apparently satisfied that he had triumphed, he contented himself with sniffing vigorously at the man's legs.

To Merc's relief.

For although he could hardly have allowed Pootles to savage the man while he lay unconscious, Merc was entirely lacking in Seraphina's casual mastery of the little dog, and would probably, he was aware, have ended up being savaged himself if he had tried to come between Pootles and his victim.

'He's okay,' Alexa announced after a quick examination. 'He's just been knocked unconscious. Hit his head too hard on the floor. Should be fine in a few minutes. Time enough to worry if he's not.'

Joyous chuckles coming gradually nearer, together with yelps from Seraphina as her daughter seized handfuls of her hair and pulled hard, announced that Lucy was being carried upstairs.

Seraphina came in.

She set Lucy down on the floor, rescuing her hair from the firm grasp of little hands. Lucy promptly threw her arms round Pootles and they began to roll around the room, getting in everyone's way with great enjoyment.

'Well?' demanded Seraphina. 'What now?'

'Fetch the police?' suggested Alexa.

'The police? I don't think so!' said Seraphina firmly. 'You wouldn't know, Alexa, being new in town, but the police here are only good for two things. Forming a guard of honour for any important visitor. And taking kickbacks for anything and everything. They come directly under the Government these days. No, Flacker Winterbotham gave Merc a free hand to round these people up by himself, without expecting the police to do anything to help.'

'So, what, then?'

As they spoke, they found themselves moving carefully around the room, in a progress more like a dance than anything else, trying hard to avoid the flailing arms and legs of what seemed at times to be a constantly attacking ball of at least two hundred dogs and babies.

'I think,' suggested Merc, 'that when this guy comes to, we might be able to get some information out of him. Then maybe we could get a better idea of our next move.'

'Suppose he won't talk?' Seraphina objected.

'Then we'll threaten him until he does!' Alexa said enthusiastically. 'Hold lighted matches to his feet, stuff like that.'

'No way.' Merc sounded firmer than she'd ever heard him.

'But he would do it to us, if he was the one in charge!'

'So? We aren't him.'

'What's the difference?' Alexa asked sulkily.

'Do you mean to say you don't know? We don't do torture!'

Seraphina intervened hastily. 'We won't need to torture him. He'll be so glad to be rescued from Pootles that he'll probably tell us everything.'

'To say nothing of Lucy,' Merc added. 'We could always set her on to pull his hair, if we do decide on torture.' He spoke sarcastically, and Alexa flushed with annoyance.

By this time, Merc noticed, he and Seraphina had been pinned down by the rotating Lucy and Pootles in one small corner of the room, while Alexa stood with her back to them, facing the far wall, clearly still very angry at what she considered their too soft hearted attitude.

It was Seraphina who first noticed that the intruder on the floor had not only recovered consciousness, but was rapidly squirming his way towards the doorway and the staircase.

'Look out!' she shouted suddenly. 'He's getting away!'

As she spoke, the man in the wolf mask rose to his feet like some monster emerging from the deep, and hurtled through the doorway towards the stairs.

They started after him.

Unfortunately, Lucy and her new Pekinese friend were still rolling around, taking up most of the floor space.

Alternatively tripping and cursing, Merc attempted to get past them without causing serious damage.

Alexa, the last to realise that their captive was escaping, rushed forward too quickly and ended up in a tangled mess at Merc's feet, just managing not to land heavily on the baby. Shrill barks indicated that Pootles had not been so lucky.

It was Seraphina who saved the situation.

Seizing her discarded broom, she managed to insert it between the intruder's legs. With a loud wail, he fell heavily for the second time that evening. This time, he started from a position almost at the head of the stairs.

The inevitable happened once again.

Bumping accurately on each step, he made his way without hesitation to the landing below. Where he came to an abrupt halt.

Merc, Alexa and Seraphina looked at each other open mouthed.

'That was a bit extreme, wasn't it, Seraphina?' said Alexa presently.

'Coming from someone who wanted to torture the poor man, that's rich!' Seraphina retorted. But with no real spirit.

She looked round at Pootles and Lucy, still rolling happily around the room.

'Right!' she said, grabbing Pootles by the scruff of his neck with one hand and managing to detach him from Lucy with the other. 'That's enough from you, mister!' And with no more ado, she pulled open the door next to the study, which opened into the bathroom, and pushed the little Pekinese inside, ignoring Lucy's wails and Pootles' barks. 'You stay there until it's safe to let you out again, boy!' She spared a thought for Mrs. Bertha Kitt, who would definitely not have approved of this action. But Mrs. Bertha Kitt, thank goodness, was still next door.

'Come on.' Merc started down the stairs. 'Let's see how he is before we start ripping each other up.'

But amazingly enough, the man was not dead. Alexa, now the acknowledged expert, examined him once more, and announced the good news with a sigh of relief. 'He's not actually dead.'

'Good.'

'He's knocked himself out again,' she added. 'That's not actually very good. He should really see a doctor when he comes round. I don't see any broken bones. There may be some sprains, though. And there's certainly lots of bruising.'

'Serves him right for breaking into our house, then!' said Seraphina defiantly.

'What's this?' asked Merc. He had been attempting to lift the unconscious man into a more comfortable position.

He was looking at a white envelope which had been half dislodged from one of the intruder's pockets by his fall.

Merc lifted the envelope and read his own name written on the front.

'What on earth?' Seraphina exclaimed.

'A message from the Twisted Rosebud, don't you think?' suggested Merc. 'It won't be the first one!'

'What can they need to say to you?' Alexa wondered doubtfully.

'Well, since it's addressed to me, I might as well open it and see,' Merc said, grinning.

The envelope contained a single folded sheet of paper. Merc read it aloud.

Chapter Thirty Four

Merc Swingly

This is a warning. Do not meddle in matters which are none of your business. We know that you have been given the task of capturing the Twisted Rosebud. You will find that you are quite unable to carry out this task, and if you persist in trying, you can only bring harm upon yourself and your family.

Be warned in time. Forget all about the Twisted Rosebud.

There will be no second warning.

Signed

The Twisted Rosebud.

Seraphina, looking briefly at Merc's face, realised that she had never seen him show such rage before.

When he spoke, his voice was cold.

'This has gone far enough,' was all he said.

But both Seraphina and Alexa shivered.

'Threats to myself,' said Merc, 'I can handle. But threats to my family are something else.'

He looked down at the unconscious man.

'It seems clear that this man came to my house to deliver this letter,' said Merc. 'I had been wondering what his reason for coming could possibly have been. There would be nothing for him here. No information to collect, nothing valuable to steal, I should think. So now we know.'

No-one felt like interrupting.

'Up until now, I was half inclined to be sorry for the Twisted Rosebud,' Merc said. 'They seemed like quite good guys who had just got a bit mixed up and were using the wrong methods. But now I see that they don't care about anyone but themselves and their own ideas.'

He paused again, thinking.

'Perhaps,' he said softly, 'we should send them a warning back.'

Alexa burst in eagerly, 'Like, maybe, one of this guy's toes?'

Merc glared at her.

'That would be their type of warning,' he said. 'It isn't mine.'

Alexa subsided.

Then came another interruption.

Lucy had no intention of allowing herself to be robbed of her new playmate. No sooner had Seraphina and Merc headed off down the stairs to see what had happened to the mysterious intruder than she darted forward and began, unnoticed by anyone in their absorption in the fate of the man who had fallen down the stairs, to try to get him back. Her chubby, not very capable, hands struggled with the handle of the bathroom door. Inside the door, her efforts were given considerable assistance by the little Pekinese, who had long ago learnt how to open door handles by jumping at them and using his weight to pull them down.

Between the two of them, it wasn't long before they achieved success. The bathroom door burst open. Out shot Pootles like an arrow from a bow. Lucy, still tugging at the handle, went over backwards. A moment later, the joyous playfellows had resumed their rolling game across the floor, to a mixture of chortling from Lucy and barking from the little dog. In a very short time, Lucy and Pootles, in their progress round the landing, reached the head of the stairs.

Suddenly, without warning, they began a rolling, bumping descent of the steps, ending up in a confused pile on top of the member of the Twisted Rosebud.

Neither of them seemed hurt.

In fact Lucy, gurgling happily, began at once to explore her soft landing mat, grabbing and pulling at his fingers and tugging at various parts of his clothes, while Pootles, separating himself from his new playmate, resumed his sniffing voyage of discovery around the stranger's legs.

'You said we'd set Lucy on him,' remarked Seraphina, 'and she seems to have taken up the idea herself.'

For the first time since he had read the letter, Merc smiled.

'I have a suggestion,' Seraphina said. 'Why don't you phone Mr. Brown? Ask his advice? Isn't that what he's there for?'

Merc hesitated. For some reason, he was reluctant to bring Mr. Brown into this.

There were murderous thoughts swirling round in his head.

In spite of his automatic reaction to Alexa's words, he somehow didn't want entirely to rule out some type of action on the lines she had suggested.

And he knew, instinctively, that Mr. Brown would completely veto this.

Though, come to think of it, who was Mr. Brown to tell him, Merc, what to do?

Seeing him hesitate, Seraphina urged him again.

'Come on, Merc. What harm can it do?'

Only decimate my options, that's all, thought Merc gloomily.

'After all,' went on Seraphina, 'the only reason we're mixed up in all this is because of the mission we were given. So let's check out our next step. We've come a good long way. We don't want to blow it now.'

'All right, all right!' grumbled Merc angrily. 'Talk about nagging women!'

But he took out his mobile and savagely punched in Mr. Brown's number.

The jingly tune of *'The Sunny Side of the Street'* assaulted his ear, then came the chirpy voice which was becoming so familiar.

'Hi, sonny boy!'

'Mr. Brown. MB. I have a bit of a problem,' began Merc cautiously. He wondered how much he needed to explain. He hadn't been exactly keeping Mr. Brown up to date. But did he need to?

He had told Mr. Brown, of course, all about the Twisted Rosebud and Flacker Winterbotham's designation of Merc as the ideal person to catch the terrorists.

'Not sure what to do here, MB,' he said.

'You worry too much, Merc! Told you not to worry about what you did in the Tiny Isles, didn't I?' said the cheerful voice. 'FW's like most humans. Give him a hint of a threat to his own skin, and he forgets everything else. Hey, don't worry, you're doing fine! So what now?'

'Listen,' said Merc. 'We've caught one of these Twisted Rosebud guys. Breaking into the house to leave a threatening letter. What do we do now?'

'Hang on,' said Mr. Brown. 'Maybe I should come over, right? No-one there who shouldn't see me, is there?'

'No. If you don't mind about this terrorist guy?'

'No way. Fine, then. This sounds like a face to face occasion to me! Be right there, sonny boy. See you!'

Then came the *'Sunny Side of the Street'* again. Mr. Brown had rung off.

'Hey, who is this Mr. Brown you guys keep talking about?' asked Alexa.

'It's a bit hard to explain,' Seraphina said. 'He sort of keeps an eye on what Merc and I are doing. Keeps us on the right tack, sort of thing?'

'And what are you and Merc doing? Some kind of mission, did you say?'

'We're supposed to stop the world from coming to an end,' Merc explained. 'Do you understand?'

Alexa's face told him the answer.

'What?'

'Look, best if you just play it by ear,' said Seraphina hastily.

'That's what we mostly have to do,' Merc put in.

'Mr. Brown – oh, well, he'll be here in a minute, maybe you'll understand better when you see him. Maybe I will, too,' added Seraphina thoughtfully.

'Haven't you seen him, then?'

'No, only Merc, so far. In fact, we only have Merc's word that there really is a Mr. Brown!'

Seraphina laughed to show she wasn't really serious. Merc was glad to think that Mr. Brown would be there any minute now. Then they would both see for themselves.

And in fact, he noticed, glancing round, that, as it happened, Mr. Brown was there already.

Merc hadn't heard the door open.

All the same, there was Mr. Brown, leaning casually against the wall beside them, listening to their conversation.

Wearing, this time, an up to date business suit, with correctly coloured power shirt and tie. (This year's colour was pale mauve.)

His unbuttoned jacket swung open sufficiently, with his hands casually stuck in his trouser pockets, to reveal the ultra cool red braces. Which, Merc thought, went really well with the mauve shirt. Not.

He still kept his baseball cap.

And his trainers.

And he was smiling in a way that made Merc uneasy.

'Um. Seraphina. Alexa. This is MB himself,' he mumbled.

Seraphina let out an undignified squawk and spun round.

Alexa looked surprised, but managed not to squeak.

'So, you've caught one of your gang already? Good work,' said Mr. Brown cheerily. He made no comment on the remarks he had overheard.

Not yet, anyway, Merc thought.

'Right, let's have a look at him,' he added.

They stepped back, allowing Mr. Brown a better view of the bundle on the floor.

Merc picked up Lucy, and Seraphina made a grab for Pootles.

Which made it possible for Mr. Brown to get an uninterrupted view of the prisoner.

Mr. Brown looked down at the man lying at the foot of the stairs.

He was still wearing his wolf mask.

'Just a suggestion,' said Mr. Brown. 'Why don't you take his mask off? It might help you to decide on your next move.'

Red faced as he wondered why on earth he hadn't done this long ago, Merc untied the strings of the possibly wolf shaped mask.

He tugged it off, and looked at the person revealed beneath.

It was Silo Clotson.

Chapter Thirty Five

'Silo!' Seraphina, in her amazement, clutched Pootles rather harder than necessary. The dog, squirming angrily in her arms, began to bark shrilly again.

The man on the floor grinned sheepishly.

'Hi, Seraphina. Merc. Alexa,' he mumbled. 'Em. Seraphina. You won't let that animal get down, will you?'

They looked at him in surprise.

'Never liked little, yappy dogs,' Silo Clotson explained unwillingly. 'One of them bit me when I was five. A terrier. Bit me when I was bending over to pick up a ball, on my – well, I still have the scar, but I can't really show you –'

'Too much information, Silo,' warned Seraphina sharply.

'Oh. Well, anyway, I don't like them.'

Merc interrupted.

'Never mind about all that,' he said. 'What on earth are you doing here, Silo? Don't tell me you're a member of the Twisted Rosebud?'

'All right, I won't.'

'But actually, you are?'

'Well. Yes. Right.'

They stared at him.

'And you delivered this letter to me? This letter making threats to my family?' Merc asked slowly. He waved the letter in Silo's face.

'But I didn't know that was what was in the letter, Merc!' Silo Clotson wailed hastily. 'I swear I wouldn't have delivered it if I'd known it was a threat! I thought it was only asking you to lay off because the Twisted Rosebud is on your side. On the side of all the ordinary people, against the bosses!'

'And you're really a member? Why didn't you say so before? When I asked you to be part of my team? To help me track the terrorists down?'

'We aren't allowed to give away any secrets,' Silo Clotson protested. 'I'd be in deep crap if anyone knew I'd said I was a member, okay?'

'I can see that,' Merc agreed. 'But why did you try to pretend that you thought Flacker Winterbotham was the Twisted Rosebud boss?'

'I thought he might be,' Silo Clotson explained. 'Nobody knows. Except maybe the inner ring. I still think it's a possibility, why not?'

'So you don't know who the leader is?' Merc was disappointed. He had hoped for a lot of information from Silo.

'What about this inner circle you mentioned?' Seraphina asked. 'Do you know who they are? Some of them at least?'

'I'm not sure,' Silo said reluctantly. 'I'd only be guessing if I gave you names.'

'This is hopeless!' said Alexa sharply. 'Let's see what he really knows, if we set Pootles on him again!'

'No! No!' Silo yelped. 'Please! I'll do my best to help you! Look. I don't go for all that threat sort of stuff. I don't want to stick with people who do that!'

'Alexa, I don't want to hear any more of that stuff from you,' Merc said. 'We don't go for threats either, right?'

He thought for a moment.

'How about,' he said, 'we put Lucy to bed now. And give Pootles back to Mrs. Bertha Kitt, who may be worrying about him. Or maybe not,' he added realistically. 'And then we all sit down and talk this out together.'

'Fine,' agreed Seraphina. Who was only too glad to get both Lucy and the struggling Pootles out of the picture.

'And, MB,' Merc went on, turning to speak to Mr. Brown, 'I guess you could come up with some helpful ideas –' His mouth dropped open.

Mr. Brown was nowhere to be seen.

They put Lucy to bed.

And returned the little dog to his owner.

'Now,' said Merc, when they were settled round the kitchen table, drinking hot chocolate. 'We need to spell out a few things.'

'Like?' Alexa asked.

'First of all, I want to know how Silo got involved with the Twisted Rosebud?'

'It was when I was made redundant from the Company,' Silo explained. 'A few of us got invitations at the same time, to come to one of the meetings. We didn't know who sent them or like that. But the invitations talked about changing stuff around and making things better for ordinary people like us, okay? So it sounded good. Nobody else seemed interested in what happened to me or any of the other guys who got sacked, right. So I went along to a few meetings, but that's about it so far, till they asked me tonight to deliver a letter. They said it would explain to you what they're really about.'

'It did,' Merc said grimly.

'See, I never meant to get mixed up in threats and stuff,' Silo said miserably. 'Especially not to you guys.'

'So. You don't know who else is in this?'

'We all wear masks,' Silo explained. 'I know some of my mates, because we got letters inviting us to join, at the same time. And, right, we talked to each other about it, before we decided to go along. Not knowing we were supposed to keep it a secret, okay?'

'But you must have some way of keeping in touch with them?' Alexa asked.

'They tell us when the next meeting is,' explained Silo. 'Apart from that, well, no.'

'So when is the next meeting?' Merc asked.

'Em. Now.'

'Now?'

'Well, in about half an hour. What is it, ten o'clock? Yeah, half an hour then.'

'And where is it?'

'Well, same as always, okay? At the company headquarters, right?'

Merc wondered.

It seemed obvious enough.

'Okay,' he said. 'So, if you sneak me in, tonight, I might get a good idea of what's going on? And of who's responsible?'

'Maybe.'

'Okay. Can you?'

Chapter Thirty Six

Merc looked hopeful.

Silo, on the other hand, looked pretty panicky.

'I don't know.'

Merc smiled.

'You can sneak me in. I know you can.'

'Look, Merc –' Silo looked round him in a desperate way '– maybe I could lend you my spare mask, and tell you the password. And you could copy what I do. Hey, I could explain all that to you beforehand, right? But I don't know –'

'What?'

'Well, what's the point? What are you going to learn that I can't tell you? Don't you trust me, or what?'

'It's not that, Silo.' Merc hesitated, seeking for a diplomatic way of concealing that Silo had actually struck the nail on the head.

Inspiration came.

'It's just that I don't want them to realise that you've told me stuff. I don't want you to get into trouble, okay?'

'Oh.'

Silo seemed convinced.

'This way,' Merc went on, 'if they catch on to the fact that some-one's there who shouldn't be, they won't know you had anything to do with it. And if they don't catch on, hey, all the better.'

'Yes?'

'Well, they wouldn't connect you with it, either way.'

To Merc, the flaw in his logic seemed glaringly obvious, but Silo didn't seem to notice.

'Fine, MS!' he said brightly. 'Then, we'd better start moving, right?'

'Right.'

Merc kissed Seraphina, gave Alexa a quick hug, and headed for the door.

'Hey, why can't I come too?' wailed Alexa.

'Oh, but I need you to stay here with me!' Seraphina said quickly. 'Suppose another Twisted Rosebud breaks in? I can't risk anything happening to Lucy when I'm here on my own.'

'Oh.' Alexa brightened up. 'You think me being here would make a difference?'

'Definitely.'

'Oh.' Alexa said no more. Her beaming smile rewarded Seraphina sufficiently for Alexa's presence.

Merc and Silo headed out at once.

They drove straight to the Company headquarters and parked.

There was a light in the upstairs rooms.

Silo whispered, 'I think the meeting would be in the room over the archway, way at the top, the one first on the right.'

'The conference room!' whispered Merc back. 'Where we had our team meeting today.'

'Right, I thought it was familiar. There's comfortable chairs, and a machine with free coffee and stuff.'

'Okay.'

They went forward cautiously. The strong outer door, made of thick oak and bound with the iron which remained as an unpleasant indication of its former existence as a bank, had been torn from it's hinges by the explosion. The maintenance team had succeeded in propping it up temporarily and it was currently wedged open to allow the members of The Twisted Rosebud access. Someone with suitable tools and considerable strength must have come first in order to sort it out and fix it open, Merc realised. Probably someone who worked for the Company, and had known what would be needed. But then, why not?

Merc became aware of a number of other dark figures surging forwards in the same direction.

'Em. About how many other people do you think are likely to be here, Silo?'

'Oh. About a hundred, I should think.'

'Oh.'

Merc hadn't anticipated so many. A cold sweat broke out on his fore-head as he realised that his confession of faith about the things he cared most about, i.e. Lucy and Seraphina, could have taken place before probably about a hundred people.

It seemed likely to be the wrong time to ask, but he had to know.

'Um. Silo.'

'Yeah?'

'You got a lift with me to the office, that night just before we went to the Tiny Isles. So were you there at the meeting where they truth drugged me?'

'Truth drugged you?'

'Yes.'

'No. I was told to come along to the Company building, right, but they just wanted me to stand guard for them outside a room. There were only a few of the top people inside.'

'Good.' Merc really meant it.

'So were you inside there, then?' asked Silo. 'You mean to tell me they actually truth drugged you?'

'Yes.'

'Wow! That means they have big plans for you, MS! They only do that when they mean to bring someone in at a really high level!'

'Oh. Well, they can forget about that,' said Merc grimly. 'There's no way they can bring me in, at any level. Especially after that letter. Threats to my family spell only one thing to me. Evil people. Not the sort of people I want anything to do with, whatever they think they stand for,'

'Oh, right, right, MS! I couldn't agree more!' babbled Silo. 'Em. Maybe we should stop talking, MS? We're getting near the meeting room. I wouldn't want anyone to hear us, okay?'

'Fair enough.'

Merc pulled the long dark robe Silo had lent him closer around his throat, tugged the hood further forward over his head, and adjusted his mask carefully.

Time to concentrate on what he was here for.

From all directions, people in masks representing dogs of different breeds, cats, lions, all types of wild animals from giraffes to crocodiles, and even a few rats and mice, were converging on the door to the conference room. Merc had time to wonder how they would all fit in.

Although, as befitted the conference room at the Company head-quarters, the room was far bigger than necessary for its normal requirements. And had comfortable seats and a coffee machine.

The door of the conference room was open.

In the doorway stood a figure, robed like Silo and himself, but wearing a mask representing a buffalo. A large, powerful figure. A figure who might have been the world heavy weight champion.

Merc felt himself flinch.

There was no way he wanted to be exposed as a spy by this animal. Or man, if that was what he was. Merc had his doubts.

Merc could see that as the approaching crowds of people came to the doorway, they were stopped by the man in the buffalo mask, and there was a muttered exchange of words.

He and Silo drew near.

'Silo. What did you say the password was?'

'Oh.'

Silo glanced round, and whispered so quietly that Merc had to strain to hear him.

'The Twisted Rosebud will grow straight, and the white flower will turn golden when it's ready.'

'Oh.'

Then Silo was going through the doorway, and it was suddenly Merc's turn.

'Password?'

'The Twisted Rosebud will grow – er – straight, and the white – em – flower! – will turn golden when it's cooked – Um, no – when it's ready!'

Merc rushed hurriedly through the last part of the password, hoping he had it right.

'Enter, friend.'

Merc heaved a sigh of relief.

He went through the doorway.

Chapter Thirty Seven

Silo Clotson was just ahead of him. He turned round, beckoned to Merc, and indicated two empty seats which he had appropriated.

Merc sank thankfully into the nearest one.

They had been among the last to arrive.

Within a few minutes, the big double doorway was swung shut.

Merc looked around.

The chair where Flacker Winterbotham had sat a week ago, when he had sent Merc off to the Tiny Isles, was empty.

But even as Merc took this in, a person robed like everyone else, but wearing a mask created to seem like another of the long extinct Buffaloes, stood up among the many masked characters, and banged loudly on the desk in front of him.

'Silence for the leader!' he shouted, in a voice which carried throughout the conference room.

He was not, Merc saw straightaway, the leader him or her self. Rather, this was a person whose job was to announce the leader, and to ensure a good hearing for them.

And even as Merc thought this, he saw a person in a mask which seemed meant to represent a Fluffy Kitten, come forward from the back of the room, and take her – yes, definitely her, Merc decided – place in what had been Flacker Winterbotham's position, in the chairman's seat.

The mask, quite a pretty, fluffy affair, covered most of the leader's face, while leaving her mouth and chin free.

There was an outburst of applause.

Then the Fluffy Kitten rose, held up one hand, and waited for the noise to die down.

'My friends,' the speaker began in a sweet but firm voice.

Yes, definitely feminine, Merc thought. Or, the thought struck him, effeminate?

'My friends, it gives me great joy to see you all here tonight. Even as we speak, plans are afoot to destroy this terrible system under which we all live. You know, and I know, that we are not free. That we are controlled by those monsters who have economic power, commercial power, over us.'

The speaker paused, to allow his or her audience a chance to express their agreement.

Which they did, with loud cheering and clapping.

Yes, thought Merc, clapping along with the rest, that's certainly true. I agree with that.

'We of the Twisted Rosebud exist to put right this wrong. We can't continue to see our people turned into mechanical objects. We want to release you from this tyranny, give you an opportunity to live freely, to make your own decisions, to be real people! Not robots who are controlled by tranquillising pills, and by consumer goods, and by a situation where you are unable to exist without buying, buying, buying, for the profit of your bosses!'

Yes, thought Merc again. How many times I've thought exactly that.

'These people need to be destroyed!'

Cheers on an escalating scale burst out on all sides of the conference room.

'I am glad – in fact, delighted! – to say that we have among our number many reformed adherents of this evil system, many who are committed to working from within, to acting from inside the system, in order to destroy these people who care only for their own profit, who are happy to see the rest of us suffer and die, so that they may make more and more money! And for what? Money can only buy so much. After the first million what can money bring? Only a higher bank balance!'

More cheers, and laughter, now on an ecstatic level.

Merc thought, 'This is all very well. But what about the people who were killed by the bombings?'

'I have important news for you, my people!' continued the sweet voice.

'I'm sure I know who that is!' thought Merc suddenly.

Just as he had thought on the night when he had been captured by the Twisted Rosebud and given the truth drug.

Until now he had almost forgotten that flash of semi recognition.

Surely that's – ? But the elusive memory, backing away into a dark cupboard in his mind and slamming the door hard, refused to emerge from hiding.

The speaker was continuing.

'Again, we have identified an appropriate target. A cruel, self-centred magnate whose only desire is to make more and more money, regardless of the pain and suffering caused by his activities to the ordinary man. We have identified someone who would be better out of this world. Someone who deserves to be got rid of. And the sooner the better!'

There was a stir throughout the conference centre. Merc thought the stir was not entirely caused by excitement and agreement.

It seemed to him that there was a mixture of uneasiness.

Not everybody wanted to see more bombing.

'But before I tell you any more details about this new target –' The speaker paused impressively.

'You all know, my friends, the importance to our movement of absolute trust, absolute secrecy. We have sworn oaths –'

Silo spoke in Merc's ear. 'I don't remember any oaths!'

'– or the equivalent,' the speaker continued smoothly. 'We know in our hearts the importance, the necessity, of loyalty, of a consistent refusal to reveal to any outsider the plans and objectives of our great society.'

There was a dramatic pause.

All round Merc, silence, broken only by gasps of fear.

'But what do I find?' the speaker said dramatically. 'What do I find?'

She raised one hand to point down the room.

'Someone has taken advantage of our trust! Someone has revealed our secrets! My friends, there is a traitor among us. Someone is opposed to our plans. And that person is attempting to undermine us!'

Another dramatic pause.

'And that traitor is here with us now!'

Merc froze. He took a horrified breath.

Chapter Thirty Eight

Strangely enough, Merc's first worry was not so much for himself as for Silo Clotson.

He had persuaded Silo to give away the Twisted Rosebud's secrets.

He had more or less bullied Silo into bringing him to this meeting.

What would happen to Silo now?

Merc himself would probably, he thought, be all right.

After all, Mr. Brown had got him into this mess, by advising him to take Silo's mask off.

Mr. Brown could get him out of it. And, thought Merc grimly, he had better do.

But would Mr. Brown look after Silo?

Merc wasn't sure.

Maybe that was Merc's own job.

Maybe if he stood up straight away and admitted to being the traitor, they would never realise that Silo had had anything to do with it?

Or maybe not.

He began to push his chair back, ready to get up.

Suddenly two burly men, big, but not quite as large as the Buffalo on the door, masked as bulls, advanced down the room, following the pointing finger of their leader.

Merc shrank back, horror stricken.

Too late!

But, no.

The bulls rushed past him, and leapt ferociously upon a slight figure seated several feet further down the room.

Female, Merc thought, from the size.

Pushing the person's chair aside, so violently that it went crashing to the floor, they dragged her, whoever she was, up onto her feet.

Then they were hauling her up towards the front of the conference room, where the leader stood stiffly waiting.

'Get rid of the mask!' was the leader's first order.

'No need,' said the captive coolly. 'I'll do that myself.'

With a swift movement she twisted free from the bulls' grasp. Then, raising both hands behind her head, she untied the strings of her mask, which, incidentally, Merc noted, was a particularly arrogant looking peacock, and quickly pulled it from her face.

Merc gasped.

Was he dreaming, or was it really Kyra Hotberthy standing there defiantly?

'You completely misunderstand my motives for coming here!' Kyra said. She spoke as loudly as the leader had done, clearly intending that everyone in the room should be able to hear her. 'I have come to warn you!'

Everyone in the conference room, it seemed, gasped in concert. Including Merc.

'I have inside information for you!' continued Kyra loudly. 'I have been allowed to sit in on the plans which are being made to destroy the Twisted Rosebud. I can keep you informed of every move of your opponents, and that's why I'm here tonight. I don't want to see this great organisation ruined.'

Merc gasped again, this time on his own. Was every member of his team really on the other side?

First Silo, and now Kyra.

He felt, for a moment, very lonely.

'How do I know that this is true?' asked the leader angrily.

'You don't,' Kyra Hotberthy said calmly. 'You'll have to take it on trust.'

'Why should I?'

'I can understand that you may not be able to make a decision just like that, Madam Kitten,' said Kyra scornfully. 'I know why you're hesitating. You're afraid to take the risk on your own authority. That's because you aren't really the leader, are you?'

'I am! I am!' spat the woman in the kitten mask. 'And don't call me Madam Kitten! My title is Leader! Because that's what I am!'

'No, you're not,' Kyra said calmly. 'I know who your real leader is, Madam Kitten. It's –'

'No!'

'Madam Kitten' sprang forward, seizing Kyra by the arms.

'If you say that sort of thing before all these people, there'll be no mercy for you! I am the only leader! Take care!'

'Then,' came Kyra's cool voice, 'you and I must talk together in private.'

Merc listened. He wasn't sure what was going on.

Then things began to clarify in his head.

Merc stood up.

He began to speak loudly in his turn.

'Fellow members of the Twisted Rosebud!' he shouted. 'Listen to me! Do we want to become terrorists, assassins? What do we really stand for? I'll tell you what we stand for, what our original aims were! We want to stop the seven companies which still remain in control of our planet! We want to prevent them from destroying this world! We want to restore a sane state of affairs where every person has a right to be free and to live lives which aren't dominated by a greedy few. And we don't want to go on with these bombings!'

To his satisfaction there was a loud cheer all round the conference room.

It seemed to Merc that more people were agreeing with his speech than objecting.

'We need to discuss our future plans,' Merc continued, 'we need to make decisions that everyone supports, not just decisions that only some people here agree with.'

There was another loud cheer.

'If there's going to be any private discussion,' Merc shouted. 'then we need a representative of the majority view to be part of it. I offer myself, fellow members, as someone you can trust to put forward your views, not just the views of the current leaders!'

By now the cheering had intensified, and people were jumping up and down, clapping and stamping their feet.

Silo pulled at Merc's sleeve.

'Good, good!' he shouted, trying to be heard over the racket. 'Go for it, MS!'

'Yeah, okay,' Merc said out of the corner of his mouth, 'but don't mention my name again, for goodness sake, friend.'

Silo collapsed.

'An excellent idea,' said Kyra Hotberthy unexpectedly. 'I move that the three of us adjourn to a private room, and talk this through.'

Merc gaped at her in surprise. To his amazement, he was almost sure he saw her left eye flicker in a split second wink.

'I agree!' he said quickly.

The leader in the Fluffy Kitten mask was left speechless.

Moving quickly up the room, Merc took the Fluffy Kitten by one arm. Kyra Hotberthy took her by the other. Moving in unison, they headed for the further door.

'Hi, MS,' Kyra muttered out of the side of her mouth.

Merc froze.

Then, 'How did you know it was me?' he asked in ultra quiet horror.

'You have a very distinctive voice, Merc,' murmured Kyra. 'But let's not say anything more just yet!'

The room had fallen silent. Apparently no-one wanted to interfere. Not even the Bulls or the Buffaloes.

Merc and Kyra, with the still silent Kitten in the middle, left the conference room.

Chapter Thirty Nine

Across the corridor they entered a much smaller room laid out for private talk between two or three people at most.

Merc sat down at the head of the table, but Kyra was the first to speak.

'Tell me, Madam Kitten.' she said sweetly, 'why do you pretend to be the leader when you know, and we know, that the real leader is someone much more powerful?'

Madam Kitten gaped at her.

'What –? You think you know things? But you're all wrong!'

'Oh, you'd be surprised how much we know,' Kyra said. 'So, tell us. How did you get into your present position? You usurper?'

'I'm not a usurper!' the Kitten flashed. 'He would have wanted me to do it! I know he would have asked me to, if he'd known.'

'Asked you?'

'Yes! He wouldn't have wanted to appear publicly, himself! He would have wanted someone to represent him. And he trusted me!'

'I see.'

Kyra Hotberthy sat quietly, thinking.

'So.'

Merc, so far, had been collecting his scattered wits.

So Kyra Hotberthy wasn't a traitor? She was acting a part? Pretending to be on the Twisted Rosebud's side? Or was she?

Merc wasn't quite sure.

But he thought it was worth the risk to act as if it was true.

'Then,' he announced, attempting to take control – after all, who was team leader around here? – 'then, who is this 'he' you keep talking about?' He took a risk. If he was wrong, he would lose cred with the Kitten. Still.

'Is it Tonky Spoutforth?'

'You know it is!' flashed the Fluffy Kitten.

'Then we need you to take us to see Tonky Spoutforth straight away. Take us to your leader, in fact.'

He was conscious of Kyra glaring at him. Well, maybe it hadn't been a very good joke.

'We mean it,' Merc said firmly.

'All right,' the Kitten muttered. 'But he's not going to be very pleased, I warn you.'

'Fine.' Merc stood up. 'The sooner the better.'

Kyra stood up, too.

Merc groaned, as he took in what he had done. What had they got themselves into?

And he really, really needed to speak to Kyra Hotberthy before anything else happened.

Before, for instance, he took the wrong position, and gave himself away to the Kitten, and then found that his instinctive trust in Kyra was all wrong, and she was definitely on the other side.

The Kitten had by now risen to her feet also.

Merc followed suit.

As they went out of the room, he managed to linger behind and grab hold of Kyra by her sleeve.

'What's going on?' he muttered. 'Whose side are you really on?'

'My own, naturally,' Kyra said sweetly.

Then she relented.

'And yours, too, Merc, of course.'

And Merc had little option but to believe her.

They left the Company building and got into the Kitten's little car.

It was late, and the streets were dark by now, in spite of the weak streetlights. The traffic was reduced. Only people on official business, and of course the many binge shoppers, were out at this time, midnight. Merc and Kyra sat together in the back of the car, while the Kitten drove.

That way, they could keep an eye on her, and make sure she didn't try to trick them in any way.

And, Merc was glad to realise, he and Kyra could talk privately, as long as they kept their voices down.

'So, what's going on, Kyra?'

'I told you this afternoon, I had a few ideas,' Kyra hissed. 'I've noticed for some time that people have been using the conference room who weren't meant to be there. Rubbish left behind. Oh, the cleaners clear it up, but often I'm in early before they get round to it. And sometimes I have late meetings. Like with you recently. And I've noticed that there's noise in the building as if something else was going on that shouldn't be.

So I've had my suspicions. And yesterday I found the robe and mask I'm wearing tonight, in the ladies' cloakroom, shoved behind one of the cubicles, like someone must have been in a hurry. So I thought I'd hover round tonight and see if I could find out what was going on. And I did!'

She looked triumphant.

'It's a pity they know now who I am,' she added. 'But if I were you, Merc, I'd keep quiet about who you are. I don't think they know that yet. So don't take your mask off unless you have to.'

That made sense, Merc realised.

'And I'm putting my own mask back on before anyone else sees me,' she added, adjusting the peacock mask over her face again.

The only thing was, Merc thought, he still had a sneaking feeling that he should be able to recognise the Kitten's voice. It had, he was pretty sure, really bad associations for him. It was a voice that made him think of someone quite scary, surely? But in a funny sort of way.

And if he ought to recognise her, then most likely she had recognised him.

He decided to say nothing to Kyra about it, and to wait and see.

The car pulled up at one of the larger houses in the city. Merc was vaguely aware that it belonged to a politician.

Sandy McPherson, the dour, serious faced Scotsman Flacker Winterbotham had been phoning on the day when Merc had been at the Board meeting.

The man who was supposed to be the token honest politician among the many who were corrupt. Although no-one actually said they were corrupt. Not if they ever wanted to say anything again and didn't much want to be offered a seat in a very hot sparky chair.

What had Sandy McPherson got to do with Tonky Spoutforth?

But then he remembered that when Tonky had been editor of the Globe, the Globe had pushed Sandy McPherson into his present position of power, constantly presenting him as honest and reliable, and a man who deserved the people's vote.

Maybe it wasn't so strange after all.

'Get out,' said the Kitten. 'If you're serious about wanting to meet Tonky Spoutforth, that is.'

'Oh, we're serious,' Merc said. 'We have important things to discuss with your leader.'

'Though not with you,' added Kyra rudely.

They moved forward, up the flight of steps to the imposing front door.

The Kitten raised the huge metal door knocker, and let it fall with a noise like thunder.

A moment later, the door flew open.

'Yes?' boomed a loud voice, and an enormous man dressed as a butler stood in their way, glaring fiercely at them in their robes and masks.

'We want to see Tonky Spoutforth,' said the Kitten.

She leant forward and whispered something in the butler's ear.

It might, Merc guessed, have been a password of some sort. Whatever it was, it apparently explained the robes and masks satisfactorily. Maybe she had said they were on their way to a fancy dress party.

The butler, his face impassive, took a step back, and bowed gravely.

'This way, sir. This way, ladies.'

Merc followed obediently as Kyra and Madam Kitten entered the house.

Chapter Forty

The butler led them along a luxuriously furnished hallway floored in light oak and thick with many coloured rugs, and into a spacious compartment which seemed to combine music room, lounge, and library.

At least, it contained a grand piano, numerous comfortable chairs and sofas covered in dark green velvet or with blue and yellow flowers on a pale creamy chintz background, and an amazing amount of books, with blue and red and brown backs which brightened the room, arranged on high shelves which covered a good part of three of the walls.

The fourth wall consisted mostly of enormous double doors, and after bowing again, and saying politely, 'If you would please to remain here while I ascertain if Mr. Spoutforth is able to receive guests, Mesdames and Sir,' the butler flung these open and disappeared through them.

'Wow!' said Merc, and was frowned down by Kyra Hotberthy.

Merc and Kyra wandered round the huge compartment, noting the statues, the oil paintings, the thick white sheepskin rugs on the polished wooden floors, and trying not to look too impressed.

Meanwhile the Kitten settled herself at ease in one of the most comfortable of the large armchairs, took out a cigarette, and began to smoke peacefully.

It was strange, Merc reflected, to see the puffs of smoke emanating from the mask of the Fluffy Kitten.

It was even stranger to realise that all this luxury belonged to a man who had the reputation of being one of the few honest men among the politicians.

The more he thought about this, the less impressed Merc was by the expensive setting.

Presently the butler came back.

'If you would care to come this way?' he said calmly.

The three guests followed him through the double doors, along another lengthy corridor, this one thickly carpeted and lined with more oil paintings and statues in niches, and finally to more double doors.

The butler stopped, coughed impressively, looked round to make sure his party had all caught up with him, and threw the doors open.

'The visitors, sir,' he intoned.

Then he stepped back and ushered them in.

They went forward into a room almost as huge as the compartment where they had been left waiting.

But this, it appeared, was a bedroom.

Directly facing the double doors, but some distance away, was an enormous four poster bed, draped with bright satins and silks in shades of yellow.

Propped up against a mountain of pillows was an elderly man.

Perhaps, thought Merc after the first surprise, not so very elderly.

The impression of age might be mainly due to the lines of pain which covered his sallow face, and the aroma of ill health which wafted from him.

If this was indeed Tonky Spoutforth, he could not be so very old.

But certainly he was a dying man.

He spoke, his voice faint and husky.

'Come nearer. Please sit.'

There was a comfortable couch on one side of the bed, and various easy chairs within a short distance on the other side.

Merc waved the two girls to the couch, and obediently drew up a soft chair for himself.

Tonky lay back against the heap of downy pillows at the head of his vast bed which propped him comfortably up, and smiled with some difficulty. Beside him on the huge bed lay a tiny black and white kitten. Tonky's left hand stroked the little creature's soft fur gently. Occasionally he lifted the kitten to his cheek, and held it against his face where he could feel its warmth and softness.

It didn't seem appropriate to Merc. Surely, he thought, with faint memories of very old films, it ought to be an enormous fluffy white cat, not a minute black and white kitten?

He stretched out his own hand to stroke the kitten. In an instant the little animal was transformed from a cuddly ball of fur into a spitting angry weapon of attack, its back arched, its fur standing on end, and its tiny pin like claws digging as deeply as they could into the back of Merc's unprotected hand.

'Ow!'

Merc hurriedly withdrew his hand, sucking at the painful stratches. Small as it was, the black and white kitten had succeeded in causing its supposed enemy considerable pain.

'Sorry,' said Spoutforth. 'Should have warned you. She's very protective of me. Must have thought you meant to attack me or something.'

The speech cost him some effort, and he ended it with a deep sigh.

Merc thought, 'Funny, more than one kitten seems to feel like that, don't they?'

It was important not to be fazed by the man's illness.

It was important to take the initiative.

'No problem,' he said, as he gathered his wits about him. The little cat had settled back into its place by Tonky's side, purring happily to itself as the man's feeble hand resumed its gentle stroking movement.

Merc watched the contented pair thoughtfully.

'Tonky Spoutforth?' he began.

'That's me. How are you? On your way to a fancy dress party, I see?'

The voice, as well as being faint and husky, was, now that Merc came to think of it, clearly working class.

And all the better for that, Merc thought loyally, remembering his own family background and his honest, independent parents.

Merc gulped. 'We want to talk to you,' he said, 'about the Twisted Rosebud. You've heard of it, of course?'

'I can't say I have.' The voice was slightly stronger. 'What is it? Some new nightclub? I've always tried to keep up with the latest fun spots. Can't go to them any more, but it's still good to hear all the gossip. Have you come to bring me up to date?'

'No, no!' Kyra Hotberthy interrupted impatiently. 'You must know what the Twisted Rosebud is! You've always known everything! Surely you – Ow!'

Merc, unable to see across the huge bed, nevertheless received the strong impression that Kyra Hotberthy had been kicked, quite hard, on the ankle by the human Fluffy Kitten, who clearly didn't want Kyra to say anything more.

'Don't worry, Tonky,' said the sweet voice of the Fluffy Kitten. 'My friend's just joking. Have you got everything you need? Can we fetch you anything?'

'No, no,' said the man, his voice growing fainter again. 'My dear friend Sandy McPherson sees to it that I have every luxury here. I can't think of a thing I don't have. Except,' he frowned for a moment, 'I don't seem to have the latest edition of the Globe? I really need to keep up to date with it, make sure I know what's going on. Maybe you could check with Dobson, the butler, you know. Ask him to fetch me a copy when you pass him on the way out, if you would be so kind? Thank you so much.'

He sighed gently and leant back against his pillows, softly closing his eyes.

'I think I might have a little doze, now,' he added quietly.

The Kitten rose to her feet, put one finger to her lips, and indicated to her companions that it was time to leave.

Merc and Kyra followed her softly out into the passage

'Well,' said Merc, 'I think we made the wrong guess there!'

'Maybe,' said Kyra argumentatively, 'but who knows? The guy may just be a first class actor. He always knew everything that was going on –'

'But you can see for yourself that's he's not the man he was, Kyra,' began Merc.

'They say he's dying,' said the Kitten abruptly. There was something like a sob in her voice, to Merc's amazement.

It was just at that moment that the lights in the corridor went out.

Kyra exclaimed aloud.

Merc, with slightly more presence of mind, made a grab for their companion.

In a few moments the lights came on again, and he found to his embarrassment, that he was holding Kyra.

He let go of her hastily and looked wildly round.

But the Fluffy Kitten had disappeared.

Chapter Forty One

'Quick!' cried Kyra. 'After her! She can't have gone far!'

But it was too late.

Rushing angrily round corners and down long passages, they tried to catch the Fluffy Kitten.

There was no sign of her.

And as they passed various footmen and maids, Merc became aware of a growing atmosphere of indignation, and of hands which attempted to seize hold of them as they passed.

Rounding a final corner, they decided to draw to a halt.

There was a door in front of them. Not the big front door by which they had come in, but certainly a door to the outside world, according to the glass panel which showed an attractive view of beautifully laid out gardens lit by moonlight.

By mutual agreement they pushed the door open and went outside.

As they made their way down a winding path through smooth lawns, flowerbeds, tall trees whose leafy branches waved softly in the breeze, and what Merc thought must be vegetable gardens, although he had never actually seen such things before, they looked at each other ruefully.

Merc wiped sweat from his forehead.

Something was puzzling him.

'I don't understand what that Fluffy Kitten person was up to!' he burst out. 'Why did she allow us to believe that Tonky Spoutforth was behind it all? She even said, or at least implied, that he'd asked her to stand in for him, didn't she? Or I suppose she actually said that he would have asked her? Why not just tell us, in a more convincing way, that she was the leader herself?'

'Perhaps,' said Kyra slowly, 'Perhaps because –'

She opened what was probably the back gate, a tall, imposing iron structure, and they went out into a reasonably familiar street.

They began to stroll in the probable direction of civilisation. Or to put it another way, of the Company building and their cars.

'I think ...' said Kyra.

She was obviously thinking aloud. Presently she said something more.

'Perhaps she isn't the leader. She thought we knew who the real leader was, so she admitted it wasn't her, and then when she saw that we had the wrong idea, she encouraged it until she could get away. As she has done.'

'Or perhaps,' said Merc, brightly, for he had also been thinking, 'she is the real leader, and she just led us in circles till she had a chance to escape. Before we took her mask off.'

'Then, you think it's someone we would recognise?'

'Yeah. I've had this weird feeling that I know her voice, all along.'

'Well,' Kyra said practically, 'maybe it will come to you. Meanwhile, we've made a right mess of what would have been a good chance to discover the main enemy. Too bad.'

'Tough,' Merc agreed. 'But, okay, 'Tomorrow is another day,' as Scarlett said. I'm going home. If I can find the way.'

Ten minutes later, not much else having been said, they arrived back at the company car park.

Seraphina and Alexa, both bubbling with excitement, were waiting up for him at home.

'Merc, I've got an idea!' Alexa cried. She had been left out of the plan to infiltrate the meeting. So, instead, she had spent the time, while waiting for Merc to return, in coming up with what seemed to her an even better plan.

'Oh?'

'The thing we need to find out most of all is, who's the leader of the Twisted Rosebud? And is it really Tonky Spoutforth? So why don't we break into Tonky Spoutforth's house? I could get in by one of the air vents, and let you in by the door. I'm small enough to squeeze in, I bet. And then we could read his private papers, and check out if he's the boss of the Twisted Rosebud or not!'

Merc looked at her coldly.

'First of all, Alexa,' he pointed out, 'because the problem has been that we didn't know where Tonky Spoutforth is living right now.'

'But I thought you would have found out all that stuff at the meeting?' Alexa said, sounding really disappointed.

'Didn't know?' Seraphina asked acutely. 'Does that mean that you do know, now?'

'Well, yes,' Merc admitted. 'But it doesn't really help.'

By the time he had outlined for them the events of the night, it was late.

'Okay, Tonky isn't the boss of the Twisted Rosebud. So maybe Silo's right, and it's Flacker Winterbotham? I could let you into Flacker Winterbotham's house instead!' urged Alexa. She was by now determined to break in somewhere. 'We could check him out, see if Silo's idea about him is right?'

'Silo's ideas aren't ever right,' Merc said.

And, 'Time you were in bed, Alexa,' said Seraphina firmly.

To Merc's amazement, Alexa obediently disappeared upstairs to her room. The spare room Silo had slept in.

'But what did you do with Silo?' asked Seraphina.

'Good heavens! I've no idea what happened to Silo,' Merc realised. He sounded, and felt, anxious.

'I'm sure he'll be okay,' Seraphina said comfortingly. 'Too late to worry about him at this time of night. We'll check up on what happened to him in the morning, right?'

Merc agreed. Reluctantly.

'After all,' Seraphina added, 'we haven't had much time to ourselves recently, have we?'

Merc gazed at her as she moved towards him, seductively unbuttoning the top few buttons of her blouse.

'I think we should try for an early night, don't you, Merc?' Seraphina said softly.

Merc nodded happily.

He put his arms round her.

Chapter Forty Two

Rolling over in bed from Seraphina, some time later, Merc finally drifted off to sleep.

His last conscious thought was the hope, without much conviction, that Silo Clotson hadn't been caught, or in any other way got into trouble.

But he realised, given Silo's personality, that this was only too real a possibility.

Presently he found himself in the familiar dream with the flying dishwashers.

And there was Griffon Longfellow.

Delicate green light, flappy wings, face like Nosher Boggs, the ex-boxer who was now a popular Nexus Luxurian bookie; the lot.

'What do you want?' Merc asked apprehensively.

'Merc Swingly!' began the Third Degree Representative.

'Yeah?'

'There is a message for you.'

'So. What is it?'

'You need to know some things.'

'Oh. Right.'

'You have done well, so far, Merc Swingly. You have listened to advice. But there are more things you need to know.'

Merc smiled weakly.

'Yes?'

'I have spoken to you before this about the need for people to have choices. Do you remember?'

'Yes,' Merc heard himself mumble. He seemed for some reason to be looking on from outside at his dream self, and listening to the conversation, while at the same time taking part in it.

'You must give people the opportunity to make choices. You must not act too soon. You must not make assumptions. You must not leave anyone without a choice. Remember that you have been given a second chance yourself. Extend that concept to the people around you.'

'Yes,' Merc said again.

'Unhappily, there are signs that you are about to forget this. My master wants you to realise the importance of remembering.'

'Oh.'

'That is all.'

Merc watched as Griffon Longfellow once more faded and dwindled into the distance.

Then there was another voice in his head.

It was Mr. Brown.

'Call me, MS.'

That was all.

But surely there was something that he needed to remember about these dreams, something that would help him to work out part of the puzzle? What was it?

Merc sank into deeper depths of sleep.

He was halfway to work the next morning, crawling along again as part of the thousand wheeled worm, when he remembered Mr. Brown's voice in his dream.

'Call me.'

He hadn't done it yet.

As the traffic once again slowed to a halt, Merc hastily got out his mobile and punched in the number.

'MB?'

'Hi, MS!'

'You said to call you?'

'Right. Danger ahead. Don't go for the obvious easy way, big guy. Remember what Griffon Longfellow just told you.'

'Um. To give people a chance to make choices?' Merc hazarded. To tell the truth, his memory of the Third Representative's message had grown rather vague.

'Got it. Here's a thought. Have you tried to get to know some of these guys you're dealing with? Found out where they're coming from? Given them a chance to change direction?'

'Um. No.'

'Don't think of people as things, MS,' said Mr. Brown. 'Don't think of them as disposable. They aren't nappies. Though most of them have probably been crapped on a lot. Try to find out about them as people.'

'Yeah.'

'Well, how's about giving it a go, then, okay?'

There was a pause, while Merc wondered which guys Mr. Brown meant. And what he meant by danger. And by 'taking the easy option'.

'Got to run now,' said the voice on his mobile. 'Ciao!'

'No-body says that now, MB – 'Merc began, before realising that the line had gone dead.

Once again, Mr. Brown had gone.

Chapter Forty Three

'Ah, there you are, MS. FW wants to see you straightaway.' The familiar words greeted Merc as he slid unobtrusively into work, hoping that no-one would notice him arriving late as usual.

'In his office,' Hyacinth added. 'He wants to hear all about your team.'

'Thanks, Hyacinth,' he said unhappily. 'I'll go on up, then.'

In his office, Flacker Winterbotham was pacing restlessly up and down.

'MS,' he exclaimed thankfully as Kyra Hotberthy showed Merc in, 'thank goodness! Come in, come in, sit down! Have a drink! Or a pill?'

Merc shook his head dumbly.

'So, tell me,' Flacker Winterbotham went on, 'how have you been get ing on? Have you found out anything about these villains yet? Do you know who's behind it all? Have you any plans for catching them?'

Merc smiled weakly.

'We have some ideas, FW,' he said. 'Some fairly clear ideas. But we need a bit of time yet. Don't worry,' he added hastily, 'we think we're getting there. You don't need to worry about yourself. You should be safe enough, I think.'

'You think?' echoed Flacker Winterbotham hollowly.

'We should catch the leader very soon!' lied Merc. 'We expect to track him down any time now!'

'Great, great!' Winterbotham said. 'I knew you were the man for the job, MS. You'll let me know straight away when you catch him?'

'Sure thing, FW,' Merc said enthusiastically. 'Just leave it to me!'

He groaned inside as he listened to his voice.

A memory from the previous night – his dream? – floated into his head.

Something about choices.

Was this what Mr. Brown had been telling him?

That he really didn't have a clue why Flacker Winterbotham was the way he was?

Merc had always just put it down to greed.

Which, okay, was probably right.

Still, it would do no harm to probe a little.

'Um. FW,' he found himself saying.

'Yeah?'

'Have you ever wondered what this Twisted Rosebud is all about?'

Flacker Winterbotham stared at him.

'No.'

'Or about why they should target you in particular?'

'Em. No, not really.'

'I just thought,' said Merc weakly, 'That – well – it might help to track them down, sort of way, if you had any thoughts about why they seem to be going for you? FW?'

Flacker Winterbotham stared at him blankly.

'Like,' ventured Merc, 'is there anyone you've sort of harmed any way? Or any group of people, maybe? Some people maybe, like, have things bad because of your, right, general lifestyle? Or something?'

'I've never harmed anyone!' Winterbotham protested indignantly. 'All I want is to be a successful businessman, what's wrong with that?'

'So. No ideas?'

Merc watched Flacker Winterbotham's face gradually change.

'Er. No. No, of course not,' he finally mumbled.

His voice no longer sounded quite so certain.

In fact, Merc could have sworn that he was remembering something.

Or perhaps a number of somethings.

'Well, never mind,' Merc said cheerfully. 'Think about it, why don't you? And if you come up with anything, well, you can let me know, right?'

'Yeah.'

'So, better be getting on with things, FW!' Merc said. 'Okay with you if I go ahead now?'

'Sure, sure, sure thing, Merc!' said his boss. 'I have every confidence in you. I don't want to hold you back. And, MS.'

He beamed.

'You can expect a really big promotion when this is all over, right?'

Merc smiled weakly again.

'Er – great, FW. I know I can trust you to do the right thing!'

He backed out of the office, still grinning.

'You handled that well!' Kyra Hotberthy greeted him tartly.

He had forgotten that she kept a link to her boss's office switched on at all times. 'So now you're committed to finding the leader of the Twisted Rosebud in a few days, right? So suppose you don't manage to find her?'

'We'll just have to see,' Merc said. 'I actually have some ideas about that. But first,' he looked shame faced, 'we need to find poor old Silo Clotson, and see if he's okay, or if anything's happened to him.'

'Fair enough,' agreed Kyra. 'Do you want me to send out an announcement for him? Come to the Conference room immediately or something like that?'

Merc looked startled.

'I never thought of that,' he admitted. 'Yeah, good idea, I suppose you can do all that stuff? Being FW's PA, you get to use the PA, sort of thing, right? I mean –' He stopped, flustered, as he listened to himself. 'Okay, go for it, why not?'

A few minutes later, as he strolled down the corridor towards the Conference room, he heard Kyra Hotberthy's voice, naturally completely distorted by the Public Address system, booming all around him.

'Will Silo Clotson please come at once to the Conference room? Silo Clotson. Silo Clotson. Please come at once to the Conference room. To the Conference room. Silo Clotson. Please come at once to the Conference room ...'

Merc shuddered. He put his hands over his ears. Actually covering his eyes unintentionally at the same time, he bumped into the Conference room door.

He brought one hand down for as brief a moment as possible, and quickly punched the door open.

Silo Clotson sprang out towards him without a moment's hesitation.

'Silo!' gasped Merc

He felt both alarmed and upset. What was happening?

'Merc!' gasped Silo. 'Merc! Thank goodness it's you! Merc, you've got to help me!'

Chapter Forty Four

How many more people were going to leap at him saying more or less those words, Merc wondered.

'So. Silo,' he said. He was doing his best to speak calmly. 'What's going on?'

He managed to disentangle himself from Silo's clutching hands.

'Come and sit down. Now, tell me the problem?'

'I don't know!' gasped Silo Clotson. 'Well, yes, I suppose I do. Help me, Merc!'

Merc went over to the nearest chair and sat down carefully.

'Okay, then, Silo. Let's take this calmly. First of all, where did you sleep last night? You didn't turn up at our place?'

'Oh. I sort of bunked down here, after everyone'd gone, right? Slept in one of the big soft chairs. Okay, really.'

'Fair enough. Though you could have come round to us. Well, I suppose there was a transport question, right? And so, what exactly is the problem?'

Silo in turn collapsed into a chair, just managing not to miss it. He groaned.

'I'm in major trouble, Merc. After you'd gone last night –'

'Yeah?'

'After you'd gone – well, see, people seemed to think that since I was with you, I must be sort of important, right? And there was a whole bunch that were saying we should go for the assassination bit. Like, the plan that Kitten woman was saying about, okay?'

'I thought most of the members voted for not doing any more of that?' Merc frowned.

'Well, yes, while you were there, yeah. But after you went –'

Silo gulped.

'After I went?' Merc encouraged him.

'This other guy got up and made a speech, and then a couple of others did too, and they were all on about how we needed to take a firm line and make our presence felt and if it took some strong affirmative action, then that was the bosses' fault for not listening to us sooner, sort of thing, and so – ' Silo trailed off miserably.

'Strong affirmative action?' Merc questioned. 'Meaning?'

'Like, killing a few more guys. Bosses, right,' added Silo hastily. 'They were all against killing innocent people, after what you said, MS! Your speech was really great, they were all really impressed!'

'But I wanted them to stop killing altogether!' Merc said furiously.

'Yeah, well.'

'So, then what?'

'Well, they talked a bit more, and then they had a vote, like, whether the Twisted Rosebud should carry on with the new assassination plans, okay?'

'And? Most of them must have voted against it, right? Nearly the whole meeting was on my side, weren't they? So how did the vote go? It must have been a very close thing, if the assassinators won?'

'Um. Well, not as such, MS,' Silo stammered.

'So? What was the result? How many voted on my side?'

'Um. Well. Me, MS.'

'You? No-one else?'

'Not as such, MS.'

Merc groaned.

He had heard of the fickleness of public support, and the short time it might last, but hadn't realised that it could come down to seconds.

'So then what?'

'Well, see, that's it, MS. They all looked at me, and the first guy, the one that started the speeches, he said he reckoned I needed to show my loyalty, seeing how I was out on a limb here with my vote, and they all cheered, and next thing he was handing me this bottle.'

Silo paused, fumbled in his pocket, and produced a small, corked glass container. 'And he said all I have to do is put this in Flacker Winterbotham's private whiskey, and it'll do for him right away. Some sort of poison, right?'

Merc stared nervously at the bottle.

'And they said if I don't do it, and Flacker Winterbotham isn't dead and done for within twenty four hours, then I'll be wiped out myself, to show what happens to people the Twisted Rosebud can't trust!'

'My goodness!' Merc said.

'So what am I going to do?' wailed Silo. 'There's no way I can find Flacker Winterbotham's own whiskey, let alone get hold of it privately!'

'No,' agreed Merc. 'The whiskey he keeps here in his office would be no good, he offers it to everybody who comes to see him. We wouldn't want to poison all his visitors at random. It would need to be his private whiskey, in his house. And there's no way we could get at that.'

He had a sudden memory of Alexa's voice last night, of her excited face.

'I could get into Flacker Winterbotham's house for you!'

Wasn't it something like that she had said?

First, it had been Tonky Spoutforth's house she had suggested.

But then Flacker Winterbotham's.

'Through an air vent!'

Yeah, that had been it.

And here was Silo with poison that would put an end to Flacker and his greed and ruthlessness for good.

It seemed like a perfect plan.

What was it Mr. Brown had warned him about?

Taking the obvious, easy path.

Treating people as if they were things. Disposable.

And he had mentioned danger.

The danger of turning into somebody who would kill? To carry out what seemed to be a good idea?

Merc made up his mind. Quite easily, in fact. This was just out of the question.

'No way, Silo,' he said.

'Yeah, I know, I can't get into his house, or anything, like I said, so I can't do it.'

'Even if you could, I don't suppose you're willing to be a murderer!' Merc reminded him sternly.

'Oh. Yes. Right,' agreed Silo hastily. 'But if I don't manage it somehow, they're going to be coming for me! I'm in such deep crap! You've got to help me, MS!'

Merc groaned.

He knew he had to help Silo.

After all, in a sense, it was he who had got Silo into this.

He had insisted on Silo taking him to the meeting.

Then he had made that reckless speech, drawing attention to himself and to his companion.

And then he had left Silo on his own, to fend for himself and make his own decisions.

Always a dangerous thing, with Silo.

He would have to think of some way of getting him out of this mess.

He did, he supposed, have some vague sort of plan.

This, unhappily, probably involved speaking to Flacker Winterbotham again and persuading him to agree to Merc's idea, and to be reasonable about it

Or something like that.

Chapter Forty Five

Merc made a couple of phone calls, one of them to Mr. Brown.

He gave it a few minutes.

Then he went back to Flacker Winterbotham's office.

There was no sign of Winterbotham.

Kyra, who had just returned from a coffee break, had, for once, no real idea where Flacker had gone.

'Well, when he turns up, ask if I can see him,' Merc said. He felt that he had done the best he could do at the moment.

He walked thoughtfully back to his office.

Unhappily, he had overlooked the fact that Hyacinth Duckworthy would be waiting there for his return.

As he walked through the door, she pounced on him.

Everyone seemed to be pouncing on him these days.

'MS! There you are at last!'

'Um. Yes?'

'You've no idea of the number of messages that have been piling up for you, MS!' said Hyacinth Duckworthy reproachfully.

Merc felt a flash of guilt. Presumably his new job entailed a certain amount of actual work, now that he came to think of it.

'Especially,' Hyacinth Duckworthy said with emphasis, 'from the Tiny Isles. You remember that you left strict instructions about what you wanted done there? Ully Beers has been messaging you continually, to report on what he's done and get your approval, and to ask your advice on the next step.'

'Probably he just wants someone to tell him he's been a good boy,' Merc said wearily. 'Okay, Hya, show me the printouts and I'll see what I should reply.'

'Well, I really think you should do something, MS. I don't want to speak out of turn, but I think that girl Kyra Hotberthy is likely to tell FW about what you've arranged out there, and if you aren't really on top of it – well, there are some back stabbers round here, even if they are sexy and pretty –'

Merc, flipping through the printouts, wasn't listening very carefully.

'And then,' went on Hyacinth Duckworthy persuasively, 'there's this one which I think must be really important, don't you? It's got all this red tape and sealing wax round it, it came in the actual post, not by email or internet messaging, and it seems to be from the Head of Worldwide Weapons, Garnie Porker. A very important man, MS!'

Merc looked at her, not really convinced.

'You really, really ought to read it, MS. Garnie Porker has probably been waiting for an answer since at least an hour ago.'

'And that's a problem?'

'Oh, yes!' Hyacinth's large blue eyes grew even larger and if possible more blue. 'Garnie Porker always gets answers to his messages fast, like, before he sends them, sort of!'

'Oh, all right, give me the letter!' Merc sighed. 'But just let me see what Ully Beers has to say first.' He skimmed quickly through the dozen messages, ranging from self satisfied to frantic, and then said, 'Just what I thought. Email him back to say, great work, everyone here's really pleased, could you, Hya? And sign it in my name, right?'

Then he took the huge, expensively embossed envelope which Hyacinth Duckworthy had been waving in his face since he walked into the office, and ripped off the large amounts of sealing wax and the red tape wound round the envelope too many times, to indicate its importance.

Inside was a big square of thick creamy paper with gold edges, the sort of thing most people used for their wedding invitations. Was Garnie Porker getting married or something? Why, on the other hand, would he be inviting Merc?

The writing was also in gold, printed in a very fancy font meant to look like hand writing without really fooling anyone.

There were also numerous gold squiggles round the margins.

At the top the gold writing, in a more important looking font, announced:

Worldwide Weapons

From the desk of Garnie Porker.

Greetings, MS!

began the letter,

Great to hear you've joined the Worldwide Productions Company Senior Management team. How's about joining me as well – for a few friendly drinks, with some of the guys you'll be working with and getting to know?

Just to encourage you, I can promise, as a special treat, that Herbie Shuffle from World Health and Chemicals will be there, as well as your own chum Flacker Winterbotham!

See you there, then!

Tuesday 8 July,

Six for six thirty, my place!

The address was flourished along the foot of the invitation.

The Arches, Boswell Place, Nexus Luxuria.

Merc gasped.

He was suddenly moving in very high circles, it seemed.

He supposed, vaguely, that that was what Mr. Brown had meant when he had said, some time ago, that Merc might be in a position to make a difference later on.

'Yeah, right, Hyacinth,' he said vaguely. 'Um. I guess I'd better RSVP, yeah? Maybe you could throw something suitable together for me to sign, could you, yeah? Thanks?'

'No problem, MS!' beamed Hyacinth Duckworthy. Her doubts about Merc, after his behaviour on the Tiny Isles, seemed to have disappeared completely. Apparently she once more regarded him as somebody worth putting a bit of effort into, somebody who it might be good to get close to.

Merc smiled happily.

He wasn't entirely sure where he was going, but it seemed likely to be somewhere that Mr. Brown and his controller wanted him to go. And that had got to be good.

He hoped.

It occurred to him that Garnie Porker had got it wrong.

It seemed quite unlikely that Flacker Winterbotham would be at this little get together.

Which reminded him.

'Hi, Hyacinth!' he said, taking care as usual not to say anything on the lines of Hiya, Hya. 'Do you think you could chase up Silo Clotson for me? He was in the Conference Room just recently?'

'Sure thing, MS,' beamed the now over friendly again Hyacinth Duckworthy, and flashed out of the office on Silo's trail.

Merc sighed.

There was always something.

He had got used to Hyacinth being a bit withdrawn, in case she got involved in his only too probable downfall. It had been really nice and peaceful, ever since the events in the Tiny Isles, not to have to be avoiding her all the time.

Now, suddenly, it seemed that he would have to start watching his step with her all over again.

Meanwhile he flicked through the dozens of messages waiting his attention.

His mind wasn't really on what he was doing, and he almost missed a message from Glooper, from the coffee shop. His second name, Merc noted, quite appropriately for the investigative work Merc had asked him to do, was Houndstooth.

Mr. Swingly

began Glooper,

Have some info for you. Might even be useful, though I don't know. Too private for email. Call round soon, okay? If you want to bother, that is.

Glooper Houndstooth.

Chapter Forty Six

Merc was pleased.

Useful information was just what he could be doing with.

Hopefully it was something which would help him to identify the leader of the Twisted Rosebud. However, he had very little opportunity to think about it.

In what seemed no time at all Hyacinth Duckworthy was back, shepherding Silo in front of her.

'Um. Great, Hyacinth. And, maybe –' he hesitated. After all she was an assistant analyst, not his PA. He didn't want her to label him as not PC.

Still, he needed to get rid of her for a few minutes.

'Er. I wonder if you would mind fetching Silo and me a cup of coffee?'

'No trouble at all, MS,' Hyacinth cooed, and, to Merc's relief, immediately disappeared.

'Right, Silo!' Merc said urgently, grabbing Silo by the sleeve and hissing in his ear. 'I think your problem's solved for the time being, okay? Flacker Winterbotham has disappeared. So even the Twisted Rosebud can't expect you to poison him, right? Just tell them that, and you should be fine until he turns up again, if ever, see?'

'Oh. Disappeared?' Silo assimilated the information slowly. 'So, you're sure of that, MS?'

'Why? What?'

'Only I thought I saw him in the corridor a minute ago?'

'Not possible!'

'Heading for the corridor with the washrooms?'

'Oh.'

Merc recovered himself.

'Thing is, Silo, I think he's lying low, right? But I'm not too sure where. But don't panic. I'll check it out.'

'Great, MS!'

'Anyway, just tell the Twisted Rosebud what I said. Tell them that Winterbotham's got offside, okay? And leave it up to me, right?'

'Right, MS!'

'So. You'd better come home with me. Go and wait in the car, right? Here, take my keys.'

Merc backed slowly out of the Conference room, thoughts churning round in his head.

The corridor with the washrooms?

Okay!

He headed in that direction.

The men's washroom seemed to be empty.

'FW?'

Merc stood in the middle of the supposedly hygienic space, and gulped the unpleasant smelling air unwillingly.

You could never be sure that men wouldn't miss their objectives, however much their bosses encouraged them with pep talks.

No answer.

Maybe he should try the Ladies?

The smell in here was much better. Merc put his head cautiously round the door, then sidled quietly in.

'FW?'

'MS? Is that you?'

'It's me.'

'Okay!'

'Where are you?'

'MS! I'm locked in the cabinet! Get me out of here!'

'Can't you just unbolt the door?'

'No! I think the bolt's stuck! Anyway, the door's jammed! I can't move it! And I can't reach the bolt!'

'Oh.'

Merc thought hard.

'Why not, FW?'

'Cause I can't get down off the toilet seat!'

'What?'

'I sat down, and then I thought I'd better put my feet up on the seat, out of sight, in case anybody sees me. If they were standing where you are, Merc, they could see my legs and feet. And they'd know I was here. So I pulled my feet up.'

'Okay. Sensible idea.'

'And then I thought I'd like to have a look under the door, so I bent my head right down to see. Not easy.'

'Not easy,' agreed Merc gravely.

'And I got the fastener of my trousers caught in my shoe buckle, and I can't get it undone, and then I got my cuff link caught too, and I can't reach the door from here or get down or anything and I don't know what to do!' ended Flacker Winterbotham on a note of fast growing hysteria. 'You've gotta help me, Merc!'

Flacker was clearly panicking.

'FW?'

'Yes?'

'Why are you in the ladies' toilets?'

'It smells better!'

Okay. No argument there.

'And I thought no one would expect to find me here!'

Fair enough.

This, Merc thought, is the guy who got the top job in the management committee of the Company.

Is it just me, or is there something wrong with this picture?

Or then again, maybe not.

'Are you sure you can't unbolt the door?'

'I can't reach the bolt, MS! I haven't got room to come down from the toilet seat. I'm twisted up in a ball! I've tried everything! I don't know what to do! I'm not used to this, I never came here before, I have my own washroom en suite with my office, I never get stuck there, it doesn't even have a bolt, for any sakes, it just shuts, no-one else comes in but me, what am I going to do, MS?'

It was fairly clear to Merc that there would be nothing much wrong with the bolt.

A bit stiff, maybe.

Flacker, already highly stressed, had simply panicked at the first sign of difficulty.

Why, it wasn't all that clear.

If he calmed down, surely he could get free from his trouser fastening?

Most men managed it every night.

Or, if someone else could get into the cubicle, it would probably be easy enough for them to disentangle him and open the bolt.

Unfortunately, it wasn't the sort of cubicle where you could climb over a gap from the one next door. The walls reached right to the ceiling.

On the other hand, there was a bit of a gap under the door.

Not really big.

There was no way Merc himself, for instance, could get under it.

Oh, well, try the obvious way first.

'Should I fetch the guy with the tools, FW? Bart Thingy, the one who knows about locks and stuff? He could probably open it from this side?'

'No!' Flacker Winterbotham's response was almost a howl. 'I don't want anyone to know where I am! You said, when you rang my mobile to warn me privately about this new assassination attempt, that it would be best to hide out for a while. And you said to disappear as quick as possible, anywhere that occurred to me, until I settled on a place no one would think of? I don't want them to find me first go off, stuck in the women's washroom!'

Chapter Forty Seven

Merc could see FW's point.

A situation like this wouldn't go down well with the staff.

It just might make them wonder why someone like Flacker was the supreme boss? And got lots more money than they did? And couldn't get himself unfastened from his trousers and out of the toilet?

And the Twisted Rosebud would find out straight away where Winterbotham was.

They'd be able to go right to the heart of things.

Or perhaps some other part of the anatomy would be more appropriate.

'Okay, FW!' Merc said. 'Look, I'll be able to get you out of here if you give me a few minutes, right?'

He walked to the far end of the washroom and took out his mobile.

'Hi, Seraphina?' he said. 'Can you get over here quick, and bring Alexa? No, I can't come for you, you'll have to take a bus. Or borrow Mrs. Bertha Kitt's car, if she'll lend it to you? Be sure you bring Alexa! I need her special skills. I'm in the ladies' toilets, right?'

Cutting short Seraphina's angry squawks, he switched off.

Then he put in the waiting time by talking some more to Flacker Winterbotham.

This was, in fact, a lot more surprising and interesting than he would have expected.

It seemed no time at all before the noise of someone hammering on the outer door of the women's washroom alerted him to the arrival of help.

It was just as well that the reception area was still a mess.

The usual guards and the usual precautions against unauthorised access were at the moment in abeyance.

Seraphina and her companions – who included Lucy: oh, right, Merc realised, Seraphina hadn't got a baby sitter – had had no problem getting in past the currently non existent guards.

Merc, looking over his shoulder, was aware of the outer door suddenly bursting open, and of the abrupt entrance of his wife and baby, their neighbour Mrs. Bertha Kitt, and their recently acquired guest, Alexa Darnhurst, from the Tiny Isles.

Right.

This was what he had been expecting.

More or less.

He could have done without Mrs. Bertha Kitt.

In her booming voice, Mrs. Bertha Kitt announced, 'Well, here we is, Pardner! What can we do for you?'

'I must say, Merc,' said Seraphina critically, 'the security round this place is absolutely hopeless! We walked in without a word from any-one. Mind you,' she added honestly, 'I think they saw Bertha and took heed, in good time, to say nothing –'

'Yeah, right,' interrupted Merc hastily. 'Look, thanks for coming, all of you. Alexa,' he grinned at the girl, 'it's you I really need. Though you couldn't have got here so quickly without Bertha and Seraphina,' he added hastily. 'Listen, do you think you can crawl under this door and open the bolt on the inside?'

'No problemo, MS,' said Alexa cheerfully. She seemed, Merc noted, to have picked up a lot of out of date expressions in her few days in Nexus Luxuria. 'Plenty of room.'

This was probably true, Merc thought, measuring her width with his eye. The inhabitants of the Tiny Isles weren't famous for their large, well fed girth.

'Um. I think it would save embarrassment all round,' said Merc quickly, 'if you and Bertha waited outside, darling? And take Lucy, of course. Only, the guy who's trapped in there might be happier if you don't see him? I'll tell you all about it later, promise!' he added quickly. 'But just for now? If you wouldn't mind too much?'

To his amazement the two women allowed him to shepherd them out-side with the baby.

'Now, Alexa,' said Merc in relief. 'Oh. Wait a moment.'

He came over to the cubicle door.

'FW?'

'Yes?' came a faint voice.

'Are you decent?'

'Well. I don't know what you would say about that. We've just been talking about that, right? I've always tried to do my best. To do the right thing, sort of. I've made my mistakes, okay. But, yeah, I've always wanted to be decent. I know there've been times when I've stepped too far out of line –'

'No, I mean. Are you dressed? Fully zipped up, right?'

'Oh. Well, actually. Well, no. See, I thought maybe I could wriggle out of the trousers and sort things out better that way, so I sort of got the zip down, and wriggled part way, but then I sort of got stuck and –'

'Well, never mind about that now. A friend of mine is coming in to help you. Don't worry, she won't give you away.'

There was a frantic squawk.

'She? MS, you can't do this to me – !'

Merc interrupted hastily.

'It's okay, FW, she's just going to unbolt the door. Then I'll come and help you with – er – the rest of the problem –'

Ignoring his boss's heart rending pleas, Merc turned back to Alexa, who, he noticed, was giggling quite a lot.

'Okay, Alexa. Stop giggling and go for it.'

Alexa dropped to the tiled floor, and squirmed forward on her stomach.

She disappeared from view.

A moment later, her voice came from inside the cubicle.

'Hey, who's this dude who's passed out?'

'Never mind that!' ordered Merc. 'Can you unbolt the door?'

'Give me a second.'

There were sounds of wriggling and of scraping metal.

Then the door was flung open.

Alexa, flushed and smiling with triumph, stood in the doorway.

Chapter Forty Eight

'Hey! Like I said, no problem! Just needed a bit of wriggling with the bolt, and you needed to hold the door up a bit, where it'd dropped down on its hinges, see? Easy-peasy!'

'Good girl! You've done something really helpful and important here, Alexa, pet! When I get home, I promise to tell you all about it. Though maybe I really shouldn't? But, hey! So what? So, can you go out now and, like, do something even harder? Persuade Seraphina and Mrs. Bertha Kitt to disappear home with Lucy as quick as possible, before this guy comes round and finds out they were here? He really won't know how to deal with it if he sees them. And if they see him! Okay?'

'Fine, MS! You're the boss!' Alexa said chirpily. She was clearly very pleased with herself, and happy to earn more praise. 'I'll disappear right away, okay?' Alexa asked, grinning.

'Great!' said Merc enthusiastically. He could hardly wait to close the door after her.

Then he approached Flacker Winterbotham cautiously.

The great man was crouched sideways in a tight ball on the cubicle seat, his head bent forward at an awkward angle, and his buttocks, in bright blue boxer shorts, with crumpled trousers stretched far too tightly over the lower parts, wedged uncomfortably against the wall.

Merc, first taking the precaution of dragging Flacker Winterbotham by the arms into the open area, worked hastily at the confused tangle of shoe buckle et cetera until he had the various items separated. It reminded him of the metal puzzles sometimes included in the better sorts of Christmas crackers, the ones that keep everyone busy and cross not only for the rest of the afternoon but for days afterwards too, and involve major rows and shouting. He wondered, as he began by taking off Flacker's shoe, why it hadn't occurred to the man to start by doing that himself, instead of going for the far more difficult trousers. But, no. This was Top Management he was talking about.

In a relatively short space of time, Flacker was free.

He would leave him to sort out his trousers for himself, Merc thought distastefully.

He swallowed a momentary panic as to what any new arrival to the ladies' room would think if they came in now, or indeed if they had come in at any point in the last few minutes.

At least Alexa wasn't still here.

He began to slap Flacker Winterbotham gently on the cheeks, and finally resorted to bringing water from the wash hand basins in his cupped hands to splash over his unconscious boss.

'FW! FW! Wake up!'

'Wha – wha – ! Who's there?'

'You need to get up, FW! And pull your trousers up! We need to get you out of here!'

Staggering and moaning, Winterbotham finally made it to his feet, adjusted his clothing as instructed, and, leaning on Merc's supporting arm, headed out of the wash room.

'We'll go by the back stairs!' Merc hissed in his ear. 'They'll bring us down to the reception area, but just not so noticeably.'

'Back stairs? What're they? Where am I? Who am I? I must be some-one important, I thought I was, or maybe not? Am I getting that all wrong? Am I just someone stupid?'

From the sound of Flacker Winterbotham's muttered response, Merc realised that his boss had never heard of the back stairs. And didn't know much about himself, if it came to that.

Which, he realised was possible enough. The back stairs were for the less important workers.

When would someone of Flacker Winterbotham's status ever have needed to use them before?

Creeping cautiously, continuing to support Flacker Winterbotham's stumbling feet, Merc made his way to the narrow, uncarpeted stairs used by people like cleaners and canteen staff, and clerical workers in a major hurry, and went slowly downwards.

It was as they approached the still abandoned reception area, where no-one but the renovating team currently worked, that Merc became aware of a worrying noise.

'Leave go of my arms!' That sounded like Alexa.

'Take your hands off her!' Wasn't that Seraphina's voice?

Then loud booming tones that couldn't be anyone but Mrs. Bertha Kitt.

'Come on, then, if you want some more!'

'Hey, big lady! What do you mean by kicking my mate just there?'

'I'll kick you even harder!' That one was Alexa again.

What was going on?

Merc dropped Flacker Winterbotham's arm.

He said to Winterbotham, 'Okay! Wait here!'

And hurtled forward.

Chapter Forty Nine

Two big men, wearing a green and gold uniform which Merc vaguely recognised as belonging to the team which had been hired to repair the bomb damage, were attempting to prevent Seraphina and the others from leaving the building. One of them was grasping a struggling Alexa by the arms. Her feet hung above the ground, and she was squirming desperately in an effort to get in more kicks.

At the same time, Merc couldn't help noticing, the man was bent over in a strangely protective attitude, and in a way seemed to be using Alexa more as a shield than as a captive.

Seraphina was tugging fruitlessly at this man's arms, while also holding on to Lucy. The baby, enthusiastically contributing to the fun, was occupied in her usual game of tugging at the nearest adult hair, in this case that of the man who was holding Alexa.

His comrade, a plump red faced man, had his own attention fully occupied. Mrs. Bertha Kitt, handbag swinging, had already smacked him round the head more than once, and as Merc watched, a further blow with the heavy black leather weapon sent him reeling backwards to collapse on the ground at her feet, one arm held up in a terrified attitude of defence.

Mrs. Bertha Kitt was turning round triumphantly to help Lucy and Seraphina deal with the first man, when she heard Merc's voice.

'Stop it! Stop it, all of you? Are you mad?'

'Not us, sonny Jim! These ladies here! Tried to brush past us without showing their passes and then went for us when we tried to stop them. Especially the big one! She's mustard!'

'Make him put Alexa down, Merc!' Seraphina shouted.

'Put her down!' Merc ordered. 'Right now.'

'But she'll just kick me again!' the man objected. He, like his mate, had been supplied in the extra large size. He was burly, and had a swarthy, pugnacious face and straggly ginger hair.

'Alexa, I want you to promise not to kick this man if he puts you down now!' Merc said. 'He's only trying to do his job. And, Bertha,' he added, 'I want you to promise that you won't hit this man if he puts Alexa down. At once.'

He noticed the immediate effect of his last words.

Carefully, facing Mrs. Bertha Kitt, but as far from her as he could manage to get, by a gradual backing movement, the ginger haired man put Alexa down.

Seraphina immediately threw her arms round the girl and hugged her protectively.

'These ladies are my guests,' said Merc sternly. 'They have every right to be here, and to leave when they want to. I'm sorry they tried to kick you –'

'Tried! Huh! ' muttered the plump red faced man on the ground. He began to scramble gingerly to his feet. 'You didn't see what the big one did to Sharkin here! Ruined him for life, I wouldn't be surprised! What's his wife going to say, huh? Your guests, are they? And who exactly might you be, then? Where's your pass, Buster?'

Merc glared at both men.

'Who employs you?' he asked.

'Miss Kyra Hotberthy, on behalf of Flacker Winterbotham himself!' retorted the burly, ginger haired Sharkin, angrily.

'Perhaps you'd like to ring Miss Hotberthy and ask her about me?' Merc suggested. 'Merc Swingly. From Eastern Fashions.'

The plump, red faced man gulped.

'If we've made a bit of a mistake –' he began feebly.

But his burly companion was made of sterner stuff.

'Prove it!' he sneered. 'We have orders to see the passes of everybody who goes in and out, right?'

Merc took out his mobile and resignedly rang Kyra Hotberthy's number.

'Kyra, we seem to have a problem here. Maybe you could help out?'

A sudden thought occurred to him.

'Excuse me.'

He darted back to the corner where he had left Flacker Winterbotham.

It wouldn't do for Kyra Hotberthy to see Winterbotham. That would undermine all Merc's plans for absolute secrecy about FW's disappearance.

'Time to move, FW!' he began as he rounded the corner. 'Scuttle down that passage and keep out of sight, right? I'll come for you when it's safe –' Then he stopped, his mouth hanging open.

Flacker Winterbotham was no longer there.

No time to wonder where he'd gone.

Merc galloped hurriedly back to where he had left his friends and family.

Kyra Hotberthy was arriving from the lift.

'What's going on here?' she inquired briskly. 'Blott, Sharkin, what are you doing? Causing more trouble?'

'Oh, it's nothing really,' said Merc, to grateful looks from the two men. 'Just a small misunderstanding. My fault really, I should have gone down with my wife and friends to see them safely out, right?'

'Nonsense!' snapped Kyra. 'Officious red tape! You two men should know the senior board members of the Company when you see them!'

'Let's say no more about it, Kyra,' Merc urged. 'Thanks for coming to sort it out. Perhaps we could have a word now?'

'Of course, MS,' Kyra beamed graciously.

'Seraphina, could you get Lucy and Alexa and Bertha out of here?' Merc hissed in an aside which he hoped no-one else could hear. 'I'll see you very shortly, right?'

Seraphina for once paid attention to what Merc wanted.

'Come on, girls,' she said, heading for the entrance, and the others followed her lead, with a final glare from Bertha at Sharkin, and a rather crude gesture at Blott from Alexa. Lucy contented herself with a gleeful giggle and a tongue stuck out in the general direction of the two men.

This time, they really did leave.

'Kyra,' Merc continued, shepherding Kyra Hotberthy, with an arm round her shoulder, back to the lift, 'I wanted to check if you've heard anything from FW? It seems strange, him disappearing like this?'

Maybe he should be confiding his plans for Winterbotham's disappearance to Kyra, he reflected, as they travelled upwards together, and he listened to her worried report that there was still no sign of the Chief Executive. But to tell the truth, for some reason he still wasn't one hundred per cent sure he could trust her.

'Too bad, Kyra,' he said finally. 'Thanks for the up-date. I guess I'll go and catch up with the paper work now.'

Waving a pleasant salute, he left Kyra Hotberthy at the door of her office, the room adjacent to Flacker Winterbotham's, and headed swiftly for his guess at Winterbotham's present location.

Thrusting open the door of the women's washroom, 'FW!' he said in an agonised whisper. 'Are you there?'

There were two closed cabinets.

Merc went quickly over to the nearest one, knocked quietly on the door with his knuckles, and murmured, 'Hullo? Is that you?'

He just hoped Flacker hadn't managed once more to lock the door beyond his own ability to open it again. No. The door swung open.

Merc's sigh of relief was cut short as a fat, middle aged woman with a red face and a look of terminal anger came bustling out. Her small, dark, beady eyes crinkled with rage and her plump reddish hands were clenched into fists. Merc automatically took a step backwards out of their range.

'*What,*' she said, '*what* do you imagine you are doing in the ladies' washroom, my good man?

Chapter Fifty

Merc groaned.

'I'm – it was – I'm sorry, a – a – mistake, sorry!' he tried to explain.

'I dare say!' the woman cut him short. 'I suppose you think this is some sort of joke! Your superiors will hear about this, young man, I assure you! I happen to be a quite important person in this Company, my dear sir!'

Merc wondered briefly who she was.

'I'm so sorry –' he attempted to say again, but was cut off abruptly.

'You need not say more. No doubt you consider that this intrusion is amusing. Let me inform you that it is very far from it. I refuse to tolerate this type of behaviour on the Company's premises. The ladies' wash-rooms should be sacrosanct!'

Merc backed hastily out of the door. The woman seemed to be swelling to twice her normal size as her rage mounted.

'Do you know who I am, young man? My name is Ms. Cordelia Lankinsop, and I am in control of the Canteen – I'm the Head Dinner Lady, a most important position, as I'm sure you know. I am a personal friend of Flacker Winterbotham, let me tell you, I bring him his coffee personally every day, and I shall speak directly to him about this, I assure you.'

You could probably do that right now, by rapping on the next cubicle, or at least I hope so, thought Merc, but was careful to control his hysterical urge to say this out loud.

He continued to back hastily out of Ms. Lankinsop's way, managing to get out of the doorway. She was following him so closely, continuing to breath out fire and slaughterings, that they were half way down the corridor before he could succeed in letting her pass.

Thankfully watching her retreating back, he slid unobtrusively into the Ladies' Washroom again.

There was still one door shut.

'FW! Are you there?' he called as quietly as possible.

The door opened cautiously and to Merc's relief Flacker Winterbotham's face peered out.

'MS! Thank goodness it's you! Get me out of here, for any sakes! And who on earth was that?' Winterbotham groaned. He wiped beads of sweat from his brow with a nervous hand.

'A personal friend of yours, she said.'

'Oh?'

'I don't know why you keep coming here to hide!' said Merc severely. 'Surely the last place anyone would think of hiding.'

'Is it? I just thought it was the last place anyone would think of looking,' Winterbotham explained.

Merc bustled him hurriedly out, first peering carefully into the corridor.

No-one in sight. Good.

'We'll go down by the back stairs again,' he said. 'That way we'll be less likely to meet Board members or people who know you well. Like Dinner Ladies. Here,' he added, inspiration striking, 'put this on.'

'This' was an ancient baseball cap which had for some reason ended up in his pocket today.

'Pull the peak well down over your face. And, hang on a minute –'

He stripped off Winterbotham's jacket and tie, turned up his shirt collar and folded the jacket inside out.

'Carry the jacket bunched up over your arm, and sort of hide behind it as much as possible. Now, keep your head down, don't look up or meet anybody's eyes if we pass them, but let's just hope we won't, and follow me.'

'Where are we going?'

'We'll talk about that when you're safely outside.'

There was no-one to pass them on the back stairway and this time they kept well away from the reception area.

Merc sighed with relief as he and Flacker Winterbotham went through the service door and pulled it shut behind them.

'My car's parked round the front. I'll just fetch it. Let's hope Silo found it okay.' A hope with a big question mark beside it, Merc realised. 'Silo'll have to know you're hiding out, can't be helped. He won't give you away. Well, not if I ask him not to. Wait for me here, Flacker. Keep out of sight behind those bins, right.'

'Right, MS.'

If he hadn't known, Merc would have had difficulty recognising the humble tones of his formerly aggressive, confident boss.

All this, Merc thought, whatever it might be doing to Merc himself, was certainly doing Flacker Winterbotham quite a bit of good.

Once in the car, which Silo had actually found successfully, to Merc's surprise and relief, he asked Winterbotham, 'Well, have you any thoughts yourself about where you could hide out?'

But apparently Flacker Winterbotham had not.

'No close friends you can trust?'

'No.'

'What about a hotel?'

'But I'd have to let them scan my ID chip, and then anyone could track me down just by looking up the police register. It doesn't cost much to get a look at it, you know.'

Merc didn't know, never having tried to keep tabs on anyone, but Flacker clearly knew all about it. Certainly, the capacity of the police to accept bribes for just about everything was known even to Merc, so why not this as well?

There seemed to be only one option left.

Merc wondered gloomily what Seraphina would say about it.

'You'll have to come home with me,' he said. 'There won't be too much room, and certainly not the luxury you're used to, but I don't see what else we can do. Silo has the spare room, and Alexa can go in with Lucy on a camp bed, so long as she's careful not to wake her. That leaves you the sofa. Not great, but you're welcome to it.'

Winterbotham's gratitude was pitiful.

As he had feared, Seraphina, though he had noticed that she had been much more flexible in her attitudes lately, greeted the arrival of yet another unexpected guest with something approaching horror.

Then, seeing the bedraggled appearance of Flacker Winterbotham, and recognising his pathetic need for some sort of help, she suddenly relented.

'Come in and sit down. Alexa and I are just getting a meal ready. I've asked Bertha if she'd like to stay and eat with us. There'll be plenty for all.'

Merc, watching Flacker Winterbotham's horrified face at the mention of Mrs. Bertha Kitt, found it hard not to burst out laughing.

'Is – is your neighbour going to be here? The big one who kicked the renovation guy in the – ?' Flacker whispered desperately to Merc.

'It's okay,' Merc cut in hurriedly. 'She won't bite you. Though her little dog might. Just joking,' he added hurriedly as he saw Flacker's face.

But Winterbotham looked anything but sure about any of it. Come to think of it, Merc wasn't any too sure himself.

Chapter Fifty One

Alexa and Seraphina between them had made an enormous pot of soya stew with plenty of the exotic spicy herbs – thought of by most people as weeds – that Alexa knew about from her island recipes; and it would be ready shortly.

It was Merc's turn to bath Lucy again, to his great delight.

The events of the last few days had almost made him forget about this until he saw his daughter gurgling happily at the sight of his arrival.

Bath time was as always a time of supreme happiness and satisfaction. Holding his warm, sweet smelling daughter in his arms, wrapped in her fluffy white towel with the ducks on the hood, Merc dried her carefully and felt a great flood of release from the day's tension.

When Lucy was safely tucked up in her cot, the incongruous group gathered round the supper table.

To Merc's surprise, Mrs. Bertha Kitt was the life and soul of the party, telling stories about her own past and her various husbands, now all dead, which amused and surprised everyone.

Particularly Seraphina, who more than once had to cough warningly at Mrs. Bertha Kitt and glance meaningfully at Alexa, who, she considered, was far too young to hear that sort of thing. In fact, probably most people were.

Afterwards, to Merc's amazement, Flacker Winterbotham, one of Seraphina's aprons tied attractively round his waist, helped Mrs. Bertha Kitt to wash and dry the dishes.

And actually seemed to be enjoying himself.

Then it was time to get down to serious discussion.

'Alexa, I think you'd better go on to bed now.'

Merc attempted to speak sufficiently firmly to leave no question about the matter, but he was overruled by both Seraphina and Bertha.

'Look what a help she was this afternoon,' said Bertha finally, in the decided type of voice that allows no argument. 'You couldn't have managed without her!'

And Merc had to agree.

Though perhaps if neither she nor Bertha had kicked the renovation guys quite so hard, they could have talked their way out more easily.

'So,' said Seraphina at last, 'are you going to tell us why Mr. Winterbotham –'

' – call me FW! –'

' – needs a place to stay?'

Merc and Silo between them explained.

About the plan to poison Flacker Winterbotham.

About Silo's dangerous involvement in it.

About the threats to Silo if he didn't carry out his orders.

About the risk to Winterbotham if the Twisted Rosebud gave the contract to someone else to assassinate him, by the same or different means – someone they didn't know about.

About how Merc had phoned to advise FW to stay under cover for the next few days, for his own sake and also for Silo's, who couldn't be expected to carry out orders to poison someone who had disappeared.

And about – and here Merc shot a warning glance at his wife, in case she came up with a normal wifely response – how Merc had every expectation of tracking down the leader of the Twisted Rosebud in the next few days.

'Oh?' Seraphina said.

'Of course!' Alexa put in enthusiastically.

'I'm sure I know the voice,' Merc explained. 'I just need a bit of peace to think it over.'

'What does Mr. Brown say about all this?' asked Seraphina.

'I haven't actually spoken to him since I phoned to tell him FW was going to disappear, earlier this afternoon,' Merc said. 'But he warned me again about not taking people at their face value. Looking beneath the surface. Maybe this is a chance for us all to do that? Get to know each other a bit?'

'An excellent idea!' boomed Mrs. Bertha Kitt. To Merc's astonishment, she gave Flacker Winterbotham a coy smile, which Winterbotham undoubtedly returned.

'Tomorrow afternoon,' Merc went on hastily, 'I've been invited to a big do at Garnie Porker's place, The Arches. I've got a sort of an idea that I might learn something there. You've been invited as well, FW, I'm told, but I don't want you to go. Too risky. Too many people will know you're meant to be there, right?'

'Right, MS,' replied FW in the strangely meek voice he had adopted to Merc recently.

Since, in fact, he had begun to see Merc as the only thing between himself and assassination.

And, okay, since he had begun to think seriously about why people might want to assassinate him.

'Now,' said Mrs. Bertha Kitt briskly, 'I suggest we settle down to a nice game of cards, or perhaps *'Take Over the World'?* You should be good at that, FW?' She nudged Flacker Winterbotham exuberantly in the ribs.

Flacker blushed richly, partly from shame at the implication, Merc saw, and partly from pleasure at the lady's attention.

Presently, when the other five were happily clustered round the *'Take Over the World'* Board, Merc announced his intention of going outside for a bit to think.

He climbed the outside stairs until he reached the flat roof of their house.

A low wall with a balcony running round all four sides ensured some degree of privacy from the neighbouring houses which crowded them in from all directions.

Sometimes, now that climate change had produced weather almost unbearably hot for some months of the year, people liked to sleep out on the roof, and it was nicer not to be too exposed to the view of neighbours on roofs close by, especially the ones with sad lives and binoculars.

Merc lay down on his back in the centre of the open roof, and enjoyed the cool breeze on his face.

He had come up here to think, but instead he allowed his mind to roam over the strange events of the last two weeks, ever since his dream of the end of the world.

He wondered vaguely if he'd been making the right decisions.

He'd wanted to. He'd certainly tried to.

But he wasn't always very wise, he admitted to himself.

And sometimes inclined to be selfish, and to choose what seemed best from his own point of view.

The night sky seemed very far above him.

He gazed up, watching the few stars gleaming against the darkness. There had been more stars to see, he remembered, even when he was a little boy. The growing pollution seemed to reduce the number that could be seen every year.

He became aware of an increasing brightness. It was as if the stars, and the whole sky, were coming closer to him. And closer.

Merc wanted to close his eyes. He couldn't seem to do it.

There was no voice to hear. But Merc knew, as the stars and the sky seemed to wrap themselves around him even more closely, like a comfort blanket, that something, some message, was being conveyed to him without the need for speech.

Someone was saying something to him.

He could just remember how, long ago, his father used to say to him, when he had first written his name by himself, or learnt something else new,

'Good boy, Merc. Good boy.'

It seemed as if someone up there was saying just that, right now.

Then, as Merc continued to listen, the same someone said, in a voice of infinite comfort,

'Don't worry. You're doing well, Merc.'

Chapter Fifty Two

The get together at Garnie Porker's place, The Arches, looked like being well attended.

Kyra Hotberthy had apparently been invited too.

Merc hadn't realised that Kyra was considered as important as that.

FW's Personal Assistant, certainly, was a woman of power, now that he thought about it.

She offered to arrange for Merc and herself to travel in one of the Company's cars, and Merc, who wasn't entirely sure where he was going, agreed gladly.

He was relieved to discover that there was apparently no question of Hyacinth Duckworthy having been invited.

'Oh, of course, certain people who think they're right in the centre of everything get invitations,' Hyacinth muttered sulkily to him, when he explained that Kyra had arranged a lift for them both. 'She seems to think she owns the company, sometimes. You watch out for her, MS, you don't know what she may be planning.'

Merc, who wasn't really listening, smiled vaguely and said, 'Oh, I think she just means to be helpful,' and left the office before Hyacinth could continue her grumbling.

She clearly didn't like Kyra, he reflected, but there didn't seem any real reason for it. Kyra must have done something to make Hyacinth distrust her so much, it seemed. But what? Maybe Hyacinth had wanted the job of PA to the Chief Executive? But she always seemed very happy – far too happy – working with Merc. He shuddered at the thought, and tried to think of something else.

The short journey took longer than he had expected, since it seemed that huge numbers of people were heading the same way, and when they eventually arrived, Merc saw at once that it would be virtually impossible to get a parking space for a considerable distance all round. The chauffeur, Joe, was the small, thin, silent coffee coloured young man with crimson dyed hair, who had driven Merc to see the aeroplane before his trip to the Tiny Isles. Merc was glad he himself wasn't driving, and waited resignedly, expecting Joe to take the car back several streets and turn them out to walk the rest of the way.

However, Kyra had other ideas.

'Take the car straight on in, Joe,' she instructed the driver. 'They'll make room for the Company, don't worry. They'd better!'

Sure enough, once through the enormous gates, Merc saw that there were in fact a few empty spaces, with notices on them reserving them for, for instance, Planetary Banking and Insurance, and among them was one clearly reserved for the Worldwide Productions Company.

The entrance was up a low, wide flight of steps and through an impressive foyer, richly carpeted in a luxurious dark red, and big enough in itself, Merc thought, to house most of the population of the Tiny Isles in considerable comfort.

He followed Kyra, who seemed to know her way, and who swept imperiously across the foyer to display their invitation cards to a pompous, rotund, balding man dressed in formal clothes which included a tail coat. Merc, about to shake hands, realised in time that this was the butler.

The butler waved up a subordinate, handed him the cards, and said,

'Marchman will announce you, Sir and Madam. If you would please follow him?'

Merc found himself entering an even grander apartment, already full of guests.

Along the sides were tables draped in starched white linen cloths, loaded with interesting looking bottles, shining cut glass wine glasses, gleaming plates, and dish upon dish of exotic food. Merc's eyes tried to pop out of his head at the sight of pheasant, grouse, chicken, ham, several sides of beef, legs of lamb, seafood of all descriptions, and all types and colours of vegetables and salads. Also too many sauces to count, all of them unfamiliar to Merc, who like most of the population of Nexus Luxuria, lived mostly on soya beans. And soup.

To one side was another table piled with dishes of strawberries, cherries, fresh pineapple, and every sort of fruit, besides numerous examples of the confectioner's art and other more solid traditional puddings. Merc's eyes shone as he identified, among the rest, the time-honoured jam roly poly pudding which he could just about remember his granny producing on very special occasions.

Behind the tables, a row of waiters and waitresses were serving the guests with whatever they chose, and on all sides of Merc and Kyra, people wandered unsteadily past with a loaded plate in one hand and a glass waving precariously in the other, trying to solve the perennial party goers' problem of how to eat anything from their plate with both hands already full.

Waiters in black ties and dinner jackets moved deftly through the crowd, offering glasses of champagne from their loaded trays.

As Merc and Kyra heard their names being announced, a heavily built figure detached himself from the crowd and came over to shake their hands.

'My dear Miss Hotberthy! What a pleasure to see you again. And looking as lovely as ever!' beamed this person. 'And so this is the famous Merc Swingly! My dear Merc – or may I call you MS? –I'm delighted to meet you at last! I've heard so much about you!'

Who from? wondered Merc. And what, exactly?

Clearly this was his host, Garnie Porker, who would have been more appropriately named Smarmy, Merc thought.

He remembered Garnie Porker vaguely from his lunch with Kyra Hotberthy in the Go-Go Room, when Kyra had pointed Garnie Porker out, dining at a nearby table, and had mentioned some of Garnie's exploits.

Merc took an instant dislike to the large, over fed, greasily smiling person who still had hold of his hand.

Garnie's own hand was unpleasantly sweaty, he noticed, and beads of sweat glistened on his forehead, which extended back well beyond what should have been his normal hairline. Thick, black curly hair clustered in a nervous way around Garnie's obtrusive ears, and his small, mean features seemed to be islanded in the middle of a large expanse of face. He was wearing a frilly light blue shirt which did nothing for his pale, spotty complexion, with a beautifully cut pin striped suit which failed miserably in its aim of disguising his grossly overweight figure.

Meanwhile, it was time Merc said something.

'Good of you to invite me, GP,' he managed.

'But neither of you are drinking,' Garnie went on. He signalled to a passing waiter. 'Sloggins! Champagne for my guests!'

Kyra and Merc obediently helped themselves to the proffered glasses from the waiter's full tray.

It was almost certainly the best champagne, Merc thought. Although he was no expert on the subject, naturally.

'You're in good time to hear my speech, my dears,' went on Garnie, who like most rich people assumed that all conversation should centre round himself, 'I'll be giving an interesting outline of the formation of World Wide Weapons, and some of my – I should say our, I suppose – greatest achievements, and then I'll be cutting the anniversary cake. Ten years since we were set up, can you believe it!'

He gestured to one of the side tables, where an enormous cake iced all over in stripes of red and blue, the colours of World Wide weapons, was reposing in solitary splendour, a huge, sharp looking knife beside it ready for the official cutting. 'Made specially for me by the world's best Master Chef – ' Garnie was continuing, but to Merc's relief he was cut short.

An enormous, middle aged man, the twin in all outstanding features – for instance, his stomach – to Garnie Porker, rushed up to Kyra Hotberthy and put both his hands on her shoulders.

'Kyra darling!' he said enthusiastically into her face. 'How lovely to see you again!'

Kyra seemed much less enthusiastic.

'Merc, this is Herbie Shuffle,' she said. She released herself from Shuffle's eagerly clutching hands, and immediately turned away, and more or less pushed Merc towards the slavering Herbie.

'You two should get to know each other,' she added, before starting a conversation with a member of the Company Board, the disgruntled Beaver Sturge, the man, Merc remembered, who had been pipped at the post in the race to be the new Chief Executive by Flacker Winterbotham. Merc, who had no desire to speak to either Porker or Shuffle, looked round uneasily for anyone else he could talk to.

To his relief, he noticed a familiar face at the edge of the crowd, a shy looking girl whom Merc presently recognised as the quite pretty Public Relations stroke Press Representative, Fancy Linnet, with the sparkling brown eyes and curly fair hair.

'Good to meet you, Herbie,' he said heartily. 'Excuse me, I must just go and have a word with our PR/PR.'

Hastily wringing Herbie Shuffle's hand, he headed off through the crowd in the direction of Fancy Linnet.

She seemed temporarily to have disappeared.

It occurred to Merc that much as he disliked the two Bosses he had met so far, his sole reason for being here, which was to find out more about the Twisted Rosebud, could hardly be furthered by avoiding these people when they seemed willing to speak to him.

He was turning back reluctantly with the purpose of striking up a conversation with either Porker or Shuffle, when a booming voice in his ear made him wonder for a moment if Mrs. Bertha Kitt had gate crashed the party.

A moment later, he recognised the lady whose arm was round his shoulder as the massive Reta Glutt, another Board member. And red hot suspect for leader of the Twisted Rosebud, according to Kyra Hotberthy.

Chapter Fifty Three

'MS!' boomed Reta Glutt. 'Great to see you! What's all this I hear about your doings in the Tiny Isles? And now it seems you've been appointed as some sort of super bodyguard stroke private eye to good old FW? Come and sit down with me over here and tell me all about it!'

Her arm still round Merc's shoulders, and waving a glass of champagne expansively in her other hand, she more or less dragged Merc across the room to a secluded sofa in a cosy alcove. She had had her bright blonde curls put up in an elaborate style for the occasion, and was wearing a far too tight red velvet designer dress, and Merc thought in horror that the effect was to make her plump red cheeks look even redder and plumper. The sabre toothed tiger look achieved by her large gleaming teeth was stronger than ever.

'What a load of cat's piss Garnie seems to be giving his guests,' she shouted, indicating the champagne. 'Never liked weak, wishy washy drinks like this one! Takes a bucketful to get you anywhere near sloshed. Time he brought out the whiskey! Waiter,' she roared, gesturing to a passing figure with a laden tray of savouries, 'get me some whiskey! Not just a couple of glasses, mind! Bring the bottle!

'Now,' she added, turning to Merc, as the despondent waiter staggered off to obey, 'tell me all!'

To Merc's supreme discomfort, she placed the hand which was not holding the glass on his knee, and gave him what he could only describe as a leer.

'A good looking young man like you has quite a future ahead of him, I bet. I think I might be able to help you along, if we make friends, see what I mean?'

She winked, and nudged Merc slyly in the ribs with her elbow.

Merc felt himself swamped by panic and champagne.

He had to get away. And quick.

'Um. Can I fetch you something to eat, Ms Glutt?'

'Think I can afford to eat this stuff, the size I am already?' joked Reta Glutt. 'But, hey, you should call me Reta, honeybunch.'

'Reta,' Merc said obediently.

An idea occurred to him. This was why he was here, after all.

'Um. Reta. I wonder if you might be the one who could help me?'

'No problem, Merc baby.'

'Thing is, Reta, I guess you know your way round in the Company far better than me. Like, you would know all about guys like Tonky Spoutforth, who used to run the Globe. You could fill me in on more background, right? Where, hey, so far he's not much more than a name to me.'

'Say on, big guy.' Reta Glutt raised her eyebrows and wriggled them suggestively. All she needed, Merc thought, to complete an excellent impression of that old time movie actor, what was his name? Groucho Marx? was a big cigar to wave around.

'I thought,' suggested Merc nervously, 'that Tonky Spoutforth might have something to do with this Twisted Rosebud I'm supposed to track down, right? But nobody seems to know much about him, and when I finally get to meet him, seems he's at death's door, okay? But I got to wondering if he was really all that ill?'

To Merc's relief, Reta Glutt took her hand off his knee in the interest of passing on some enjoyable gossip.

'Well, Merc baby, I can't help you too much on this one. From what I hear, yeah, he's in a bad state. But, hey, how do I know? This is just the stuff hanging on the grape vine.'

'Oh.' Merc paused to think.

'Mind you,' went on Reta Glutt, 'from what I hear, his daughter's the one you should really be looking into. Twice as fierce as the old man. Mustard mixed with dynamite, right? Not that I know where you'd find her. Maybe she isn't even in Nexus Luxuria. Still, I reckon she wouldn't be too far from the old man when he's in such a bad way.'

'Daughter?' Merc asked eagerly. 'He has a daughter?'

'Oh, yeah, and a girl who's been following in father's footsteps and then some. According to my sources she hit the roof when the paper was closed down. Burst into a Company Board meeting and threw a chair at the Company boss of the time, Buster Panter. At least, I think it was her. Or else one of the journalists? Before I was on the board, myself. Pity. I'd have liked to see that.'

'But wasn't she arrested?'

'Nah, they just wanted to hush everything up. Couldn't afford to have people getting stirred up. That was the whole reason for closing down the Globe, see? It was getting people too interested in what the Company was up to. Last thing they wanted was more discussion and scandal, maybe people beginning to question why they let the Company run their lives.'

'Yeah,' said Merc thoughtfully. 'So, Reta. What else can you tell me about this daughter?'

'Not a lot. I never met her.'

'Well, has she a name? I mean, do you know it?'

'Oh, yeah, I know her name,' said Reta Glutt. 'A bit of a daft, romantic name I always thought. She's called Rosebud.'

Merc gasped.

Had he found the answer to his search for the Twisted Rosebud's leader?

Had the Fluffy Kitten who had been in control at the Twisted Rosebud meeting a few nights ago been in fact Tonky Spoutforth's daughter, Rosebud?

The name seemed to make it clear that there was a definite connection.

Merc wondered.

He didn't know anyone called Rosebud.

And under this Government, it was almost impossible to change your name, and still be able to do even basic things like buy food.

Your name and other stuff was inserted on a chip planted under the skin of your right hand at birth, and couldn't, as far as Merc knew, be removed. For women, it could be added to when they got married, but nothing could be wiped.

But maybe someone had found a way of overwriting the chip? Worth looking into.

He must ask Silo, the team's computer expert.

Or even Hyacinth Duckworthy, who was clearly quite a bit of a whiz kid.

Meanwhile, Reta Glutt had replaced her hand on Merc's leg. Time to move.

Using his previous excuse, Merc stood up.

'I see our Press Officer over there,' he said apologetically. 'I need to have a word with her before she disappears from sight. Catch you again shortly, Reta.'

Ignoring the scowl on Reta Glutt's face, he moved off hurriedly through the crowd, making for the spot where he had, in fact, caught another glimpse of Fancy Linnet.

Chapter 54

This time he managed to catch her.

'Fancy! Hi!'

Fancy looked round, and her pretty face looked pleased. She was dressed much more simply and cheaply, Merc noticed, in a blue dress patterned with little white roses, than Reta Glutt, with her expensive designer style red velvet gown, or the other well off party guests; but still managed to look a lot more attractive.

'I was hoping to have a chat with you,' Merc began. 'I wanted to fill you in on some of the developments in the Tiny Isles, since my trip there. And then maybe pick your brains a bit? About the Twisted Rosebud, that is.'

'Sure thing, MS,' Fancy Linnet smiled. She lowered her brown eyes modestly. 'Should we get out of this crowd?'

'Good idea.'

'This way.'

Fancy Linnet led Merc across the room, and into a side area where there were only a few people. A door at the back of this space led on into a small side room, which was conveniently empty.

'Now, MS,' said Fancy Linnet sweetly, 'Let's sit down and be comfortable while we talk.'

She settled herself gracefully on an enormous white fleecy sofa, and patted the space beside her. Merc found himself sitting down, in spite of some unwelcome and, he hoped, unnecessary reflections about frying pans and fires.

'You were going to tell me something about the Tiny Isles?' Fancy Linnet suggested.

'Yeah, I thought you might like to do a short piece on how things are changing there?'

'Changing?'

'Yeah.' Merc felt slightly embarrassed. Still.

'I didn't think the conditions out there were too good,' Merc explained. 'So, hey, I've set up a few things, like, air conditioning in the factory buildings, and right, before they get to that, new buildings with a lot more space and safety precautions for earthquakes and stuff. And the hours and wages are getting a thorough overhaul.'

Fancy was looking thunderstruck. Her jaw had fallen several feet, leaving the rest of her pretty face looking a bit unfinished.

'You can say, if you like,' Merc went on, quite oblivious of the reaction he was getting, 'that the Company feels it should do everything it can to improve the lives of its employees. And maybe say that we hope to see our fellow companies following our lead?'

'And,' Fancy Linnet found her voice sufficiently to ask, 'does Flacker Winterbotham agree to all this?'

Merc hesitated. But it couldn't do any harm.

'Flacker Winterbotham is shocked at the way previous Chief Executives of the Nexus Luxuria Production Company treated their staff, before last year's takeover by Worldwide Productions,' said Merc firmly. 'He wants to make it clear that the former conditions were not in any way his responsibility and that no-one should hold him to blame in any way for these. He is considering further changes, but these will not be announced until the plans are complete. But I can let you know that they will be more than surprising!'

It was certainly true, Merc reflected that Flacker Winterbotham didn't want to be held responsible, or blamed, for anything the Company had done so far. He hoped it might be equally true that FW would be glad to make any changes that would rescue him from the Twisted Rosebud's attentions. Which reminded him –

'The other thing I wanted to talk to you about, Fancy –'

'Yes?' breathed Fancy Linnet, somehow or other managing to wriggle even closer to him, and looking up at him with her wide open brown eyes. Her curly fair hair brushed lightly against Merc's shoulder. 'Yes, Merc?'

'This Twisted Rosebud,' said Merc firmly, squirming back as much as he could without outright rudeness. 'Do you have any helpful thoughts about it? For instance, do you know anything about Tonky Spoutforth? Or his daughter?'

Fancy's eyes opened even wider, to Merc's amazement. He hadn't thought that that would be possible.

'Do you?' Merc repeated.

'Not as such, MS,' Fancy told him. 'I've heard lots of gossip, right, but I don't know how far it can be trusted.'

'Well, supposing you just tell me whatever gossip you've heard,' Merc suggested. 'Then,' he went on, forgetting any necessity to be tactful, 'if it seems to me to be rubbish, I won't need to pay any attention to it.'

'I suppose I've heard quite a lot, MS,' Fancy Linnet said apologetically. 'But I haven't paid all that much attention to it myself. I suppose I've heard a lot of rumours about Tonky Spoutforth, as you might expect. But whether he's actually involved in any sort of aggressive terrorism, well, I just don't know. I wouldn't have thought it of him.'

She paused, and blushed. 'I knew him, you see. I was a very junior reporter for the Globe in its last years. That's where I got my training, and that's what made me able to apply for my present job. But Tonky always paid attention to even the junior staff, and he talked to me several times, and gave me some helpful tips. Took me out to dinner, once. And he never seemed to me to be the sort of man who would blow people up –'

'Okay,' Merc said. 'I wondered about that myself. But his daughter, now? From what I hear, she's another sort altogether? Maybe you could tell me – ?'

His question was cut short.

Suddenly there was a loud noise like an explosion which seemed to come from the main room nearby.

Merc sprang to his feet.

'What on earth –!' he shouted.

Fancy Linnet shrieked, and buried her face in her hands.

Suddenly the atmosphere seemed to be full of dust, and a smell of, was it burning? Something like that.

Merc rushed to the door and flung it open.

At once the burning smell grew immensely stronger.

They could hear cries and wails that reminded Merc uncomfortably of his end of the world dreams.

Had he failed, after all? Was this the end?

But a moment's thought told him that it was more likely to be further action by the Twisted Rosebud.

Merc bolted frantically back into the main reception rooms.

Pushing through the crowds of frightened people, he looked round in all directions. The focus of the panic and screaming was over by the furthest side table.

A number of people were staggering around, pale and terrified.

On the floor, surely past help, Garnie Porker lay still, unable to move or speak.

Chapter Fifty Five

Merc had felt nothing but dislike for Garnie Porker when he had met him a short while ago.

And what he already knew about the man hadn't helped.

Nevertheless, he knew he had no option but to gallop over to where Porker lay on the floor, kneel down beside him, and do what he could.

No-one else, he couldn't help noticing, was doing anything.

Except standing gazing helplessly, or running aimlessly about screaming hysterically, or looking shocked and horrified.

Merc felt for Garnie Porker's pulse.

There was something there, he thought, but it was very faint.

Without pause for thought, Merc bent over the recumbent man and began mouth to mouth resuscitation.

It wasn't the pleasantest thing he had ever done. And for some time nothing seemed to be happening. Merc kept going.

He felt hopeless, felt like giving up.

Suddenly someone was kneeling beside him.

'I'll take over for a bit, Merc.'

It was the cool, efficient voice of Kyra Hotberthy. Except, Merc noticed, that the cool voice seemed, for once, to have been shocked into a slight tremble.

Kyra carefully replaced Merc and continued the mouth to mouth resuscitation.

It seemed pretty useless.

Then suddenly Merc noticed that the faint flutter under his fingers, where he still held Garnie Porker's wrist, was gradually growing stronger.

Kyra continued to blow air into the man's lungs. Abruptly, Porker gave a funny little gasp, then a gulp.

Merc helped Kyra to raise him up, to help with his breathing, and saw with satisfaction that Garnie Porker was starting to draw in air by himself.

Colour came back into Garnie Porker's face. He opened his eyes, and looked up at Merc.

'Wha – what – ?'

'Don't try to talk,' Merc advised him briefly. Supporting Porker in his arms, he looked round impatiently.

'Has anyone sent for a doctor?'

Apparently not.

'Then do it!'

Mobiles were hurriedly produced and numbers punched in.

Less than ten minutes later, five important looking doctors hurried into the reception room. To be followed a few minutes later by three more.

Clearly, Garnie Porker was going to get sufficient medical care.

Merc watched as the gang of doctors, arguing among themselves as to who should have priority in giving Garnie Porker treatment, arranged for the still weak Chief Executive to be carried to his own room, and busily bustled out after him.

Time to find out what had happened.

Merc looked round for someone who could be expected to have been observant. His eye picked out Kyra Hotberthy as the only possibility.

'So, Kyra, what in Heaven's name is going on here?'

Kyra Hotberthy, her face still pale and shocked looking in spite of her bronze skin, began to explain.

'It might have been another bomb. I think. No way of telling. But one minute Garnie Porker was standing at the buffet table. And the next there was this awful noise, a sort of crackling, and the air was full of a burning smell, and there was Garnie lying flat on the floor. I thought he was dead!'

'So, why just him?'

'I don't know. It can't have been a very powerful bomb, I suppose. Maybe more like an electric shock, now I think of it? Maybe he did something to trigger it off? Set off a detonator that did something to a circuit?'

'What was he doing just before the explosion?' asked Merc.

'Well. He was making a sort of speech. There was this cake, sort of celebrating the tenth anniversary of Worldwide Weapons, right? So Garnie made this speech, and then he struck a match to light the candles on the cake, and then he plunged in the knife to cut it – oh!' Kyra gasped. 'Maybe – do you think? Was there something, like maybe a live wire, inside the cake? Did he make the connection when he cut in with the knife?'

'That seems very likely.' Merc spoke more concisely than usual. 'At least it seems that the bomb, or I think you're probably right, the electric shock, was meant for him, not for everyone here.'

'I guess.'

'So maybe the Twisted Rosebud is learning slightly better ways.'

Merc looked round him again.

The faces of half the people there were expressing shock, but the rest seemed more satisfied than anything else. As if they were quite glad that someone had tried to destroy another human being.

Merc felt a sudden disgust.

Was it worth while trying to help people like this? he wondered. It was a serious question. Wouldn't the world be a lot better without most of the selfish, greedy crowd who were callously watching him, unconcerned and uncaring about what had been happening to a fellow human being?

Suddenly it was all too much.

'Okay, I'm going now,' he announced abruptly. 'Kyra, what about the car? You want to hang on here a while? I'll leave the car for you, then, will I? Okay? I can walk over and pick up my own car from the Company car park, and head on home.'

Then he left the super-sized mansion, and its super-sized crowd of rich and mindless business people, now busily gossiping, but not forgetting to gobble up what was left of the food their host had provided, and drink his champagne. A host who had come within an inch of death. And had been left unaided by every one of them.

Merc didn't like the guy, but he was completely repulsed by the callous selfishness he had felt emanating from the crowd as they had stood, open eyed, watching the action as if it was a film put on for their amusement, and making no effort to help him in his attempt to save Garnie Porker's life.

He felt a fresh wave of anger boiling up in him as he made his way through the streets of the city in the direction of the Company buildings.

No one had seemed to care, or been willing to help in any way, except Kyra Hotberthy. Who hadn't even liked the man, he remembered.

It felt good to walk, after the stifling luxury of the last few hours.

Halfway back, it occurred to him that he hadn't responded to Glooper Houndstooth's message yet.

True, he had been busy. There hadn't been a moment when it would have been easy to fit Glooper in. Moreover, all desire to track down the Twisted Rosebud seemed to have left him since his recent view of the gloating faces round Garnie Porker.

Who was he helping, here?

Who was worth helping?

Wouldn't it have been a good thing if instead of an electric shock aimed at one man, it had been a bomb, and a more powerful one at that? If it had taken out some of those gloaters as well as Garnie Porker?

Wait a minute, Merc, said an inner voice in his head. Take out? You mean, kill, or tear to pieces, or seriously maim and destroy, don't you?

Merc's anger cooled, and was replaced by horror at his recent thoughts. No, nothing could justify that sort of action.

And, anyway, he had asked Glooper to get information for him, and it didn't seem right to ignore Glooper, when he had sent to tell Merc that he had some useful news.

Especially when he knew that Glooper would be fully expecting to be ignored.

And would tell Merc so at some length when he next saw him.

With a sigh, Merc fished out his mobile and messaged Glooper.

r u there? can I cum round?

The reply flashed back a moment later.

yep! cum on.

Merc turned aside, and made for Glooper's coffee shop.

He wondered vaguely what Glooper had found out, and if it was really so important.

Chapter Fifty Six

The shop, as was often the case when Merc called in, was empty except for Glooper himself standing behind his huge coffee urn.

Seeing Merc, he drooped forward, wiping his spotless hands on his shining white apron.

'Mr. S! You've actually come to see me!' he said in his mournful voice. 'So, you aren't too busy, then? You weren't doing something else that mattered? Or even something that didn't matter? Come and sit down. I'll fix you some coffee.'

Merc sat down at an empty table, draped in a shining clean white cloth.

Glooper moved slowly about behind the counter, and presently deposited a brimming coffee cup on the table in front of Merc, with the greatest of care. Not a single spot landed on the white tablecloth.

'I don't know if you'll like this,' he said sadly. 'No-one does, much, I find. But there it is.'

Merc, who tried not to lie as a rule, thought it best to ignore this.

'So. Glooper. You have something for me?'

'Certainly have, Mr. S. Of course, you're surprised, I expected that. I know you didn't think I'd be much use.'

'And?'

Glooper came to the point unexpectedly quickly.

'You wanted some stuff re that guy Spoutforth, Mr. S. It just so happens I was talking about him to one of my mates, well, when I say mate, he's a guy who comes in here regularly, like, I don't know why, and turns out he knew Tonky well, a few years back when Tonky was still editing the Globe. I got this guy chatting yesterday afternoon, and, see, I recorded it for you. Under the table, right, so's he wouldn't know, just in case he raised any objections. Bit fuzzy, but you can make most of it out. Anything you don't catch, ask me. Like, with hearing it sorta first hand, I know what he was saying, mostly. Well, some of it. Well, maybe.'

Glooper sighed his woebegone sigh again.

'More coffee?' he added, solicitously.

'Um. No, ta, this is great,' Merc mumbled, fearful of being forced out of politeness to swallow a second cup. 'So, go ahead, then, Glooper.'

Glooper Houndstooth set a miniature recorder on the table and pressed a button.

There was a strange, buzzing noise.

'You're at the end. That's the blank bit,' said Merc helpfully. 'Go to the start.'

'Technology!' Glooper said, shaking his head despondently. 'Always been a bit allergic to it.'

Merc, wondering how Glooper managed to live in the modern world in that case, took the recorder from him.

He further wondered if Glooper had actually managed to record anything at all.

Merc didn't think of himself as a techno expert, but he'd been working things like this more or less since he was in nappies. He noticed that it was a pretty old fashioned object, very similar to the one he'd been given on his fifth birthday.

A few seconds fiddling and he heard Glooper's mournful voice.

'So, Wilkie, tell me more. Sounds a real interesting guy.'

Glooper managed to make this sound more like 'extremely boring guy,' but Merc realised that Glooper had been doing his best.

Then came another voice, presumably the unknown Wilkie's.

'Yeah, you can say that again. Did more for journalism, did old Tonky, than anybody else I ever heard of. Wasn't content to dish out the stories on the Press Releases, know what I mean? No, Tonky was out there, finding out the true story for himself, or sending one of us to get it.

Didn't mind what the risks were, especially if it was a risk to his staff, ha! ha!

No, I'm joking, he was a fair boss, took lots of the risks himself, right? And some of the stories he brought back were first class, I can tell you. Tonky wanted to make sure the truth got out there, and wasn't just smothered at a high level, see?

He had a story one time nearly shook up the Government, not to mention Big Business.

A corruption scandal, sorta thing.

Tonky had it all set up on the front page, but Buster Panter, the guy who was, like, running stuff right then, swooped down on the Globe Offices and made them wipe the story, and all the backup files too, see, so's it couldn't be used.

He said Tonky had it all wrong, he didn't want to see him with egg on his face, he would sort him out with the true facts, and he claimed he did.

There wasn't any corruption, he said, apart from one guy who was taking backhanders to give a contract to the wrong person, he said, and that guy had been sacked weeks ago. The guy who was Tonky's source was an opportunist who wanted to get into a position of power himself, by bringing disgrace on all his rivals, and manufacturing lies and false evidence about them, and Buster Panter said he was surprised Tonky hadn't seen through him sooner.

Well, Tonky couldn't check up with this guy, Lenny Cudsley, his source, because he had somehow or other disappeared. Didn't turn up until months later, when they found his body in the river, wearing one of them concrete jackets – very fashionable round here, about then, I'm told. Only identified by his chip.

It was suicide, okay? I don't think so.

And Tonky couldn't reconstruct the story, they'd made such a mess of his files.'

Glooper's voice said, *'Maybe just as well for him.'*

'Didn't make much difference in the end. Not long after, he had another snorter of a story, about the links between Big Business and the World Government, not that it would have been exactly news to most people with any sense, but seeing it in black and white might have woken people up a bit.

But this one was too much.

Soon as they heard about it, the Bosses closed the old Globe down.

Buster Panter was the main action man, I heard. Got the rest of them stirred up to get rid of Tonky.

Oh, not the way they dealt with the other guy, Cudsley.

Tonky wasn't put in the river.

But he was deported from Nexus Luxuria, back to the little island he came from, and that was the end of him in politics or journalism, see? Might as well have been dead.

Glooper's voice came again. *I hear he came back, though. Maybe a couple of years, or a year ago?*

Wilkie's voice said, *Yeah, I heard that too. Don't know how he could have managed it, but he always had a lot of good friends, old Tonky –'*

Merc pressed the off switch abruptly.

Two big men had come into the coffee shop, and were sitting down at a nearby table.

Merc, glancing quickly over his shoulder, recognised them as the two members of the renovation team who had tried to evict Seraphina, Lucy, Alexa and Mrs. Bertha Kitt from the Company buildings, to their own discomfiture.

Chapter Fifty Seven

Blott and Sharkin, those were their names. Both quite big, around six feet, and heavily built, giving an impression of strength. One of them over-weight with a round, reddish face and colourless eyes which suggested very definitely that he had less than common sense. The other burly, with thinning carroty hair and a sharp face.

Not particularly bright guys, Merc had thought in his short meeting with them.

Still, he didn't want them, or anyone else come to that, to hear Glooper's recording.

'Hi, Glooper!' one of them called out. Blott, Merc thought. The fattish one with the red face. 'How's about some coffee over here? And an extra size muffin or two, or five.'

Glooper rose carefully to his feet.

Sharkin, his sparse ginger hair flopping over his glistening forehead, smiled obsequiously at Merc.

'It's Mr. Swingly, isn't it? Hi, Merc, how're you doing?'

Merc, slightly surprised, nodded in a friendly way, but didn't feel called upon to say more than, 'Hi.'

Sharkin persisted.

'Some mistake, us not recognising you the other day. We'll know you in future. Won't we Blott?'

'Oh, yes. We'll know you in future,' contributed Blott.

Merc couldn't help thinking there was something strange about the way this was said.

'And I'll know you guys,' he replied.

To his surprise, Blott jerked the coffee cup Glooper had just placed in front of him, and spilt most of the contents on the clean white table-cloth. Glooper looked at the rapidly spreading stain with horror, then hurried to fetch a fresh cloth, which he insisted on substituting for the spoilt one.

'No harm meant, Mr. Swingly!' Blott gasped out, ignoring Glooper's activities.

'Just our little joke, Mr. Swingly!' Sharkin added, grinning savagely.

Blott seized the plate of huge muffins Glooper had just set down on the once more spotless cloth, and stuffed two of them into his mouth at once.

A feat Merc had never observed before.

'Come on, Sharkin!' he said as soon as he could speak. 'I'm outa here!'

Between them they lifted the remaining muffins from the plate, thrust them into their mouths, and made for the door.

'Hey!' Glooper bellowed, managing to insert his small figure between Blott and Sharkin and the doorway, apparently unaware of the risk involved. 'I'm not giving free hand outs here! This ain't the Salvation Army! I'm trying to stay away from the bankruptcy courts for a while, okay? (Though I daresay I'll be there soon enough, mind you.) Two coffees, five whopper sized muffins, pay your check, right?'

Sharkin, plunging a hand into his pocket, pulled out a handful of coins and threw them hastily on the table.

'Keep the change!' he mumbled.

Blott made for the door.

Merc wondered if it was just his imagination, or was there smoke coming out of Blott's mouth?

Glooper rolled forward to examine the coins. By the time he had turned back to them, the two men were gone.

'Weirdos!' Glooper said peaceably. His anger had evaporated as quickly as it had arrived. 'Probably haven't paid enough.' He counted the coins. They added up to more than four times the amount on the check. Glooper wasn't sure if he should be pleased or not. Was there a catch?

He came back and sat down by Merc again. 'I guess he didn't mean to give me quite so much extra cash. Though, mind you, the muffins today were pretty extra special. I get all the leftovers from the cook at Garnie Porker's, see? Me and her are walking out together. That was some stuff called chilli peppers that she gave me, that I thought would spice the muffins up a bit. Great stuff, she said they were. Better than cranberries or blueberries.'

From the street, choking noises could be heard.

'Red hot chilli peppers, I think she said,' Glooper added.

The choking noises were now interspersed with groans.

'Do you think they're enjoying the muffins?' Glooper asked. He went to the door and looked out. Across the street was an old fashioned water trough for thirsty dogs and horses. Blott and Sharkin, side by side, were leaning over it, their faces immersed beneath the water.

'Hey, come and see this, Mr. S!' Glooper exclaimed. Merc moved over to the doorway.

As he and Glooper watched with curiosity, the water began to bubble as if coming to the boil.

Merc quickly lost interest in the two men.

'Come on, Glooper, let's have the rest of this talk.'

'There isn't much more, really.'

Merc pressed the on switch, and Wilkie's voice resumed where he had left off.

He knew a lot of politicians as well as businessmen. The sort who still have their private aircraft, and a secret supply of fuel. One of them might have flown him in. Only a guess, mind. And someone might be keeping him out of sight in one of those big houses they all have. Feeding him, and stuff like that, so's he'd never need to give away his identity, buying things, right?

Sandy McPherson, now. He might be doing some of that. He was a good mate of Tonky's.

The recorder ground to a halt.

'That's it,' Glooper said.

Merc asked, 'You didn't find out anything about Spoutforth's family?'

Glooper looked disappointed.

'Nah, didn't think of it. I might have known I'd get it all wrong.'

'Never mind, Glooper,' Merc said quickly, seeing Glooper's face. 'You did a good job. Really great. I don't know if you want to put this on a professional footing, but I really think you deserve to get something for helping so much. I really appreciate all you've done.'

He offered Glooper a handful of notes, hoping the coffee shop owner wasn't going to take offence. But Glooper only seemed surprised to be rewarded for his efforts.

Merc finished his coffee and stood up to go, shaking Glooper's hand vigorously, and trying to look delighted with the information provided.

As he left the coffee shop, however, he thought back over what he had heard, and realised that most of it wasn't news.

He already knew that Tonky Spoutforth was here in Nexus Luxuria, although he had not, in fact, flown in. Kyra had tracked him down on one of the regular transport ships. He knew that Tonky was being looked after and protected by Sandy McPherson in his luxurious house.

Wilkie's rambling chat had been helpful more by way of background than for anything else.

Extra insight into the motivation of the people who ran the Twisted Rosebud.

Especially the leader, if that was what she was, the Fluffy Kitten.

Tonky Spoutforth's daughter?

But there were considerable problems about that idea.

Tonky was a sick man. He could stay indoors all day and avoid the security cameras which read everyone's identity chip at supermarket checkouts, and such places. But how could Tonky's daughter, if she wanted to take an active part in leading the organisation, and to move about freely, as he knew at first hand she did, avoid being identified, and probably arrested, straight away?

Anyway, enough for one night.

He would head on home, and talk it over with Seraphina. Seraphina was clever and had a lot of common sense as well. She might have some ideas which would help to sort out the remaining questions, even if she couldn't come up with the answers. Then there was Alexa, who thought she knew all the answers, and wasn't so far wrong about that, if it came to it.

He ought to be quite near the Company car park and Headquarters by now, Merc thought. He noticed, looking round him, that he had already been going in more or less the right direction on automatic pilot.

He realised that he had done something else automatically, too. He had taken out his mobile phone.

Yeah.

Time to talk it over with Mr. Brown, as well.

He rang the number.

'MB?'

'Hi, MS!' came the chirpy voice.

'Have you any advice for me?'

'I've already given you all the advice you need, MS. Haven't you been listening?'

'Right, yeah, thanks, MB, but I just –'

Merc broke off for a moment to get his thoughts together.

'Like, what should I do next?'

'Don't worry about that.' There was a funny little laugh. 'You won't actually need to do anything, right now. Things are moving.'

Merc couldn't think of anything to say.

'But, MS!'

'Yeah?'

'You're a good guy. You're doing good. You've been learning a lot. But just one thing you need to learn a bit more about.'

Merc listened.

'That's a good name you have. Ever thought about it?'

'Not as such.'

'Well, think about it now. It's a good name. Merc. But it needs another letter.'

'Why?'

'Yeah,' said Mr. Brown. 'That's right.'

And rang off.

Merc was glad to notice that he had stopped saying 'Ciao!'

Merc walked on. He was thinking hard. He was beginning to feel tired, and quite thankful that he would soon be at the Company car park, and able to drive home, when he became aware of footsteps behind him.

Footsteps which trod heavily in the same direction, but always keeping behind him.

Footsteps which he now realised he had been noticing subconsciously for some time.

Chapter Fifty Eight

Merc stopped and listened.

The footsteps stopped also. But not immediately. Merc was just aware of them for a moment after he himself had stopped.

He walked on.

Presently he realised that he could hear the footsteps again.

It was growing dark.

Merc wasn't exactly nervous.

But he would have felt happier if he had been in a better lit, more populated street, instead of the empty alleyway which he had turned into because it was the nearest way to the Company car park from Glooper's.

Most of the roads in Nexus Luxuria were made for the convenience of cars, even now that since the world wide oil shortage the only cars in existence were run on electricity. But this was a remnant of the pedestrian zones which had long ago been a feature of city life.

It was a narrow, dilapidated alley, paved with brick, stone, and even – originally a decorative feature – with cobble stones.

There were no cars, and no room for anything but two, or at the most three, people to walk side by side.

He stopped again.

The footsteps continued for a moment, then they also stopped.

Merc, who wasn't normally worried about the danger of muggers, found himself growing nervous.

Was there anything he could use as a weapon, if it came to that and he needed one?

Stooping, he lifted a loose cobble stone in his right hand, and swung round to face his pursuers.

'Who's there?' he called out in challenging tones.

Silence.

Merc wondered if he had been imagining things.

Shrugging, he walked on. Not omitting, however, to keep a firm grip on the cobble stone.

Presently he became aware that he could hear the footsteps again.

Suddenly there was a shuffling sound immediately behind him.

Quickly, he swung round, the stone raised in his right hand.

Too late.

Something dark and evil smelling, probably an unwashed item from somebody's linen basket, he didn't want to know more than that about it, was smothering his head and face.

He could see nothing, and found it hard, and not very pleasant anyway, to breathe.

Then hands were grabbing him, and he found himself unable to move, and a moment later a blow on his head put an end to all further thought for the time being.

Merc came to himself in a darkness so profound that he wondered for some minutes if he was still unconscious.

His head was swimming round and he could see a medley of bright lights, vaguely reminiscent of a fun fare, floating about among the darkness. He had no idea at first where he was or what had been happening. Gradually the confusion began to clear. He became aware again of his body, and could feel things.

He was lying on what seemed to be fairly soft carpet, or maybe a rug, he thought. Not on a concrete floor. So. Not an underground cellar, then.

It took him a while longer to clear his mind and to remember what had been happening and how he had got here.

Two people were arguing.

'Like, this is so boooo – ring.'

'So, tough.'

'But we could have a game of cards. Or roll the bones?'

'Hello? Have you noticed that the light's off, Blott?'

'Yeah, but it has an on switch, right, Sharkin?'

'Oh, great, so we turn it on, and when the guy comes to, he sees our faces? Hello? Then we have to chuck him in the river, okay? And then the Boss gets mad at us, because you heard the Boss saying, Blott, or am I wrong, that there was no way we were to damage him, right?'

'Right,' agreed Blott, gloomily.

'So, right, we haven't damaged him. Or not much.'

There was a silence, occupied on Merc's part by some feverish thinking, coupled with relief that Sharkin had thought the thing through before turning the light on. Blott? Sharkin? Where had he heard those names before? They seemed, through his concussion clouded mind, to be vaguely familiar. If his head would stop spinning quite so fast, he thought it possible that he would be able to remember and identify the names, and the people attached to them, quite easily.

He moved one cramped and uncomfortable leg.

The two men seemed to notice the movement, darkness or not.

'Seems to be back to himself, okay,' he heard Sharkin's voice saying.

'So. What should we do with him now?'

'You know the Boss said we weren't to do anything. We just wait, okay, till the Boss gets here.'

Angry as he was, Merc couldn't help feeling a profound relief to hear this.

He rolled his tongue round his mouth, and realised that he wasn't gagged or in any other way prevented from speaking.

'Can't we have some light?' he asked, risking it.

There was a sudden silence.

Not just the absence of voices, but a stillness, a lack of movement.

'No-one wants to let you see their faces,' said a rough voice, which Merc recognised as one of the people, he thought Sharkin, who had been speaking previously.

'Aren't you wearing masks, then?'

'Well. No.'

'I thought all muggers had masks.'

'We have some.' Blott sounded indignant.

'We just haven't got them on at the minute,' Sharkin explained sounding almost apologetic, as if discovered in an oversight.

'Well, if you have some, why not just put them on?' Merc suggested reasonably. 'I guess you'd like a bit of light as much as I would.'

'Okay, Blott?'

'Why not, Sharkin?'

Merc waited.

Then he blinked.

A strong light was flooding into his eyes, forcing him to adjust to its powerful beam.

Two bulldog masks peered down at him where he was lying on the ground.

Well, not exactly on the ground.

He had clearly been carried from the alleyway into a house or building of some sort.

He was lying on a big, soft rug, as he had guessed. A bright, crimson rug, which he thought had been placed there on purpose. This was a hopeful sign.

The Boss, whoever that might be, clearly had some concern for his comfort.

Which seemed strange for someone who hadn't hesitated to attack and kidnap him.

'Um. Sorry for the inconvenience,' said the first bulldog. From the voice, Merc identified him as Blott.

'The Boss will be here any minute now,' said the second bulldog. Sharkin, obviously. 'We don't mean to do you any harm, right? The Boss just wants a few words with you, see?'

'Fine,' said Merc.

He moved his arms and legs cautiously, and noticed that while his arms were securely fastened, his legs seemed to be free.

A mistake, he rather thought.

Struggling round onto his back, he managed to manoeuvre himself into a sitting position.

Meanwhile, there was food for reflection.

Blott. Sharkin. The effects of concussion were wearing off. Even in his present still fuzzy state of mind, he had by now managed to place the names. They were the two members of the renovation team who had been dealt with so successfully by Mrs. Bertha Kitt, Alexa, Lucy and Seraphina.

Presently his head stopped swimming quite so badly, and after some moments of concentration he managed to identify them further.

They were the two men who had come into Glooper's café.

And there was another thing.

He was sure that his captors, now that he saw them in their bulldog masks, were the two henchmen who had supported the Fluffy Kitten at the meeting of the Twisted Rosebud which he had managed to infiltrate. They had been the Leader's right hand men, at that meeting. So Blott and Sharkin were not just some random muggers, as he had thought at first!

They were fairly senior members of the Twisted Rosebud!

Merc's discovery gave him an amazing amount of satisfaction.

They must have deliberately followed him into Glooper Houndstooth's coffee shop, intending to catch up with him in a suitable place.

Not the brightest people, clearly.

They had put on their masks, but had spoken to each other by their names, forgetting that Merc would recognise these.

Merc felt quite pleased with himself.

He wasn't doing too badly, then!

Identifying two senior members of the Twisted Rosebud!

Finding out some stuff that mattered!

Adrenalin flowed through his system in an encouraging flood.

'So, when do you expect this boss of yours to get here?' he asked pleasantly.

Chapter Fifty Nine

'Oh, any minute now,' Blott assured him. 'We rang her on the mobile just as soon as ever we were sure we had you.'

'She really doesn't want to hurt you!' Sharkin added. 'We were told to take great care.'

She? Merc thought, but carefully didn't say it aloud.

What else would they let out if he encouraged them to talk?

'Yeah?'

'She just wants to talk to you!' Sharkin went on. 'She thinks you can be a great addition to our cause, see? Help us do the things we're aiming at. She thinks you've misunderstood our objectives.'

'And she would prefer the opportunity to explain this for herself, strangely enough!' said a cool, sweet voice behind Sharkin and Blott.

A figure came forward into Merc's view.

It was the Fluffy Kitten.

'You can go, now, boys,' she said. 'I can deal with the prisoner by myself.'

'Yes, ma'am!'

'Yes, ma'am!'

The two bulldogs fell over themselves trying to leave, clearly more than alarmed at the idea of causing any more annoyance to their Boss.

'Now, Merc,' said the cool, sweet, voice of the Fluffy Kitten, 'I think you and I can come to a better understanding if we just try to be reasonable, and don't assume that we have to fight.'

She came forward gracefully into the room, as the door closed, not quite with a bang, behind Blott and Sharkin.

'Just one question,' Merc said. 'How do you always know where to find me? How did you know I'd be coming away from Garnie Porker's tonight? And on foot, too?'

'Oh, that was no problem.' The Kitten laughed. It was a silvery laugh, but it grated unpleasantly on Merc's ears.

'Not everyone's on your side who pretends to be,' she said. 'People tell me things. One in particular. She really has you fooled, doesn't she? But it's my team she's on, not yours! I knew you were leaving on foot just as soon as you set out. Heading for the Company car park to pick up your car. It made things quite convenient for me.'

Merc stared at her. Team? There was only one woman on his team, if that was what the Fluffy Kitten meant. Then he asked, 'And what can you possibly want with me?'

'I've wanted to bring you in on our plans for quite some time now, Merc,' the Fluffy Kitten said. 'I think you can add quite a bit to our organisation. I'm sure the aims of the Twisted Rosebud aren't so very different from your own. Remember the truth test you did for us? It showed how close you were to thinking on the same lines as ourselves. Maybe some of our actions aren't what you would choose?'

The Fluffy Kitten, smoothing back the pretty and abundant hair of her mask with a very feminine gesture, moved a little closer to Merc.

'I'm willing to listen to your views, Merc. But I think you, just as much as us, are eager to bring about our objectives. Think of the present situation, with seven multi-national companies ruling the entire planet, and doing things that are destroying us all. Causing pollution, climate change, slavery – under another name – in the Third World factories, and all the rest of the horrors of our modern life style.

'You, like us, find this state of affairs repulsive. You know it needs to be changed. And I know you believe that using drugs, to persuade people that they are quite happy with this way of life, is a bad thing, too. If our ideas about how to bring the necessary changes about don't suit you, then maybe we'll all have to rethink.'

She had gone into speech mode, Merc thought.

Probably said this sort of stuff at the Twisted Rosebud meetings all the time. Not that it wasn't true.

The Fluffy Kitten, clearly aiming for a sweetly reasonable attitude, sat down on the rug next to Merc, leant against the wall beside him with her arms round her raised knees, and waited for his response.

'Yes,' said Merc slowly. 'A lot of what you say is right, no question.'

He leaned back against the wall in turn. Staying well clear of the Fluffy Kitten, however.

Unless he was picking up the wrong signals, and he didn't think he was, he had some experience of this sort of stuff, too much actually, it would be a good idea to stay right outside touching distance.

'You see!' beamed the Fluffy Kitten. Under her half mask, which covered her head and neck, but was cut to allow some freedom to her wide red mouth and pretty chin, she smiled. The mask cast a concealing shadow across her mouth but her small white teeth glinted in the light. 'I knew we would agree when we talked about it.'

'But –' Merc went on.

'But?'

'Yes, but.'

Merc sighed.

How to put across what he wanted to say?

'Who are we to decide who should be destroyed, Kitten?' he began. 'Are we so very good ourselves? Shouldn't everyone be given a chance to change? How do you know that the people you kill wouldn't be very different, wouldn't be ready to help bring about the sort of world you want, if they were given the chance? Given an opportunity to think about it? I haven't always been so very unselfish, myself. I'm willing to bet you haven't either. Why not try talking things out with the guys you think are your enemies? Who knows, you might find they were willing to be your friends?'

The Fluffy Kitten stood up abruptly. Her hands formed themselves into claws.

Instead of listening to Merc, she began to scream. Then her words started to pour out, falling over themselves in her eagerness to express her defiance. Her antagonism, her fury at Merc's words, shrilled through every fierce syllable.

'You don't know what these people have done!' she hissed. 'You don't have any idea how evil they are! The world would be well rid of them!'

'And what about the things you've done, Kitten?' Merc asked calmly. 'Wouldn't the world be well rid of you? Lots of people probably think so.'

'I was wrong!' the Kitten shouted. 'I thought I could make some-thing of you! You're useless! I don't want to talk to you any more! Blott! Sharkin! Come here!'

Merc felt an unwelcome shiver run down his spine.

What had he let himself in for now?

At the same time something went click in his head.

That voice.

He had been sure, from the first time he heard it, that he knew it. That he recognised the speaker.

It was someone he knew quite well.

Blott and Sharkin were coming back. He could hear the heavy, thumping tread.

'Quick!' said the voice of the Fluffy Kitten. 'I want him tied up securely. Safe enough to be left here without guards. Get it done.'

Merc felt himself bundled into a heap, lying on the floor once again. He was still on the soft rug, he was glad to notice. It made things just that little bit better, somehow.

Then the light which had, without him really noticing this, been a source of comfort and strength to him, suddenly went out.

Chapter Sixty

Blott and Sharkin were manhandling him, rolling him from side to side as they rather inexpertly tied his legs together – so much for the tiny hope instilled in him by that amount of freedom, Merc thought ruefully – and thrusting an unpleasant tasting cloth into his mouth. They followed this up by tying another length of cloth round his mouth to keep the gag in place.

Merc began to feel rather hopeless.

'That'll do it, Blott.'

'Can he breathe, Sharkin?' The second voice was more worried, less confident.

'Course he can. Who cares, anyway?'

'Don't think the Boss wants us to kill him. More just give him a scare, like.'

'Oh. Well.'

'Maybe we should loosen the gag a bit. Make sure it isn't over his nose.'

'Fair enough.'

To the relief of Merc, who now realised that he had, certainly, been finding it a struggle to breathe for the last few minutes, one of the men untied the cloth round his mouth and adjusted it so that his nose was clear.

'Okay. Let's go.'

He heard the retreating footsteps of Blott and Sharkin.

Time to think a bit.

The Kitten – and he thought he more than probably knew now who she was – was pretty definitely, as far as he could see, a psychopath.

He didn't think she wanted to kill him.

Everything he knew about her was against that idea.

But even slight opposition had brought about an extreme reaction, an anger beyond the bounds of what was normal.

She would be back later on, he was pretty sure.

Should he pretend to have been convinced by her arguments? To be on her side now?

Would she believe him? Come to that, could he act the part well enough?

He wondered.

Worth a try, maybe.

But it would make it impossible for him to continue to try to make her see sense. In fact, if she thought she had changed Merc's mind, wouldn't that just reinforce her in her awful plans?

He didn't want to be responsible in any way for whatever further atrocities she might carry out.

Then there was what Mr. Brown had said. About not using people, or thinking of them as things.

He had seen how Flacker Winterbotham had changed. A bit, anyhow.

Didn't the Kitten have a right to be allowed to change too, not just to be used, and reinforced in her wrong ideas, just so that Merc himself could escape?

Maybe it would be a better plan to try to loosen his bonds?

Neither Blott nor Sharkin had given any impression of knowing what they were doing particularly well.

The ropes might not be all that well tied.

Merc began to wriggle and to pull his hands apart in an effort to loosen the ropes.

About ten minutes later, he reluctantly came to the conclusion that all he was doing was tightening the knots.

If he could have managed to get his hands free, he could have got hold of his mobile phone and rung Mr. Brown, he thought.

His mind drifted back to some of the things Mr. Brown had said.

Something about being able to go anywhere that Merc went, wasn't there?

Perhaps Mr. Brown already knew where Merc was, then?

He couldn't speak through the gag.

But perhaps that didn't matter?

He thought, 'Okay, Mr. Brown, if you're there, what about it?'

'Merc,' said Mr. Brown's voice, inside Merc's head.

'Hey, listen, can you get me out of this?'

'Haven't you any ideas yourself, sonny Jim?'

'No. Not really. If I could get my hands free –'

'Yes?'

'– I'd give that Kitten a lesson she needs!'

'And don't you need any lessons, boy?'

'Well. Yeah. I expect so.' Merc felt his face go red, inside the gag.

'Just a tip, sonny. There's justice. Like, giving people what they deserve. And there's mercy. Like, giving them another chance. You can pick which one you want to run with. But it has to be the same for everybody, right? Mean to say. You can't pick mercy for yourself, and justice for all the rest of the guys, see?'

'Yeah.'

'So, which are you going to go for?'

The thought of being given what he deserved made Merc's blood run cold.

'But. Doesn't justice matter, then?'

'Oh, sure it matters. But he's taken care of all that. Himself. I thought you knew that?'

Merc's jaw would have dropped except that it was held securely in place by a bunch of someone's smelly washing.

'Well, it's up to you, sonny boy. No-one's twisting your arm, get it?'

Mr. Brown's voice faded away.

He hadn't offered any real help, Merc reflected.

Or maybe he had?

Merc was still thinking it through when he heard a tiny sound.

It seemed to come from high up on one of the walls.

A slight, scratching noise.

Then, abruptly, this became a fearsome clatter as something apparently fell with a thump onto the edge of the floor, where there were stained wooden boards, Merc had noticed, instead of the thick rug where he was lying.

A moment latter, there was another, more careful thump.

There was the sound, he thought, of someone standing up.

A moment later he was aware of that someone's breath close to his face, as the unknown person bent over him.

Then a soft, whispering voice.

'Merc? Are you okay?'

It was Alexa.

Chapter Sixty One

Merc, trying incautiously to speak through his gag, almost choked himself.

Then he was aware of the gag loosening, as Alexa's hands worked quickly, releasing him in an amazingly short time.

'Keep still!' she commanded. 'And keep quiet. We don't want them to hear us.'

Merc reflected that after the clatter she had made on her entrance, anyone likely to hear them must have already done so, but he said nothing, except, 'If you put the light on you'll find it easier to see what you're doing.'

It took Alexa rather a longer time to untie Merc's arms and legs.

But at last it was done.

Merc rolled over cautiously, flexing cramped muscles and letting out an occasional unplanned 'Ow!'

'How on earth did you get here, Alexa?' he whispered when he was able to concentrate on anything but his cramps.

'Through the ventilator on the wall up there.'

'But how – what I meant was, how did you know where to come?'

'Seraphina was getting worried about you,' Alexa explained. 'But there was no way she could go out looking, with Lucy to cart along. And she didn't fancy leaving me to look after Lucy either. So I went next door and asked Bertha if she would drive round a bit and see if she could see you. And she offered – I didn't hint at all, well, hardly at all – she offered to take me along.'

'What about Silo and Flacker?'

'They were scared to go. They don't want to be seen, right. And Seraphina didn't trust either of them to look after Lucy, even with me there, like. Not since Flacker tried to help change her nappy and ended up putting it round both her legs, so as she couldn't walk. He's a looper, but I kinda like him. So does Bertha, I reckon.'

Alexa grinned.

'So, what then?'

'Well, me and Bertha scouted around for a while and then we saw you sorta mooching along in the back alleyways, like, and we stopped the car to get to speak to you. But, hey, just as we were getting out, we saw these two hoods jump you. Bertha could have dealt with them, I guess, but by the time she'd got herself well out of the car – she, like, sticks a bit, see – they had you gripped under the arms and were hustling you along pretty fast. So we thought we'd better just chase after them, like, till we found out what was up.'

'And?'

'They had you inside the building here before we could catch up. We hung about outside for a bit and looked around. Guess you know it's t he Company offices? – then we tried different ways of getting in, but it was all like locked up, so then I climbed up the outside balcony and on up to the top, and right, there was this ventilator thingy, so I reckoned I could like get through if the frame wasn't there. So, like, I punched it out with both my feet, holding on to the roof edge with my hands, and sorta swinging at it, see? And it fell out pretty quick, so then I got in and glad to say the floor wasn't too far down and I was able to jump okay without like breaking any bones. I think.'

She grinned again.

'Bertha thought maybe she could find a way in if she went on looking, a way big enough for her, I mean.'

'Alexa, you're a star!' Merc told her fervently. 'But, I don't want to be a pain, but what now? Aren't you trapped as well as me?'

'No way!' Alexa said cheerfully. 'If we can't get this door opened from inside without a key, and, hey, most doors open that way, right? They're only locked from the outside – then we'll wait for those guys to come back, and lam into them. You and me can sort them out, no problem. Pity Bertha isn't inside with us, mind you. Like, she'd soon show them what's what.'

While agreeing that Mrs. Bertha Kitt would be an undoubted addition to their action team, Merc was slightly worried about the rest of Alexa's plan.

'Let's look at the door first,' he suggested sensibly.

Unfortunately, the lock, unusually as Alexa had correctly pointed out, didn't in fact open from the inside without a key.

'Okay,' said Merc. 'This is what we do. One of us on each side of the doorway, as soon as we hear any sound of them coming back. I know they were only leaving me for a short while to let me think things over. You take my jacket, and I'll use my shirt.' He began to remove the articles as he spoke, reflecting that it was a good thing he had been dressed up for Garnie Porker's get together, in a buttoned shirt and jacket instead of just his usual T shirt. Pity, mind you, that he hadn't got a T shirt type vest on, under his shirt. It would make things less embarrassing. Still, first things first. 'As they come in, throw the clothes over their heads and hold them, and try to trip them up at the same time. They'll be disorientated for long enough for us to get out of the door and slam it on them. I hope. Then, if the key's in the lock, we'll turn it, and run for it. They aren't specially bright guys. I think we might get away with it.'

'Shouldn't we hit them over the head?' Alexa asked hopefully.

'With?'

Certainly the room seemed completely bare of suitable weapons.

Looking round, Merc recognised it as an empty storeroom. Quite a big one.

The sort of place where incoming goods were held in a halfway house before being transferred on, to the right office.

Apparently, everything had recently been shifted to its new home.

Or else the place had been deliberately emptied to make a good prison cell.

'Anyway, Alexa, when you hit someone hard enough over the head to knock them out, you can kill them or cause severe brain damage. I'm not doing that. Even to Blott and Sharkin. They probably do have some sort of brains that could be damaged. Well, I think Sharkin has, anyway.'

'Gosh, is that who it is?' asked Alexa excitedly. 'The two guys who tried to stop us getting out of the Company building yesterday? Hey, I really wish Bertha was here! She'd show them!'

'Never mind Bertha. Here, take this jacket. Do you think you can manage to get it over someone's head and trip them? Maybe you'd better practice on me.'

So the next ten minutes were spent rather strenuously, until Merc, stumbling again to his feet, and breathing deeply, pronounced that they were both expert enough.

Then it was a question of waiting until Blott and Sharkin, with or without the Fluffy Kitten, Merc couldn't help reflecting, arrived.

And if the Fluffy Kitten was there as well, making the odds three to two, and one of the two pretty small, he would just have to hope for the best.

When they had been sitting, one on each side of the door, for what seemed a long time but which Merc's watch told him had only been about five minutes, Alexa said, 'Shouldn't we put the light out?'

'Good idea.'

Then, sitting in the dark, the waiting seemed longer than ever.

They both heard the sound at the same moment.

Someone approaching along the corridor outside.

Chapter Sixty Two

Merc leaned forward cautiously across the closed door to give Alexa a little warning tap on the arm, and at the same time realised that Alexa was leaning forward to signal to him.

As their hands collided in the darkness, Alexa gave a stifled giggle which Merc was hard put to it not to echo.

Then came the sound of the key grating in the lock.

Merc leapt to his feet, hoping Alexa was remembering to do the same.

A moment later two shadowy figures crossed the threshold, one after the other.

Merc allowed the first man – from his plump outline it was Blott – to come forward into the room far enough to allow Alexa a chance to attack his comrade. Then he flung his shirt over the first man's head, keeping his arms pinned to his sides, and with his left foot kicked his legs from under him. Blott, if that was who it was, tumbled to the ground with a terrified squawk, and Merc felt the other man, tripped equally neatly by Alexa, follow him down.

Then they were out of the room, pulling the door shut behind them, and Merc was feeling for the key.

Unfortunately that was where things stopped working just so well.

No key.

Right.

'Come on!' he said briefly to Alexa. Seizing her arm he began to hurry her along the corridor before their two captives could recover.

Someone was blocking their way.

With a groan, Merc saw that it was the Fluffy Kitten.

Not a problem, he thought.

Grabbing the Kitten's shoulders, he started to push her aside.

Then stopped.

Something was sticking into his ribs.

Looking down, Merc didn't need the Kitten to tell him that it was a gun.

'Run, Alexa!' he yelled.

'Don't run, Alexa,' the Kitten said coolly. 'Unless you don't mind if I shoot Merc Swingly, here. And then you, after that, of course. Unless you think you can get past me and to the far end of this quite long corridor before I can aim for you?'

Alexa, her way of escape impeded by Merc and the Kitten, stood frozen.

Behind her, the door finally burst open, and Blott and Sharkin emerged, holding on to each other for support and looking rather battered and the worse for wear.

Now what?

Merc groaned.

Surely it wasn't still too late to escape.

The gun jammed tightly into his ribcage alerted him to the realities.

'This is too stupid,' he said after a moment. 'You can't keep us here for ever. People will be coming in in the morning.'

'I've no intention of keeping you here,' said the Kitten. 'This was only a temporary cell. I've found the Company headquarters a useful extra place for meetings and so on. It's so central, and so above suspicion, and so stupidly without scanners. But I have my own little place for anything more permanent. Blott! Sharkin! Pull yourselves together and take the little girl's arms. I hope you can manage her between you!'

In spite of the sarcastic note in the Kitten's voice, Sharkin ventured to disagree.

'Ah, but you don't know what she's like, boss! A real little wildcat! We had enough trouble with her last time!'

'That's right,' corroborated Blott heavily. 'At least the other one isn't here. That big woman the size of an elephant who kicked Sharkin where she shouldn't have. No-one could deal with her, Boss –'

'Get moving!' said the Kitten, in a sharper tone than any Merc had as yet heard from her. 'She won't struggle. She doesn't want me to shoot her friend, does she?'

'No,' said Alexa quietly.

'Go in front with her. Then I can keep an eye on her as well as him. Go on!'

Blott and Sharkin, still muttering, took hold of Alexa's arms and began to march her into position in front of Merc and the Kitten.

The five of them started to move slowly along the corridor.

Merc turned over several plans in his head.

None of them seemed to avoid the outcome of a bullet through his own ribs, or through Alexa. Which ruled them out.

Presently he spoke.

'I wish you'd explain something to me.'

'Yes?'

'I know now who you are, you see. But I still don't know if you are really Tonky Spoutforth's daughter? And if you are, how you manage to go about under a different name? Is there some way of overwriting the chip? And have you discovered it?'

The Kitten laughed.

'So you know who I am, Merc?' she said. There was, Merc noticed, a bitter sound to her voice. 'It took you long enough, didn't it? Perhaps you just haven't paid enough attention to me most of the time?'

'Sorry,' Merc mumbled.

'Oh, don't worry. I think you'll pay a little more from now on, won't you?'

She laughed.

'No, I'm not Tonky Spoutforth's daughter. Your gossiping sources got that wrong. I'm his step daughter. That's why I have a different surname. But he's been as good as a real father to me. That's how I've thought of him since he married my mother, after my own father died. And that's why I had to do something about those brutes who ruined his life, just for the sake of their own selfish need for power and money. Do you understand?'

'Yes, I do,' said Merc honestly. He also knew that the Kitten's story was very familiar, and he knew where he had heard it. There was something wrong here. And something which didn't seem possible. He asked the necessary question. 'There's still one thing. How come Spoutforth's daughter stroke step daughter was called Rosebud, but you manage to use another first name now – don't you?'

'Easy.' The Kitten's voice was scornful. 'It's a nickname. I picked it myself, and made everyone use it, for years, since my fourth birthday, in fact. That was when I realised that the rose is not only my favourite flower, but the most important and popular flower with everyone else as well. But as you apparently know, I'm not using it just at present. Quite a handy thing, to be able to go back to your real name, the name on the chip, when you want to hide your personality, don't you think?'

Chapter Sixty Three

They were coming to the first break in the corridor.

Just ahead of Alexa and her captors, another corridor cut off to the left, round a sharp corner.

The Kitten, Merc thought, was becoming distracted.

Telling him about herself had taken her attention, however slightly, off the gun, which he imagined wasn't pressed quite so tightly against his ribs.

Was there a chance here?

It happened as Blott and Sharkin, dragging the angry faced Alexa, began to pass the entrance to the branch corridor.

With the sort of roar a tiger might have given leaping from its open cage, a huge figure loomed up beside them, came swooping out from the corridor they were passing, and landed with all its weight on both Blott and Sharkin, knocking them to the ground, with Alexa between them.

It took Merc a moment to realise that it was Mrs. Bertha Kitt.

Blott and Sharkin were quicker off the mark.

'It's her! It's her!' they shrieked in unison.

Struggling to their feet, and brushing off the grasping hands of their attacker, Blott and Sharkin, frantically pushing each other out of the way, and tripping over each other's legs and feet at frequent intervals, went plunging away up the corridor, waving their arms and still shrieking, with Mrs. Bertha Kitt in hot pursuit.

They left the helplessly laughing Alexa still sprawled across the floor where they had all fallen.

This was his chance, Merc realised.

The gun was no longer pressed closely into his ribs. Instead, the Kitten was waving it wildly in the air.

With a quick movement, Merc knocked the gun out of the Kitten's hand. It flew somewhere across the floor with a clatter.

The Kitten lost her head.

'Blott! Sharkin! Come back!' she howled. Abandoning the need to keep Merc under the control of her gun, in fact abandoning the gun, she threw caution to the winds and went leaping up the corridor after her two henchmen and their attacker.

Merc, taken aback by the swift change in the position, stood where he was while Alexa, picking herself up, came rushing up to him.

'I told you Bertha was looking for another way in,' Alexa said between giggles. 'Looks like she found it.'

'Now what?' Merc wondered aloud.

'Maybe we should get moving, ourselves.'

They hurried down the corridor, ready to dodge out of sight, at the least sound of the Kitten coming back, for now there were any number of open doors and side corridors around.

But the only person to appear was unmistakably Mrs. Bertha Kitt, whooping exultantly to herself as she bounded along.

'Lost them!' she announced as soon as she came within bellowing range of them. 'They know their way round this place a lot better than me.'

'Bertha, great to see you! Thanks!' said Merc.

'You too, young man. So, why are you wandering round here half naked, eh?'

'Oh. I used my shirt and jacket to catch those two guys. Me and Alexa.'

'Well,' said Mrs. Bertha Kitt, 'not wanting to be too critical, but it seems to have been a waste of your outfit. Not that I'm complaining, mind.' She gave Merc a friendly wink.

Merc, blushing, hurried to change the subject.

'How did you get in, Bertha? And can we all get out that way, do you think?'

'Should think so,' said Mrs. Bertha Kitt cheerfully. 'The front door was closed, but with all the damage to the reception area, it didn't really make much difference. I soon found that it was off its hinges, only really propped up and secured by ropes. So I was able to lift it the rest of the way off, quite easily. I put it back, so no-one would realise I'd come in, but it won't take too long to lift again.'

Merc, who had a clear memory of the enormous front door, gazed at his neighbour in awe. He made a silent decision never again to keep her lawn mower for longer than he had promised, before returning it.

'That's great, Bertha!' he said. 'Shall we go, then?'

'Like that?' asked Alexa, grinning.

Merc blushed again.

'Better pick up my shirt and jacket first, okay?' he mumbled.

So they did.

Then they made off down the corridor towards the reception area.

Merc was fairly sure he knew the way, even though this was a part of the Company buildings he was less familiar with. Halfway there, they came around a corner and almost tripped over Blott and Sharkin, collapsed in a heap against each other and leaning against one of the walls.

Merc examined them carefully.

'They're all right,' he said finally. 'They've been knocked unconscious, seem to have banged their heads against the wall, but they look as if they'll be coming round fairly soon. They both seem to have been hit, probably by the Fluffy Kitten. Maybe she lost her temper with them, for making such a mess of things, and just lashed out at them. I wouldn't be too surprised at anything that lady would do when she loses her temper.'

'Do you want to take them with us?' Mrs. Bertha Kitt asked, but Merc shook his head.

'Not a lot of point,' he said. 'They can't tell us anything I'm not pretty sure about already. But maybe we should have a look round for the Fluffy Kitten. I wouldn't mind finding her. There are still quite a few things I want to talk to her about.'

They looked round.

In fact they went on looking round until both Alexa and Mrs. Bertha Kitt were heartily sick of looking, and Alexa was driven to reminding Merc that Seraphina was waiting anxiously for his return.

But of the Fluffy Kitten, there was no sign.

Chapter Sixty Four

Merc's car was still safely parked in the Company car park.

'Get in,' he said, 'and I'll drive you back to wherever you left your own car, Bertha. Then maybe we can all get home.'

The roads were emptier than usual. It didn't take too long to get back.

When they reached the house, the door flew open at the sound of the car and what seemed like a mob of people came pouring out.

On further inspection, it was only Seraphina, Flacker Winterbotham and Silo Clotson.

But when they had crowded back indoors, together with Alexa and Mrs. Bertha Kitt, all talking busily, Merc realised with a groan that any hope of a quiet night would have to be abandoned.

The first half hour was spent in recounting, to constant interruptions, questions and corrections, what had been happening to Merc, and then to Alexa and Mrs. Bertha Kitt as well, since Merc left for Garnie Porker's party.

Then it was Seraphina's turn.

Everything, she said, had been quiet enough up until an hour ago.

Flacker and Silo had decided to go out for some fresh air. They had taken a stroll through the neighbouring streets, and Seraphina had seized the opportunity, first, to check on Lucy, and second, to sit down and relax. She was too polite to say so, but reading between the lines, Merc knew that she had been pretty pleased to get a bit of time to herself at last.

Then Flacker and Silo had come bursting back in. Full of dismaying news.

At this point Silo and Flacker, speaking in antiphonal bursts, though not particularly musically, took over the story.

'We were followed!'

'We thought they were going to jump us!'

'Flacker tripped over a lump of stone and swore, and I definitely heard someone whispering, 'That's him!''

'So Silo said, 'Run!' and, right, it looked like the best option.'

'We only just got back here in time! We could hear them after us!'

'So, let me get this right,' Merc asked, 'you thought you were being followed by some dangerous guys, so you brought them back here to Seraphina and Lucy?'

'We hadn't anywhere else to go!'

'They were after us!'

'It's okay, Merc,' Seraphina intervened. 'No-one's tried to attack the house or anything. Maybe whoever it was lost the trail?'

'They were just behind us!' Silo babbled.

'So, now they know where Flacker's hiding? You, too, Silo, if they're interested, right?'

'Well, yeah, MS, but they don't seem to be doing anything about it so far,' Flacker pointed out hopefully.

'Who was it? Have you any idea?'

'Well, like, we sort of thought, the Twisted Rosebud?'

'Okay, Silo, brilliant suggestion, but I meant, like, actual people as such?'

'Oh.'

'And how many were there?'

'Oh, a lot!'

'No, Silo, I guess just two. But we didn't know if maybe they were armed?' Flacker shot a shamefaced look sideways at Mrs. Bertha Kitt, who immediately responded.

'Quite right, Flacker. No sense in getting into a fight right then. Now we have a good chance to plan something. I vote we set up a trap, and if they decide to break in again, then we'll be able to catch them.'

Flacker smiled gratefully.

'So,' said Merc finally, 'we don't know who it was, but at a good guess, not Blott and Sharkin, who were still knocked unconscious at the time, and not likely to be the Fluffy Kitten, who wouldn't have had time to get here from the Company Offices. People we don't know, I guess.'

'Yes,' said Seraphina, 'maybe just minor characters. Members of the Twisted Rosebud, without many scenes, and no speaking lines. That would explain why they didn't attack the house straightaway.'

'And it means they probably went off to report to someone senior. Maybe to the Kitten herself, if they could find her,' said Merc slowly. 'So when they get organised, they'll be back with reinforcements. Or someone will.'

'So, how about this trap?'

'Yeah, good idea, Bertha. Why don't you girls, and Silo, work something out? I guess we have a bit of time yet. Meantime, Flacker and me need to have a bit of a talk. Okay, FW?'

Flacker Winterbotham, looking puzzled, followed Merc out of the room.

'Let's go up to the roof, FW,' Merc suggested. 'It's nice and cool up there.'

They climbed the outside steps and stood side by side on the roof, leaning over the narrow parapet on their elbows, and gazing out over the multiplication of bright lights which was all that showed of Nexus Luxuria by night.

'Funny how beautiful it looks from up here, Flacker,' Merc said. 'Not so good when you get a bit closer up, right?'

'I suppose.'

'Lot of pretty unhappy people there.'

'Yeah?'

'Oh, definitely. Why do you think that would be, FW?'

'Um. Something to do with the Company, do you mean, MS? The way we run their lives?'

'Well, what do you think, Flacker?'

There was a long pause.

Merc began again.

'I was speaking to the PR/PR today, at Garnie Porker's do.'

'Yeah?'

'Fancy Linnet. Pretty little thing.'

He paused.

'I told her about the changes the Company was making to its factory, and its whole system, in the Tiny Isles.'

Flacker said nothing.

'I told her,' Merc went on deliberately, 'that the changes had your full agreement and support.'

'Oh, sure thing, MS,' Flacker Winterbotham babbled hurriedly. 'Quite right. Changes needed. Quite right.'

Merc smiled.

'I also told her,' he went on. 'That there would be some big changes here at headquarters in Nexus Luxuria, at the Company, Worldwide Productions, as well. I didn't give her any details, but I said you'd be announcing them soon. Okay by you, FW?'

'Um. Sure. Sure. Er. What changes, exactly, MS?'

'That's something you and me need to discuss, FW. But maybe the sort of changes that might make these Twisted Rosebud guys a bit less eager to blow your head off.'

Flacker Winterbotham gulped.

'And maybe the sort of changes that might make those people out there –' he waved one hand at the lights of Nexus Luxuria – 'might make their lives not quite so unhappy. Mind you,' Merc added conscientiously, 'I've always thought whether people are happy or not depends mostly on what they're like inside. Still, we can take away a lot of the outside obstacles to happiness, I guess.'

He smiled at Flacker Winterbotham's face, with its expression of horror.

'I should think Bertha would be pretty pleased with you, too,' he added.

Flacker's face brightened.

'Oh. You think?'

'Definitely.'

'Oh. Well, good, then.'

'And now,' Merc said, 'maybe we should be going down. See what these guys have worked out by way of a trap.'

They made their way back to the living room.

With some difficulty.

The outside door which opened into the kitchen was solidly blocked with large objects which seemed to range from the fridge to the kitchen table.

Using more than normal strength, they succeeded in pushing these far enough aside to allow Merc, by far the slimmer of the two men, to squeeze painfully through the narrow opening.

A final shove allowed Flacker Winterbotham just about enough room to follow him.

The kitchen floor was littered with a fine selection of Lucy's toys, mostly either ball shaped, so that Merc found his feet sliding each time he stepped on one, or large and cumbersome. Flacker Winterbotham, not at his most poised, and at no time a contender for the world's most graceful heavyweight, successfully managed to trip over first the doll's house, and then the push along horsy.

The noise level was sufficient to bring Mrs. Bertha Kitt to the other side of the closed door into the next room, bellowing at the top of her voice,

'Stop right there! I warn you, I'm armed!'

'Bertha! It's us. What's going on?'

'Merc?'

'Yes! Did you forget we were up on the roof?'

'Ah.'

Seraphina's voice cut in.

'You wanted traps, Merc. Traps are what you've got.'

'Well, you'd better let us in, now,' said Merc, trying for patience.

'Silo, can you help me move this?' said Bertha's voice.

Then there was a thunderous sound of heavy furniture being dragged away, and a few minutes later, Alexa's head could be seen peeping round the now partly open door.

'Did you block up the outside kitchen door again, when you came through?'

'No,' said Merc grimly. 'Okay, FW, maybe you would do that?'

Flacker Winterbotham, moving to obey, tripped over the toy baby pushchair this time, to the amusement of everyone except himself.

Then he and Merc squeezed with difficulty into the living room.

'The kitchen door mustn't be jammed enough,' said Alexa anxiously. 'Silo, maybe you could move the washing machine against it as well?'

Silo, nodding happily, went to carry out his task.

'We've put lots of stuff against the front door as well,' Alexa explained. 'And more of Lucy's toys to ambush anyone who manages to get in. But we didn't think anyone could move the barricades enough to get through any of the doors.'

'Apparently we were wrong,' said Mrs. Bertha Kitt. 'But for sure, they won't be able to get in without being heard.'

'And we've done our best with the upstairs windows, too,' Seraphina added. 'We've put high furniture against them all, heavy stuff that would be hard to move if you're trying to climb through a window at the same time.'

'And we broke some glasses and put the sharp pieces along the window sills,' Alexa said brightly. 'That was my idea!'

'And what's this about being armed?' Merc demanded. 'Where did you get a gun, Bertha?'

'I picked up that one the Fluffy Kitten dropped,' Mrs. Bertha Kitt explained. 'Didn't you notice? I saw it when we went back for your shirt. I tucked it into my belt under my jacket in case it might come in useful.'

Merc looked at her helplessly.

'Well, for goodness sake, Bertha, don't go firing it,' was all he could find to say.

'I won't,' Bertha promised. 'That is, unless I really have to.'

Merc didn't feel very reassured. However.

'I guess we should make out a plan of defence, now,' he said. 'Let's sit down and get comfortable. How about some coffee or something?'

'I'll put the kettle on,' offered Seraphina. 'Before we block up the door from here to the kitchen again.'

'Only thing is there don't seem to be any chairs or things to sit on. They're all blocking the doors.'

They ended up scattering cushions in a circle in the middle of the room, and making themselves as comfortable as possible on these.

Merc, not usually very observant about that sort of thing, couldn't help noticing that Flacker Winterbotham and Mrs. Bertha Kitt were sharing a double sized bolster type cushion.

They seemed very happy about it.

'So,' he said, nursing his mug of coffee in both hands. 'Has anyone any ideas about what we should do?'

Chapter Sixty Five

'I think we should stay together in this room. As Bertha says, no-one can get in without us hearing them,' said his wife.

'But, Seraphina,' objected Alexa, 'it won't be much good hearing them if we can't stop them getting in.'

'I've got this gun, don't forget,' Bertha put in enthusiastically. 'We can threaten them and tie them up.'

'Maybe,' said Seraphina doubtfully. 'Doesn't that depend how many of them there are?'

'The Twisted Rosebud don't usually send more than one or two on a mission,' offered Silo.

'Right, you have inside information, Silo,' Merc remembered. 'So, maybe only two people attacking at once. But what if they send in reinforcements?'

There was a gloomy silence.

'I think we'll have to face that if it happens,' decided Merc finally.

Seraphina stood up.

'I think I'll just go and check on Lucy,' she said, and left to go up to Lucy by the open plan stairway in one corner of the room.

'Why not phone the police?' Alexa asked. 'I mean, this is some fun, okay, and I don't want to spoil things, but maybe?'

'Like we told you before, Alexa, the police are useless,' Merc explained kindly. 'They do nothing these days except take bribes and book cars for parking in the wrong place. You must have been hearing stories about the old days. People who are well enough off, like FW here, have their own private bodyguards now, and the rest of us rely on things going on well enough in general, right?'

The three others who had lived in Nexus Luxuria for longer than Alexa nodded agreement.

'That's one reason why I keep a dog,' added Mrs. Bertha Kitt. 'Pootles would scare away any intruder who tried to break into my house, that's for sure!'

Suddenly she stiffened, and put her hand to her mouth.

'Pootles! Oh, my goodness, I forgot all about him! I must go and fetch him at once! He'll be all on his own all this time, and missing his mummy!'

'Bertha, he'll be far safer in your house than here,' Merc said reasonably. 'You can't possibly risk going out there right now. Anything could happen.'

'I'll go,' said Flacker Winterbotham suddenly.

And was rewarded by a beaming smile from Bertha.

'Flacker, that's really sweet of you. But Pootles doesn't know you, he might not be easy to get hold of.'

And how, thought Merc.

'No, I'll go for him myself.'

Mrs. Bertha Kitt surged to her feet.

'No, Bertha,' said Merc. 'We can't afford to have anyone leaving here. The Twisted Rosebud may be just outside. Suppose they grab you as you come out? Suppose they push their way in once the barricades have been moved to let you through? It won't work, okay?'

'But Pootles!' wailed Mrs. Bertha Kitt, no longer seeming strong and tough. Her lower lip trembled. 'What if they go next door? I couldn't bear it if anything happened to him.'

More than one person in the room shared the thought that if any of the Twisted Rosebud went in next door, it wouldn't be Pootles who would regret it.

'What's wrong, Bertha?' asked Seraphina, coming back down the stairs.

'Pootles!' wailed Mrs. Bertha Kitt. 'They won't let me go out to fetch him from next door! Ooooh!'

'Sorry, Bertha,' said Seraphina. 'I forgot to tell you. Pootles is sleeping happily in his basket in Lucy's room. I fetched him after you and Alexa went to find Merc. I thought it might be a good idea to have him here.'

'Oh, Seraphina!'

'No-one will get into Lucy's room without us knowing, that's for sure.'

'And without being scared witless, too,' Silo contributed thoughtlessly, then hastily began to mumble apologies in the face of Mrs. Bertha Kitt's glare. 'I – I – mean – he's a great watch dog – !'

'Never mind all that!' Merc interrupted hastily. 'Now, is there anything else we should do now?'

'How about a game of cards?' suggested Silo.

'No, I meant – ' began Merc. Then realised that it wasn't such a bad suggestion.

'Right on, Silo,' he said instead. 'Where did we leave the pack?'

They were halfway through their third game of Cheat – and Flacker Winterbotham was proving to be extremely expert, not entirely to Merc's surprise. So far, he had been beaten only by Alexa – when they heard the noise.

It was, as Mrs. Bertha Kitt had pointed out, something that couldn't have been missed.

A loud crashing sound, accompanied by howls of agony.

It sounded, Merc thought, like someone who had put his knee down heavily on large sharp pieces of broken glass, jumped hurriedly back, and then fallen backwards, with his ladder, from the height of a first story window.

Which was not surprising, since that was what it was.

The intruder, whoever he was, and Merc rather hoped it was Sharkin, didn't seem to have been killed.

Dead people didn't shout so much.

There were further sounds, whisperings, shushing, and then what were probably the footsteps of several people stealthily withdrawing to a safe distance.

'It worked!' Alexa cried gleefully. 'I knew the broken glass would fix them!'

'Quiet!' ordered Merc sharply. 'We want to hear what they're planning next. They won't give up as easily as that.'

Everyone listened intently.

But there was nothing to be heard except an indecipherable muttering and some hard to make out movements.

Presently these died away.

Chapter Sixty Six

'Okay,' said Seraphina, 'I'm going up to check on Lucy again. It wasn't her room, but it might have woken her up.'

'Fine,' said Merc absently. He was wondering if there was any way he could get a message out to the Fluffy Kitten, that is, if she was outside. He took out his mobile and looked at it thoughtfully.

Just then it rang.

Kyra Hotberthy.

'Hi, Kyra.'

'MS. Where are you?'

'At home, Kyra. Where else?'

'Oh. I was worried. I heard a rumour –'

'Oh?'

'That you'd been mugged. Or whatever.'

'Where did you hear that?'

'Oh, I don't know. People talking, that's all.'

'Oh.'

'So. It wasn't true? You're okay?'

'I'm fine, Kyra.'

'You sound strange, MS. Something's been happening, right?'

'Don't you know, Kyra?'

Kyra's voice sharpened. 'How would I know?'

'Just wondered.'

'Okay, we need to get together and talk,' Kyra said angrily. 'I'm coming round, okay? I'll be there in half an hour.'

She rang off.

Merc was still standing looking at his phone when Seraphina came back down.

'Lucy and Pootles are both fast asleep,' she reported. 'But the window of our room's badly cracked, Merc. Looks like it was bashed with something, before the broken glass on the window sill did its work.'

'Good work, there, Alexa,' put in Merc. 'And the rest of you, right?' he added hastily in the face of annoyed looks from the other planners.

'Listen,' he went on quickly. 'I think I've got a pretty good idea about who runs the Twisted Rosebud now. I sort of definitely know who the Fluffy Kitten is.'

'Well, aren't you going to tell us?' demanded Mrs. Bertha Kitt.

'Yes, right, sure I am. I've had several ideas, okay? See, her voice sounded familiar all along. But I couldn't just place it. I think she changed it a bit, made it more sort of forceful, when she put the Kitten mask on. But still, it had to be someone I know, see? There's this Reta Glutt woman from the Board, I thought it might have been her, but this is a case where size definitely matters. And her voice isn't right. She's, like, loud, and I don't think she could keep the volume down enough. Not all the time. It's hard to do that when you're naturally loud.' He tried not to look towards Mrs. Bertha Kitt.

Who immediately said, 'Oh, I don't know. Not that I've got such a loud voice myself, but if I had, I'm sure I could keep it down for the sake of a disguise –'

'Of course you could, Bertha!' Flacker Winterbotham encouraged her enthusiastically, then, as she looked at him suspiciously, 'not that it's loud enough to really count, Bertha! You have such a soft, gentle voice –' he babbled, until Merc helpfully shut him up by continuing his explanation.

'Then there's Fancy Linnet, the PR/PR girl, she has a soft enough voice, and I wondered about her for a while, but somehow, it didn't fit. It had to be someone I knew well. Then it dawned on me.

'It's –'

He was interrupted by a loud crash.

Broken glass from the window of the living room splintered all round them.

They looked down, frozen, at a round metal object which someone had hurled through the window. Probably everyone recognised it at once. A grenade.

It lay on the floor at their feet, spluttering and hissing.

For a second no-one moved or breathed.

Then Silo lumbered to his feet. Moving faster than Merc would have believed possible, he swooped down upon the grenade. Scooped it up. And in one athletic movement hurled it back through the window in the direction it had come from.

'Silo! No!' shouted Merc.

Too late.

There was a second's pause while the grenade travelled through the air.

Then an unearthly scream, almost drowned by the noise of the explosion.

Merc leapt for the window, flung it open, and scrambled through, followed closely by Seraphina and Alexa, then, not so closely, by the other three.

There were sounds of running steps.

The rest of the Twisted Rosebud, all those who could, were leaving.

Fast.

It seemed likely that none of them would be back.

But on the ground, a hundred feet away from the window, the grenade had found its target.

The tattered remains of someone.

Someone scattered in bits over the surrounding area.

Merc knelt down. And found himself weeping.

Seraphina put her arm round him.

'I didn't mean it,' Silo was saying in horrorstricken tones. 'I just wanted to get it out of the room before it went off. I didn't mean this to happen.'

'It's the Fluffy Kitten, isn't it, Merc?' asked Seraphina quietly.

'Yes.'

They could see that there were still some remnants of a furry mask. They were clinging to the strangely untouched face above the shattered body.

'But who is it?' Alexa asked frantically. 'Do we still have no idea who it is?'

'Merc knows,' Mrs. Bertha Kitt told her.

'Yes. I know,' Merc said. He pulled the remains of the kitten's mask gently away from her face. 'I should have known all along. It's the girl who used to be my assistant. It's Hyacinth Duckworthy.'

Chapter Sixty Seven

They were interrupted.

Driving furiously, Kyra Hotberthy swung round the corner in her bright scarlet car.

She parked at an angle and leapt out.

'What's happening? What's happening?'

Then she saw the remains of Hyacinth Duckworthy, scattered across the road, and was silent, staring.

No-one felt much like speaking.

Finally Kyra pulled herself together.

'I heard the explosion,' she said. 'I thought –'

'You thought what?' asked Merc quietly.

'I thought the Twisted Rosebud might have got you or FW.'

'But instead it was your boss, Kyra?'

Kyra's jaw dropped.

'Hey, no, MS. You've got it all wrong.'

'You're telling me you aren't part of the Twisted Rosebud, Kyra? That you haven't been working with Hyacinth all along? That was a clever little act you put on with her, the night Silo and I went to your meeting. Stand up and have a row with the Fluffy Kitten – with Hyacinth. Pretend to be against her. How could I possibly suspect you then? You saw me come in, didn't you, Kyra, and you recognised me in spite of the mask. So you set me up. Threw me off your trail.

'But there were too many other things. Too many coincidences. Too many times when you knew where I would be, and then so did the Twisted Rosebud. The night when we were to meet at your office, before going off to the Tiny Isles. And the Twisted Rosebud was waiting for me. And today, when you knew I was going to Garnie Porker's, and exactly when

I left on foot, and the Twisted Rosebud were able to grab me again. For instance.'

'MS, you've got it all wrong. Don't you see that Hyacinth knew as much as I did about where you would be? If not more? I'm certain she knew you were coming to the office that night!'

Merc suddenly remembered telling Hyacinth that he had a meeting in the office with Kyra. He had been delighted to have an excuse not to take her out to dinner, hadn't he?

'And surely you've seen how against the Twisted Rosebud I've always been?' Kyra spoke earnestly. They looked at her.

She looked around in turn at the circle of accusing, or in Silo's case puzzled, faces.

'Maybe.' Merc spoke slowly. Now that he saw Kyra again, for the first time since his suspicion of her had crystallised, he was suddenly unsure again. Something in him still insisted that Kyra was someone he should trust. 'I know you've helped me sometimes. When no-one else bothered to. But one thing's sure, Kyra, you're going to have to do a lot more explaining. Hey, why don't we go inside? Not much point in standing in the street.'

'What about poor Hyacinth?' Seraphina spoke for nearly the first time since the explosion. 'We can't just leave her here.'

Merc stepped forward and put his jacket over as much of the shattered body as he could.

'We'll need to let someone know. She'll have to be taken away. Cremated. But meanwhile, I guess we could all do with a hot drink of some sort.'

They trooped inside. Merc made the necessary phone calls.

'Will anyone else try to attack us?' asked Alexa.

She was shivering, and her eyes had become big and luminous.

'I don't think so,' Merc tried to reassure her. 'I think that's the end of the Twisted Rosebud. I don't see guys like Blott and Sharkin carrying on without their boss to give them a regular shove. Still, there may be some tougher ones. Do you know, Kyra? That's where I need to hear more from you! I guess we'll leave the outside barricades in place just for now. But maybe we could open up the way into the kitchen.'

'More coffee for everyone?' asked Bertha, when some of the furniture blocking the door from living room to kitchen had been shifted. She was holding Flacker Winterbotham's hand tightly. 'Let's you and me make it, Flacker.'

They went into the kitchen together, pushing aside the remains of the heavy furniture which still partly blocked the way.

'Aren't they sweet?' said Seraphina. 'Did you see how he was holding her hand? Don't you think we should all do that far more, Silo?'

She cast a meaningful glance at Merc, evidently aiming her words at him.

'Um,' said Silo. 'Er – I don't think I know her really well enough yet, do I, Seraphina?'

Merc tried not to laugh. He could hear Bertha's voice faintly from the kitchen as she murmured in Flacker Winterbotham's ear, 'That could have been you, Flacker, couldn't it? Thank heavens it wasn't!'

'It could have been all of us,' Merc said vigorously, turning to the others. 'If it hadn't been for Silo. Silo's a real hero. He saved all our lives.'

Silo brightened up a little. 'I didn't mean for to kill anyone, MS,' he said. 'I just grabbed the thing and sort of chucked it back, just to get it away.'

'I know, Silo,' Merc said quietly. 'It's just the way things worked out. But I don't think that grenade was meant just for Flacker. Oh, he was part of the target, certainly. But if it had gone off, the grenade would have killed everyone in the room. We were all so close to it. And I think the Kitten knew exactly who was in this room. And meant to kill all of us.'

There was a pause.

'Well,' said Seraphina briskly, 'I can't offer any of you a chair until the barricades come down, but do grab a cushion, everybody. And let's hear from Kyra, and get this business sorted out as quickly as possible.'

They settled themselves in a circle.

'You're right, I need to tell you about my own part in all this, MS,' began Kyra Hotberthy. 'But first off, I'd be glad if you could fill me in a bit. What exactly has the Kitten – I suppose we should start just calling her Hyacinth, but it seems so strange! – what has she been telling you? And what made you think I was on her side?'

'Let's wait for the coffee,' said Alexa quickly. She was still shaking. 'I – I don't feel up to much yet. Maybe it'll help.'

'This,' remarked Kyra, 'is where most people would have a round of pink pills. And probably some whisky. But as you'll remember, Merc, neither you nor I believe in popping pills all day as a way out of our problems. And I guess that goes for Seraphina too? Don't know about the rest of you?'

Merc saw Silo looking puzzled. But then, nothing new there.

'Let's leave all that until later, when we've got a hot drink in us, like Alexa says, and when Flacker and Bertha can hear it at the same time,' he said quickly. 'Hey, here comes the coffee.'

Chapter Sixty Eight

They settled themselves in a comfortable circle on the cushions spread round the floor, nursing their hot coffee in hands which were still inclined to shiver. The effects of shock hadn't yet worn off.

Seraphina asked, 'How did you know it was Hyacinth, Merc?'

'I should have known it was her the first time I heard her voice,' Merc admitted. 'It was really familiar. For a while I wondered if the voice that I seemed to know so well was Kyra's, but then it occurred to me that Kyra has a slight accent. So her voice isn't at all like the one I heard. Then, at the meeting, when I saw Kyra and the leader, the Fluffy Kitten, together, it was clear that the familiar voice definitely wasn't Kyra's.

'So why was this voice so well known to me, and yet not easy to recognise? I worked it out that it was because when the person was dressed in her Kitten disguise, she sounded so much more in charge. So different. So much the Boss. It threw me for a long time. But when she had me caught and locked in that storeroom, she sounded much more like her normal self, and suddenly it clicked.'

'She locked you in a storeroom?' questioned Kyra Hotberthy. 'Tell me more!'

'Don't you know?'

'No. I don't.' Kyra glared at him.

So Merc reluctantly explained, yet again, what had been happening to him since he left Garnie Porker's.

'And I know she said something that made you suspect me,' Kyra Hotberthy said quietly. 'So what was it?'

'She mentioned knowing I would be leaving my car in the Company car park and heading back there. And she said she'd got the info from someone – a female someone – who I thought was on my team. But who wasn't, really.' Merc spoke reluctantly. 'Who else could that have been, Kyra? And who else knew?'

'She was lying, Merc! She's always been jealous of me,' added Kyra in a quiet, reflective voice. 'It's as if she knew –' She broke off for a moment. Then she said more vigorously, 'And Hyacinth knew you were going to Garnie Porker's! She gave you the invitation! She saw us leave in the Company car. After that, she would only have to set some-one on to watch, and to follow you when you came out.'

'Oh.' Merc looked at her. 'I suppose that's what Blott and Sharkin were doing. I know they followed me into Glooper's Coffee Shop. I guess they were following me all the time, back from when I left Garnie Porker's. Right.'

'And as for me knowing where you would be, and then the Twisted Rosebud knowing –' Kyra paused. 'Don't you realise Hyacinth Duck-worthy kept track of you all the time? It was a regular joke on the grape vine. She was nuts about you, MS. That's why she wanted to get you involved in the Twisted Rosebud. She wanted you working with her, close to her.'

Seraphina – who was gradually getting back to normal – made a sound like 'Ho!' But decided, in the circumstances, to say no more.

'I found it hard to believe Hyacinth was the Kitten,' Merc said. 'But once I'd recognised her voice, I knew for sure. Even though she sounded different. It was so clearly her, once I knew. She said I should have known straight away. I just never paid enough attention to her. I guess that's true.' He sighed.

'And a good thing, too!' Seraphina interpolated in an annoyed voice.

'I can't help feeling sorry for her,' Merc added. 'After all, her father was treated really badly, and it's only natural she should have been angry on his behalf –'

'Her father?' interrupted Kyra.

'Yeah. Tonky Spoutforth. Her stepfather, really.'

'Her stepfather!' Kyra Hotberthy exploded. Red in the face. 'So that's what she told you!'

They all stared at her in surprise.

Kyra recovered her usual calm. She sipped slowly at her coffee, then looked up. 'Listen, MS,' she said. 'I didn't mean to tell anyone this, because it obviously makes me an even more suspicious character, but I think it's time the truth came out. Hyacinth Duckworthy wasn't Tonky Spoutforth's stepdaughter. I am.'

Six pairs of eyes opened wide in amazement.

'She told me,' said Merc slowly, 'that her surname was different, because he was her stepfather. And that she called herself Rosebud, because roses were her favourite flower. A flower she liked better, though she didn't quite say this, just implied it, than her real flower name, Hyacinth. It seemed to make sense.'

'Oh, it makes sense, all right. But it's a pack of lies.'

'I did wonder,' Merc admitted. 'Her story was so much like the one you told me, Kyra, about your own life. Why was that, do you know?'

They waited.

'Tonky Spoutforth was my Dad's best friend,' Kyra said. 'When my Dad died – as I told you when we met, Merc – Tonky married my mum. My mum was completely shattered. Couldn't have faced looking after me. Her health was ruined by the so-called Happy Honey pills. She died quite soon afterwards. So Tonky looked after me instead, right? He brought me with him to Nexus Luxuria when he moved here and set up the Global Recorder. He called me his little Rose, or Rosebud. No particular reason. Just a pet name.'

'Oh.'

'Yes. Hyacinth used to work for the Globe at one time. She hero-worshipped my Dad. Tonky, I mean, I thought of him as my Dad by then. All his staff hero-worshipped him, okay? When he was fired, I remember hearing that she burst into Company headquarters and made a major row. Then she disappeared for a year. When she turned up working with you, MS, I recognised her, from a couple of times when I went into Dad's office, years ago, to get a lift home with him during the school holidays. But I didn't bother to say anything. I thought she had got over her fit, and just wanted a quiet job.

'She never seemed to recognise me. I was away at University, of course, for several years, after the Company head hunted me, so she never really met me as an adult. But I wondered, just now, if deep down she sort of half recognised me when I came back to Nexus Luxuria with Flacker Winterbotham, as his PA, when he got the new job as Chief Executive of the Company after the takeover.

'It seems as if she half knew who I was all the time, without really realising she did. Maybe that was why she was always so jealous of me, and tried to turn you against me. So, hey, I got it wrong. She hadn't got over anything. She was always plotting quietly away in secret.'

'She wanted to be Tonky's daughter,' Merc said slowly. 'That's why she stole your life story, Kyra, and pretended it was hers. So Hyacinth wasn't Rosebud, after all?'

'No,' said Kyra. 'She was the Twisted Rosebud. But I was the real Rose.'

Chapter Sixty Nine

'And you didn't set up a conspiracy to get back at the company for what they did to your Dad?' Alexa asked.

'No.'

Kyra looked round at them.

'But I have to admit.'

She paused again. This was difficult, Merc could see.

'I knew my Dad had come back, and was staying with Sandy McPherson. And I knew he was dying. He'd no idea of revenge or anything. He just wanted to end his days in Nexus Luxuria, where he'd lived and worked for so long. Funnily enough, right? But it made me so angry to see what the Seven Companies had done to him. I really wanted to teach somebody a lesson. Especially Flacker Winterbotham, since he was the new Chief.

'I got myself unto Flacker Winterbotham's staff as soon as he got the appointment, with the idea of getting close to him, and using that to get back at him somehow.' Kyra flushed. 'Not very good. Sorry, Flacker.'

Flacker Winterbotham started, went red about the ears in his turn, and spoke. Merc had never heard him speak like that before.

'It's me that should be saying sorry, Kyra. I've used everybody. Never thought about anyone but myself. I – I –'

He broke off, and Mrs. Bertha Kitt cuddled his head on her shoulder, and said, 'There, there, pet.'

Merc, who knew Flacker Winterbotham had changed a little bit, but wasn't expecting anything so wholesale, stared in amazement.

This change was definitely a genuine end of year clear out, not just a few unreal reductions on a load of bought in cheapies.

Then he looked back at Kyra Hotberthy.

'But, Kyra,' he said. 'I still can't help wondering –'

'Why I was always on the spot when the Twisted Rosebud went into action?' Kyra smiled. 'Well, there's a reason for that. Though I'm not sure if you'll believe it. But I hope you will. I've been trying to tell you for a long time. I meant to, that night at the office, but your head was so groggy that I thought I'd better leave it. Then I came along to your room to tell you, just after we arrived in the Tiny Isles, but that didn't work out either, if you remember. And after that, you seemed suddenly to have got suspicious of me – I didn't know why.'

'That was Hyacinth,' Merc realised. 'Warning me against you! She did that several times. So, are you going to tell me now whatever it is?'

'Yes,' said Kyra. She hesitated, still obviously nervous. 'I've been scoping the Twisted Rosebud out for a long time. I picked up some stuff on the grapevine. Like, being FW's PA, people told me stuff. Thought I could put a word in for them, maybe. So, hey, I kept an eye on what was going on.'

'Why?' asked Merc.

'Why?'

'Yeah, what was it to you?'

'Well, I'll tell you.'

She paused.

'It was all tied up together with what the Companies had done to my Dad, wanting to do something to them, and wondering if these Twisted Rosebud guys could be the people to help me. But the more I found out about them, the more I saw they weren't. They seemed to me to be just as evil as the Companies, in a different way. Blowing up innocent people – well, people as innocent as anyone ever is, right? – people who just happened to be in the wrong place at the wrong time. It made me question my whole plan of getting back at the Companies.'

'So you never thought your Dad – Tonky Spoutforth – was the real le der of the Twisted Rosebud?'

'No way. He just wasn't that sort of guy.'

'That was all a bluff?'

'Hey, it wasn't my suggestion!'

'No, right, it was Silo's,' Merc remembered.

'I just did the research for you. Though mind you, I have to say that I knew all along Tonky was back, and staying with Sandy McPherson. But I couldn't tell you that, not without giving away my connection to him. I wasn't ready for that just then.'

'So. The whole thing with the Fluffy Kitten, getting her to take us to see Tonky Spoutforth – ?' Merc paused.

'But that was you, wasn't it, Merc? Not me?' Kyra reminded him. 'It was really awkward for me, actually. I was still trying to keep Tonky right out of it. I didn't want to risk him landing in more trouble. I knew enough about the Twisted Rosebud then to have made up my mind that I wasn't on their side. But I didn't know who the Kitten was, or anything. I still wanted to find out more. And there was something else. I had another reason for wanting to find out.' She paused. This was the hard bit.

Time for a little thinking, Merc realised. Why had he been so suspicious of Kyra Hotberthy? Even after he knew that it wasn't her voice which sounded familiar?

He was clear now that it had been because of the ideas about her put into his head by Hyacinth Duckworthy. Both as herself, and then, later, as the Fluffy Kitten.

And yet, all the time, hadn't there been something inside him struggling to believe that Kyra wasn't on the wrong side? Something that was trying to tell him that he really should be trusting her, working with her?

Something to do with Silo Clotson – ?

'I – well, I'd been given a sort of task to do. I, like, I had this dream,' Kyra said awkwardly. 'Before this all started. Well, sort of a dream. I don't know what you'd call it, really.'

Merc and Seraphina shot each other looks of wild surmise.

'It was the end of the world, see? Rocks bouncing off each other –'

'Flying dishwashers,' contributed Merc.

'People's heads exploding,' went on Kyra.

Seraphina and Merc glanced surreptitiously at Silo Clotson, who, however, appeared oblivious.

'A big sort of Dinosaur,' Kyra said.

'– with flappy wings –' Seraphina added.

'And a face like Nosher Boggs the bookie.'

'And a green light.'

'And a warning.'

'And a message –'

'Go back.' This was Merc.

'A second chance. An opportunity for people to make choices!' Kyra said.

'Hey!'

'You had it too!'

'But did you – ?'

They stared at each other.

'So that was why you said that about Silo's head! That evening in the office!' Merc shouted. 'And I thought I'd misunderstood you! But I hadn't! No wonder I thought we should be working together!'

'Until you started suspecting me,' Kyra put in.

'Yeah.' Merc felt ashamed. Mr. Brown had told him to trust his instincts. And he knew now that his instinct, all along, to trust Kyra, had been right. If it hadn't been for Hyacinth Duckworthy's insinuations, he would have trusted Kyra all along.

'So, we all had the same dream? Or whatever?' said Seraphina. 'How could that possibly happen?'

'So what's the big surprise?' said another voice.

Mr. Brown.

Unnoticed by anyone, he had appeared, and was standing, mobile in one hand, complete with immaculate business suit and red baseball cap, leaning nonchalantly against the barricade just inside the living room door.

Chapter Seventy

'Did you think you were the only ones?' asked Mr. Brown. He was grinning in the familiar way.

'Well. I thought. Yes, I suppose –' Merc stuttered.

'I suppose not,' said Mr. Brown. He grinned even more broadly.

'As if!' he said.

They looked at him.

'Everyone gets that chance,' said Mr. Brown. 'All of you. You, Flacker. Bertha. Silo. Alexa. As well as the people who have the actual warning dream. You've all had a chance. If it hasn't been Gryphon Longfellow getting in touch directly, it's been guys like Merc, or Seraphina, or Kyra, passing on the message. Don't pretend you've never heard them!'

Faces were red. Heads were hung.

'But, MB.'

'Yes, Merc?'

'I don't know about the rest of the guys. But, right, I didn't do much of a job of passing on the message. I – I – I suppose I thought no-one would believe me. Or whatever.'

'You didn't do everything you could, Merc,' said Mr. Brown. 'But, hey, you did a fair bit. It's okay, boy. What did I tell you about mercy? It's for you, as well, okay?'

'Right,' he added briskly, 'so, now, I guess we won't hear any more from the Twisted Rosebud. Without their leader, they wouldn't have much idea. I take it you aren't still suspecting poor old Kyra, here, of being involved? No? Good! But the way things are, the way the Seven Companies are running this planet, there'll be another lot along any minute, right, not prepared to put up with things the way they are, wanting to bomb the companies out of existence? So, what still needs to be done, what changes do we need, to take away their motivation?'

There was a blank silence.

'Quite a lot, I guess,' said Flacker Winterbotham eventually.

'Correct!' said Mr. Brown. 'And who would be the best people to do it?'

Flacker looked at him.

'Um. Me, for one. Maybe?' he hazarded.

'Good! You've got it, FW!'

'But. I'll need help!

'So? You have Merc and Seraphina. And Kyra. Not to mention Alexa. And Silo. And – I understand –' Mr. Brown suddenly looked coy, 'Mrs. Bertha Kitt, am I right?'

'You certainly are!' said Bertha briskly. 'Don't you worry about a thing, MB. I'll soon sort this man out!'

'Course you will, Bertha!' beamed Mr. Brown. 'Well, hey, I'll just leave you to get on with it, then? Any time you want me, you've got my mobile number, okay?'

'But, Mr. Brown!' Alexa suddenly erupted. Her basic stubbornness, her refusal to be put down or fobbed off, pushed her forward, where adults, if not angels, feared to tread.

'Yes?'

'Will any of this make any difference? Isn't the world going to end sometime soon, anyway?'

Merc gulped.

That was exactly what he would have said.

If he had had the guts.

Okay, he had guts, all right.

Which were currently making their churning, uncontrolled presence felt in the depths of his stomach, in no uncertain terms.

Mr. Brown beamed at the girl.

'It may not make a difference to the big picture, Alexa. But what about the flip side? The B movie?'

'Huh?'

'The small picture, Alexa? How things go for a few – or maybe even a lot – of individuals? Who have to get by in this sorry old world in the meantime? Before everything gets sorted out?'

'Oh.' Alexa thought hard. 'I never thought about that,' she admitted.

'It's the individuals who count, Alexa. What sort of lives they have. It was meant to be great, see? But people mucked it up. And sooner or later, it'll get to the stage where it has to stop. But meanwhile. How individual lives go. That's what matters. The big picture, yeah, I'm not saying it's not important. But you can leave that to him, okay? What you need to worry about is the small picture. The old men and women, and the kids, and the guys – male and female, that is, don't get me wrong, if anyone was ever politically correct, it's him, okay? – the people struggling with a daily job – well, it's all of them, get me?'

Suddenly Mr. Brown wasn't there any more.

'Whew!' said Flacker Winterbotham, wiping the sweat from his forehead with the back of his hand. 'Some guy, right?'

'Right!' agreed Merc fervently.

They stared at each other for a moment, wondering what had just happened. Wondering what came next.

Mrs. Bertha Kitt was the first to recover.

'Amazing!' she said. 'We seem to have got ourselves a job, right everybody?'

'Seems so, Bertha,' Merc said, and the others nodded.

'Now,' said Mrs. Bertha Kitt briskly. 'Let's get down to it. We'll start by making out a list of the changes we want to see in this bad old state of affairs, right?'

'Right, Bertha,' they all agreed.

And, with all of them giving a bit of help to Silo – finding him a pencil and paper, working on his spelling, et cetera – they started, hopefully, to make out a list.

'Some sort of set up to give the homeless people somewhere to live,' was Merc's first contribution.

'A proper redundancy package for company employees,' suggested Silo.

'A law to reduce the number of Happy Honey pills people can buy.' That was Kyra.

'Proper control of factory buildings and hours of work on the Tiny Isles,' Alexa said firmly.

'A free press, with the old Global Recorder operating again,' Flacker surprised everyone by saying.

'Great idea, Flacker!' enthused Mrs Bertha Kitt. 'And how about more places where little doggies are allowed to run free?'

They looked at her. But no-one liked to comment.

And so the list continued.

A blueprint for change.

Not for a perfect set up.

But, just maybe, for a possibly slightly better world.

In the small picture.

About the author

Gerry McCullough has been writing poems and stories since childhood. Brought up in north Belfast, she graduated in English and Philosophy from Queen's University, Belfast, then went on to gain an MA in English.

She lives just outside Belfast, in Northern Ireland, has four grown up children and is married to author, media producer and broadcaster, Raymond McCullough, with whom she co-edited the Irish magazine, *Bread*, (published by *Kingdom Come Trust*), from 1990-96. In 1995 they published a non-fiction book called, *Ireland – now the good news!*

Over the past few years Gerry has had more than fifty short stories published in UK, Irish and American magazines, anthologies and annuals – as well as broadcast on *BBC Radio Ulster* – plus poems and articles published in several Northern Ireland and UK magazines. She has also read from her novels, poems and short stories at several Irish literary events.

Gerry won the *Cúirt International Literary Award* for 2005 (Galway); was shortlisted for the 2008 *Brian Moore Award* (Belfast); shortlisted for the 2009 *Cúirt Award*; and commended in the 2009 *Seán O'Faolain Short Story Competition*, (Cork).

Belfast Girls, her first full-length Irish novel, was first published (by *Night Publishing*, UK) in November 2010 (re-issued July 2012 by *Precious Oil). Danger Danger* was published by *Precious Oil Publications* in October 2011; followed by *The Seanachie: Tales of Old Seamus* in January 2012 (a first collection of humorous Irish short stories, previously published in a weekly Irish magazine); *Angel in Flight* (the first Angel Murphy thriller) in June 2012; *Lady Molly and the Snapper* – a young adult novel time travel adventure set in Dublin (August 2012); *Angel in Belfast* (the 2nd Angel Murphy thriller) in June 2013; *Johnny McClintock's War* in August 2014, *The Seanachie 2: Norah on the Beach* in September

2014; *Hel's Heroes* in June 2015 and *Dreams, Visions, Nightmares* (a collection of eight literary and award-winning Irish short stories), in January 2016.

More info at: *__http://gerrymccullough.com__*

Gerry
McCullough

author of *Danny Boyd, Lady Jane*, etc.

Belfast Girls

The story of three girls – Sheila, Phil and Mary – growing up into the new emerging post-conflict Belfast of money, drugs, high fashion and crime; and of their lives and loves.

Sheila, a supermodel, is kidnapped. Phil is sent to prison. Mary, surviving a drug overdose, has a spiritual awakening.

It is also the story of the men who matter to them –

John Branagh, former candidate for the priesthood, a modern Darcy, someone to love or hate. Will he and Sheila ever get together? Davy Hagan, drug dealer, 'mad, bad and dangerous to know'. Is Phil also mad to have anything to do with him?

Although from different religious backgrounds, starting off as childhood friends, the girls manage to hold on to that friendship in spite of everything.

A book about contemporary Ireland and modern life. A book which both men and women can enjoy – thriller, romance, comedy, drama – and much more ….

"fascinating ... original ... multilayered ... expertly travels from one genre to the next"
Kellie Chambers, Ulster Tatler (*Book of the Month*)

"romance at the core ... enriched with breathtaking action, mystery, suspense and some tear-jerking moments of tragedy.
Sheila M. Belshaw, author

"What starts out as a crime thriller quickly evolves into a literary festival beyond the boundary of genres"
PD Allen, author

"a masterclass, and a vivid dissection of the human condition in all of its inglorious foibles"
WeeScottishLassie

Belfast Girls

Gerry McCullough

Published by

Precious Oil
PUBLICATIONS
www.preciousoil.com/publications

Chapter One

Jan 21, 2007

The street lights of Belfast glistened on the dark pavements where, even now, with the troubles officially over, few people cared to walk alone at night. John Branagh drove slowly, carefully, through the icy streets.

In the distance, he could see the lights of the *Magnifico Hotel*, a bright contrasting centre of noise, warmth and colour.

He felt again the excitement of the news he'd heard today.

Hey, he'd actually made the grade at last – full-time reporter for BBC TV, right there on the local news programme, not just a trainee, any longer. Unbelievable.

The back end shifted a little as he turned a corner. He gripped the wheel tighter and slowed down even more. There was black ice on the roads tonight. Gotta be careful.

So, he needed to work hard, show them he was keen. This interview, now, in this hotel? This guy Speers? If it turned out good enough, maybe he could go back to Fat Barney and twist his arm, get him to commission it for local TV, the Hearts and Minds programme maybe? Or even – he let his ambition soar – go national? Or how's about one of those specials everybody seemed to be into right now?

There were other thoughts in his mind but as usual he pushed them down out of sight. Sheila Doherty would be somewhere in the hotel tonight, but he had plenty of other stuff to think about to steer his attention away from past unhappiness. No need to focus on anything right now but his career and its hopeful prospects.

Montgomery Speers, better get the name right, new Member of the Legislative Assembly, wanted to give his personal views on the peace process and how it was working out. Yeah. Wanted some publicity, more like. Anti, of course, or who'd care? But that was just how people were.

John curled his lip. He had to follow it up. It could give his career the kick start it needed.

But he didn't have to like it.

* * *

Inside the *Magnifico Hotel*, in the centre of newly regenerated Belfast, all was bustle and chatter, especially in the crowded space behind the catwalk. The familiar fashion show smell, a mixture of cosmetics and hair dryers, was overwhelming.

Sheila Doherty sat before her mirror, and felt a cold wave of unhappiness surge over her. How ironic it was, that title the papers gave her, today's most super supermodel. She closed her eyes and put her hands to her ears, trying to shut everything out for just one snatched moment of peace and silence.

Every now and then it came again. The pain. The despair. A face hovered before her mind's eye, the white, angry face of John Branagh, dark hair falling forward over his furious grey eyes. She deliberately blocked the thought, opening her eyes again. She needed to slip on the mask, get ready to continue on the surface of things where her life was perfect.

"Comb that curl over more to the side, will you, Chrissie?" she asked, "so it shows in front of my ear. Yeah, that's right – if you just spray it there – thanks, pet."

The hairdresser obediently fixed the curl in place. Sheila's long red-gold hair gleamed in the reflection of three mirrors positioned to show every angle. Everything had to be perfect – as perfect as her life was supposed to be. The occasion was too important to allow for mistakes.

Her fine-boned face with its clear translucent skin, like ivory, and crowned with the startling contrast of her hair, looked back at her from the mirror, green eyes shining between thick black lashes – black only because of the mascara.

She examined herself critically, considering her appearance as if it were an artefact which had to be without flaw to pass a test.

She stood up.

"Brilliant, pet," she said. "Now the dress."

The woman held out the dress for Sheila to step into, then carefully

pulled the ivory satin shape up around the slim body and zipped it at the back. The dress flowed round her, taking and emphasising her long fluid lines, her body slight and fragile as a daydream. She walked over to the door, ready to emerge onto the catwalk. She was very aware that this was the most important moment of one of the major fashion shows of her year.

The lights in the body of the hall were dimmed, those focussed on the catwalk went up, and music cut loudly through the sudden silence. Francis Delmara stepped forward and began to introduce his new spring line.

For Sheila, ready now for some minutes and waiting just out of sight, the tension revealed itself as a creeping feeling along her spine. She felt suddenly cold and her stomach fluttered.

It was time and, dead on cue, she stepped lightly out onto the catwalk and stood holding the pose for a long five seconds, as instructed, before swirling forward to allow possible buyers a fuller view.

She was greeted by gasps of admiration, then a burst of applause. Ignoring the reaction, she kept her head held high, her face calm and remote, as far above human passion as some elusive, intangible figure of Celtic myth, a Sidhe, a dweller in the hollow hills, distant beyond man's possessing – just as Delmara had taught her.

This was her own individual style, the style which had earned her the nickname 'Ice Maiden' from the American journalist Harrington Smith. She moved forward along the catwalk, turned this way and that, and finally swept a low curtsey to the audience before standing there, poised and motionless.

Delmara was silent at first to allow the sight of Sheila in one of his most beautiful creations its maximum impact. Then he began to draw attention to the various details of the dress.

It was time for Sheila to withdraw. Once out of sight, she began a swift, organised change to her next outfit, while Delmara's other models were in front.

No time yet for her to relax, but the show seemed set for success.

* * *

MLA, Montgomery Speers, sitting in the first row of seats, the celebrity seats, with his latest blonde girlfriend by his side, allowed himself to feel relieved.

Francis Delmara had persuaded him to put money into Delmara Fashions and particularly into financing Delmara's supermodel, Sheila

Doherty, and he was present tonight in order to see for himself if his investment was safe. He thought, even so early in the show, that it was.

He was a broad shouldered man in his early forties, medium height, medium build, red-cheeked, and running slightly to fat. There was nothing particularly striking about his appearance except for the piercing dark eyes set beneath heavy, jutting eyebrows. His impressive presence stemmed from his personality, from the aura of power and aggression which surrounded him.

A businessman first and foremost, he had flirted with political involvement for several years. He had stood successfully for election to the local council, feeling the water cautiously with one toe while he made up his mind. Would he take the plunge and throw himself whole-heartedly into politics?

The new Assembly gave him his opportunity, if he wanted to take it. More than one of the constituencies offered him the chance to stand for a seat. He was a financial power in several different towns where his computer hardware companies provided much needed jobs. He was elected to the seat of his choice with no trouble. The next move was to build up his profile, grab an important post once things got going, and progress up the hierarchy.

In an hour or so, when the Fashion Show was over, he would meet this young TV reporter for some preliminary discussion of a possible interview or of an appearance on a discussion panel. He was slightly annoyed that someone so junior had been lined up to talk to him. John Branagh, that was the name, wasn't it? Never heard of him. Should have been someone better known, at least. Still, this was only the preliminary. They would roll out the big guns for him soon enough when he was more firmly established. Meanwhile his thoughts lingered on the beautiful Sheila Doherty.

If he wanted her, he could buy her, he was sure. And more and more as he watched her, he knew that, yes, he wanted her.

* * *

A fifteen minute break, while the audience drank the free wine and ate the free canapés. Behind the scenes again, Sheila checked hair and makeup. A small mascara smear needed to be removed, a touch more blusher applied. In a few minutes she was ready but something held her back.

Chapter 1

She stared at herself in the mirror and saw a cool, beautiful woman, the epitome of poise and grace. She knew that famous, rich, important men over two continents would give all their wealth and status to possess her, or so they said. She was an icon according to the papers. That meant, surely, something unreal, something artificial, painted or made of stone.

And what was the good? There was only one man she wanted. John Branagh. And he'd pushed her away. He believed she was a whore – a tart – someone not worth touching. What did she do to deserve that?

It wasn't fair! she told herself passionately. He went by rules that were medieval. No-one nowadays thought the odd kiss mattered that much. Oh, she was wrong. She'd hurt him, she knew she had. But if he'd given her half a chance, she'd have apologised – told him how sorry she was. Instead of that, he'd called her such names – how could she still love him after that? But she knew she did.

How did she get to this place, she wondered, the dream of romantic fiction, the dream of so many girls, a place she hated now, where men thought of her more and more as a thing, an object to be desired, not a person? When did her life go so badly wrong? She thought back to her childhood, to the skinny, ginger-haired girl she once was. Okay, she hated how she looked but otherwise, surely, she was happy. Or was that only a false memory?

"Sheila - where are you?"

The hairdresser poked her head round the door and saw Sheila with every sign of relief.

"Thank goodness! Come on, love, only got a couple of minutes! Delmara says I've to check your hair. Wants it tied back for this one."

* * *

The evening was almost at its climax. The show began with evening dress, and now it was to end with evening dress – but this time with Delmara's most beautiful and exotic lines. Sheila stood up and shook out her frock, a cloud of short ice-blue chiffon, sewn with glittering silver beads and feathers. She and Chrissie between them swept up her hair, allowing a few loose curls to hang down her back and one side of her face, fixed it swiftly into place with two combs, and clipped on more silver feathers.

She fastened on long white earrings with a pearly sheen and slipped her feet into the stiletto heeled silver shoes left ready and waiting. She moved over to the doorway for her cue. There was no time to think or to feel the usual butterflies. Chloe came off and she counted to three and went on.

There was an immediate burst of applause.

To the loud music of Snow Patrol, Sheila half floated, half danced along the catwalk, her arms raised ballerina fashion. When she had given sufficient time to allow the audience their fill of gasps and appreciation, she moved back and April and Chloe appeared in frocks with a similar effect of chiffon and feathers, but with differences in style and colour. It was Delmara's spring look for evening wear and she could tell at once that the audience loved it.

The three girls danced and circled each other, striking dramatic poses as the music died down sufficiently to allow Delmara to comment on the different features of the frocks.

With one part of her mind Sheila was aware of the audience, warm and relaxed now, full of good food and drink, their minds absorbed in beauty and fashion, ready to spend a lot of money. Dimly in the background she heard the sounds of voices shouting and feet running.

The door to the ballroom burst open.

People began to scream.

It was something Sheila had heard about for years now, the subject of local black humour, but had never before seen.

Three figures, black tights pulled over flattened faces as masks, uniformly terrifying in black leather jackets and jeans, surged into the room.

The three sub-machine guns cradled in their arms sent deafening bursts of gunfire upwards. Falling plaster dust and stifling clouds of gun smoke filled the air.

For one long second they stood just inside the entrance way, crouched over their weapons, looking round. One of them stepped forward and grabbed Montgomery Speers by the arm.

"Move it, mister!" he said. He dragged Speers forcefully to one side, the weapon poking him hard in the chest.

A second man gestured roughly with his gun in the general direction of Sheila.

"You!" he said harshly. "Yes, you with the red hair! Get over here!"

Chapter Two

1993

There were so many things about her life that Sheila Doherty hated, especially her appearance, her skinniness and her hair, which was a very bright red. She was eight, and just beginning to notice boys. She knew how important it was that other people should think she looked good, and how impossible. How awful it was to be called 'Ginger', to be considered too tall, too thin, too ugly. She hated being called after in the streets, and in the school playground.

When church, Sunday dinner and Sunday school were over, Sheila wandered out into the back garden. Boredom attacked her.

The back garden was not very large and there was nothing much to do there. There was a square of grass, a border bright with flowers in spring and summer, but mostly brown or green on this dull October afternoon, and an empty rabbit hutch against the far wall.

Sheila could vaguely remember the rabbit, a furry, cuddly focus of love a few years ago when she was five or six, and her short but violent grief at his unexplained death from some unidentified rabbit disease.

She mooched over the grass, kicking aimlessly at the few still remaining fallen leaves, and leaned against the wizened old apple tree in the corner near the hutch. Although she was not to leave the garden or go out into the street by herself, it was good for her to be out in the fresh air, her mother said. It might give her a bit more colour.

Sheila's pale skin and red hair, from her father Frank's side of the family, were a source of constant irritation to both Sheila and her mother Kathy. Both would have preferred almost any other combination, but particularly the dark hair and blue eyes for which Kathy had been so widely admired in her youth – as she often told Sheila with some complacency.

Sheila kicked a few more leaves and wished something would happen. If only she had a sister, or even a brother. It would be fun to have someone to play with.

Suddenly a large ball thudded at her feet.

Sheila jumped and said, "Sugar!" Then she blushed, for she didn't often use what Kathy would call bad language. She picked up the ball and stood with it in her hands, looking cautiously around.

It seemed to have come over the wall which ran between her family's garden and the house next door.

She watched. Two hands were gripping hard on the top of the wall. Then a head rose slowly above the edge.

Black curly hair, blue eyes wide open in inquiry, a mouth which broke into a friendly grin as its owner saw Sheila.

"Hi. Can I come and get my ball?"

Sheila nodded silently.

The girl scrambled over the wall, leaving muddy smears on her light blue jeans as she did so. She advanced on Sheila and took the ball which Sheila held out to her.

"What's your name?"

"Sheila. What's yours?"

"Philomena Mary Maguire, but I get called Phil."

They looked at each other steadily for a moment. Then Phil again took the initiative.

"We've come to live next door, here. We moved in yesterday. Is this your house?"

"Yes."

"What's it like, here? Mammy said it would be fun to have a garden. Is it? Do you like it?"

Sheila had never thought about it. She had always had a garden. Didn't everybody?

"Let's play with your football," she said.

"Okay." Phil looked back. Another head had risen above the wall. Brown hair, not as dark as Phil's, grey eyes, a round freckled face with a friendly grin.

"This is my brother Gerry," said Phil. "Can he come over, too?"

"Yes, g-great!" stammered Sheila.

A moment later, Gerry, who was obviously a year or so older than Phil but still small for his age, had scrambled over the wall and given

8

the football a vigorous kick, only just missing Kathy's favourite rosebush. Sheila giggled. This was going to be fun.

They played happily together for the rest of the afternoon. Phil and Gerry were inclined to take the lead and to suggest new games.

Sheila didn't mind. It was interesting. Phil was fascinated by the rabbit hutch and the apple tree. She made Sheila see the back garden with new eyes, as an exciting place of endless possibilities.

"We could make a swing from the tree if we had some rope," Gerry suggested enthusiastically. "We could use the clothes line."

"I don't think my mammy would let me –" Sheila began.

But he had already pulled down the line and was starting to tie it to the tree. So Sheila and Phil joined in and helped him. It was great.

The afternoon whizzed by, and there was Sheila's mother, woken up from her Sunday afternoon nap, calling Sheila already for her tea.

"I won't be allowed out after tea," Sheila said. "It'll be too dark. Maybe I'll see you at school tomorrow?"

"St Columba's, mine's called," said Phil. "I won't know anybody yet, so it'd be nice if you were there."

Sheila was disappointed. "I go to Alexander Primary, so I won't see you. But we could play after school?" she suggested hopefully.

"Okay," said Phil. "See you, then."

She and Gerry scrambled back over the wall and Sheila went in. St Columba's was the nearby Catholic primary school, she knew. Alexander Primary was Protestant. She thought maybe she wouldn't mention her new friends to her mother, just yet, though Kathy would have to know sometime that the new neighbours were Catholic.

From then on Sheila and Phil were inseparable.

Gerry was a good friend too, but he had his own mates to hang around with usually and, as they all got older, it was only occasionally that he would join in with Phil and Sheila's games. After all, they were only girls.

It was Phil who stood up for Sheila now when people called her 'Ginger,' or 'Carrots', and made fun of her.

"You leave her alone or I'll twist your elephant ears off!" she ordered Chrissie Murphy when she tried to pull Sheila's hair.

And, "Leave off my mate or I'll get my big brother to give you such a hidin'!" when Sandy Bell was teasing Sheila more than usual.

Occasionally Sheila would turn to Gerry to help her and the 'big brother' would soon deal with any persistent trouble makers, going so far as to punch big Geordie Patterson in the eye on one memorable occasion.

When they moved on to secondary school, although they were still separated during the school day, their friendship remained strong.

It was against all the rules, they knew, vaguely, for a Catholic and a Protestant to be best friends but, thought Sheila and Phil, who cared?

Danger Danger

Two lives in parallel – twin sisters separated at birth, but their lives take strangely similar and dangerous roads until the final collision which hurls each of them to the edge of disaster.

Katie and her gambling boyfriend Dec find themselves threatened with peril from the people Dec has cheated.

Jo-Anne (Annie) through her boyfriend Steven finds herself in the hands of much more dangerous crooks.

Can they survive and achieve safety and happiness?

"starts with a bang and never quite lets up on the tension ... it will hook you from the beginning and keep you spell bound until the very last sentence."

Ellen Fritz, *Books 4 Tomorrow*

"The emotional intensity of the characters is beautifully drawn …
You care for these people."
Stacey Danson, *author*

an amazing, page turning, stunning novel ... equal to Belfast Girls *in every respect. I can't wait for her next novel to be published.*

Teresa Geering, *author*

an attention-grabbing plot, strong writing, and vivid characterization,
... fast-paced and highly addictive

L. Anne Carrington, *author*

Angel in Flight:

the first Angel Murphy thriller

Is it a bird? Is it a plane? No, it's a low-flying Angel!

You've heard of Lara Croft. You've heard of Modesty Blaise. Well, here comes Angel Murphy!

Angel, a 'feisty wee Belfast girl' on holiday in Greece, sorts out a villain who wants to make millions for his pharmaceutical company by preventing the use of a newly discovered malaria vaccine.

Angel has a broken marriage behind her and is wary of men, but perhaps her meeting with Josh Smith, who tells her he's with Interpol, may change her mind?

Fun, action, thrills, romance in a beautiful setting – so much to enjoy!

"it's a fast-paced read, ... exciting, and you can not put this book down"
Thomas Baker, *Santiago, Chile*

"I could not stop reading! ... a gripping thriller from beginning to the end"
SanMarie Lamprecht

"a fast-paced, exciting read. From the moment I read the first line, I was hooked"
Cheryl Bradshaw, *author, Wyoming, USA*

"a sassy bigger then life heroine in an action packed adventure thriller in Greece"
Book Review Buzz

Angel in Belfast:

the 2nd Angel Murphy thriller

Angel Murphy is back, in true kick boxing form!

Alone in his cottage near a remote Irish village, Fitz, lead singer of the popular band *Raving*, hears the cries of the paparazzi outside and likens them in his own mind to wolves in a feeding frenzy.

Next morning Fitz is found unconscious, seeming unlikely to survive, and is rushed to hospital. Has he been driven to OD? Or is someone else behind this?

His friends call in Angeline Murphy, 'Angel to her friends, devil to her enemies,' to find out the truth. But it takes all Angel's courage and skills to survive the many dangers she faces and to discover the real villain and deal with him.

> *"brings the city and its people ... to life with evocative description and scintillating dialogue"*
>
> **Elinor Carlisle**, Berkshire,UK

> *"I could not stop reading! ... a gripping thriller from beginning to the end"*
>
> **SanMarie Lamprecht**

> *"makes the troubled city of Belfast vibrant and appealing"*
>
> **P A Lanstone**, UK

> *"I felt like I had been transported to Belfast's often tough, gritty streets"*
>
> **Bobbi Lerman**, USA

> *"love the fact that we are reintroduced to characters from Belfast Girls"*
>
> **Michele Young**, UK

Johnny McClintock's War

One man's struggle against the hammer blows of life

The story of one man's struggle to maintain his faith in spite of everything life throws at him.

As the outbreak of the First World War looms closer, John Henry McClintock, a Northern Irish Protestant by upbringing, meets Rose Flanagan, a Catholic, at a gospel tent mission – and falls in love with her.

When Johnny enlists and sets off to fight in the War he finds himself surrounded by death and tragedy, which pushes his trust in God to the limit.

After more than five years absence he returns home to a bitter, war torn Ireland, where both he and Rose are seen as traitors to their own sides.

John Henry and Rose overcome all opposition and, finally, marry. But a few years later comes the hardest blow of all. Can John Henry still hang on to his faith in God?

"wonderful story of a man's journey in trying to hang on to his faith against all odds"

Ann Ellison, Amazon.com

"had me captured from the start and it moves at a fair pace throughout"

Tom Elder, author, Amazon.com

"The creativity and imagination of the author is evident ... excellent book"

Thomas Baker, Santiago, Chile

"characters you will truly care about, and a gut-wrenching emotional ride"

Tom Winton, author, USA (Amazon.com)

"a book that will hold you spellbound until the very last sentence"

Sheila Mary Belshaw, author (UK, Menorca & Cape Town)

Hel's Heroes

Hel wants a hero like the ones she writes about, but does one exist?

A contemporary romance and an historic romance in one book!

Helen McFadden – Hel for short – is a successful writer of Historic Romance for the eBook market. But one day she decides that she needs to get out and experience a bit of real life. She is soon clubbing, partying and generally having a good time – and men are springing up in her life from all directions.

There's Jason, the actor, Paddy the happy-go-lucky businessman, Jordie the footballer, Markie the pop star, even Pete, her old friend.

But do any of them measure up to the heroes she writes about – especially Jack, the highwayman in her current book?

Will Hel ever learn to relate to a real man and stop expecting to meet a clone of one of her heroes?

"A fast paced, gripping tale of two romances ... and a woman's introduction to real life."

Thea, Amazon.co.uk

"What I enjoyed best ... is the author's ability to put us at Helen's side."

Barbara Silkstone, Amazon.com

"an entertaining book: a real page-turner that brings a smile to one's face"

Ronald W. Sharp, Amazon.co.uk

"an outstanding and cleverly crafted novel ... The twist at the end is awesome."

Rukia the Reader, Amazon.co.uk

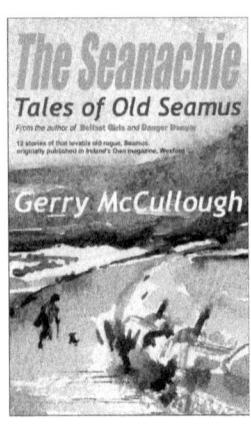

Tales of Old Seamus

The Seanachie:
Tales of Old Seamus

Gerry McCullough

A humorous series of Irish stories, set in the fictional Donegal village of Ardnakil and featuring that lovable rogue, 'Old Seamus' – the Séanachie.

All of these stories have previously been published in the popular Irish weekly magazine, Ireland's Own, based in Wexford, Ireland.

"heart warming tales ... beautifully told with subtle Irish humour"

Babs Morton, author, UK

"an irresistible old rogue, but he's the kind people love to sit and listen to for hours on end whenever the opportunity presents itself"

G. Polley, author and blogger, Sapporo, Japan

"This magnificent storyteller has done it again. Each individual story has it's own Gaelic charm"

Teresa Geering, author, UK

"evocative characterisation brings these stories to life in a delightful, absorbing way"

Elinor Carlisle, author , Reading, UK

The Seanachie 2:

Norah on the Beach *and other stories*

Gerry McCullough

Another humorous series of Irish stories, set in the fictional Donegal village of Ardnakil and once again featuring that lovable rogue, *'Old Seamus'* – the Séanachie.

All of these stories have previously been published in the popular Irish weekly magazine, *Ireland's Own*, based in Wexford, Ireland.

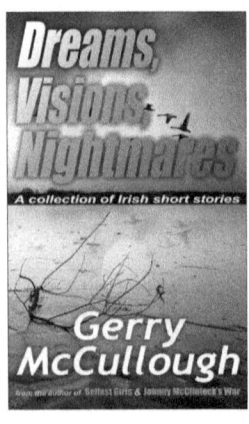

Dreams, Visions, Nightmares

A collection of eight literary and award-winning Irish stories, (newly expanded and edited):

Primroses (winner of *Cuirt international Literary Award*, Galway 2005, published in *West 47* magazine and *Cuirt Annual* 2005)

Pink Silk (published in *Verbal* magazine, Derry, 2008)

Shadows (published in *Brazen City*, Belfast 2008)

Giving Up (commended in *Seán O'Faolain Short Story Competition*, Cork 2009; published in *Sharp Sticks, Driven Nails*, Dublin 2010)

Slipping (published in *Ulla's Nib* magazine, Belfast 2009, winning Star Prize)

Ballystravey, 1988 (published by *Luciole Press*, California 2009; shortlisted for *Cuirt Award*, Galway 2010; published in *Crime after Crime* anthology, USA)

Stevie's Luck (shortlisted for the *Brian Moore Award*, Belfast, 2008)

Dark Night (Extended into full length novel, *Johnny McClintock's War* – published in 2014)

Lady Molly & The Snapper

A young adult time travel adventure, set in Ireland and on the high seas

Gerry McCullough

Brother and sister Jik and Nora are bored and angry. Why does their Dad spend so much time since their mother's death drinking and ignoring them? Why must he come home at all hours and fall downstairs like a fool?

Nora goes to church and lights a candle. The cross-looking sailor saint she particularly likes seems to grow enormous and come to life. Nora is too frightened to stay.

Nora and Jik go down secretly to their father's boat, the *Lady Molly*, at Howth Marina. There they meet The Snapper, the same cross-looking saint in a sailor's cap, who takes them back in time on the yacht, *Lady Molly,* to meet Cuchulain, the legendary Irish warrior, and others.

Jik and Nora plan to use their travels to find some way of stopping their father from drinking – but it's fun, too! Or is it? When they meet the Druid priest who follows them into modern times, teams up with school bully Marty Flanagan, and threatens them, things start getting out of hand.

Meanwhile, Nora is more than interested in Sean, the boy they keep bumping into in the past ...

<u>Prophetic fiction by **Raymond McCullough**</u>:

In Six Hours

... the world changed:

In just six hours the Middle East – and the world – will change forever

A friendship forged in war leads four men on separate journeys to their final destiny in a Middle East heading for meltdown

As bitter enemies race towards nuclear conflict, only a miracle can save Israel from the hostile Islamic forces surrounding her. The USA, Russia and the western world are playing with fire in the Middle East, as Iran rushes towards a nuclear climax.

While fighting the Taliban with the ISAF forces in 2012, four young men from very different backgrounds meet in Kabul, Afghanistan:

Shaul *'Solly'* Levine, an Orthodox Jew from New York City;

Micky *'Dev'* Devlin, an Irish Catholic from Boston;

Brandon *'Doubtin'* Thomas, a black Pentecostal from N. Carolina;

Khan Ali *'Zai'* Yusufzai, a Muslim Pashtun from Afghanistan.

They discover that they have more in common than they first thought and make a pact that one day they'll meet up again in Jerusalem after the prophesied Six Hour War in the Middle East, taking separate ways to a common destiny.

Meanwhile, they will keep in touch with one another as much as possible and work towards making that meeting a possibility. Will these prophecies come to pass? Will Israel itself survive the coming nuclear holocaust?

This apocalyptic thriller moves from war, to a couple of budding romances in very different locations, to more war and then the ultimate Middle East war. But even in the midst of conflict, new relationships are being formed. Action, friendship, romance ... and yet more action.

"McCullough writes with conviction and clearly knows his subject well ... [his] fluid prose draws you in and his logic and characterisation make for a believable compelling drama. Highly recommended!!!"
Juliet B Madison, author, UK

"So well written and very descriptive, you actually think you're there. Raymond has obvious knowledge of the areas he has written about as that and his passionate way of writing shine throughout. Must read book"
Tom Elder, author, USA

Non-fiction by *Sheila Mary Taylor*:

Count to Ten:
Fly with a miracle

Few things worse can happen to a mother than for her child to be diagnosed with cancer. It started as a pain, that became a 'hot spot', grew into a tumour, ultimately threatening Andrew's life. At the very least, his leg would have to be amputated, a chilling prospect.

The true story of how Andrew and his family coped with the days, weeks, months and years that followed his diagnosis, of the reliefs, the triumphs, the relapses and the outright screaming panics.

It is a testament to Andrew's passionate determination to pursue his adventurous dreams even in the face of death itself. It is also a testament to a revolutionary new treatment that was applied with care, expertise and wisdom by the dedicated team at the London Bone Tumour Clinic.

It is so easy to love your children. It is so hard to hang onto hope, especially onto their hope – the hope they need to carry on.

"An uplifting and emotionally charged book. Highly recommended."
Sooz Burke, author, Australia

"personal, sensitive, powerful, heart-breaking, uplifting and compelling all at once"
WeeScottishLassie, UK

"a road of many zig-zag turns, bends and bumps, share the journey with them, a wonderful book, I highly recommend it."
Janice Donnelly, UK

Non-fiction books from

A Wee Taste a' Craic:

All the Irish craic from the popular
Celtic Roots Radio shows, 2-25

Raymond McCullough

*I absolutely loved this! I found it to be very informative
about Irish life culture, language and traditions.*
Elinor Carlisle (author, Reading, UK)

*a unique insight into the Northern Irish people
& their self deprecating sense of humour*
Strawberry

Ireland – now the good news!

The best of *'Bread'* Vols. 1 & 2 –

personal testimonies and church/fellowship
profiles from around Ireland

Edited by: *Raymond & Gerry McCullough*

"...fresh Bread – deals with the real issues facing the church in Ireland today"
Ken Newell, minster of Fitzroy Presbyterian Church, Belfast

The Whore and her Mother:

9/11, *Babylon* and the *Return of the King*

Raymond McCullough

Could the writings of the ancient Hebrew prophets be relevant to events taking place in the world today?
These Hebrew prophets – Isaiah, Jeremiah, Habbakuk and the apostle John, in *The Revelation* – wrote extensively about a latter day city and empire which would dominate, exploit and corrupt all the nations of the world. They referred to it as Babylon the Great, or Mega-Babylon, and they foretold that its fall – 'in one day' – would devastate the economies of the whole world. Have these prophecies been fulfilled already?

Is Mega-Babylon the Roman Catholic Church?
A world super-church?
Rebuilt ancient Babylon?
Brussels, Jerusalem, or somewhere entirely different?
Should this city/nation have a large Jewish population?
Why all the talk about merchants, cargoes, commodities, trade?

Can we rely on the words of these ancient prophets?
If so, what else did they foretell that is still to be fulfilled?
Do they refer to other major nations – USA, Russia, China, Europe?
What about militant Islam?

"AMAZED when I read this book ... in awe of your extensive knowledge on so many levels: Christian, Jewish, and Muslim culture; the Jewish diaspora ... Greek & Hebrew; ... thought-provoking and troublesome ... many will be offended, but you consistently build your case instead of being sensationalistic."
James Revoir, author of *Priceless Stones*

Oh What Rapture!

Is a *'Secret Rapture'* going to spare believers from the tribulation to come?

Raymond McCullough

Many are convinced that very soon an event referred to as *'The Rapture'* will take place, where bible believers all over the world will suddenly disappear, leaving society at a loss to explain this disappearance of so many. Many non-fiction books, fiction thrillers and movies have capitalised on this theme, earning a fat revenue for their authors/producers.

But is this really what the bible teaches?
Is *'The Rapture'* genuine, or a deceptive false hope?

Are those who trust in it being duped, so that they fail to prepare themselves for what is coming?
And are they being disobedient to the clear command of the Lord?

Written by the author of *Amazon* best-selling book, *The Whore and her Mother*, also on the topic of bible prophecy, this volume focusses on the false teaching of a *'secret and separate Rapture'* – an event which is NOT supported by scripture!

This book investigates the scriptures used to back up the *'secret Rapture'* theory and clearly compares them to the other scriptures concerning the return of the Messiah, Jesus (Yeshua). The evident truth is revealed and the origins of the false *'secret Rapture'* doctrine are exposed.

Believers around the world are taught to expect persecution, sometimes even death, for their faith. More have been killed in the past century than in previous centuries combined – in China, Cambodia, Vietnam, Nigeria, Syria, Iran, Iraq, Egypt, Indonesia, etc. Yet many believers in the west confidently expect to avoid any persecution and be *'beamed up'* out of any coming tribulation!

If you thought believers were soon going to be lifted out of a worsening world situation, be prepared to meet the exciting challenge of scripture head on!

"Interesting and gave food for thought ... definitely worth a read"
Kindle customer, UK

www.ingramcontent.com/pod-product-compliance
Lightning Source LLC
Chambersburg PA
CBHW070642180626
46817CB00006B/2205